She Had Not Meant
To Love Him

Natalya smiled, avoiding his eyes, as her confusion mounted and she felt a hot flush stealing up her throat to her cheeks. His proximity created a wild, surging rush of violently disturbing emotions, making her heart race.

She felt his bare skin under her hands. The glowing, golden warmth within her made her weak. His arms gathered her closer, and she felt an instant of panic, an impulse to delay this ultimate commitment, but it was swept aside by the rush of her feelings which carried her along, making her completely helpless.

His touch brought to life a bittersweet need which seemed to spring from the very core of her being.

LOVE'S GENTLE AGONY

AGONY

by

Aaron Fletcher

A DELL/LORELEI BOOK

Published by
Lorelei Publishing Co., Inc.
Two Park Avenue
New York, N.Y. 10016

For information address
Lorelei Publishing Co., Inc.
Two Park Avenue
New York, N.Y. 10016

ISBN: 0-440-04972-5

Printed in the United States of America

First printing—October 1978

Distributed by Dell Distributing, Inc.
1 Dag Hammarskjold Plaza
New York, N.Y. 10017

PART I

The Count and the Gypsy

CHAPTER I

Most of the tiny, weathered houses along the narrow, twisting street were tightly locked, the doors and shutters bolted and the men and women at labor in the fields adjacent to the city. But a few of the houses had people at home, the doors open in the hope that a breeze would stir the torrid air which lay between the buildings like a suffocating blanket, thick with the fetid stench of sewage in the gutters. An old woman was visible in the gloomy interior of the first house with an open door, and Saiforella hobbled on past, hunched over her cane. Those whose bodies were warped with the ravages of time were observant, and they frequently saw through her disguise. The next few houses were locked, then there was another open door. The woman moving around inside the house was thirty or less, and she had the indications of relative prosperity about her, sturdy shoes on her feet, and clothing which looked fairly new, with no worn places or patches. Saiforella shuffled across the street and looked into the house as she tapped the end of the cane against the stoop.

"Good day, fair one," Saiforella cackled, pitching her voice high and making it crack and quaver to conceal the clear timbre of her natural voice. "May good fortune always smile upon you and your loved ones."

The woman walked toward the door, frowning darkly. "Away with you! I want no Gypsies here."

Saiforella fumbled a couple of the copper bangles out of the cloth belt around her waist under the soiled, ragged folds of the cloak, and rattled them together as she held them out. "A pretty bangle for your arm, fair one? Only ten kopecks each, or fifteen the pair."

"I want no bangles. Now get away from my door."

"Pretty beads for your lovely neck?" Saiforella said, replacing the bangles and taking out a string of the glass beads and shaking them. "Pretty colors to match your pretty eyes."

"No! Get away from my door before I call a soldier!"

There was a cradle on the other side of the room, in front of the stove which filled most of the wall, and Saiforella tucked the beads back into her cloth belt and took out a rattle, small pieces of hardwood on a colored string. "A rattle to amuse your beautiful baby so its laughter will cheer your heart? Only five kopecks, lovely woman." The woman hesitated, and Saiforella shook it harder. "See how it rattles? Show it to the baby and see how the child laughs."

"She is asleep . . ." The woman shrugged with resignation, taking the rattle. "Very well, I will get your money." She turned away, then quickly turned back as Saiforella stepped over the sill, glancing to the right and left. "Stay on the street! I'll have the soldiers on you if you steal here!"

"I only wished to shade myself from the sun, lovely one," Saiforella muttered. She fumbled in the cloth belt for a twist of grass and chicken feathers tied with a colored string. "And to give you this. Put it on the baby's cradle, and the child will be protected from sickness."

8

The woman frowned suspiciously and took the bit of grass and feathers between the tips of two fingers. "What is it?"

"A powerful amulet to protect your child. There has been death on this street, has there not? I can feel it hovering near and breathing on the back of my neck even as I talk to you, because I have the gift for detecting such things. Go ahead and put it on the cradle, lovely one. I want no money for it, and I give it to you because I would not have your beautiful baby ill." She took a lump of charcoal from her belt and scratched marks on one side of the doorjamb. "Or you, so I will make the symbols to keep death from your door." She scratched marks on the other side of the doorjamb and tucked the charcoal back into her belt. "There, fair one. Now everyone in this house will be protected, and it is a gift from me to you."

Disbelief and superstitious willingness to believe battled on the woman's face, and superstition won. She smiled and nodded. "Thank you. I will get your money for you."

"It is nothing, lovely one," Saiforella replied, darting another look to the right and left inside the door as the woman turned away. There was nothing within reach, and she leaned back on the cane. "It is an honor for me to be able to exercise my powers in your behalf."

"Several have already died of the summer sicknesses this year," the woman said, taking an earthenware pot down from the stove and removing a coin from it. She walked back to the door, holding out the coin. "They say Gypsies have powers such as you claim, and I trust we will have no sickness here."

"It will pass by now," Saiforella said, taking the coin, and she suddenly leaned toward the woman. "Stay! Let me see your hand again!"

9

The woman looked at her with a puzzled frown, cautiously extending her hand. "What is it?"

A man's blouse and trousers and a woman's dress were hanging on the shutters by the door to dry, and a couple small, bag-like garments for the baby were spread on the windowsill to dry. There were no indications that the woman had other children, and the pronoun she had used in referring to the baby hadn't been lost on Saiforella. She pulled at the woman's finger, looking at her hand, and nodded and cackled gleefully. "You have a male child in your belly."

"I do?" the woman exclaimed in an elated tone, spreading her palm wider as she leaned over and looked at it herself. "How can you tell?"

"This line here. See how faint it is? Your husband must plant his seed in your belly tonight to fix it, or it will leave with your next monthly blood."

"But he did two nights ago."

"It did not fix the male child. See this line here, here, and here? These are male children which left with your monthly blood. On this side of the deep line are male children, and on this side are female. See this thick line? It is a female child which was born to you. The one in the cradle is female, is it not?"

"Indeed it is."

"Then I was correct, you see. But your man's seed must be very weak for so many children to have left you. Your womb is healthy and strong, because I can tell by this line here." She shook her head and sighed heavily, worming her hand inside the folds of the cloak and taking out one of the tiny phials of colored water. "Here, put this in his tea. After he drinks this, three years will bring you three fine, healthy sons."

The woman took the phial, looking at it hopefully, then looked at Saiforella with a reluctant shake of her head. "How much is it? Perhaps I cannot afford it."

Saiforella shrugged, turning away from the door and leaning on the cane with both hands. "It is priceless," she said sadly. "The woman who had the power of making the potion is dead and did not pass her secret on, and that is the last I have. But you have been kind to me, so simply give me what you can for it."

The woman looked at the phial, chewing her lower lip as she thought, and shrugged apologetically as she looked back at Saiforella. "I only have sixty kopecks, auntie. Perhaps I can afford fifty."

Saiforella lifted and dropped one hand in a resigned gesture. "It will do, because you have been kind to an old woman who has no home. Give me the fifty kopecks, and pray for my soul when you next go to church."

The woman smiled and nodded happily, turning away from the door and returning to the stove. Saiforella glanced along the deserted street in both directions, listening to the clink of coins with a practiced ear as the woman dug in the bottom of the earthenware pot. There were at least a couple of rubles, some coppers and perhaps more in the pot, and a different tactic might have brought more for the phial. But fifty kopecks was as much as she usually got. She turned back to the door as the woman came back across the room, the coins in one hand and a loaf of dark bread in the other.

"Take this with you also, auntie. I would give you more, but it is all I have."

"Your kindness is the greatest gift I will receive this day, fair one," Saiforella replied, tucking the coins into the belt and taking the loaf of bread under her arm. "Put the potion in your man's tea tonight, and name your first son after this day of the week so he will have good fortune."

"I shall, auntie. Travel safely."

11

"Remain in good health, lovely one," Saiforella replied, turning away from the door. There was a slit in the front of her dress just below the cloth belt around her waist, and it opened into a long bag sewn inside the dress and hanging between her legs. She tucked the loaf of bread under the cloak, glancing over her shoulder as she shuffled away. The woman had left the doorway. Saiforella pushed the loaf of bread through the slit, and the pewter cup, copper pot, tin plate, and other odds and ends stolen from houses on other streets rattled faintly as the bread fell into the bag on top of them.

Her throat was sore from forcing the croaking, quavering note, and she was sweltering in the bulky clothes. She wore wooden clogs on her feet, and a drab, shapeless grey dress which was ragged, patched, and stained. The tattered cloak draped over the dress, and a hood shadowed her face. A horsehair wig of a dirty grey color was fastened inside the hood, and the straggly, lank hair hung down over her face. There were splotches on her cheeks and forehead which were made of berry seeds mixed with paste, simulating an advanced stage of the lues. Paste and grime were plastered on her slender hands, making them look like withered, scaly claws. Rags sewn into the back of the dress gave her a hunched, stooped appearance as she bent over her cane and hobbled along with the shuffling gait she had perfected. When she talked, she kept her lips pulled in over her teeth to conceal their pearly glint. And she kept her eyes averted, downcast, or hooded behind slitted eyelids. They were a deep blue, an unusual color for a Gypsy, and their clear, lustrous sheen would betray the fact that she had yet to reach her twentieth year.

The woman in a house further along the street was greedy and avaricious, with cold, hard eyes. She wanted a ring, a bead of red glass set in brass, and she let Saiforella enter the house while she put it on her finger and looked at it. The man's chair was just inside the door to take advantage of any evening breeze when he came home from work, and some of his things were around it. Saiforella's quick glance spotted the pipe and tobacco pot as soon as she entered. They were on the floor on the other side of the chair, where they wouldn't be missed immediately. The pipe looked valuable, some kind of dark wood which was delicately carved and chased with a design in silver. The pot looked even more valuable, solid silver with tiny figures on the lid and around the sides of the bowl. But the pot couldn't be dropped into the bag, because any tobacco in it would spill out and part of it would be lost in the bag.

The woman extended her hand at arm's length, looking at the ring in the light. "Are you sure it is a ruby?"

"Brought by caravan from the Orient, lovely one, and traded from one band of my people to the other until it came into my hands, at a price of everything I owned."

"And this is real gold?"

"As true as the shine in your beautiful eyes, and blended with base metal only to the degree necessary to give it strength to hold the precious stone."

"I will give you a ruble for it."

"I would make you a present of it, beautiful one, but it is the only thing of value I possess. I must have five rubles."

The woman looked at her with a taut, hard smile. "I will not take it off, and I shall call the soldiers and tell them you stole from me if you do not sell it to me for a ruble."

Saiforella slowly bent over her cane and made choked, weeping sounds, nodding and gesturing affir-

13

matively with her hand as she watched the woman through slitted eyelids. The woman smiled triumphantly, looking at the ring again as she went to get the money. Halfway across the room, she remembered that she shouldn't turn her back and she quickly looked over her shoulder at Saiforella and watched her as she walked on across the room and took a pewter vase from a shelf. It had been only a second or two, but it had been long enough. Saiforella had moved swiftly, deliberately enough to keep her clothes from rustling and her clogs from scraping, but rapidly enough to gather up the pipe and tobacco pot. The pipe was in the bag, the pot was tucked under the cloth belt around her waist, and she was hunched over the cane again. The woman came back across the room with two fifty kopeck pieces, rattling them in her hand, and she looked at Saiforella with a sneering smile and dropped them to the floor in front of her. Saiforella lowered herself shakily to her hands and knees, gathered up the coins, and struggled to her feet again. The woman made a sound of contempt in her throat as she turned away, and she smiled with satisfaction as she lifted her hand and looked at the ring again. Saiforella deftly plucked a scarf from under a coat hanging on a peg by the door as she left.

She hobbled on along the street, dropping the lid of the tobacco pot into the bag and emptying the tobacco into the scarf, and there was a clink of coins. She dropped the pot into the bag, glanced around, and pulled a fold of the cloak aside and looked at the to-. bacco in the scarf, stirring it with a finger. The man had been hiding money in his tobacco pot. She counted the coins, hissing with delight. There was a total of two rubles and thirty kopecks in copper coins, a substantial amount of money. And the dealer in her band who furnished her trade wares would charge only ten kopecks or so for the ring, so there would be a profit of ninety kopecks on it. She tied a knot in the scarf to hold the tobacco in it, dropped it into the bag, and put the coins in the belt.

Two soldiers hailed her in the next street, and she waited for them as they walked toward her, officious frowns on their faces. One of them was a noncommissioned officer, which made it even more dangerous. If they searched her, and they might, all would be lost. The *dortch* was tucked under the right side of her belt, convenient to her right hand, but it was a final resort. A ball of metal four inches in diameter and covered with a tight skin of leather, with a short chain and a leather wrist loop on the other end of the chain. Her mother had made her practice constantly with it since the age of thirteen, and with the loop around her right wrist and the ball in her hand in the position to cast, she could knock an insect out of the air or crack a man's skull. But if she used it on soldiers, her entire band might be arrested.

"This is not the place for Gypsies, old hag. Gypsies are supposed to stay at the fairground, not roam the streets and steal everything in sight. What have you stolen today, old woman?"

"I have stolen nothing, your honor. I am an honest woman, selling baubles and trinkets to buy food so that I—"

"Don't lie to me, or it will be worse for you, old crone. Let's see what you look like under . . . gah! Stand away from her! God knows how many men have had their members fall off from only passing her on the street!"

"It has been many years since a man's member has troubled me, but the finest member a man might possess would be poorly represented by your mustache, your honor." She took one of the tiny phials of water

15

from the belt and held it out. "Here, put a drop of this on each side of your mustache every morning, and you shall have the finest mustache in your regiment within the month."

He took the phial, looking at it with a doubtful frown. "What is in it?"

"I do not know, because I am only an old and ignorant woman, your honor. But it is a compound of essences which make great mustaches on men, and there is no question of that. My fourth son used it, and his mustaches are beyond the sides of his face."

"Will it make a black mustache, like a Gypsy?"

"It retains the natural color of the hair, your honor. And I gladly make you a present of it, because I am grateful to those who makes the streets safe for old people such as me." She looked at the other soldier. "Would you like a present, your honor? Perhaps a pretty bangle for the arm of your lovely wife or beloved?"

The first soldier was sniffing the phial suspiciously, and he looked up and guffawed. "He needs more than that, old woman. He has been unable to make a woman cast her eye in his direction."

"Liar," the soldier muttered, flushing darkly and looking away with a frown.

"Then a love philter is what you need," Saiforella cackled, taking out one of the twists of grass and feathers. "Here, take this, your honor."

"What do I do with this?"

"Urinate on it, let it dry, then put it into the pocket or anywhere on the person of the woman who catches your eye. She will follow you to the ends of the earth and be your slave."

He looked at it, his mouth hanging open, then looked back at her. "Are you telling me the truth, old woman? Will it do that?"

16

"My second son used the same kind of philter to marry the most beautiful woman in his band, and he is so ugly my husband accused me of lying with a goat."

They were soldiers, filled with self importance, but they were also peasants. They came from generations of serfs, and the superstitions of the serfs were a part of them. The noncommissioned officer dug in his pocket and took out a ten kopeck coin. "Very well, auntie. Be gone with you, and do not let us catch you away from the fairgrounds again."

"Bless you for your kindness, your honor," Saiforella said, bowing over her cane as she took the coin. The other soldier gave her ten kopecks, and she bowed as she took it. "And you, your honor. Bless you for your kindness and for making the streets safe for an ignorant old woman. And for your bravery against our enemies. And for all the services you do our country. Bless you."

"Be gone, then."

Saiforella nodded and bowed, turning and shuffling away. "I do as you command, your honor. Bless you. Bless you both."

They stood and watched her for a moment as she hobbled slowly along the street, then she heard them turn and walk back in the direction from which they had come, their boots scraping in the dried mud of the street and their murmurs of conversation fading. Sweat trickled down her sides and itched on her face and in her hair, and it was only partly from the heat. There had been other encounters with soldiers during the past days, but they had been more casual, a shouted curse or warning and a fist shaken at her. One had run at her and hit her with a stick, knocking her down, but it had been out of boredom and in idle, brutal humor to give him and his comrades a laugh. This encounter had been more serious. They had been about

17

to search her. It was likely that the complaints of those from whom she had taken tokens during the past days were beginning to mount up, as they frequently did, and the soldiers were being instructed to be more watchful and strict. In that event, the streets had become unsafe for her. In any event, the day was over for her. The encounter had unnerved her, and her lack of confidence would be communicated to those she met, making them more wary and stingy with their coins.

The development fit in with other things, because Panna, the leader of her band, had announced that they would shortly be leaving and the fair was drawing to a close. There was always a depressing melancholy about the end of a fair, even when they were leaving enroute to another one. It was as though the crowds, noise, and excitement acquired a kind of life of its own, and that the end was the death of something uniquely precious. She had objected to Panna's decision as a matter of form, and she had known the objection wouldn't make any difference in the outcome. All the others had agreed with Panna, because few of the men and none of the other women debated Panna's decisions except in private. But her position in the band was something of an anomaly. As the daughter and only child of Rael Hator, king of the Chota clan of the Halebi tribe until his death seven years before, she was of royal blood and had certain prerogatives, including disputing with the leader of her band when she wished.

But there were also disadvantages to her situation. She had had an abundance of suitors in the winter camp each year since the age of fifteen, but those who were willing to do without a dowry because of her beauty were of insufficient stature in the clan and those who had an appropriate station to marry a woman of royal blood needed a dowry to maintain her. It was a vexing situation, and in the meantime she and her mother were paupers. The rich furs, luxurious clothes, array of gold bangles on her arms, and the fine, large, gaily-decorated wagon she remembered as a child were things of the past. Possessions and money had slipped away, and she and her mother shared a wagon with the Torgau family, paying a rent of three rubles a month for a small section in the rear of it.

Another unusual thing about her status in the band was that she was the only one who lived on peddling trinkets and taking tokens from house to house in the cities where the fairs were located. Any Gypsy was proficient in taking tokens and did so when a safe opportunity arose, but to do it for a living was a dangerous undertaking, dangerous for her, and also dangerous for the band as a whole, because they could be implicated if she were caught. But she had no husband to support her, she hadn't the knowledge of people required to cast fortunes, and she had no other trade. And if she revealed her beauty to dance for money, it would be an open invitation to be raped by the first Army or Government official who saw her.

The Torgau family wagon was crowded, and there had been less than subtle hints that they would gladly forego the three rubles per month to have all of their wagon to themselves. Panna was always courteous and polite to her, even in the midst of a dispute, but it was clear that he would be more than pleased to see her married or with another band. None of it had ever come into the open, because it would be a disgrace to the band if there was less than full hospitality rendered to any Gypsy, particularly a woman of royal blood. The other members of the band enjoyed the status accruing to the band by hosting a princess, and there were frequent small gifts of food and other kindnesses. But they worried about the possibility of trouble falling upon them because of the way she earned her livelihood. If some reasonable solution to the situation presented itself, everyone would be pleased. And no one would be pleased more than she.

On the way back to the fairgrounds, there was a narrow mews off the right side of the street, lined with houses even smaller and more shabby than those along the street. The house on the corner was locked and shuttered, but clothes were hanging out of a window on the side of the house facing the mews. Saiforella dropped her cane and leaned over it, sweeping the street and mews with her eyes as she slowly and painfully picked up the cane and supported herself on it again. There was no one moving along the street or in the mews. The open doors were out of the line of sight of the side of the house. She shuffled toward the mews.

There were also two cabbages on the windowsill where the clothes were draped, and a dog lay in the shade by the side of the house. The dog growled threateningly, uncurling and coming toward her. She wormed her hand into the strap on the *dortch,* gathered the ball in her hand, and pulled the chain from under the belt. A dog was a good and valuable animal, the symbol of a closely-related tribe, and she had no desire to kill or seriously injure it. She shook her cane at the dog, hissing, and the dog bared its teeth and snarled viciously as it charged. Her right arm snapped out, and the ball flew to the end of the chain. It touched the top of the dog's head, and she snapped her wrist to pop the ball back into her hand as the dog slammed to the dirt on its stomach. She stepped across its body, tucking the chain back under her belt and glancing around again as she reached up with the cane to knock the clothes down.

There were two men's blouses, one almost new and the other somewhat worn, and a woman's dress in good condition. She wadded and stuffed them through the slit in the front of her dress, then knocked the cabbages down with the cane, deftly catching them and pushing them through the slit. The dog struggled to its feet and fell onto its side. She bent over it, and dragged it to its original position. The dog growled weakly, its eyes unfocussed and dazed. She arranged its legs under it, then straightened up and glanced around as she hobbled back into the street.

The city of Diakonskii supported a garrison and agriculture, with no substantial industry or trade, and the fair was a relatively small one. It was a mass of tents and hastily-erected wooden booths arranged in rows on the open ground by the river which ran past the city, and there were dealers in sheepskins, metal products, fabrics, leather, and household items, as well as tea shops, taverns, and amusement booths. The dirt aisles between the tents and booths had been churned into dust which had settled over the area in a powdery film of dull brown, and the gaily-colored pennants which had been draped on some of the booths and tents hung limply in the stifling heat of late afternoon. There were only a few people wandering about, because the large crowds came at night when the soldiers and the field laborers would be free. Then the lanterns would be hung and the torches lighted, and the dust and shabbiness of the tents and booths would disappear in the soft glow of the dancing yellow light. The dealers would vie with each other in their extravagant claims, and hordes of soldiers and peasants would push back and forth between the amusement booths, hoping to buy a moment of happiness with the coppers they clutched.

21

The Gypsy caravan was located in a corner by the canal which ran through the city and met the river, where the stench of sewage and other filth was almost overpowering in the hot air. The wagons stood in a circle, with a few tattered booths and a stage which would be used during the evening on the side facing the rest of the fairground. Some used their wagons for trade, as her mother used their space in the rear of the Torgau wagon to earn money by casting fortunes, and those wagons were always placed on the side of the circle by the fairground. The tribe specialized in working with metals, and most of the people in the fairground during the day came to the corner where the Gypsy caravan was located, women bringing pots, pans, and kettles to be patched, overseers bringing farm tools for repairs, and mechanics and small tradesmen of the city bringing broken equipment or implements of their trade to be repaired. The forges and benches were set up at both sides of the circle, and a dozen or more men of the caravan were at work over them, hammering, soldering, and filing. Customers stood in clusters around the forges and benches, some resigned and others impatient at the delay, all of them sweating in the torrid heat and conversing desultorily. When one of the men finished a job, there would be an outburst of shouting and pushing, everyone demanding to be next. The ones who looked most prosperous would take precedence, as they did in everything, and the shouting would die away to mutters and grumbles.

A few of the women of the caravan were moving among the customers, trying to peddle their wares, and Saiforella could see her mother looking for likely prospects who might be talked into having their fortune cast. The booth owned by Kostich, the dealer in trinkets, baubles, clothing, and sundries, was one of the few open. His wife and second oldest son were standing in front of it, shouting and beckoning at passers-by, and he and his oldest son were working at one of the forges. Saiforella's mother smiled and nodded to her surreptitiously as she hobbled past, and she returned the nod and ambled slowly toward Kostich's booth. His wife glanced at her, and called to one of the small children in the rear of the booth to fetch his father. Saiforella continued on past the booth toward the Kostich wagon.

Kostich was always polite, conscious of her status and wary of the Hator temper, which usually surprised Saiforella as much as anyone. She emptied the bag and spread the things out on the floor, keeping the loaf of bread and the cabbages, then took the remaining bangles, beads, and rings out of her belt. They were his, because she had never accumulated enough money to buy her own stock of wares. He counted them, then looked through the items she had taken out of the bag. His face was sweaty and his hands grimy from the forge, and he was clearly in a hurry to get back to it. It was hot in the wagon, and the sounds from outside filtered through the wooden walls. She waited as he looked through the things again, counted the remaining bangles, beads, and rings once more, and chewed his lip as he counted in his mind.

"Seven rubles and fifty kopecks to settle, Princess," he said with an apologetic smile and shrug. "That is the best I can do."

It was little enough, but she had money in her belt which would bring it up to an average day. "It will do," she said, rolling one of the cabbages over to the things in front of him. "For your wife."

"We are grateful, Princess," he said, digging in his money belt under his shirt. He counted the coins into her hand, then began gathering up the things. "It was a good day, was it not?"

She shrugged, rising from the floor and moving toward the door as she pushed the coins into her belt. "Good enough, but one always wishes for a better one. Perhaps tomorrow will be better."

"Tomorrow? We leave tonight, Princess."

She silently nodded, opening the door, and closed it behind her as she went down the steps at the rear of the wagon.

. The horses were tethered on ropes inside the circle of wagons, hanging their heads and dozing in the sun. Their smell was fresh, clean, and familiar in her nostrils, then the sour stench of the canal returned as she went between two wagons on the other side of the circle. She sat down in the shade of one of the wagons, leaning back against a wheel and relaxing. The wagon was near the edge of the canal. A dead dog lay in the trickle of thick, slimy water in the bottom of the canal, and birds were hovering over it and picking at it.

Light footsteps came around the rear of the wagon, and her mother smiled down at her. "Greetings, my lovely. Was it a good day for you?"

"I have twelve rubles and sixty kopecks."

Her mother knelt by her, taking her hand and patting it. "The money is nothing, beloved. No one bothered you, did they?"

"There were two soldiers, but they were little trouble."

Her mother sighed, patting her hand again. "The troubles of this place will be behind us soon, beautiful daughter, because we will be leaving after the fair closes tonight." She squeezed Saiforella's hand between hers, her smile anxious; she was more cautious of the Hator temper than most because of her proximity to it, and it always embarrassed her when Saiforella publicly questioned Panna's orders and decisions. "It is good that we are leaving. We will take the paste off, and you will be able to wear a pretty skirt and blouse and your gold earrings, my princess."

Saiforella glanced at her mother and nodded and shrugged disinterestedly as she looked away.

"Come. There is cabbage soup in the wagon."

Her mother was considerate of her to the point of sacrificing opportunities to make money, and there were still people around the forges who might be coaxed into having their fortunes cast. Saiforella shook her head. "The day is not yet done. I will wait here."

"It is done for us, beautiful one. They who are here now clutch their kopecks as though they were gold. Come."

Saiforella nodded, gathering herself to rise to her feet, and her mother took her arm and helped her up. They went back across the circle, and into the rear of the Torgau wagon.

Their compartment was partitioned off by a mat of tattered rags sewn together and suspended from the curved ceiling of the wagon. It was crowded with their belongings, the rolled pallets on which they slept, a trunk, a stack of utensils, and clothing, and it was sweltering from the sun beaming down on the wagon. Her mother propped the door open a couple of inches to let in air, then rooted among the pots and pans in the corner. Saiforella took off the cloak, wig, and dress, and sat in her ragged petticoat on the lumpy pallet on which she slept.

The soup was thin and sour, a few pieces of cabbage swimming in tepid water, and they each had a piece of the bread and a cup of kvass which had been diluted with water and which tasted of the river mud. When they finished eating, Saiforella lay on her pallet and looked through a tiny crack between two boards in the side of the wagon. All the wagons looked dirty and shabby, and the horses were thin. It had been a poor year for everyone, and money was scarce. The previous year, her mother's money box had contained a substantial stack of rubles when they had gone to the winter camp. But each month they had to pay Torgau three rubles for their space in the wagon, food cost a few kopecks each day, and they had been down to their last few kopecks when the yearly trek from fair to fair had started. Their money was now far less than it had been at the same time the previous year. The coming winter would be hard.

Silvana's wife came into view through the crack, followed by a woman of the streets from the city. Soon it would be dark, and Silvana's wife would dance on the stage. Men would crowd around the stage to throw coins and try to peek up her skirt as she danced. When she left the stage, some would follow her. All the *gadjo* thought Gypsy women were whores and Gypsy men whoremasters for their wives and sisters, and some would talk to Silvana and offer him coins to lie with his wife. Silvana would take those who were too drunk to know the difference to his wagon to lie with the prostitute from the city, and Silvana's wife would wait in the compartment at the front of the wagon until they had all taken their turn and left. Then she would go back to the stage and dance again.

Saiforella turned on the pallet and watched her mother, who had finished cleaning the bowls and putting them away. She was sewing on a blouse cut from a square of bright yellow muslin Saiforella had taken from a house in Makariev, the city where they had been previous to Diakonskii. The next fair was at Nizhnii, but it would be at least two or three weeks before it started, and it was a bad time because there was no opportunity to earn the money that was still needed for food and rent. There were few places they

26

could go to wait for the fair at Nizhnii to begin. The remote and desolate location where they made winter camp with the other caravans was far away, and Gypsy caravans were usually tolerated only where fairs were being held.

"Where are we gonig?"

"To a village of which Panna has heard. The landowner there is said to be a kind man, and Panna believes he will let us stay there."

"And if he will not?"

Her mother looked at her with an anxious, placating smile. "They say he is a very kind man, Princess. And there are no soldiers or officials there, only villagers. I will have your blouse finished to go with your skirt, and you will be able to wear your pretty clothes and your earnings, my beauty."

Saiforella looked away, sighing. There were so few opportunities to walk in the sunshine without her disguise, open and unafraid. Perhaps for a time she could dream of rich clothes, bountiful food, gold bangles on her arms, and a large, gaily-painted and decorated wagon pulled by four powerful, sleek horses, and she could forget that she was one of a band of migrant doves in a world of hawks and vultures.

"What is the name of this village?"

"It is called Sherevskoye. The *gadjin* who owns it is a man called Sheremetev."

CHAPTER II

The sun burned down mercilessly from a brassy, cloud-less sky, and in the distance the road faded into a dancing blur of rising heat waves. Count Sheremetev's horse plodded slowly along the road, followed by the carriage in which his wife and her maids rode. Behind the carriage was a long line of carts and wagons loaded with baggage, provisions, and house serfs. Distant features in the landscape gradually came closer, neared, then passed. There were villages, clusters of rude houses around a tiny square and a small church surmounted by a domed spire. Occasionally they passed serfs along the road, sometimes one or two with their hoes or other tools on their shoulders, or a cluster of men and women in worn, dusty clothing and clumsy boots, with children trotting along behind. All of them moved off the road and bowed deeply as the proces-sion passed, the men uncovering their heads and the children staring fearfully and curiously. They crossed creeks spanned by bridges made of heavy, hand-hewn timbers which rumbled hollowly under hoofs and wheels, and beyond the low hills lay the valley, with the road going through the center of it to the next hill.

It was drearily monotonous. The villages, creeks, forests, fields, groups of serfs, and other features

28

seemed to repeat themselves endlessly. The count had traveled the road many times and knew he was nearing his destination, but the journey was long and tedious, one valley or hill much like the rest, and an hour or a day much like the one before or after it. The broad expanse of rolling terrain seemed like a gigantic treadmill which would continue to flow by forever.

Gavril Pavlovich Yakovlev, the village headman, was waiting where the road to the village turned off the high road, the rest of the welcoming retinue behind him. There were four village elders, the pink skin of their scalps showing through thin, white hair as they held their hats in both hands, the clerk, cringing, grinning, and moving his ink-stained fingers nervously, and the village priest, fat and sweating in his long cassock. The idiot Pavlo was peering around a tree a few yards away grimacing grotesquely and shrugging frantically, giving the impression that he either had something he urgently needed to communicate or an agonizing need to urinate. The ancient, crippled hag who scooted around on thick pads of tattered rags tied to her hands and knees had lived through another winter and had made it to the high road with the welcoming party, and she crouched in the weeds at the side of the road, gaping up open-mouthed through the tangle of dirty white hair which had escaped from the scrap of torn rag on her head.

The count reined up his horse, and the carriage, carts, and wagons stopped behind him. The headman stepped forward, and the count leaned over and extended his right hand, which the headman kissed reverently and began his welcoming speech.

The speech never varied. The pink opening of the headman's mouth in the thick mat of his mustache and beard uttered the same words he had said the year before that. Or even many years before, because this headman looked much like the previous headman. It was one of the moments when time and events seemed to reach a juncture with themselves, crossing and blending and bringing into question the very existence of reality.

The peasants' beards were combed and their hair was freshly trimmed. They had on their best clothes, clean white cotton blouses belted at the waist and hanging down over baggy trousers tucked into heavy boots which shone with thick coatings of grease mixed with soot. Lookouts would have been posted to give them ample warning of the arrival, and they had undoubtedly been waiting for hours. There was an agonizing pathos about their anxious preparations and eagerness to please, as well as in the expressions on their faces. Others dealt with their serfs impersonally, but a combination of personality and experience had given Sheremete a deep sense of responsibility toward them. They had responded with loyalty and devotion, and the relationship between master and serf was much more complex than was usual. At times he felt envious of others whose considerations were less complicated and cluttered, and at other times he felt resentful over the intrusions of serfs' affairs upon his time and energies. But somehow it seemed worth it.

The headman continued talking. It was a momentous event to them, and one to be savored fully and dealt with ceremoniously. The count could feel the sweat trickling down his cheeks as he patiently waited. The delay was irritating to his wife, Marya Pavlovna. He could hear her scolding one of her maids in the carriage. Her voice became louder, more angry, then there was a sound of a slap and one of the maids squealed and began weeping. Marya Pavlovna's attitudes toward serfs were unmixed and untroubled by considerations other than her own needs and desires.

But her mercurial moods included kindness and generosity, and her maids regarded her with a combination of awe, fear, and affection. There was a sound of another slap, and the maid's sobs became louder. One of the elders glanced at the carriage then quickly looked back at the count. Yakovlev continued talking. The house serfs riding on the carts and wagons stirred, some of them climbing down to peer, point, and giggle at Pavlo.

Yakovlev finished, and he moved forward and reached for the count's hand. The count smiled and nodded, leaning down and letting the headman kiss his hand again, then he sat up in the saddle and gathered the reins to turn his horse onto the road to the village. Pavlo darted from behind the tree with a penetrating squeal, and began bounding rapidly along the road toward the village in long, soaring leaps, turning sidewards and looking back at the count, and uttering a shriek with each leap. The house serfs laughed uproariously, climbing back into the carts and wagons. Marya Pavlovna slapped the maid again. The headman and elders turned to lead the way along the road, and the clerk and priest stepped aside to follow the carts and wagons. The count held his horse back to a slow walk, following the headman and elders. The carriage squeaked and rattled as it turned onto the road after him. The carts and wagons began moving again.

The road was lined with large limewood trees on both sides, shady and cool after the high road. It was level for a few yards, then it went up the side of a low hill. Pavlo was far ahead, disappearing over the top of the hill, still leaping and shrieking. The headman and elders breathed heavily, and the horses labored up the incline. At the top of the slope there was a panoramic view of fields, some harvested, some yet to be harvested, and others plowed for replanting, a pattern of squares of different colors and sizes, spotted with the tiny dots of serfs moving like clusters of ants in the distance. The dark line of the deep forest spread across the hills beyond the fields, curving like a scythe. There were isolated homesteads of woodcutters and herdsmen along the edge of the forest and scattered among the fields, and a few versts away there were two jumbled groups of houses which made up the outlying villages. The avenue of limewood trees ended at the bottom of the hill, at the main village; Sherevskoye, with the towering, brooding stone hulk of the estate manor surrounded by its gardens, stables, and outbuildings overlooking the village and the broad, shining blue ribbon of the river. The count glanced back as his horse followed the headman and elders across the top of the slope. The wagons and carts were spread out along the avenue, the horses leaning into the harness and straining with effort. The clerk was behind the last wagon, trying to keep up. The priest was far behind the clerk. The crippled old hag had come only a short distance, leaning forward to plant the pads on her hands on the road ahead of her and then dragging herself forward on the pads on her knees.

The wide gate in the stone fence in front of the manor was standing open, the windows were open, and the contingent of house serfs who had been sent ahead to ready the house were in a line at the edge of the courtyard. The horses' hoofs clattered on the stove pavings and the carts and wagons rumbled through the gate. The count dismounted and handed the reins to a house serf, followed by Marya Pavlovna who lumbered out of the carriage and walked up the steps, redfaced and overweight, hot and irritable, pinching and slapping at two of her maids. The count looked at her, smiling fondly. She had been hopelessly spoiled as a child, which was more or less usual, and it had carried over into adulthood, which wasn't unusual. But the pettishness which had been aggravating at twenty had become what was a somehow appealing and engaging childishness at forty. She glared at him, tossed her head, and marched through the front door as a house serf opened it for her and her maids.

The count spoke with the headman and the elders for a moment, then they took their leave, bowing and backing away. The courtyard was a bedlam as the rest of the carts and wagons came through the gate. Horses snorted and stamped, drivers exchanged comments, and the house serfs milled about, laughing and chattering. The house steward shouted and waved to restore order and organize unloading parties. Two of Marya Pavlovna's maids climbed back and forth on a wagon, digging frantically for something she wanted, and serfs began carrying things inside. The count made his way through the wagons and serfs to the steps, and went inside.

It was an old house, and as a child he had spent many long, drowsy summer afternoons exploring forgotten corners and odd rooms in haphazard arrangement on the upper floors, sometimes finding broken toys, bits of yellowed letters, and other fragments left in the wake of the passage of some forgotten ancestor of years before. The builder had been one in whom the Cossack blood had been undiluted, and it was much like a fort, with the windows on the third floor and those on the second floor over the wings positioned to give overlapping fields of fire to protect the lower windows and entrances. Some more accustomed to the modern Italian and French styles of architecture were slyly derisive about it, but it was well built and comfortable. And it had protected the family during the Pugachev uprising, when many noble families had been slaughtered.

33

The entry hall was massive, the ceiling soaring up to the height of the second floor, with staircases on both sides leading up to a mezzanine connecting the hallways leading into the second floor wings. An arched doorway on the left of the entry hall led into the ballroom, and doorways on the right led into the drawing rooms and formal dining room. The count walked the length of the entry hall, past the staircases, and through a doorway into his study. The furniture was dark with age, heavy and old fashioned, familiar from childhood. The six tall, dome-shaped windows looking onto the back garden were open, and the cool, fresh breeze filled the room with the scents of the river and the fields.

A door between the two center windows opened onto the stone veranda along the rear of the house. He went through the doorway, crossed the veranda, and sat down on the stone ballustrade along the edge of it and looked around the garden. The shade trees were old and gnarled, the shrubbery arrangements neatly trimmed, and the flower beds carefully edged and weeded. The boughs on two apple trees near the back of the garden were sagging under the weight of the fruit on them.

Marya Pavlovna's angry voice came through an open window above him. He glanced up, then looked away, sighing with resignation. Part of the reason for her mood was reflected by the apples on the trees. The summer season was well advanced, and it was much later than the time they usually arrived at the summer estate. It had been a hot and uncomfortable trip, and the summer visitation of cholera in Moscow had been nearing its apex by the time they left, carts rumbling through the streets in the slums and collecting piles of corpses to take to the lime pits outside the city. Marya Pavlovna's mother and two brothers had died of cholera during her childhood, and while there were few families which hadn't had their losses from cholera, the memory seemed to affect her more deeply than most. The thought of death seemed to prey on her mind.

Another reason for her continuing dissatisfaction was that they lived in Moscow, banned from the court at St. Petersburg because of an impertinent comment the count had made to Czar Paul. Aleksander had been czar since 1801, six years before, and the ban had been continued by him. Part of the reason for the delay in the city had been the anticipated arrival of Prince Yusupov, a friend of the count since their days together in the Izmaylovsky Regiment, and an intimate of Czar Aleksander. Yusupov had come to Moscow to conduct a meeting of the Academy of Arts, arriving some six weeks later than his original schedule, and despite his hurry to finish his business and leave the cholera–ridden city, he had been cordial and friendly to the count. He had promised to do what he could to assist Sheremetev in gaining readmittance to court, but his promises had been less than concrete and specific.

Prince Yusupov was one among many intermediaries whose support he had enlisted, thus far to no avail. At some point there had to be a judgement as to whether or not the objective was worth the effort. Moscow wasn't Siberia, there was a congenial social circle, and there were clubs and theaters. The summer estate was comfortable and much closer to Moscow than St. Petersburg, and there were business affairs and other matters to fill his time.

But there was also duty. He wasn't available at court to fulfill tasks and commissions, and the reason he wasn't there was his doing. It was his obligation to make amends. There was also the consideration that Marya Pavlovna would be much happier in St. Petersburg. And there was his son, Vassily Ivanovich, ten years old and in boarding school, who was the sole heir of the Sheremetev family and whose long range interests would be poorly served by his family's isolation from court. So he would continue trying.

Two house serfs were placing his books, papers, writing materials, and other miscellanea on shelves and tables in the study. He went through the study and into the adjacent room, his bedchamber, where his valet was sorting clothes and other belongings and putting them away. The count sent him for water and began undressing. The valet returned with a couple of house serfs carrying buckets of water and a tub, and Sheremetev stood in the tub and washed while the valet poured the water over him.

For the trip he had worn fashionable clothing in the French style, linen trousers which fit closely around the waist, hips, and thighs, a ruffled shirt, an uncomfortably long and heavy frock coat with a high collar, and a peaked felt hat, and he felt cool, refreshed and more comfortable after bathing away the dust and sweat of the day and dressing in the clothing he usually wore on the estate when not receiving visitors; a long blouse of soft holland with a wide belt around the waist to gather it, and loose linen trousers tucked into knee boots. The valet brought a light meal of raisins and nuts, cheese, bread, and a bottle of wine. He ate, then walked through the manor, slapping his riding crop against his leg and looking around.

It was late afternoon, and the sunshine streaming through the windows on the west side of the manor was a soft gold, picking out motes of dust hanging in the air. Groups of house serfs moved around, under the watchful eyes of the house steward and housekeeper. The count walked into the huge ballroom. Tall windows covered with heavy drapes filled one of the long walls, and the other was covered with tapestries hung on gilded rods. At the opposite end of the room there was a raised dais for the musicians, and dozens of chairs upholstered in striped fabric were ranged along the walls. On each side of the arched entrance from the entry hall were long sideboards for refreshments.

But the room seemed very empty. His boots stirred whispers of sound which echoed back from the walls. The pink and silver paint on the plaster ceiling was faded, and he could see cobwebs in the corners and on some of the chandeliers. The drapes, tapestries, and the fabric on the chairs looked faded. As a child, he could remember times when the ballroom had been a blaze of light and crowded with guests, but in later years many had moved their summer residences to other areas. It was now fashionable to spend the summer in the vicinity of Czarskoe Selo, the czar's summer residence near St. Petersburg. Until a few years before, there had been a military garrison twenty versts away, and there had been young officers to invite to dinner so they could flirt with and pay court to Marya Pavlovna. But the garrison had been closed. There were only a few summer residences within a reasonable distance, and the past summers had been characterized by a lack of social activity. He found it refreshing, but Marya Pavlovna became bored very quickly.

The house quietened as the serfs finished their tasks and retired to the servants' hall for their meal. There was a feeling of anticlimax in the arrival, as though something were left undone. Sheremetev left the ballroom, walked up the stairs on one side of the entry hall, turned down the corridor, and stopped in front of the door of Marya Pavlovna's sitting room, rapping on it with his riding crop.

A maid opened the door a crack, then opened it wider and stepped back. Marya Pavlovna was lying on a long sofa in front of the windows, a cloth on her forehead. A weeping maid was picking up pieces of a china vase which had been smashed against the wall. Most of the maids were conspicuously absent. Marya Pavlovna turned her head slightly to look at him, then closed her eyes again.

"Are you resting well, Marasha?"

"I have a headache."

He walked across the room toward her. "Perhaps lavender on your temples would help."

"If I had a maid to put it on, instead of these clumsy oxen!"

He pulled a chair away from the wall and around to the front of the sofa, and he sat down, tapping his riding crop against his knee. "Then I will do it for you."

That brought a weary smile, and a maid giggled. "With your great hands?" his wife murmured. "Indeed my temples would be crushed . . ." Her voice and her smile faded, and she sighed heavily. "It is lonely already. Autumn will not come soon enough for me."

"You're weary, Marasha. Things will seem more cheerful tomorrow."

"Not when I awaken and I am here. We might be in Siberia, but for this insufferable heat."

"It is clear that you know little of Siberia."

"And scarcely more of St. Petersburg, it has been so long since I have been there. When will we be able to return to court?"

He sighed and shook his head as he stood up and moved toward the door. "That remains to be seen. Have a glass of wine, and perhaps it will ease your headache."

She moved on the couch and sighed irritably. "Did you come to inquire after entertainment this evening, Ivan Nikolayevich?" she asked in a spiteful tone. "If you did, then I must disappoint you, because I am indisposed."

The maids giggled. The count contained a sudden flash of anger, looking back at her as he opened the door. "I came to inquire about your comfort, Marya Pavlovna. Perhaps you will feel better tomorrow."

"La, such restraint," she murmured. "Is this my great Cossack, Ivan Nikolay'vich? It surpasses belief that this is the one who inspired the czar's anger and got himself exiled."

He tapped his riding crop against his leg, looking away and shrugging. "Moscow is hardly exile, madame. And hopefully, moderation has come with maturity."

She sighed heavily and turned her head back, looking up at the ceiling. "I would that the lesson had come sooner."

He nodded, turning toward the doorway. "And I, madame," he replied quietly, walking through the doorway, and he closed the door behind himself.

He went back downstairs and out the front door, and walked slowly down the steps. The gardener, an old, wizened man, was walking along the side of the courtyard toward the gate with a couple of tools over his shoulder, and he grinned and bowed deeply as the count nodded to him. The count walked through the gate to the road. Pavlo was sitting on the ground outside the gate, and he sprang up with a piercing screech and bounded away when he saw Sheremetev. The count looked down the road at the village, slapping his leg restlessly with his riding crop, then turned and started walking along the avenue between the trees, toward the top of the rise overlooking the village and river.

The surface of the road between the limewoods was corrugated with fascines embedded in the dirt, bundles of sticks laboriously gathered, tied together, and sunk into the mud during the spring thaw to stabilize the roadbed. They were scarcely noticed by most, a vibration under the wheels of a carriage and nothing more, but they meant something more to him. At fifteen he had been banished to the summer estate for a winter by his father because of an indiscretion with one of his mother's younger maids. The summer previous to that, the road to the village had been rough and pitted, which he had barely noticed but which had brought the village headman of the time a reprimand from his father, and the villagers had been making preparations to repair the road when he, his valet, and his tutor arrived by troika from St. Petersburg for his winter of punishment.

There had been a shortage of firewood in the village. Each day the villagers had streamed out into the forest to dig fallen limbs from under the snow, but the houses had been frigid and many of the women and children had been ill, because most of the wood had gone into the hoarded stacks of fascines the headman had levied on each household to repair the road when the spring thaw began. Standing timber was landowner's property, but he had told the headman to have the willow thickets along the river thinned to provide extra wood, knowing that his father wouldn't observe it. Later, out of sheer boredom, he had helped them make fascines and repair the road when the spring thaw began. So he noticed the corrugations in the road, because he knew that each foot required hours of work.

During the winter he had spent at the estate, two children had been killed and partially eaten by wolves driven from the forests by hunger. An old man and an old woman had died, and a younger woman had died during childbirth. A man had fallen through the rotten ice on the river when the thaw began, and had never been seen again. Before that winter, the village had been something forgotten between summers. Since then, it had been a living entity peopled by human beings. Then there had been five years at school in England during the reign of Catherine the Great, when the British had replaced the French influence at St. Petersburg. The tiny isle had seemed claustrophobically small after the vast reaches of Russia, but there had been an expansiveness of a different sort among people who regarded their churchmen with a tolerant skepticism, flung the contents of chamber pots at unpopular nobles, and had been known to shout obscenities at their sovereign when passing by in a coach.

After Sheremetev inherited the estate, he had gained the reputation of being indulgent and tolerant, patient and slow to order the knout for any but the most surly and intractable. He retired serfs from the labor of the fields at a relatively young age, letting them share in the produce of the village while they puttered about at odd jobs and visited with each other, and he had introduced cottage industry so the villagers could improve their lot. The crops were substantially more abundant than they had been during his father's time, and the two smaller outlying villages represented expansions he had made to the original estate. In both instances, they had been properties heavily mortgaged by owners who gambled to excess, and in both instances deputations from the villages had come to him and asked him to buy the property and village. In one instance he had been short of ready money, and the villagers had made up part of the money and loaned it to him.

Most landed nobles wouldn't have allowed the old, crippled hag and the idiot to remain in their village. But the old, crippled hag had once been a young woman, perhaps comely and desirable, and she had worked long and hard. And one who clung to life with such tenacity deserved at least the opportunity to keep clinging. The headman didn't like Pavlo, because he frequently introduced the ridiculous into matters that the headman considered weighty. But it seemed possible that the far edge of the ecstasy of insanity might be in touch with some higher order of things.

The clear, ringing sound of a shepherd's birchbark pipe hung in the late afternoon air. A cheerful, melodic chant came from several directions as the workers came in from the fields, men's and women's voices blending and the rhythms of the different groups in different directions mixing together in a somehow harmonious whole. The voices of children playing in the village streets rang out. There was an odor of woodsmoke blending with the scent of the fields, and a soft haze hung over the river. The air was cooler, and the sun was setting in a bed of crimson fire.

A girl drove a gaggle of geese along the avenue with a long, willow stick. She was sixteen or seventeen, her bare feet dirty and her coarse features red from the sun. Her clothes were ragged, faded, and patched, an apron over a voluminous skirt which came halfway down her calves, an ill-fitting blouse, and a scarf around her head. But there was a suggestion of the curves of large breasts under the loose clothes, and her hips moved with a lithe, natural swing as she walked. She flushed, giggled, and curtsied awkwardly as she passed him, and he smiled and nodded. His smile faded, and he looked at her as she walked on. She glanced over her shoulder, then looked at him more closely. Her face flushed furiously, and she began walking slower and swinging her hips in instinctive provocation and invitation. The geese slowed and began picking in the grass around one of the limewoods. She dug at the dirt with her bare toes and looked at him from the corners of her eyes.

42

He sighed, turned, and walked on along the road away from her. The lesson of the winter on the estate had been learned, and it had been reinforced by experience. Much of his relationship with his serfs was based on mutual respect, and he had a responsibility toward the Sheremetev name and bloodlines. But his Cossack ancestors had bequeathed him the blue eyes, tall, powerful build, the healthy constitution which made his fifty years rest lightly upon him, and a fiery temperament which had resulted in his being banned from the court at St. Petersburg and which made him glance over his shoulder regretfully as he walked on and the girl continued driving her geese toward the village.

Dusk fell as he stood at the top of the rise and leaned against the trunk of one of the limewood trees, looking down at the village and the river. He walked back down the avenue to the manor house. Tapers and lamps had been lit in the entry hall and up the staircases, and the house serfs were moving around quietly. His valet was lighting tapers in his bedchamber as he walked in. The valet took the count's riding crop and put it on a shelf, and helped him off with his boots. Sheremetev sat down in a chair, relaxing with wriggling his toes. The girl driving the geese was still on his mind.

"Vodka."

The valet nodded, crossing the room to take a bottle and a glass from a shelf.

CHAPTER III

"The *starets* will not eat the potatoes, *barin*."

The headman's voice was quiet and apologetic, his eyes moving up to meet the count's then sliding uneasily away again. The count sighed heavily and slapped his leg with his riding crop, containing his anger. The morning had started poorly, the rays of the rising sun coming through the windows of the study and awakening him as he sprawled in a chair with an empty vodka bottle on the floor, a burning nausea churning in his stomach, an agonizing headache pounding in his temples, and his mind reeling in a foggy, muddled state between sobriety and drunkenness. Then a glance at the clerk's books had put him into a rage. He used the records as a basis for making decisions affecting the people in the village, and they were hopelessly inaccurate. And he had given the clerk a week to get them into order, promising him the knout if he failed.

But the distaste of the holy man for potatoes was much more serious than untidy and inaccurate books. Serfs clung tenaciously to tradition, even when it was clearly irrational. A villager would plow a field in the same direction and pattern that he had used for years, a direction and pattern set for him by his father be-

44

fore him, and it was only with the greatest difficulty that he could be persuaded to begin plowing on the other side of the field and cut across previous furrows. The introduction of cottage industry had been only grudgingly accepted and by only a few younger families, even though their earnings in weaving fabric and making felt boots produced several times their annual earnings in farming. Similarly, they hadn't liked the potatoes the previous year, when the count had made them plant them on an experimental basis. The yield had been beyond his most optimistic expectations, and he had committed a lot of the land to them this year. But he could only make them grow potatoes. He couldn't make them eat potatoes. The serfs were very superstitious, and they wouldn't eat them if the holy man wouldn't. There had been problems on some of the czar's properties where the German overseers had introduced potatoes. They had been blamed for everything from cholera to impotence and it had been necessary to send a convoy of sleighs to carry grain from the stockpiles maintained against famine in order to feed serfs who were starving while surrounded by tons of potatoes. He had expected less difficulty from his serfs, because he had made a point of eating them himself in the presence of the villagers the year before, smacking his lips and exclaiming how delicious they were. But if the holy man wouldn't eat them, they wouldn't.

"Perhaps they weren't boiled properly. As I told you last year, they are best with ample seasoning and pieces of cabbage."

"Different ways have been tried, your honor."

"Have the villagers been eating the potatoes?"

"Some, your honor."

"Have you?"

45

The headman cleared his throat uncomfortably and looked away again. "Not for some time, your honor. All I had have been eaten."

The count nodded skeptically. The motion made his headache throb, and he tucked his riding crop under his arm and rubbed his forehead. They were standing in front of the headman's house at the end of the village street, the count's horse standing by them. Several children were standing between adjacent houses and staring open-mouthed, and women doing chores watched them surreptitiously. Four old men were standing at a polite distance looking on.

"Will you enter my house, your honor? The sun is hot."

It was the second time the invitation had been given, and the count forced a smile to soften the negative. His main purpose in stopping to talk to the headman had been to get his mind off his anger at the village clerk. And he had discovered a problem of much greater magnitude. He pulled the horse closer, preparing to mount. "No, I will go and speak with the *starets*."

"Perhaps you will have a bowl of tea before you go, your honor."

An earlier bowl of tea his valet had brought him had promptly come back up, as had the quart or so of water he had drunk to slake his raging thirst, and the handful of raisins he had cautiously swallowed. "No, perhaps another time."

"A cup of vodka could serve to lighten the problems of the moment," the headman said diffidently. "I would have one, but I am not as young and strong in the mind as my *barin*, and I would be unable to see to my duties properly."

The count hesitated. It was unquestionably obvious that he had imbibed too freely the night before, and the headman's attitude all during the conversation had reflected that he recognized it. The count felt a remote disgust with himself, as he always did when he drank too much, but the headache was a gnawing torment. He nodded, moving back away from the horse and holding the reins loosely. "Perhaps it would, Gavril Pavlovich."

The headman smiled widely and bowed, backing away, and he turned and went into his house, calling his wife. The count put his riding crop under his arm and rubbed his forehead again as he looked around. The children were motionless and staring. The elders smiled and bowed politely when his glance crossed them. The air was hot and still in the street, and there was a strong odor of urine and feces. The count had tried to establish some rules of hygiene in the village, and everyone had listened and agreed gravely. And then they had continued to urinate and defecate between their houses. At times it felt as though he were standing in the middle of the river and trying to hold back the water with his arms.

The headman returned with a large cup of vodka. It was cheap and raw, fiery and powerful, and it burned a trail down to his stomach. For a moment the nausea surged, becoming imperative, then it subsided. The amount was substantial, but courtesy required that he drink it all. He finished it and handed the cup back to the headman, thanking him. The headman replied in a quiet voice, smiling and bowing as the count mounted his horse and turned it into the street. The elders bowed as he rode past them, and he nodded. Pavlo darted from between two houses on the left side of the street, uttering a shrill whoop, and raced between two houses on the right side of the street.

Of all Sheremetev had learned in England, doubtful skepticism toward those who announced themselves

47

as interpreters of divine will was the most enduring. And the structure and composition of the Church, as well as the conduct of many of its members, had done little to allay his skepticism. The black clergy, the monastic elite, had their leaders in the czar's councils and constituted a spiritual arm of the Government. The white clergy, those who lived among the laity as parish priests, performed yeoman's work dictated by their superiors. In both groups, there were too many who were grasping and greedy. The black clergy reaped rich rewards in personal gain and influence in political circles, and the white clergy, who were usually barely literate and had memorized the services and Biblical passages necessary to fulfill ritual duties, preyed on the serfs. The count had once heard of a priest in a nearby village who had refused to perform the funeral services for a penniless woman's dead child until she had borrowed some money to pay for it. He had gone to the village to see if the story were true, and it had been. He had paid for the funeral service for the woman, and after it was over, he had beaten the priest through the village with his riding crop.

But the holy men were a group apart. Devotees to a life of pious vagabondage and begging, they were officially ignored by the Church. But they were revered and regarded with superstitious awe by the serfs. Some were unquestionably sincere, and several had attained wide reputation as mystics possessing channels of access to higher powers. Others were simply charlatans, vagrants or deserters from the Army hiding under matted beards, filthy rags, and nonsensical jabber. Regardless of their origins and sincerity, a landowner who placed himself in opposition to them would find that his serfs were giving him lip service but doing holy man's bidding.

The street through the village turned into a narrow, dusty road between tall willows and reeds along the high water mark of the river on the left and the fields on the low hill to the right. The vodka had helped. The count's headache was diminishing rapidly, and his stomach felt better. The sunshine seemed bright rather than glaring, and the cool breeze rustling through the willows was fresh with the damp scent of the river. A few serfs moved along the road between the fields and the village, and he nodded to them as they moved to the side of the road and bowed deeply.

Further along the road there was a shallow valley between the low hills on the right. A narrow creek lined with tall birch trees ran through the valley, and the road curved to the left around the marshy, overgrown area of willows, reeds, briars, and brambles where the creek fed into the river. He reined his horse to a stop at the bridge of heavy, weathered timbers across the creek. It was an area he knew well. The wolves used the concealment of the creekline to approach the road during winter, when the birches along the creek were bare and skeletal, and women and children who had to pass that way were always accompanied by men carrying stout clubs. During hard winters, when the wolves were starved, packs of them would sometimes attack in an attempt to kill and drag away a child while the men were kept busy fighting.

There were remains of an ancient, ruined structure in the thicket, hidden from the road by the foliage. The serfs had always been superstitious about the place, but as a child he had prowled through it and explored it. The stone walls in the thicket appeared to have been erected centuries before, constructed of large, heavy blocks of which had slipped apart and sagged as they gradually sank into the soft earth. The purpose of the structure was a mystery lost in the mists of the passage of ages, along with the forgotten ones who had built and used it. He had questioned the village headman as a child, and the old man had used pebbles to count back to sixteen generations of his forebears who had lived in the village. The ruin had been there before then, looking as it still did. In digging around it, he had uncovered crude carvings of men with outsized genitals and women with large, globular breasts. His father had found them among his things and had thrown them away, concerned that they might lure his mind away from his studies and along paths unsuitable for his age. Which they had.

A well-trodden path went from the side of the road into the thicket, the path used by the villagers to bring food to the holy man and supplicate for assistance in becoming pregnant, healing an ill child, winning at cards, gaining someone's love, and the various other worries and concerns of humanity in general. Sheremetev tied his horse to a willow at the side of the path, then walked into the thicket, bending and pushing branches aside with his riding crop. It was shady and cool there, the bright sunlight becoming a green twilight as it filtered through the foliage, and the soft ground and rotting leaves spongy under his boots. The black bulk of the ruined walls became a dark shadow through the foliage, then the path widened into a grassy opening.

The holy man was sitting against the wall, his legs stretched out in front of him and his hands folded on his lap. He was thin and angular, his wild growth of hair, beard, and mustache matted into a shaggy, uncombed mass of greyish-brown which concealed all of his face except his eyes, which were closed, presumably in meditation. He was clothed in tattered, dirty rags, his chest and hairy shanks showing through holes and tears. His feet were bare. The weathered remains of a lean-to were at the end of the wall, the shelter the villagers had built for him, and earthenware bowls and an earthenware water jug stood on the ground near him. Dried, crusted lumps of boiled potato were in one of the bowls.

There had been a suggestion of movement as the count stepped into the clearing, as though the holy man might have been lying in a more comfortable position on the grass and had assumed a position more appropriate to his calling upon hearing someone approaching. The count waited, tapping his leg with his riding crop. The holy man's eyelids fluttered, then opened. His eyes were sharp, shrewd, and penetrating, the eyes of a merchant rather than of a mendicant.

"How are you called?"

The holy man's mustache and beard moved slightly as he replied in a low voice. "Who asks how I am called?"

The count looked at him in silence for a long moment, then slowly walked forward until the toes of his boots were almost touching the holy man's bare feet. The holy man blinked, his eyes suddenly wary as the count stared down at him coldly. "I am Count Ivan Nikolayevich Sheremetov, the owner of these lands. And you will address me in a manner befitting my station."

"I answer only to God, and it is only He who is to be addressed—"

The holy man's voice broke off in a squeal of surprise and pain as the riding crop slashed down across the top of one of his bare feet. He jerked the foot up under him, then pulled his other leg up as the count struck at it with the riding crop. He crouched against the wall, lifting his arms to protect his face and head as he looked up at the count in fright. Sheremetov straightened up and stepped back.

"How are you called?"

"I am called Platon, your honor."

The count nodded, pointing at the bowl of spoiled potatoes with his riding crop. "You waste food. It appears that the wisdom you are reported to possess does little credit to such a wise name."

The holy man blinked vacantly, the reference exceeding the depth of his education. He looked at the bowl then back up at the count. "Potatoes, the food of the devil. I eat only natural food, and that which is—"

"I have eaten potatoes and have suffered no ill effects. Potatoes are healthful and nourishing."

"Devil's balls. I will not eat potatoes."

The count nodded again. "If you will not eat potatoes, then you must leave. It is my wish that the people of this village eat potatoes, and they will not eat them if the holy man does not. So I must find a holy man whose hunger is greater than yours. Leave immediately, and do not exchange words with the people of the village as you go."

"God directs my movements and my actions, and He has commanded me to tarry here. I shall consult Him again and see if He wishes me to—"

"You have no need to consult with God—you have consulted with me. You shall either leave or eat potatoes."

"I shall *not* eat potatoes, and I must consult with God to determine if he wishes for me to leave or to—"

His voice broke off in a yelp of fright as the riding crop sang through the air, and it changed into a screech of pain as the crop thudded heavily against his back. He howled shrilly, curling up into a ball on the ground with his arms over his head, and the count bent over him, swinging the riding crop in long, hard blows. Sheremetov reached down and grasped his tangled hair, jerking him up off the ground. The holy man began screaming shrilly, writhing and trying to twist away. Dull red marks began showing on his dirty, pasty skin through the holes in his rags, and his shrieks became louder as his struggles became more frantic. The count released him and dropped him to the ground, then kicked him solidly in the side, driving him back against the wall. The holy man curled up on the ground by the wall, whimpering with fright and pain.

The count was breathing heavily with exertion. He drew in a deep breath, wiping the sweat from his face with his sleeve. There was still a slight feeling of detachment from the vodka, but his headache was beginning to return. He drew in another deep breath, looking down at the holy man. "You shall eat potatoes."

The holy man cowered against the wall, looking up at him in terror. "I will consult with God and ask his permission, your honor, and I—"

"No. You shall eat potatoes."

"Perhaps it would be better if I departed, as you said, your honor. I will not exchange words with the people of the—"

"No," the count said quietly, shaking his head. "I have spent too much time in debating with you, and I have changed my mind. I wish for you to stay. And for you to eat potatoes."

"Your honor, I must consult with God. I cannot defile myself with food which is unclean and not meant for humans to consume, because—"

He broke off with a squeal and began scrabbling along the wall to get away as the count snarled with anger and bent over him. The count stamped his boot down onto the holy man's back, knocking the breath

53

from him and crushing him against the ground, and he looped the strap on the grip of the riding crop over his wrist to free his hands. The holy man babbled with panic, clawing at the ground and trying to get away, and the count seized his shoulders and lifted him. He put his right hand firmly around the holy man's throat, dragging him to his feet. The holy man's eyes bulged, and his mouth became visible in the mass of his beard as he made strangled, choking noises. The count gathered his strength, and he tightened his hand around the holy man's throat and lifted his feet off the ground, holding him at arm's length. The holy man's feet flailed in the air and he clawed at the count's rigid, knotted forearm through the sleeve of his blouse as his eyes bulged wider and hoarse, muffled gasps came from his throat. His mouth opened wider and his tongue jutted out, and his struggles began diminishing. He pawed weakly at the count's arm as his body became limp. The count lifted him higher, then threw him against the wall. He smacked into the stone wall with a meaty thud, and fell to the ground.

The headache was pounding in the count's temples again. He felt hot and sweaty, and a dull, frustrated anger churned within him. The only remaining effect of the vodka was a bothersome detachment from his surroundings which served only to make his mind sluggish and torpid and did nothing to isolate him from the irritation he felt and the agony in his head. He wiped his hand against his trousers. The holy man had a sour, acrid stench about him, and his hand felt soiled and greasy. The holy man moved feebly on the ground, fumbling at his throat and breathing in deep, shuddering gasps.

"You try my patience, Platon. If you anger me further, I shall choke the life from you and continue holding your throat until your soul departs from your body through your anus. When your soul appears before God soiled with dung, you will wish you had heeded me."

The holy man looked up at him in disbelief, then in utter terror. His mouth worked soundlessly, and he continued fumbling at his throat. The count motioned toward the water jug with his riding crop. The holy man crawled to it, drank and swallowed with an effort, then spoke in a hoarse whisper.

"The villagers would not permit you to kill me. Or if you did, they would rise up and avenge my death in such a manner as to—"

"My villagers would not rise up against me, regardless of the reason. And they would not know of your death, or how it happened." He nudged the holy man with his toe, pointing toward a clump of brush. "Look at that brush in the patch of grass. If I killed you, I would take the water jug and carry water from the river and wet the grass around the brush, then I would set fire to the brush. When the brush burned and the grass dried, it would appear a miracle, would it not? The brush consumed by fire, without scorching the grass. And I would tell the villagers that God had appeared as a firebrand in the brush, calling you to him, and that three angels in white robes came for you and bore you away. The villagers would revere you and worship your memory, would they not? For all the advantage it would be to you, with the fish in the river feeding on your body and your soul appearing before God stained with dung because it left your body through your anus. And another holy man living here and becoming fat on the potatoes and other food brought to him by the villagers."

The holy man looked down at the ground. There

55

was a long silence. He sighed deeply, shaking his head, and spoke in a rasping whisper. "You are a cruel man, your honor."

"I achieve my ends, and I will not have the people in this village starve this winter because you do not like potatoes. I will have potatoes brought to you, and you shall eat them in the presence of the village headman and elders."

The holy man nodded dispiritedly. "I shall do as you command, your honor. But if there is sin, then it is upon you."

The count nodded, grunting with satisfaction and turning toward the path. "I shall bear it gladly, Platon. I have seen people starve, and I would bear any sin to keep that from happening here. But there is no sin in eating potatoes, and I am sure that you will shortly become accustomed to them and find them tasty. Go sit against the wall, and I will have your meal brought to you."

The holy man made a sound in his throat, crawling toward the wall with the water jug, and the count began walking back along the path. There was a sudden commotion in the thick growth at the side of the path, sounding like some large animal charging out at him, and Sheremetev, startled, leaped back and lifted the riding crop. Pavlo burst out onto the path, his clothes torn and his face scratched from briars, his eyes gleaming with an intense, insane light, and his face flushed and sweating. He opened his mouth wide and uttered a penetrating screech at the count. The count snarled with sudden anger, jumping forward and striking with the riding crop. It hissed through empty air, Pavlo darting away along the path, shrieking excitedly. The count started running after him, but he was slow and clumsy compared to the fleet Pavlo. Pavlo sped along the path, looking over his shoulder at the count, and ran headlong into the horse standing at the end of the path. He bounced off the horse and fell to the ground, and the horse made a sound of alarm and wheeled, kicking him solidly as he started getting to his feet. Sheremetev caught up with him, the riding crop lifted to strike. But for some reason he froze, withholding the blow. Pavlo looked up at him for a long, dragging instant, then he leaped up with a whinneying, laughing sound, ran out onto the road, and began bounding with long, springing strides toward the village, uttering a ringing shriek with each leap. The count still held the riding crop up, tense with anger, then he lowered it and chuckled wearily, patting the horse's neck and talking to him to calm him.

He started to untie the reins and mount the horse, then hesitated. A dozen serfs were working in a field up the rise from the creek, and they were exchanging comments and pointing toward Pavlo as he bounded toward the village. They were a long distance away, and their laughter and shouts were a whisper on the edge of audibility. He felt weak from not having eaten and from exertion, and the headache was excruciating, swelling and ebbing in his temples. He walked around the horse and out onto the road, cupping his hands together and shouting at the serfs. They turned and looked toward him. He waved his arm in a beckoning gesture. A couple of women dropped their tools and began trotting along the furrows in his direction. Three or more made a hesitant movement, looking at each other and at him. He turned and walked back into the shade of the willows. The two women ran toward him, and the others began digging in the furrows again.

The horse picked delicately at long, tender shoots of grass with his silky, rubbery lips. The count took the bit out of the horse's mouth so he could eat more easily, then leaned against a willow and wiped the sweat from his face with his sleeve. Insects sang and chirped in the foliage, and the sunshine was so bright that it hurt his eyes. He closed them, leaning back against the willow. The few hours of restless sleep in the chair had aggravated rather than dispelled the fatigue from the journey from Moscow. And the headache seemed to be getting even worse.

The first woman crossed the road, a hundred feet in front of the second one, and bowed as she stopped at the edge of it. She was an older woman, her face dark and seamed and her body stout under her shapeless garments. "You called me, your honor?"

"Go to the village and tell the headman that the *starets* is hungry and wishes to have potatoes and cabbage. And tell him to bring the elders with him to pay honor to the *starets* when he brings the potatoes and cabbage."

She looked at him numbly, her lower lip sagging, then she collected herself and bowed again. "I do as you command, your honor."

She shuffled away with a heavy gait between a walk and a trot. The other woman leaped lightly over the ditch on the other side of the road and crossed it toward him. She was a younger woman, much younger. Her clothes were also bundlesome and shapeless, thick and heavy to protect her from the sun, and worn, faded, and patched from hard usage. But there were indications of a lithe body under the clothes. Her breasts moved resiliently, and her step was light and quick as she crossed the road. Her features were coarse and red under the shawl, but not unattractive. She curtsied awkwardly at the side of the road and started to speak. Then her eyes met his, and she closed her mouth and looked at him in silence. Her face became redder, her eyes dropped, and an embarrassed smile played around the corners of her mouth. She moved

58

her feet slightly, and there was a subtle change in her posture. Her breasts were more prominent. The curve of her hips was more accentuated.

There were dark spots of sweat between her breasts and around her waist, and sweat shone on her face. He remembered the small stone carvings he had found in the ruin years before, and he knew what had motivated the one who had carved them. They had been grotesque and misshapen when considered as a representation of a human being, but they had possessed a grace beyond the most delicate and precise carving when considered in the abstract. The one who had carved them had looked upon a woman such as the one standing on the edge of the road, and he had expressed his response in lines of stone. The woman was gravid and fertile, as receptive and fruitful as Mother Earth, the essence of womanhood. And somehow he felt representative of the carved male images. The one who had carved those images had expressed the concept well.

He had wanted only one messenger, but he couldn't send her back to the field. The only wise course would be to remove the temptation from sight. "Go to the manor and tell the first house serf you see that I am here and I wish to have vodka brought here to me."

She curtsied and turned away. He looked at her, sighing. She glanced over her shoulder, and a wide smile spread across her face as she looked at him. He smiled wryly. She began hurrying along the road.

CHAPTER IV

"How much are you able to produce each day?"

"Twenty five arshin, when my wife and I both work on the looms, your honor."

"All of this quality?"

"Yes, your honor."

The count held the cloth toward the light from the door, feeling it and looking at it. He had expected some improvement in quality from the increase in proficiency which would result from experience, but the improvement was far greater than he had anticipated. The cloth rivaled the expensive, imported Dutch linen sold by merchants in St. Petersburg and Moscow in evenness, fineness, and sheen.

There were other reasons to feel pleased. The holy man had eaten the potatoes and cabbage while the headman and elders watched and the count sat at the edge of the clearing and drank the vodka his valet poured for him, and even if the holy man ate with less than good appetite and gusto, it had been convincing enough for the headman and elders. In addition to that problem being resolved, there had been unexpected expansion in the cottage industry. Felt boots were being made in five more houses, and two recently married couples wanted loans to buy looms for weaving fabric. It had also occurred to him that he could use the influence of the holy man to encourage an even more rapid growth of the cottage industry, now that he was amenable to suggestions.

It would solve several problems. Since his childhood, the village had almost doubled in size while the amount of farm land under tillage had remained constant. Acquiring the two adjacent properties had helped to an extent, because there had been relatively few workers in comparison with the size of the properties, and some land had been fallow. But it was a stop-gap at best. Inevitably, there would come a time when the population would exceed the output of the available land, regardless of how much he reduced his revenue requirements on the serfs, and it would come in the latter years of his ownership, depending upon how long he lived, or in the first years of his son's. His policies had resulted in an unusual growth in the population, and he didn't want to pass on problems that he himself had created.

The situation could be resolved with the proper mix of farming and cottage industry. By custom, he owned either a portion of the labor of the serfs or was due a cash payment of *obrok,* a sum of money in lieu of the labor. The woodcutters, herdsmen, a few fishermen, and a couple of serfs who owned barges and who traded between the villages along the river, had always paid *obrok* instead of working. The approaching population problem had been obvious for some time, and he had always set the *obrok* payments low and granted generous loans to any who wished to enter a trade instead of farming. The cottage industry had been an attractive idea at the beginning, because the village was located on the river and had resident owners of barges who could transport the finished products to market. It had seemed unpromising for a long time, but with the sudden interest in cottage industry among the villagers, it appeared that a solution might be forthcoming. Particularly with the assistance of the holy man.

The linen seemed to swim before his eyes, the lines in the fabric blurring and blending together. The headache was completely gone again, but the vodka had made him a little unsteady. And the cheerful, alcoholic glow enhanced the feeling of pleasure over the way the day was turning out after its inauspicious beginning. But there was a minor problem which he hadn't foreseen. As he had dismounted in front of the house and before the man's wife had come out to hold his horse, he had seen the child who was sitting quietly in a corner helping the woman on a loom. The child was of an age to be going to the classes the priest conducted on the rudiments of reading, writing, and arithmetic. The count folded the cloth and handed it back to the man, and pointed toward the child with his riding crop. "Only children of an age to work in the fields should work at weaving or making boots. He should be learning how to read and write."

"I shall do as you command, your honor."

"The cloth you are making is of good quality and should bring a good price. I congratulate you on your skill."

"You do me great honor, your honor. My wife's mother and father have talked about buying looms, and I would sell them these if I had the money to buy better ones. It could be that I have the money if some of the *obrok* is to be returned this year, as you have so generously done in past years."

"The clerk's accounts are in such a state that I cannot tell the beginning from the end. When they are corrected, I will see how much *obrok* I will be able to return."

"You are very kind, your honor."

The count nodded, turning away and crossing the room toward the ikons mounted in a wide niche in the side wall. It was hot and stuffy in the room, and his feet felt clumsy and heavy. As he bowed to the ikons, he had to shift his weight to keep from falling forward. He straightened up and turned toward the door. The doorway seemed to move from side to side as he walked toward it.

His head cleared somewhat in the relatively cooler air of the street. The woman handed him the reins, and he turned the horse and lifted himself into the saddle. The man and woman stood in front of the door and bowed deeply, and he smiled and nodded as he turned the horse away from the house. The pangs of hunger in his stomach reminded him that it was afternoon and he hadn't eaten, but it wasn't an imperative hunger. And it would be a good time to begin looking at some of the forest to see which trees the woodcutters had marked for his permission to cut down. It was always a matter of interest to him, because many estates had been completely deforested through injudicious cutting of timber. He passed the elders again, nodding to them as they bowed. An old woman was carrying a basket of potatoes along the street, and he nodded to her with a pleased smile.

The horse plodded along the street and out of the village along the road again. It was nearing the hottest hour of the day, and even the sounds of the insects seemed to be muted. Many of the serfs in the fields were sitting in the shade at the edge of the fields, eating the food brought to them from the village, and resting. The quiet was shattered by a squeal as Pavlo darted out of the willows on the left side of the road, effortlessly leaped the ditch and low stone wall at the side of the road, and raced up the hill along a path at the edge of a field. The count chuckled, watching him. As Pavlo neared the crest of the hill, he leaped another stone wall to avoid passing a group of serfs sitting on the ground, and disappeared into a thicket of brush at the edge of a small copse of trees. There was an explosion of outraged feminine shrieks, and a large, heavyset woman emerged from the brush, pulling her skirt down with one hand and dragging Pavlo with the other. She began thumping him with her free hand. Another woman emerged from the brush, shaking her skirt down, and she seized Pavlo's other arm and began beating him. Pavlo's yelps and the women's angry shouts carried across the field to the road, along with the sounds of hilarity from serfs who were watching and rolling about on the ground in convulsive laughter. The count chuckled again, opening a pocket behind the saddle and taking out the vodka bottle. He looked at the level in it, took a drink, pushed the cork back into the bottle and put it back into the pocket.

He passed the holy man's thicket, thinking about persuading him to encourage more of the villagers to take up weaving and making felt boots. It had been a trying day for the holy man; and it would be wise to wait for a few days. Many holy men had a taste for vodka, even though they publicly refused it. A few bottles of cheap vodka which could be hidden in the thicket would be a small price for his complete cooperation.

The slow, steady motion of the horse and the heat were soporific, and the count's eyelids became heavy. His head nodded. He snapped back awake and blinked his eyes as he sagged to one side in the saddle, and he reined in the horse and looked around. The path where he wanted to turn off and ride up the hill was behind him. He turned the horse around, reined him off the road and onto the path, and let the reins go slack again as the horse labored heavily up the hill.

The trees had been marked by wrapping a bough around the trunk and weaving it tightly into place. His approval was indicated when he left the bough in place and informed the woodcutters through the village headman that he had inspected that section of forest. When he had inherited the estate, the woodcutters had found, to their surprise and dismay, that he could remember which trees had been marked to cut down and would promptly levy fines for cutting down trees without permission. He had no difficulty in remembering, because he knew how he wanted the forests thinned and he could immediately spot fresh stumps which were too close together. He rode slowly back and forth through the trees, looking at the stumps. A few were fresh, most were of varying shades of darkness from weather, and some were rotting. Saplings were planted near each stump. Several of the oldest ones were much too high, those which had been cut before his time and before he ordered the woodcutters to cut low to the ground to keep from wasting wood. All of the saplings had been planted during his time, and the older ones had developed into trees, some of which were beginning to be cut. A branch flipped back from his hand as he pushed it aside and knocked his hat off, and he climbed down from the horse to retrieve it. He put it back on, wiped the sweat from his face with his sleeve, and climbed back into the saddle. It seemed to take more effort than usual. He took the vodka bottle out of the pocket behind the saddle, took a drink, and replaced it.

He rode through the patch of forest, looking at the stumps and the trees which had been marked, then rode back through on another sweep a short distance further along the length of the forest. There was a lump on the ground which looked suspiciously like a stump which had been covered with dirt and leaves, a tactic a couple of the woodcutters had tried on him, but when he dismounted and kicked the leaves away it was only a rock. He rode back to the edge of the forest and paused for a moment. The sun was beginning to incline toward the west, and the serfs were at work in the fields again. Their slow, monotonous chant sounded muffled and distant in the hot, still air. He glanced along the river and at the village as he started to turn the horse back into the forest, and then he stiffened in the saddle and tightened the reins as he lifted his hand to shade his eyes.

A line of wagons was in the process of pulling onto the wide, grassy flood shelf between the river and the village. There were fifteen or more of them, most of them large wagons pulled by four horses, and they were painted in bright colors which gleamed in the sunlight. They had large rear wheels and small front ones, and the beds were built up into tall, wooden walls and a curved roof. The horses were richly caparisoned, with ribbons and tall plumes on their bridles which were visible even at a distance, and the sunlight drew sparks of fire from the bits of metal and bells of their harness. Gypsies. He turned his horse toward the path.

The village headman was walking along the road, and he stood and waited when he saw the count riding along the road toward him. In the count's absence, he would have driven them away, but when the count was in residence in the village, he was deferred to automatically. As Sheremetev approached, the headman pointed toward the river and started to tell him about the gypsies. The count silently nodded, and the headman began following him back toward the village.

They could be arrested at any time, because they were always in violation of the law against vagabonds. In practice, however, they were only arrested when

66

suspected of something more serious, which was frequent enough. They were tolerated and allowed to travel between the fairs during spring, summer, and autumn, and they disappeared somewhere for the winter. They were also known to be dedicated, skillful thiefs, and he didn't want them anywhere near his village.

The count rode his horse between two of the houses and down onto the wide flood shelf which angled gradually down toward the river. Their horses were good stock, large and powerful, but they looked somewhat thin and overworked. And the bright paint on the wagons looked faded and weathered at closer range. The wagons were in a wide circle, the horses still hitched to them. Most of the people were moving about inside the circle, laughing and talking. Children and a few old people from the village were standing at a prudent distance, looking at the wagons curiously. Several of the gypsies saw the count approaching, and they turned and shouted toward the center of the circle. A man came between two of the wagons and walked toward the count.

He was a tall, well built man in his forties. His clothing was similar in style to Sheremetev's, but his blouse was gleaming crimson silk with deep sleeves and tight cuffs, and was belted with a brilliant blue sash which was tied at one side, with the ends hanging down. His trousers were dark and loose, stuffed into heavy boots, and the scarf wrapped around his head matched the sash around his waist. His beard and mustache was thick and black, and a gold earring dangled from one of his earlobes. His white teeth gleamed in a wide smile as he approached the count and bowed deeply with a flourish of his arm. "Have I the pleasure of addressing the landowner, *monsieur?*" he asked in good French.

"I am Count Ivan Nikolayevich Sheremetev, the owner of these lands," the count replied in the same language.

"I am delighted to meet you, *monsieur le comte*," the man said, bowing again. "I am called Panna, and I am the leader of this band of poor travelers."

"Then it is you with whom I wish to speak. You and your people may not tarry here. You must leave immediately."

"*Alors, monsieur le comte.* We are workers in metal, and we only wish to ply our trade with the good people in the village here, repairing that which they might discard as useless. And entertain them, perhaps. Our animals are weary and we have come far, *monsieur le comte,* and we will cause no—"

"*En voilà assez!* I have no wish to debate with you, and I do not intend to have gypsies camped by my village. You may water your animals at the river and let them rest for a time, but you must be back on the high road before sunset or I shall . . ."

His voice trailed off into silence as he saw her. Several of the gypsies had come between the wagons and were standing in a loose group behind their leader, listening to the conversation with worried expressions. She was by herself, standing in front of a large rear wheel on a wagon. She was young, eighteen or twenty, and a small, slender woman. Her skirt was a dark green color, fitting tightly around her waist and flaring out over her hips in thick folds which fell to her ankles, with a broad band of yellow near the hem. Her blouse was yellow, cut low and exposing her shoulders, arms, and a suggestion of the cleavage between her breasts. A scarf the same color as the blouse was wound around the gleaming mass of blue-black hair, but much of it spilled out of the confines of the scarf and fell down her back in heavy, pleasantly disarranged tresses. Her features were fine and delicate, and stunningly beautiful. She had large eyes, set well apart, and they seemed to be blue. Her nose was small and pert, her lips wide and full. She was looking at him, and the expression on her face was one of interest and an almost childish curiosity. He had seen gypsies many times before, but he had never really observed their style of clothing before. The other women looked dull compared to her.

The man said something, hesitated and glanced over his shoulder, then looked back at the count. The count looked at the man again. "Pardon?"

"I will be personally responsible for the conduct of all of my people, *monsieur le comte*. And I assure you there will be no trouble, because they obey my commands. We wish only to spend a few days, entertain your people and repair their things, rest our animals and make repairs to our wagons, and buy some food . . ."

The man continued talking as the count looked at her again. She was still gazing at him, and she appeared unconscious of the fact that he was returning her gaze. Her lips were parted slightly, and the pink tip of her tongue moved along her lower lip. She was much more slender and smaller than most Russian women. Her arms looked almost frail, and her shoulders were thin and delicate. Her small hands were clasped together in front of her. Her skin was an ivory color, a dusky white, and it looked soft and smooth. She was fascinating.

Color suddenly flooded into her cheeks, and she moved away from the wheel and edged toward the rear of the wagon, as though she had just noticed his stare. An older woman came from the other side of the wagon, looked at her and at the count, and pulled her around the rear of the wagon.

The count drew in a deep breath and released it in

a sigh. He felt muddled and confused, and the vodka made it hard to think clearly. The wagons were distinctly shabby, and the people looked tired and pathetic. The man had stopped talking and was looking at him with a hopeful smile. His request seemed to be a small thing.

"Very well, you may remain. But if there is a single item stolen in the village, every woman in your group will have her head shaven and every man will be branded as a thief."

"It is only right for you to protect your people, *monsieur le comte,* but it is not unknown for a person to mislay a thing and believe it to be stolen."

The comment indicated honesty. If they had intended to steal, the man would agree with anything in order to get to stay so they would have the opportunity. Instead, he wanted an assurance that there would be no false accusations. The count turned in the saddle and looked at the headman. "If any villager says falsely that something has been stolen by your people, he will be punished with the knout," he said in Russian.

"Are you permitting them to remain, your honor?" the headman asked in a surprised tone, not understanding the conversation in French.

"I am."

The headman bowed. "The villagers will be informed of your command, your honor."

The man began thanking him effusively, smiling widely and bowing, and the count nodded and turned his horse away, riding back toward the village. The headman followed him, and the gypsy leader turned toward his people, waving his arms and rattling something in their language. A cheer rose among them, and they ran back into the circle of wagons, whooping with exhilaration. A lilting song broke out among them, becoming louder as others joined in. A flute, then an accordion began playing the melody. The count stopped his horse at the houses, and turned to see if the young woman was in sight. People were singing and dancing happily around the wagons, unhitching the horses, taking things out of the wagons, and talking and laughing excitedly. The young woman wasn't among them. The count turned back around in the saddle and rode between two of the houses to the street.

He was hungry, but he didn't feel like going to his home. The thought of returning to the forest didn't appeal to him either. He wanted to return to the gypsy wagons and look through them for the woman, but that would create animosity, and for good reason. He sighed, turning the horse to ride back toward the forest.

The affairs of the village always interested him. They were variegated—the fields, the forests, the accounts of the woodcutters, fishermen, barge owners, and others, and the personal concerns of the villagers. Each year an old couple or two retired from the fields, and newly married couples took their places in the fields as a family unit. There was the amount of *obrok* payment to determine, requests for loans to consider, and the many other details which always filled the summers with activity. But it was all suddenly flat, dull, and uninteresting. He rode back and forth through the forest, taking drinks from the bottle of vodka. His route and movements through the forest were from habit, because he scarcely saw the fresh stumps and the trees which were marked. And he wasn't interested in them. In his mind's eye, he saw the slender young woman standing in front of the tall wagon wheel and looking at him. He wondered if her eyes were really blue.

A limb knocked his hat off again, and he almost slipped and fell from the horse when he started to dismount. He put it back on and clambered back onto the horse, looking around. It seemed that he had been riding back and forth in the patch of forest for a long time, but he appeared to be somewhere near the center of it. A few minutes later the trees began thinning out in front of him and he saw that he had come in the wrong direction, and he turned the horse and went back the other way.

It was late afternoon, and there was a soft and golden quality to the light over the landscape. Smoke was rising from a few chimneys and from fires the gypsies had built among their wagons. Some of the serfs had already left the fields, and there was a group of them, children, and old people near the wagons, talking or bartering with some of the gypsies. Other gypsies were moving along the street between the houses, selling or bartering things or possibly searching for those with metalware to repair. Pavlo was bounding around the wagons in a wide circle, and a couple of dogs from the wagons were racing along behind him, either chasing him or running with him.

Women from the wagons were at the river bank, washing children and clothes, and ripples spread out in the water as the children leaped and splashed. Others had spread out further along the bank, and there were movements in the reeds and willows from well above the open space adjacent to the village to far below it. A couple of men were fishing in the quiet backwaters in the reeds, and others appeared to be bathing. Sheremetev saw a movement and a flash of yellow in an isolated opening in the reeds near the holy man's thicket. He shaded his eyes with his hand, peering closely. There was a small cove in the river bank, with thick, tall reeds growing out into the water, and a tiny patch of greensward surrounded by willows. A lone woman was moving about at the edge of the water. Her blouse and a wide band on her skirt were bright yellow. He picked up the reins and turned the horse toward the path down the hill.

During childhood summers at the estate, he had frequently prowled along the bank, finding small, concealed openings in the reeds and willows where the currents of the river during its flood had scoured them of growth and allowed grass to grow. Woodcutters usually poked through the edge of the reeds for a long distance along the river when the flood subsided, finding and retrieving wood washed down from upriver, and lovers sometimes met in hidden, isolated spots among the willows and reeds. But the vast majority of the villagers knew little about the river except the open spot where water was drawn and clothes were washed, because they had no time, energy, or interest to waste on that which didn't produce food or money. It was ever-changing, the glade of one year becoming a thicket the next, with a few openings and paths made by dogs in the village hunting the burrowing animals which dug dens in the marshy ground. The odor of woodsmoke hung in the reeds and willows as the horse picked its way along a narrow, curving path in the growth, and the sounds of the village seemed to come from a long distance away.

Time and distance were muddled in his mind in the absence of clear and distinct references. The opening where he had seen the woman from the hill had been ahead of him and off to the left when he turned the horse onto the path by the holy man's thicket, and now it seemed that he might have come too far and it was behind him and to his right. The ground under the horses's hoofs was becoming more marshy, and it was possible that he had ridden out onto a point by the cove where the opening was located, or even far past it. There was a narrow path which turned off to the right, a dim and ill-defined line through the reeds and tall, rank weeds, and he turned the horse onto it. But a few yards further on it curved to the left. He started to turn the horse around, then loosened the reins and let it walk slowly on as he shrugged and reached to take the vodka bottle out of the pocket on the saddle. Then he remembered that the bottle was empty.

The horse stopped at a low, thick stone wall. Sheremetev looked at it, puzzled. It was the same kind of stone and construction as the ruin in the holy man's thicket, but here the destruction wrought by the ravages of time had been much more thorough. The heavy stones had sunk deeper into the earth, and were within the high water mark of the river during years of deeper floods, which had made debris accumulate around them. The ground was fairly high, almost dry under the horse's hoofs, and the reeds were thinner. There were a few thin willow saplings scattered among them, and he dismounted, tied the reins to a willow, and looked at the wall.

There was a whisper of sound, just on the edge of audibility over the rustle of the light breeze through the reeds and the hushed noises from the village the sound of a woman singing. The wall in front of him was about waist high, and he struggled up onto it, almost tumbling across it, and planted his feet firmly to keep from weaving as he turned his head from side to side and listened. The reeds and willows were still well above him, but they were much thinner and he could see further than he had from the horse. He heard the monotonous rise and fall of a woman's voice absently singing as she did some chore, but a clear, ringing, pleasant voice, in a characteristically gypsy rhythm and intonation. There was a flash of color through the growth, a bright yellow. He began walking along the wall.

The girl uttered a startled exclamation of fright and

74

surprise as he stepped into the opening, putting her hands to her mouth and looking at him with wide eyes, then slowly lowered her hands and looked at him apprehensively. Her hair was damp, piled loosely up on her head with loose wisps hanging around her ears and the sides of her face, and her blouse clung to her moistly from her bath in the river. She had been washing clothes, bright skirts and blouses, and they were hung on reeds and willows to dry. Her eyes moved up and down him as he stood a few feet from her, looking at her, and she forced a faint smile as she plucked at her skirt with her fingers and bobbed in a motion of a curtsy.

"You frightened me, your honor," she said in Russian.

Her Russian was good, with a lilting accent which made her seem exotically attractive. He collected himself, trying to make his smile casual and friendly. "It wasn't my intention to frighten you. I heard you singing and came to see who it was."

"Perhaps I shouldn't be here. I wished to have privacy to bathe and to wash my clothes, but perhaps I have abused your hospitality by wandering on your property and—"

"You may go anywhere you wish and do as you wish on my lands."

It came out much too emphatically, seeming harsh and crude rather than the polite invitation he had wished to express. The wary apprehension deepened in her eyes, and her smooth cheeks turned slightly more pale. She was still trying to smile courteously, respectfully, and confidently, but it was strained. Her eyes were huge, and they were blue, the deep, rich blue of the sky on a cloudless day in spring. Her breathing was faster than normal, making her breasts surge in the thin fabric of her blouse. She turned her head and

75

looked at her clothes. "You are too kind, your honor . . ."

"What are you called?"

"Saiforella, your honor. Of the family of Hator."

It was a pretty name, and it seemed to fit her. Her chin came up a fraction as she said her family name, as though it were a name of some importance. He nodded. "An attractive name, as is the one who bears it. I am called—"

"I know your name, your honor. We traveled without stopping so we might reach this village after the fair at Diakonskii, because it is widely known that Count Ivan Nikolayevich is a kind and generous *barin.*"

The compliment embarrassed and confused him vaguely. She stirred reactions in him that were somewhat apart from kindness and generosity. He nodded silently, looking away.

"It is late, and I should return to my wagon . . ."

"Stay and talk with me. Your clothes aren't yet dry."

The caution in her expression became more pronounced, and she looked at him and dropped her eyes. "My mother will be anxious . . ."

"Your mother? You do not have a husband?"

She looked at him again, her eyes moving over his face. A slow smile spread across her face, and her white teeth showed between full lips. There was amusement and something approaching coquetry in her smile as she lifted her eyebrows archly. "Why do you ask, your honor?"

He felt confused again, and it was difficult to look into the shining blue of her wide eyes. "You are of an age to have a husband," he muttered, shrugging and looking away.

She nodded, and her smile faded as she looked away. "I am, but I am a Hator, your honor," she replied.

She sighed softly, taking a step toward the clothes hanging on the reeds and willows. "I must return to my wagon . . ."

He stepped to her, taking her arm. "No, stay and talk with me."

Her face paled and her eyes widened with fright as she pulled away from him, and he instinctively tightened his hand on her arm to hold her. She looked up at him, her lips trembling and a pulse beating at the side of her silky throat, and he looked down at her. His impulsive movement to hold her had been motivated by the desire to detain her so he could be in her presence and look at her. But as she looked up at him, frightened and trembling like a young, wild doe, other more primitive responses stirred within him. The fragrance of her hair and body filled his nostrils, and her slender arm was warm and smooth in his hand. Color rushed back to her face and she flushed as his eyes devoured her beauty, and she pulled the neckline of her blouse higher as his eyes moved down to her breasts. He took her other arm, pulling her closer to him.

"No, your honor . . . please . . . please, no . . ."

The anguished wail of despair which rose to her lips was smothered as he clasped her in his powerful arms and lifted her, crushing her to him and kissing her hungrily. She struggled in his arms like a small, captive animal, but her strength was nothing compared to his and the breath was forced from her lungs. He fell to the ground with her, and her cry of terror was a faint moan under his lips as he tore at her clothes and his.

The numbing fog of alcohol combined with the fiery lust her young and delicate beauty had generated within him, stripping aside his inhibitions and his control over bestial desires, and the Cossack within him was

77

unleashed. He took her savagely, ignoring her cries and whimpers of pain in his mindless drive to satisfy the craving which seethed within him, and her struggles diminished as she lay pinioned under his surging body and the pain and deeper injuries to her spirit robbed her of strength and the will to resist. She lay motionless and helpless, a chance and unwilling victim of his drunken desire.

When it was over, she lay on the ground motionless for a time. He lay by her, gasping and panting. One of her hands moved falteringly, pulling at her clothes in an instinctive movement to cover her nakedness, then she slowly sat up and began pushing herself to her feet. He started to get up, reaching for her, and she quickly moved away with a cry of terror. Her lips were bruised, her hair was hanging over her shoulders and down her back, and tears were streaming from her eyes. He hesitated, then sat back with a deep groan and rubbed his face with his hands, trying to collect himself as the full realization of what he had done began dawning on him. She straightened her clothes, snatched her washing from the willows, and disappeared into the reeds.

CHAPTER V

Saiforella lay on her pallet facing the side of the wagon, numb with despair and grief. Her mother had guessed what had happened even before she pieced it together from the barely-coherent gasps and sobs, and others had seen her running to the wagon. They had gathered silently, and Panna had called her mother outside. Her mother's voice had been a broken whisper as she sobbed and talked to Panna. The deep voices of the men had rumbled as they muttered darkly among themselves. Then Panna's firm voice had spoken. Her mother had come back into the wagon, and the voices had moved away from the wagon as the people dispersed. Her mother had talked in a quiet whisper, telling her what had been said. Restitution or retribution was in order, but the count was a powerful man. The men were angry, but they would follow Panna's orders. Nothing would be done in haste. The outcome remained to be determined.

And life had gone on. Darkness had fallen, and the serfs had come to the wagons. Trinkets and baubles had been peddled, and housewares had been repaired. Booths had sold tea, bread, and cake, the same as the villagers had in their houses a short walk away and perhaps even a poorer quality, but made delectable because of the polite smiles and bows with which it was served. The stage had been put up, the streamers had been hung, and the torches had been lighted. The villagers had crowded around as the acts paraded for them; the trained dogs, the dancers, jugglers tossing their hoops and bats, then all the musicians and singers in the band playing and singing.

The laughter, shouts, and sounds of the music came through the walls of the wagon to Saiforella. She had always been isolated from the merriment except when among her own in the winter camp, because she possessed a quality of beauty which was dangerous.

And it had brought her downfall. The agony of her sorrow was made more intense by the knowledge that it had been her own fault. She had unwisely exposed herself to the gaze of a powerful and highly-placed *gadjin*, in a moment of foolishness wasting all the efforts of her mother and the other women in the band who had done so much to protect her since her beauty had ripened. And even more unwisely, she had ventured along the bank of the river without an escort, contrary to the constant reminders of her mother and the others. But the trip had been long, hard, and tiring, the wagons leaving Diakonskii after dark, traveling through the night and continuing on through the day toward Sherevskoye. The *gadjin* had been a truly kind-looking man, as Panna had been told. A stern but just face, beardless but not strange-looking because of it, even a handsome man. Tall and powerful, massive compared to the men in the gypsy band. A person of high birth, as she was among her people, and one of the first she had seen. Eyes the color of hers, if somewhat tinged with red from strong drink, and a dashing figure as he sat his fine horse, but flushed and ugly in the grip of his animal passions.

Everything had changed. There would still be suitors at the winter camp, but their advances would be more casual than ardent and there wouldn't be as many. It happened to gypsy women occasionally, and ever afterwards a shadow hung over them. The band would be in disgrace because a woman of the Hator family had been raped while in their safekeeping. Panna's leadership would be questioned, because he was expected to exercise control over her. There would be arguments, accusations, and recriminations at the winter camp. The council might designate a husband for her, a widower or other older man, regardless of her wishes. All because of a moment of poor judgment.

The hours had passed. Someone had scratched quietly at the door and handed in a bowl of lentil soup, one of her favorite meals. But the soup had grown cold as she lay on her pallet in her stained and muddy clothes. The villagers had left, and the torches extinguished. The noises died away around the wagons, and the camp settled for the night. Her sobs changed to dry gasps and shudders as her tears became exhausted, and her mother still knelt by her pallet in silent sorrow and sympathy.

A dog barked on the other side of the circle, then became quiet as a man spoke sharply. There was a distant murmur of men's voices, then silence again. Several minutes later the horses moved restlessly as someone crossed the circle toward their wagon. The footsteps came closer, then there was a gleam of a lantern under the door and the sound of a heavy boot on the step.

"Bala?"

It was Panna. Her mother rose silently, went to the door, and opened it. The light of the lantern was bright after the darkness as Panna came up the steps. He came into the wagon and quietly closed the door, and her mother moved the bowl of cold soup to one

81

side and sat back down. Panna's boots scraped against the floor as he knelt and put the lantern down. There was a surreptitious sound on the other side of the rag partition as the Torgau family moved closer to listen.

"The *gadjin* came to my wagon. He tells me he was drunk, and he is sorry for what he did."

"He is sorry?" Saiforella's mother snapped. "His sorrow is mirth compared to ours. My daughter is—"

"Enough," Panna interrupted in a weary tone. "It is done. The *gadjin* was drunk, and your daughter was foolish. What remains now is to decide on what we can do with the situation at hand."

Saiforella's hopeless despondency faded as resentment and anger built up within her. Panna's tone seemed too casually resigned, and she didn't need him to tell her she had been foolish. She turned on the pallet, pushing her hair out of her eyes and looking at Panna. "I am sure that your wisdom combined with that of the *gadjin* is sufficient to discover means of capturing the stars in your hands," she said sarcastically, then cleared her throat impatiently as her voice quavered from weeping. "What device have you decided upon to return my virginity?"

Panna's face flushed with irritation and Saiforella's mother looked at her with a placating expression and reached out to pat her arm. Saiforella pushed her mother's hand away and glared at Panna. He looked away, taking a deep breath and sighing, then looked back at her. "You shall marry him."

It took a moment for the full meaning to register. Saiforella's frown became puzzled. Her mother shook her head as she looked at Panna. "But he has a wife, does he not?"

"Yes, but there is precedent. If you will recall, your daughter's paternal grandfather was a mercenary captain of the guard in a city far to the west of here, and he had a wife both in the city and with a band of the tribes. There have also been many instances when women of great beauty of the tribes have married *gadjo* of high birth. There have also been several instances when our kings have had wives in more than one band. I have discussed this with the *gadjin,* and he has agreed to perform the marriage ceremony with the princess and consider her his wife."

"But what of his *gadjo* wife?" Saiforella's mother asked. "Will she not object?"

"I doubt if she will know," Panna replied dryly. "She cannot talk to the villagers, because she knows the language of the people very poorly. She speaks only French, which is common with Russian women of her station."

"But how is he to be a husband to my daughter?"

"The same way that her paternal grandfather was a husband to his wife in the band of the tribes. I have told him that I will keep her in the band, and he has said that he will support her in a manner befitting her birth. The council will find no fault with this arrangement, because there is ample precedent and because it resolves this difficult situation . . ."

They talked on, and Saiforella listened to them absently, pondering. At first it seemed impossible. Her people rarely married among the *gadjo,* regardless of what Panna said, because of their different ways of life. Occasionally a *gadjin* would join a band, however, or a beautiful child would be stolen and reared with a band, and there was no prejudice against them because of their race.

But as she thought about it, the solution began to seem very attractive. All the problems she had envisioned would be erased. Her status among the people would be enhanced, because married women were always more respected. And it would be additionally beneficial because her husband would be of high birth. As she became older and more wise, she could gradually achieve the status of queen among her people and sit with the men in council during the winter encampment. There were other advantages which Panna and her mother were discussing.

". . . Shankal and his wife are old, and they have been wanting to sell their wagon and move in with their youngest son and his wife. The *gadjin* said that he would gladly buy a wagon for you and the princess, together with other things you need. And he is a man of great wealth . . ."

There would be a fine, large wagon and beautiful horses, thick, warm furs for the winter and cool, soft silks against her skin in summer. They would eat only the best of food, and gifts could be given to the other wagons. She would have gold bangles for her arms, and large, heavy gold earrings for her ears. It would no longer be necessary to grovel in the houses of peasants and risk arrest by soldiers to collect tokens worth a few kopecks.

They had stopped talking, and both of them were looking at her. She turned her face away, gesturing in casual indifference with her hand. "I shall consider it."

"You shall marry him," Panna said firmly. "I am the leader here, and I have decided. I will go get the *gadjin* now, and you shall eat bread and salt with him in front of witnesses."

Saiforella looked at him coldly. "You shall address me with respect, Panna."

He sighed wearily, lifting his hands and dropping them. "I meant no disrespect, Saiforella of the family Hator, but we all suffer shame until this is rectified. You are under my jurisdiction, and I command you to marry the *gadjin* tonight."

She pursed her lips and looked at him in silence

84

for a long moment, then slowly nodded. "Very well," she murmured, then she leaned forward and pointed a finger at him, hissing angrily. "And henceforce you shall not refer to him as *gadjin*."

He opened his mouth to reply, closed it, then smiled in resignation and let her have the last word, nodding. Her mother uttered a happy sound, rising and reaching for the lantern on the hook on the wall, and knelt and lit it from the flame in Panna's. Panna picked up his lantern and left, and her mother bustled about, putting things in order. She took out another skirt and blouse for Saiforella to put on, and Saiforella shook her head firmly and waved them away. He must see what he had done to her.

Panna returned a few minutes later, knocking quietly on the door, and her mother opened it. The count was behind him, following him up the steps and into the wagon. His clothing was disheveled, his eyes were red, and his face was pale and lined, as though he had been sleeping. He looked at Saiforella, smiling regretfully, and she glared at him. His eyes dropped, and she sniffed with satisfaction. Her mother plucked at her skirt, frowning warningly, and she pushed her mother's hand away.

It took only a moment. Her mother broke a piece of bread from a loaf and divided it, and put the stone salt cellar between them. Panna spoke to the count in the liquid language they used between them, and the count nodded, dipped the piece of bread in the salt, and ate it. He looked as though he were about to choke on it. Saiforella dipped her piece of bread in the salt and ate it in her turn. Panna spoke again, and the count felt in his pockets for a coin. He didn't have one with him. Panna smiled, taking out his purse, and he handed him a ruble. The count put it in his pocket, took it back out, and handed it to Saiforella. Saiforella handed it to her mother, and she leaned over and put it away in one of the small wooden boxes. It was over.

Her mother beamed and clucked happily, and Torgau and his wife made excited noises on the other side of the rag partition. Panna and the count rose, moving toward the door and conversing in the foreign language again. The count turned at the door and politely took his leave in Russian, and her mother replied. Saiforella looked at him with a stony expression, then looked away. Panna chuckled and said something in the foreign language. The count nodded and smiled, Panna said something else, and they both laughed as they went out the door, closed it, and clumped down the steps.

Saiforella hadn't been sure what was going to happen. It had occurred to her that he might want her mother to go elsewhere. so he could claim his conjugal rights, and she had intended to deny him until he humiliated himself and begged her so the Torgau family could hear and spread it all through the band. But he had another wife, a *gadjo* wife, and he had returned to her. Saiforella's mother was at the side of the partition, chuckling happily and whispering with Torgau's wife. Saiforella snapped her fingers and pointed at the bowl of cold soup. Her mother moved away from the partition, took a horn spoon from a box, and handed her the bowl and the spoon, then she slid back to the partition and began whispering with Torgau's wife again. Saiforella stirred the cold soup with the spoon and began eating it. The problems were resolved, but her initial pleasure had turned to resentment. She had been raped, then spurned. She pondered the possibilities for retaliation.

The next morning word spread about what had happened, and everyone in the caravan was jubilant. What had seemed dire adversity had turned into the best of fortune. Instead of disgrace being brought upon the band, its status had taken a giant leap forward because of Saiforella's situation. Saiforella's mother bartered with Shankal and his wife over cloth hangings, pots and pans, a stove, and other things in their wagon, and men helped them move the remainder of their belongings to the wagon belonging to their youngest son. Shortly before midday, the village headman came to the wagons and asked for Panna and Saiforella's mother. Saiforella's mother put on her best dress and scarf, and they went to the village. An hour later they returned, Saiforella's mother tightly clutching a heavy leather purse inside her dress. When she had paid for the wagon, horses, and other things, there was still over a thousand rubles in the purse.

The move into the Shankal wagon was hurried, in order to get it cleaned and have everything in order in event the count came that night. The wagon was spotless by late afternoon, and Saiforella's mother prepared a large meal of fish, soup, and boiled turnips. They had all the bread and undiluted kvass they wanted with the meal, an unaccustomed luxury, and after they ate her mother prepared fish cakes and tarts in event the count came that night and was hungry. But he didn't come.

The following day, her mother bought a pig in the village, and several women helped her cook it for a wedding celebration feast. It was during the afternoon so it would be over by the time the villagers finished work and came to the wagons, and there was singing and dancing as everyone gorged themselves. To Saiforella, it seemed a little flat, pointless, and anticlimactic, but everyone else enjoyed it.

Kostich sold her ten gold bangles and a pair of golden earrings almost as large as bangles for thirty rubles, and her mother shopped through the wagons for expensive linens and silk to make new clothes for her. Kostich's oldest son was chosen by Panna as the driver for the wagon and caretaker for the four horses, and his wage was established at five rubles per month. It was a position of trust and responsibility, and he threw himself into his tasks enthusiastically, strutting about and leading the horses to water and graze, and accumulating leather and metal to repair and decorate the harness. Through Saiforella, the problem of where the caravan would stop each year between the fair at Diakonskii and the fair at Nizhnii had been finally solved, and Panna cultivated a friendship with the village headman and repeatedly warned everyone in the caravan that no tokens were to be taken from the villagers.

As a married woman, Saiforella had more latitude in conduct, and she moved freely about the camp and wore her new finery to watch the entertainment in the evenings. She had every reason to be happy. She was the wealthiest wagon owner in the caravan. The wagon was massively large, meals were abundant, the smooth fabrics of the new clothes her mother kept making were cool and caressing against her skin, her bangles clattered on her arms satisfyingly, and her new earrings were heavy on her ears and swayed against the sides of her face when she turned her head. She had a cooling bath each night, and her bed was soft and comfortable. Everyone in the camp, including the men, listened closely and politely whenever she spoke.

But the nights passed, and the count still didn't come to the wagon. Her mother was unconcerned about it, but Saiforella's resentment grew. She thought of more humiliations for him and of more acid remarks to make to him, but they festered in her mind for lack of an outlet.

She glimpsed him occasionally from afar as he rode his horse through the village, but he never came to the wagons. Six days after their arrival at the village, he sent the village headman for her mother and talked to her at the headman's house. He asked her mother what had been spent and discussed what would be needed for monthly expenses, and gave her some more money. Saiforella interpreted it as a less than subtle insult and as the ultimate rejection. He didn't even want to talk to her. She was the wagon owner and his wife, and the matters should have been discussed with her. When her mother returned to the wagon, Saiforella exploded in fury and screamed and cursed at her, throwing things around the wagon until her mother scuttled back out the door. Then she lay on her pallet and wept bitter tears of impotent rage, biting, kicking, and scratching at the pallet.

The next day she saw him riding his horse toward the high road, a carriage following him. That afternoon, Saiforella's mother cautiously and hesitantly brought the subject up, telling her that the village headman had told Panna that the count was going to visit with friends at a nearby summer estate. Saiforella curled her lips with disdain, spat on the floor, and slammed her heel down to express her rage.

He was gone for two days. The morning after he returned, the headman came to Panna and told him that the count had brought guests back to the village with him and that he would bring them to the wagons that evening to be entertained. The news touched off a flurry of activity. The finest buntings were brought out and washed, and fresh pitch torches made. The area in front of the stage which had been trampled down by the serfs watching the nightly entertainment was strewn with discarded bits of food and garbage, and it was meticulously cleaned. The wagons on the stage side of the circle were washed, and all the performers had their costumes refurbished. Instruments were polished and tuned, and everyone got out their best clothes. The headman impressed several of the villagers to help wherever they could, and during the afternoon four ornate, upholstered chairs and four small tables for refreshments were sent down from the manor house. Saiforella walked around the camp and watched the preparations, finding the entire undertaking vastly boring.

The activity became frantic as the sun began to sink and final details were taken care of. The villagers began to collect in a wide semicircle far back from the stage, all of them wearing their best clothes. The four chairs and four small tables were in a row on the carefully-swept ground in front of the stage. The entertainers gathered at the side of the stage, and the musicians sat down on their bench at the rear of it. Hamza's trained dogs yelped excitedly, and he spoke sharply to them to keep them sitting in a row, panting and trembling. The jugglers rattled their bats and hoops, exchanging terse comments and quiet chuckles. The four small girls designated to serve the refreshments clung to their mothers and shivered nervously. The three girls who would do the young girl's dance giggled among themselves and rattled the strings of tiny bells on their ankles.

Saiforella wore one of her new skirts, one her mother had made of alternating vertical panels of yellow, black, and crimson muslin. It fit tightly to accentuate her tiny waist, and fell in heavy folds around her ankles, weighted with tiny bits of metal sewn into the hem. Her blouse was crimson muslin, with a scarf of the same material wound through her hair and tied at the back. She sat on the driver's seat of one of the wagons which was close enough to the stage for her to

90

see but where she would be out of the light cast by the torches around the edge of the stage.

The torches were lit, and the flickering, wavering light covered the stage and cast a glow all around it. The gypsies clustered at the sides of the stage in their best clothes, bright splashes of crimsons, purples, greens and yellows, and the light from the torches gleamed on white teeth against dusky skins and dark mustaches and shone on gold earrings and bangles. On the distant edge of the light from the torches, the semicircle of villagers was barely visible, unmoving as they waited. Time passed. The frogs croaked in the marsh, and insects darted around the spluttering torches. The tea for the guests was sent back to a wagon to be kept hot on a brazier, the tarts and cakes were covered to keep insects off them, and the vodka and wine were put into water to cool. More time passed. People looked at Panna and muttered questions, and he replied with silent shrugs. The musicians plucked the strings of their instruments, and a tamborine jangled idly. Some of the children sat down on the ground. Saiforella kicked off her sandals and lay down on the seat, settling herself comfortably and closing her eyes.

There was a stir among the serfs, and Saiforella sat up, yawning and rubbing her eyes. It was far past the time Panna had been told to have everything ready, and they were finally arriving. House serfs were carrying four lanterns at shoulder height, and two men and two women were walking in the pool of light between the lanterns. Panna snapped an order, and a couple of men began replacing torches which had burned down. A rippling wave of movement flowed through the villagers as they parted and bowed deeply. The four lanterns and four people moved through the path made by the villagers. The count and his wife were in front. He was dressed in light brown trousers which fit him tightly, shiny boots up to his knees, a ruffled shirt, a coat with a high collar and long tails, and a tall hat. The countess was a very stout woman, wearing an expensive-looking pink silk gown with a wide, flounced skirt, with a loosely draped wrap of silk spotted with sequins over her shoulders. She was looking over her shoulder and making some comment to a couple behind them, and they were laughing. The other man was dressed in clothes similar to those worn by the count, and he was older and fatter, his stomach bulging out in his tight trousers. Both of the women looked much alike, pale, pampered, and fat.

There were half a dozen house serfs besides those carrying the lanterns, and one ran forward to dust the chairs with a cloth as another circled around the chairs and sprayed the air with heliotrope scent. The four came closer, and the light of the torches played on their faces. The count looked dissatisfied, as though he didn't want to be there. The others looked bored. There was a bustle of house serfs as they sat down, then the house serfs gathered behind them. Panna hopped lightly onto the stage, smiling widely and bowing deeply, and began his speech. He spoke in the language he and the count used in addressing each other and Saiforella couldn't understand him, but it was obviously the usual speech for important performances. There was a flurry as women at the side of the stage prepared the trays of refershments, then the four small girls carried them out to the tables placed between the chairs.

None of the visitors were listening to Panna. The other man and woman appeared to perceive something amusing about one of the musicians, and they exchanged laughing comments in a loud voice. The countess spread a fan with a flick of her wrist and laughed with them. The count glanced at them and looked away. The four small girls put the trays on the tables, curtsied, and ran back to the side of the stage. The countess looked at her tray, moved one of the tarts with her finger, and made a comment in a sarcastic tone. The other man and woman laughed. Panna finished talking and looked at them uncertainly. The count smiled slightly and nodded. Panna bowed deeply, and walked toward the side of the stage, motioning to Hamza to begin with the dogs.

They had come to be entertained, but they hadn't brought with them the necessary anticipation of enjoyment. Where there should have been receptiveness, there was derision. Where there should have been interest, there was jaded indifference. The dogs yapped and leaped over the sticks, and they paraded on their rear legs. They scurried in circles and hopped over each other in patterns, and they tumbled and rolled. The count looked at the ground in front of him with an absent expression. The two women laughed and talked. The other man industriously probed a nostril with a forefinger and examined the particle he extracted. One of the house serfs moved forward and murmured to the countess, motioning toward the tray on the table by her, and she looked over her shoulder at him, laughing and nodding toward the tray. The house serf took a cake, bit into it, then spit it out with an expression of distaste. The two women laughed uproariously. The count turned his head and looked at the house serf with a solid expression. The house serf moved back.

The atmosphere changed. The excitement which had accumulated during the day-long preparations soured and died, fading into a bitter, dreary gloom which hung over the group around the stage. The magic of the moment was lost, something intangible but crucially important to the interaction of performers and observers draining away in the face of the ridicule, scorn, and indifference of those sitting in front of the stage. Even the dogs seemed to perceive it, their usual nervous energy changing to a subdued and leaden relief that it was over as they trotted to the edge of the stage and leaped off. The jugglers began. The usual fine edge of their performance wasn't there, and their shouts and leaps as the hoops and bats flew through the air was a spiritless and grotesque sham of their usual frenzy of movement. The strumming of the musicians was dull and heavy. The crowd around the stage was quiet, rather than clamoring to spur the performers to greater efforts. The jugglers finished and bowed off the stage. The four distinguished visitors didn't appear to notice that they had left.

It had happened before. There were sometimes outside circumstances which put crowds into a disgruntled and belligerent mood, and they were surly and difficult to please. But most of the time, serfs were eager to be entertained, unashamed of the element of childishness in the attitude required for the full realization of the most poignant enjoyment.

Fiery anger was building up within Saiforella. Her people had prepared to give of themselves, and their gift had been scorned, as she had lain in the wagon night after night, intending to punish the count a little but willing to give herself to him as a wife. Her offering had been spurned as well. The four found her people a source of contemptuous amusement, those whose ancestors had been wearing the skins of wild animals, huddling in caves and gnawing on raw bones when hers had possessed a culture, way of life, and sophisticated system of laws and customs built up over centuries. The group clustered about the stage, a proud and independent people, were quietly resentful and wounded by the affront. The three girls were doing the girl's dance, expertly going through the steps as their skirts swayed and their small arms weaved in the motions of the story. Silvana's wife was moving closer to the stage, her face drawn and resigned as she prepared to get on the stage to do the woman's dance, anxious to get it over and be done.

Saiforella climbed down from the seat of the wagon.

Panna saw her moving through the people toward the side of the stage. He glanced at the count and looked back at her thoughtfully, pondering the wisdom of her showing herself. He moved toward her as she approached Silvana's wife. "Perhaps it would be better if you remained out of sight. Your husband's other wife might—"

"Bah!" she spat. "How would that fat, dull-witted cow know who I am? Give me your bells, Mura."

"Why do you want her bells?" Panna asked, looking alarmed. "You cannot dance here."

"Why not? I am a married woman, am I not?"

"She can dance much better than I can," Silvana's wife said, smiling at Saiforella with relief and handing her the anklets of bells.

Panna shook his head doubtfully. "No, your husband might be angry if you dance, and it would be—"

"You take too much upon yourself, Panna. *I* am his wife, not you, and I know better."

Panna was unsure, turning again to look at the count, and he turned back to Saiforella and shook his head. The three girls were finishing their dance, and Saiforella whirled away from Panna with an impatient hiss, pushing through the people toward the stage. He started to reach out to stop her, hesitated, then looked back at the count again and frowned worriedly, scratching his beard. The three girls were at the edge of the stage, curtsying. There was muted applause from the

95

villagers on the edge of the light. Some of the house serfs behind the four chairs were sitting on the ground, and others were lying down. The three girls trotted to the side of the stage, and Saiforella reached up to help them down, patting them and smiling at them.

A murmur of surprise came from the gypsies as she leaped lightly onto the stage. On the edge of her vision, she saw the count as he sat up straight in his chair and looked at her. The two women were talking to the other man, and he was ignoring them as he sat up in his chair and stared. The musicians looked at her with puzzled expressions. She kicked off her sandals and lifted one foot, then the other, putting the rings of bells around her ankles. Fignon, the lead musician, cleared his throat with a soft sound and began strumming three notes on his balalaika to set the rhythm for a dance.

Silence fell. There was only the strumming of the single balalaika and the hissing and popping sound of the torches around the stage as the flames licked upwards. Even the sounds of the frogs and insects seemed muted. The two women had stopped talking, and were looking at her. The faces on both sides of the stage were turned up toward her. There was no movement. The atmosphere was sour, tense, and discordant after the failed performances. Saiforella gathered herself.

The bells around her ankles jangled as she walked across the stage with a swinging stride, smiling widely at Fignon and shaking her bangles down around her wrists. "Hai, Fignon!" she shouted gaily. "Are you here or elsewhere? Is that Fignon playing, or is it the plinking of a *gadjin*?" She leaned toward him, snapping her fingers in his face and stamping one of her bare heels against the stage, making the bells jangle rhythmically. "Play, Fignon, play! Play!"

96

He laughed and nodded, nudging his son and sitting straighter on the bench as he strummed harder. His son began playing the three notes on his balalaika, and the concertinas and the accordion began whistling and honking with the balalaikas. The violins picked up the tune, and the tamborines began thumping and rattling as the two women slapped and shook them. But all of it was only noise, dull and dragging, and not music.

Saiforella snarled with impatience, darting to one of the women and snatching her tamborine from her. "Must I teach you to play the tamborine, Bediya?" she shouted, laughing as she beat the tamborine and shook it. "Is there a gypsy who cannot play the tamborine?" She backed away from the musicians, pounding the tamborine and looking at them. "Where is my music? Am I to dance to this? I am not a turtle! Have all of you remained here among the *gadjo* until you have become like them? Play! Play!" She ran back to Fignon, slamming the tamborine against her left fist, her elbow, and shaking it in his face. "How am I to dance without music, Fignon? Where is your heart? Play, Fignon, play!" She beat and shook the tamborine and stamped her heels against the stage as she moved to the violins. "Are you dead, Kafeta?" she shouted, shaking the tamborine at him. "Did you come here to be buried or to play music? Is your bow as worthless as your member? Play! Play! Play!"

The self consciousness and humiliation the four noble visitors had generated among the musicians was rapidly dissipating, and they were laughing and beginning to put themselves into it. The notes of the violins were taking on a hint of wild, plaintive wailing, and the concertinas and accordion had sweetened. The balalaikas were beginning to sing. She tossed the tamborine back to Bediya, and she stood in front of them, clapping her hands together and stamping her feet. The rhythm was beginning to breathe a life of its own, but it was still far from the pounding which became one with the pulse. The musicians needed help.

She moved toward one side of the stage, making the boards vibrate under her feet as she slammed her heels down, and her bangles clattered and flashed in the yellow light of the torches as she pounded her hands together. "Am I in a graveyard?" she shouted down at the faces. "Am I to dance for the dead? Do *gadjo* ride in these beautiful wagons, or am I among gypsies?" They laughed and nodded to each other, clapping their hands and catching the beat and mood of the music. She jerked her scarf out of her hair and threw it down, then moved across to the other side of the stage, stamping her feet, clapping her hands, and shaking her head until her hair whipped madly about her shoulders. Those on the other side of the stage had already picked it up, clapping their hands together and shouting encouragement to the musicians. She threw her head back and uttered a penetrating note, trilling it with her tongue against her front teeth. Shrill whoops burst out on both sides of the stage in reply, and the clapping of hands became a pulsing force of noise in rhythm with the instruments.

And it was music for a dance. It was far beyond the pallid, lifeless performance which was staged to entertain *gadjo*. The beat had taken the intensity of the music of the winter camps, when they played and danced for each other in the sheer joy of their music. It was the wild, unrestrained rhythm of their freedom, the music which came from the deep forests and the boundless steppes. The villagers had been caught up by it and they were also clapping their hands and shouting, not understanding but responding to something which had been stirred within them. The sound echoed back and forth across the river and beyond.

The shouts and whoops from the sides of the stage became louder as they called to Saiforella to begin the dance. She teased them, laughing with exultant joy as she stamped back and forth across the stage, swinging her hips from side to side and throwing her hair about as she clapped her hands. They began screaming, demanding the dance. She moved back to the center of the stage, feeling the rhythm and letting it become one with her, and she looked at Fignon.

"Haleb!"

Fignon nodded, rising from the bench and moving forward a step, and he lifted the neck of his balalaika to signal to the other musicians to break into the melody. She poised, spreading her arms wide and lifting herself to her toes. Fignon bent forward, dropping the neck of his balalaika, and the music soared off into its wild run as he sat back down. She spun toward one side of the stage, her feet moving in firm, rapid steps to shake the bells in rhythm with the music as her skirt swirled about her, and she caught herself and made her skirt wrap firmly around her legs and thighs from its momentum as she started her spin toward the other side of the stage. It whipped back out and swirled again as she went through the opening steps of the dance.

It was the story of Haleb, the founder of the tribe Halebi, who had become a nomad because he had unwittingly forged the nails which held Jesus of Nazareth to the cross. The Roman soldier had been given sixty coppers to buy nails, but he had bought wine with part of the money and had only forty coppers left. The darting runs from side to side on the stage were his search for a smith who would make four nails for forty coppers, becoming faster and faster as smith after smith refused to make them for such a small sum. Then he found Haleb, a poor smith with a large family who had little work.

She spun and leaped, going through the symbolic motions of heating and forming the nails, then dropping them into the tub to temper them. But the fourth and last nail remained red and hot, turning the water in the tub into steam without becoming cool. She ran back and forth in the movements of carrying more water from the river to pour into the tub, only to have it turn into steam. Her movements slowed and became more languid, relating Haleb's growing concern that the failure of the water to cool the nail was a portentous omen of some sort, and she bowed backwards and almost touched the stage with her shoulders, going through the motions of questioning the Roman soldier on the intended use for the nails. Then she personified horror and consternation, sinking to her knees and whipping her hair from side to side in despair, and she went through the motions of Haleb trying to buy the three nails back, offering his wife, his children, his pitiful house, and his tools and forge. She sprang to her feet and stamped across the stage, simulating the Roman soldier's firm tread as he left with the three nails, deciding to use only one to nail both feet to the cross.

The narrative returned to Haleb, who found the last nail in front of his doorstep, still hot and smoking. Hurriedly he gathered his belongings and family and journeyed to Damascus, only to find that the nail had followed him and caught up with him on the day after he arrived. Saiforella went through Haleb's motions in obtaining a wagon, gathering his family, and departing on an unending odyssey, always one day ahead of the nail.

The tempo quickened toward the climax. Haleb's

sons matured, found wives, and bought wagons, and they followed their father. Cousins joined the caravan from other tribes of wanderers, and they multiplied and became a tribe. Joy and comfort were found in the freedom of the open spaces away from the cities as they journeyed from place to place, earning money as itinerant smiths, then returning to the open road to sing their songs and celebrate their feasts. The climax came and she extemporized on the ritual and traditional steps and movements of the dance, doubling and tripling the rhythm of the music with her stamping heels as she curved her arms over her head and spun rapidly from side to side, her skirt swirling straight out around her waist and the night air touching her legs and thighs. Sweat was damp on her face and body, her breath was short, and her energy was flagging. She summoned her reserves, whipping herself to greater efforts as she leaped and spun in steps which conformed to tradition but which were hers alone and set her apart from others who danced the Haleb. Then the final crashing runs of the music came, and she went into a final spin, twirling on one foot in the center of the stage. She held it, feeling for the last note, then dropped to the stage with her skirt spread out around her and her forehead on her arm as the music stopped.

The applause was deafening. Those by the stage had gone wild, screaming hoarsely, and even the musicians were applauding. The villagers were howling and clapping their hands madly. She lifted her head, pushing her hair out of her face, and looked at the four in front of the stage. The count was looking at her with an expression of mingled anger and desire. The two women's faces expressed raw, undisguised hatred. The other man was standing and clapping his hands furiously, shouting at the top of his voice. He trotted forward, digging in his coat pocket, and took a leather purse out of his pocket. He leaned forward over the stage, and pushed it into her blouse between her breasts.

He clutched the edge of the stage and started clambering awkwardly onto it as she sat up, taking the purse out of her blouse. The count was suddenly on his feet and moving forward, his face red with rage. Panna and a couple of other men ran around to the front of the stage, and they laughed and talked to him with ingratiating jocularity as they pulled him away from the stage. One of the men reached over and took the purse from Saiforella, and he pushed it back into the man's pocket. Saiforella rose to her feet, looking down at them. The count stopped and looked up at her with a thunderous, threatening expression. The other man tried to get his purse back out of his pocket to throw it to her. She smiled down at him, backing away from the edge of the stage and throwing kisses to him with both hands, then she turned and walked toward the side of the stage, swinging her hips from side to side and smiling invitingly over her shoulder at him. He broke loose from Panna and the other men, and he knocked a torch off the front of the stage as he began trying to pull himself onto it. A couple more men came around to help hold him. The count moved forward, pushed Panna and the others out of the way, took the man's collar and jerked him off the edge of the stage, holding him effortlessly.

Saiforella knelt at the side of the stage, gathering up her scarf and sandals and taking off the anklet rings, and she stood back up and looked at them again over her shoulder. The count was glaring at her in fury. The other man pawed aimlessly at the air as the count held him by the collar. She laughed, tossing her head to throw her hair back and make her earrings swing, and she put one hand on her waist and moved her hips provocatively. The count's face became crimson. The other man struggled harder against the count's grip. She laughed again as she leaped lightly from the stage and tossed the anklets to Silvana's wife.

CHAPTER VI

There was a feeling of accomplishment and success, yet one of anticlimax. The *gadjo* had been jerked from their sneering nonchalance and made to observe the beauty and glory of the music of her people as few *gadjo* had before, and each had been shaken to his foundations. But Saiforella felt that an element had been missing, that her retribution was incomplete. She thought about it as she undressed, tossed her clothes aside and poured a bucket of water over herself as she stood on the grating. Then she shrugged it off and dismissed it from her mind as she dried herself and put on another blouse and skirt. The spirits of her people had been lifted from the gloom cast over them by the *gadjo,* and that was the most important consideration.

The sounds outside diminished as she lay on her pallet, looking around the wagon and yawning. It was luxuriously comfortable and beautiful with the dim, yellow light of the lantern shining on the wall hangings, and it wasn't beyond the realm of possibility that Saiforella had jeopardized all the luxuries they had recently acquired. But some things were more important than riches. Any nomad could become wealthy by settling in one place and accumulating possessions, but there were things which weren't negotiable and couldn't be bartered. Her dance had been an impulsive act, but long and thoughtful consideration would have produced the same decision.

The door opened, and her mother came in, carrying tarts, cakes, and fishcakes in her skirt. She smiled at Saiforella, closing the door, and her smile became reproachful as she knelt by a chest and began putting the food into a bowl. "Your husband is angry with you, beloved."

Saiforella curled her lip with disdain, and she drew in a breath and swallowed it, and belched hollowly.

"He is your husband, loved one."

"He is a *gadjin*. Bring me a fishcake."

Her mother picked up the bowl and dusted crumbs off her skirt as she crossed to Saiforella's pallet. "They did not like our food."

"They did not wish to like it. It is good food, but they think of us as we do of them. They are able to show how they feel, but we cannot. But we leave our dung on their lands and take tokens from their houses, and that is enough."

Her mother sighed and shook her head worriedly, munching a cake, and suddenly smiled. "You have never danced better than tonight, beautiful one."

Saiforella grunted, chewing, and leaned over for a water jug by the pallet. "It was for our people, not them. To them, the stumbling of a drunk would be dancing." She took a drink from the jug, replaced it, and lay back down on the pallet and looked up at the ceiling, sucking her teeth.

"You are tired," her mother said, picking up the bowl and rising. "You will feel better tomorrow."

Saiforella shrugged indifferently and yawned. Her mother put the bowl on a chest at the side of the wagon, trimmed the lamp wick and turned it low, and went around the side of the cloth partition to her small sleeping area at the front of the wagon. Saiforella listened to her mother unrolling her pallet and lying down, settling herself for the night. The vague, bothersome feeling that had troubled her earlier returned. She thought about the dance, and the expressions on the women's faces. Then she smiled as she thought about how the count and the other man had reacted, and she chuckled softly as she turned onto her side to go to sleep.

The barking of a dog awakened her. The camp had settled for the night, and the sound of two men's voices carried between the wagons in the stillness. The voices stopped, and heavy footsteps came toward her wagon. She heard her mother's clothes rustle as she got up from her pallet, and a board in the floor of the wagon squeaked as she moved toward the partition. Heavy boots thumped against the bottom step, and there was a brusque knock on the door. Her mother came around the end of the partition, picked up the lamp and turned up the wick, and went to the door to open it. She backed away from the door, smiling and bowing, and put the lamp down on a chest as she walked back toward the end of the partition to return to her sleeping area.

Sheremetev had taken off his coat and hat, and he was still wearing the same shirt, trousers, and boots. The grey in his hair and mustache made him look distinguished, and he was a tall, powerful, handsome man. He was frowning darkly.

"You shall never do anything like that again. Never."

She sat up and looked at him, an expression of exaggerated bewilderment on her face. "Who is this? Who is this man who gives me commands?"

"You know who I am," he snapped.

She frowned thoughtfully, shading her eyes with her

hand and leaning toward him to look at him closely, then she sat back and put her finger on her chin. "Could this be my husband?" she murmured in a musing tone, then she shook her head. "No, I do not believe so. My husband is not so fat."

He tensed and his face flushed. "I did not come here for foolishness, woman. I came here to tell you that you shall act with decorum in the ftuure, and not like a woman of the streets."

She stiffened, her lips becoming a straight line, and she slowly gathered herself and rose to her feet, glaring at him. "A woman of the streets?" she said softly. "And this from one who attacks maidens." She drew in a deep breath and shouted at the top of her voice. "Go back to your fat slut, *gadjo* whoreson!"

He looked shocked, then became rigid with outraged anger. "You shall address me with respect, woman!" he stormed.

"Respect?" she jeered, her lips curling back from her teeth and her earrings shining in the soft light as she slowly advanced toward him, her head thrust forward and her fingers curved into claws. "Respect for a *gadjo* bastard? I will show you my respect!" She leaped forward and spat in his face.

He growled with rage, snatching at her, and she twisted away from his hands as he seized her shoulder. Her blouse began tearing, and he gripped it and pulled, trying to drag her to him. She leaped away, and the blouse tore off her and bared her to the waist. He moved toward her again, and she danced lightly around him, her naked breasts bobbing as she laughed mockingly.

"I shall thrash you, woman!"

"And the wolves shall gnaw your bones, *gadjin!* Go thrash the fat slut you had with you before, and you will lie more safely on your pallet!"

107

He stopped trying to catch her and stood in the middle of the wagon and glared at her, breathing heavily with anger. "We are said to be husband and wife, but what can be done can also be undone, woman! You try my patience too far!"

She put her hands on her hips and looked at him witth an expression of contempt, shrugging. "Is that what you wish? Is that why you came here?" She turned, glancing around, then went to the wall, opened a box, took out the coin he had given her, and threw it at him. "There, *gadjin*!" she shouted as the coin bounced off the wall behind him. "There is your coin, so take it and leave! I am a Hator, and there are many who would have me for a wife! Even after a fat swine has raped me!"

He ground his teeth together, trembling with rage, and he slowly shook his head. "No. You are mine, and you shall do as I say. If I must beat you, then I will do so. And I will have my rights with you."

She tossed her head back and laughed, and lifted one hand as he started to move toward her again. "No, wait. Wait. You wish to have your rights with me? Very well, you shall have them." She glanced around again, ran to a chest and opened it, and took out a bottle of vodka. "But first drink this," she said, her lips curling and her tone a sneer. "Your manhood is in vodka, is it not? Drink this so you will not shame yourself before your wife."

He growled wordlessly, advancing toward her and reaching for her, and she leaped to one side and threw the bottle at him. It grazed the side of his head, and he staggered to one side as the bottle exploded against the wall of the wagon in a shower of glass and vodka. He put his hand to his temple and shook his head to clear it, and she snatched up an earthenware water jug, leaped toward him, and swung it at his head. He dodged the water jug and caught her arms, and the jug crashed to the floor and broke. She tried to pull away from him, her hair flying as she jerked herself from side to side, then she leaped toward him and scratched at him. He pushed her arms down and twisted them behind her back, and he put one arm around her and lifted her feet from the floor. She kicked out at him, and stubbed her bare toes against his boots. He looked down at her and smiled triumphantly as she stopped kicking, and she turned her head to one side and sank her teeth into his bicep. His smile changed to a grimace of agony as her teeth penetrated his skin through his sleeve, and he moved one hand up her back, seized her hair, and pulled her head back. She wriggled and twisted in his arms, trying to free herself, and her teeth snapped together as she tried to reach him to bite him again. He held her tightly as he carried her across the wagon to the pallet.

They were panting heavily with anger and exertion as he pushed her down on the pallet, holding her down with his weight. He gripped her tightly with one arm, pushing her clothes down, and jerked them off her legs. She suddenly relaxed and stopped struggling, and looked up at him as she lay naked on the pallet. His eyes moved over her face studying her expression, and he cautiously relaxed his grip on her. She smiled brilliantly, moving her hands slowly up his arms and shoulders to his neck, and she dug her fingernails into the back of his neck and pulled his lips down to hers. He kissed her, anger turning into passion, and he lifted his head and looked down at her again, breathing heavily with desire. She lifted her head, gathered her hair in her hands and pulled it to one side, and made an impatient sound in her throat as she fumbled at his belt. He began tugging at his clothes.

Her slender body was soft and pliant under his, lithe

and receptive. He restrained himself, the impatience from his fiery, demanding desire making him awkward, and he tried to be gentle with her. She gasped as he took her, then she dug her fingernails into his back and thrust herself at him as he hesitated. His body moved in a surging rush, and her body responded to his. She pulled his lips down to hers again, wrapping her arms around his neck, and he kissed her and held her tightly as the primitive, heated rhythm made them one. The headlong, unchecked pace made the sensations racing through him careen to an abrupt flood of ecstasy, then the writhing of her body and the murmurs in her throat renewed his strength. Time collapsed, seconds becoming languorously long to be savored with deliberate and casual enjoyment as hours flicked by in the space between two heartbeats. She was exquisite, with a seductiveness which was instinctive and an inborn part of her nature.

They lay quietly on the pallet, and he held her and caressed her, his lips moving over her face. She was satisfied. One of the main purposes of the dance had been obscured in her mind, and her realization of that purpose and its fulfillment had come at the same time.

Her ivory skin was silky against him and under his hands, and he breathed the fresh, warm scent of her body and hair. He glowed with contentment and self-congratulation, and he was fascinated by her. She seemed to embody many different people, the shy, frightened girl at the river, the alluring, seductive siren who had danced on the stage, the shrieking violent fury who had fought him, and the passionate, demanding woman who now lay in his arms. And, lying there, she seemed someone different again. There was a large birthmark on her left breast, a brown mark shaped like a *tau* in sharp contrast to her skin. The top line of the

110

mark went from one side of her breast to the other, and the vertical line followed the swelling curve of her breast and ended just above the nipple. He touched it with his finger.

"It is the mark of the Hator," she murmured softly in her lilting accent.

"All of your family are born with such a mark?"

"Yes. Those who do not are not considered Hator. It is called the brand of the Pharaoh."

"Why is it called that?"

"Many generations ago, when my people were journeying in Egypt, the head of the Hator planted his seed in the Pharaoh's family. As punishment, the Pharaoh branded him with the cross of the Hator. We have had the mark since."

For the first time, it occurred to him that gypsies had their own myths and traditions. It was consistent with the fact that they had royal families, as hers was, and it was logical in view of their long history. There were references to gypsies by historians from centuries before. He pushed her hair back from the side of her face and moved one of her heavy earrings with his finger.

"Will you eat?"

He was more weary than hungry, but he was painfully conscious of how rudely his wife and guests had acted at the entertainment, and he was ashamed of it. They had been scornful of the refreshments offered, and he didn't wish to offend her by leaving the impression that eating her food was beneath him. More than that, he had no wish to stir the vicious temper which had been more than evident. "Yes," he said.

She pulled away from him and sat up, slipping on a pair of sandals, then rose and moved around the wagon in a total lack of self-consciousness which made her even more alluring and desirable. Bits of glass and pieces of the earthenware jug crunched under her sandals as she collected bowls, cups, and a bottle and put them on the floor by the pallet.

"You will have to drink kvass, because you broke the vodka my mother bought for when you came."

"*I* broke it?" he snorted, smiling at her. "You broke it!"

She giggled, kicking off the sandals and sitting by him on the pallet. "I tossed it to you, but you didn't catch it." Her smile faded as she poured kvass into the cups, and she sighed and shrugged whimsically. "It is no fault of mine that I am a Hator and have the temper of a Hator."

He grunted doubtfully, taking one of the fishcakes and biting into it, and lifted his eyebrows. It was delicious, hot with spices and with a crisp crust. "This is good. How is it made?"

"With fish, potatoes, and spices. Potatoes cost little money, because many of the serfs will not eat them. Near Novgorod and at other places, they will use them only as food for swine."

He nodded, taking another fishcake, then thought about what she had said. It was a use for potatoes which hadn't occurred to him. He took a drink of kvass and bit into the fishcake. "You must not dance again as you did tonight."

She was sitting by him with her legs folded under her, hair hanging around the sides of her face and the golden gleam of her earrings showing through it in the soft light. A shadow of the anger which had gleamed in her eyes shone again as she looked at him. She flipped her hair back with one hand, reached for her cup and took a drink of kvass. "Your people see lust in the dance, and mine see beauty and art. I have never danced before *gadjo* before, and I will not do it again."

112

It was mildly irritating to the count to meet resistance to his wishes. But it wasn't an unreasonable compromise to permit her to dance for her people, as long as she didn't display herself to those who might take advantage of her. He nodded. "If you had never done it before, why did you tonight?"

"To make you remember that I was here."

He smiled at her and took another drink of kvass, and looked away. Things had been confused and muddled in his mind the night they had performed the marriage ceremony of her people, and they had seemed to move very rapidly. The regret and remorse over what he had done had been overwhelming in his mind, and he had agreed to Panna's suggestion because it seemed to be the only solution. But the thought of having two wives was abhorrent, even though eating a piece of bread with her and giving her a coin fell far short of a marriage ceremony in his mind. Many things had kept him away from her while he tried to sort it out in his mind, not least among which was the stability of his marriage. Marya Pavlovna didn't look for transgressions, but her reaction had always been prompt and severe when something had been brought to her attention which hinted of unfaithfulness. It was unlikely that she would find out, because she had no communication with the village except through the house serfs, who considered themselves so superior to the villagers that their contacts were few. And, as he looked at Saiforella and thought about her, the calamitous possibilities seemed less than they had before.

"I will not forget again."

She looked at him with a sultry smile, nodding. "It will be better if you do not." Her smile faded as she reached for the bottle to pour more kvass into their cups. "Our caravan will be leaving soon enough to go to the fair at Nizhnii."

Panna had mentioned it to him. While he had been puzzling over the situation in which he was entangled, it had seemed like a sought-after solution in that she would be gone. And now it was something he didn't want to contemplate. He pushed it aside in his mind to think of later, taking a drink of kvass. "I always thought gypsy women were quiet and obedient."

"Are you telling me that I am a disobedient woman? I am not. Panna is our leader, and I have always followed his commands without question except when he was wrong."

Her tone indicated that she perceived no conflict in what she had said, but it seemed something less than obedience to him. There was resentment in her eyes which had the potential of turning into anger, and he silently nodded, dropping the subject. Sheremetev took another drink of kvass, then lay back on the pallet. She looked down at him, pushed the bowls and cups away, and moved closer to him. She lay across his chest, smiling down at him. He pushed her hair back over her shoulders, looking up at her, and moved his hands over her slender bare shoulders. She bent lower and kissed him.

CHAPTER VII

Marya Pavlovna became ill, and the count sent a rider to Moscow for an apothecary. Saiforella probed his troubled mood and found out the problem, and she recommended an old crone in the band named Sarhana. The count was doubtful about Saiforella's true motivations and demurred, but Marya Pavlovna began to get worse and her maids showed indications of being reluctant to care for her properly, apparently afraid she had the dreaded cholera. The count became desperate, and finally asked Panna about Sarhana. He recommended her without qualification, and the count told him to send her to the manor.

Sarhanna was a woman of advanced years, her shriveled body bowed from hardship and toil and swathed in heavy, shapeless clothes. Her beak of a nose and pointed chin almost met across her toothless mouth, large earrings dangled from the sides of the large, bright scarf wrapped around her head, and her beady eyes were sharp and penetrating. Marya Pavlovna's maids were terrified of her, but Marya Pavlovna was in a state of semiconsciousness and barely aware of her surroundings.

She began to improve almost at once. Sarhana hovered over her for a day and a night without rest, pouring infusions between her lips and waving talismans and chanting, and by the time Marya Pavlovna was fully conscious of what was happening around her, she was accustomed to Sarhana and her appearance. Communication between them was limited to the few words of Russian that Marya Pavlovna knew, because Sarhana didn't know French, but it seemed to suffice. Marya Pavlovna had suffered for years from aches and pains in her legs and back, and when she became somewhat better, Sarhanna began massaging her legs and back daily, bringing Marya Pavlovna the first relief she had known for years.

The apothecary arrived, brusquely ordered Sarhana back to the caravan, and began a regimen of drenching and bleeding. Marya Pavlovna's condition deteriorated rapidly, and the count ordered the apothecary to return to Moscow and sent for Sarhana again. Sarhana moved her pallet into the corner of Marya Pavlovna's bed-chamber, curling up on it to catch snatches of sleep between treatments, and Marya Pavlovna began improving again.

The time approached for the caravan to leave for the fair at Nizhnii. The count discussed it with Panna to see if the departure could be delayed, and he found that their annual route was as firmly established as it was with migratory fowl. But it had been a poor year, and several of the gypsy families needed money for major repairs to wagons and for new draft animals. Two of the barges used by barge owners in the village to ferry commodities up and down the river were becoming old and leaky, and several more villagers wanted looms to weave cloth. The count and Panna talked about it and Panna held a meeting, and the people in five wagons agreed to stay to make the barges and looms, planning on catching up with the main body of the caravan at the winter camp. Saiforella and her mother remained, and Sarhana moved her small bundle of belongings into the corner of one of the wagons.

The main part of the caravan left early one morning, and the count sat on his horse at the top of the hill and watched them moving along the avenue of lime-woods toward the high road. The people who remained stood in a group at the top of the rise in the avenue overlooking the high road, waving as the line of brightly colored wagons rumbled along the high road and passed out of sight over the first hill. Then they turned and walked back down the avenue toward the village and the six wagons remaining by the river. The count watched them, pondering the long range effects of his desires and his wife's illness, outside circumstances which had altered the established course of the migration of a part of a Gypsy band.

Marya Pavlovna's health improved to the point where they could again visit and entertain others whose summer estates were within reasonable distance. They entertained more than they visited, because Marya Pavlovna was reluctant to be away from Sarhana. Marya Pavlovna worried about her eventual separation from Sarhana, and she importuned the count to do something about it. He talked to Sarhana, asking if she would join the household as an employee, and met an adamant, unwavering refusal; she was a nomad, regarding life in an established household with something approaching revulsion, and she wanted to have her own people near her. He tried to explain the situation to Marya Pavlovna, and his explanations were met with angry outbursts. There had been a time when he thought Marya Pavlovna had a bad temper, but his experience with Saiforella's had given him a new standard of judgment.

At the same time, Marya Pavlovna began to suspect

that he had some intense personal interest among the Gypsies. His absences from the manor had gone unremarked, because they weren't inconsistent with their pattern of life. In Moscow, their circles of friends overlapped somewhat, but Sheremetev was frequently absent on business both during the day and at night. They had slept separately for several years, as was customary, and their personal contact had been limited to meals together or conversations, the occasional nights they spent together, and entertainments in which they participated.

A couple of Marya Pavlovna's maids started taking walks along the river near the wagons, which was totally uncharacteristic for house serfs and particularly maids, and it seemed certain that Marya Pavlovna had sent them to see who was occupying the wagons which were left. The count ordered the headman to have a couple of men from the village follow the maids and harass them, knowing that the maids would then hide in the vicinity of the manor to avoid meeting the men and tell Marya Pavlovna that they had been to the river. But maids loved gossip, and it was a foregone conclusion that they would tell Marya Povlovna something interesting, even if they had to concoct it. In addition Saiforella and her mother were gathering reeds and willows to weave chicken coops to hang under their wagon, and it wasn't impossible that the maids had seen Saiforella before he had seen the maids. So he waited a couple of days, then told Marya Pavlovna that the headman had caught a couple of the village men chasing after her maids and keeping them from walking along the river as they apparently wished, and the men had been punished. That afternoon there was a disturbance in Marya Pavlovna's rooms as she punished the two maids for lying to her.

Marya Pavlovna began making herself more congenial and available to him, possibly with the idea of checking for herself. But some subtle chemistry which Saiforella had catalyzed within the count made him surprise himself, and any test she might have had in mind was totally inconclusive.

The time passed very rapidly. The affairs of the village and the fields were in good order, and he frequently walked along the river with Saiforella. They explored the coves and backwaters along the river and found tiny, hidden glades to eat the food and drink the kvass she brought, and they sat and talked for hours. Their more tender and private moments were occasionally interrupted by the unwanted presence of Pavlo, shrieking and bounding about, but the count's anger was allayed by Saiforella's high regard for Pavlo. She told the count that she had run Pavlo down and caught him a couple of weeks after the caravan had arrived at the village, and she had cut a swatch of hair from Pavlo's head and woven it into a talisman she wore around her neck.

A number of times he was almost on the point of suggesting that he rent a house in Moscow for her and her mother to spend the winter there, but he didn't bring the subject up because he didn't want to hear her refusal. And he was apprehensive of the final outcome if he managed to talk her into it. Czar Paul had once caused a number of wild waterfowl to be caught and their wings clipped to decorate the ponds around his summer estate. When the days had shortened and the leaves had started turning, the waterfowl had all killed themselves in trying to fly.

His reactions were mixed when he found that both Marya Pavlovna and Saiforella were pregnant. He was surprised, bemused, somewhat proud, disgusted with himself for being proud, and more than a little ashamed because of the situation he had created. Saiforella was

119

ecstatically gleeful and didn't appear to perceive his reservations. Her pleasure was infectious, but he was also bothered by the fact that he had committed a Sheremetev to the life of a homeless nomad. Marya Pavlovna was resentfully resigned because of the miscarriages and stillbirths she had experienced, dreading the ordeal and discomfort which she anticipated would be unproductive. But Sarhana seemed to have detected Marya Pavlovna's delicate condition before she realized it herself, because she was in the process of concocting large amounts of potions for Marya Pavlovna to take during her pregnancy, and preparing amulets for Marya Pavlovna to wear on her person.

From the back copies of the news sheets the count received from Moscow, he learned that the summer epidemic of cholera was more or less over, and there were numerous mentions of people who had returned from their summer estates. The barges the gypsies constructed on the riverbank were finished and launched, and those who had been working on the barges began helping the others finish the looms. The days became measurably shorter, the mornings became crisp, and the finger of autumn began touching the forests and the limewood trees along the avenue to the high road. The pleasure of walking along the river with Saiforella became bittersweet, the moments passing all too swiftly. Then the dreaded time inevitably came. The count paid the gypsies for making the barges and looms, a day was spent in preparations, and the six wagons left for the winter camp. He sat on his horse at the top of the rise and watched them moving away along the high road, waving to Saiforella as she stood in the back door of her wagon and waved to him until they were out of sight.

Marya Pavlovna was disconsolate over Sarhana's departure, and there was constant weeping among her maids. The count was morose and despondent himself, but he also felt guilty for what he had done and he tried to comfort her. But she was resentful toward him because of her pregnancy and his failure to force Sarhana to remain, and was as ill-tempered with him as with her maids. He began seeing to the affairs of the village and the villagers again, and making preparations to return to Moscow.

It seemed logical that departing the *mise en scene* where he had met and known Saiforella would bring at least some lessening of the deep melancholy which gripped him, but it failed even to abate it. Sheremetev felt deepening sadness upon leaving the village, and it remained after his return to Moscow. The house seemed claustrophobic, but still he didn't feel like leaving it, and it was days before he received his business manager because his interest in his business affairs had waned.

The house was located on Old Konyushennaya Street, in the center of one of the better if less faddish residential districts, and had been inherited from an uncle. The amenities were somewhat primitive because it was an old house, but it was located behind tall, stone walls which isolated it from the noise and bustle of the city, the gardens and stables were extensive, and he had liked the house as a child. After remaining there for a week without leaving the house, he began taking rides, out the Dragomilovsky Gate and through the fields around the city. Then he began crossing the Moskva at Luzhniki and walking through the Sparrow Hills overlooking the river. It became his favorite place. As autumn deepened toward winter, he saw the trees finish changing color and shed their leaves, and he watched the last flights of wild waterfowl settling into the marshes and reeds along the Moskva to rest for a time then arise again to wing south. And he thought of

Saiforella, wending her way along a road somewhere en route to a desolate and deserted place on the vast steppes. He thought about their walks along the river at Sherevskoye, and he thought about the dangers of the road and the hardships of the winter on the steppes.

Several invitations to visit were received from friends in the city, but Marya Pavlovna was still moody and reentering the social rounds of the city was distasteful and seemed pointless to the count. Then his son Vassily Ivanovich was allowed to leave boarding school and spend some time at home to celebrate his eleventh nameday. The letters he brought with him indicated he was doing well in school, and it occurred to the count that it wasn't too early to be casting about for means of establishing the beginnings of his son's position in life. He talked to Vassily about it at length and discussed it briefly with his wife, then made arrangements for him to enter the Yamburgsky Regiment of Uhlans upon his graduation from boarding school. In the process of making the arrangements, it is necessary to visit several acquaintances and former comrades in arms who had influence in the Yamburgskys, and he also found it necessary to take care of a few business affairs which had become urgent because of his lack of attention. His interest in obtaining the czar's approval to reenter court life at St. Petersburg also revived, and he threw himself into his business affairs again.

The count and his wife began receiving some people and visiting a few, and they began going to the French Theater at the Arbatsky Gate when a particularly interesting play was on the program, but the winter was unusually severe and they remained at home more than they had in the past. Marya Pavlovna's pregnancy became more obvious, but the nausea she had experienced in previous pregnancies seemed to be prevented by the potions Sarhana had given her. Marya Pavlovna also credited the talismans with helping her to feel better, and she soundly thrashed a maid who inadvertently burned one along with some discarded bits of cloth left over from altering a gown.

It snowed heavily and blew into deep drifts along the sides of the streets, then the temperature plummeted. Christmas came, and Vassily Ivanovich came home for the holiday while Moscow was gripped by the frigid cold. He brought two friends with him whose parents were out of the country as envoys of the czar, and the count was pleased with his son's choice of friends, because they were both from old, well established families. Sheremetev spent more time than usual with his son because of the inclement weather, and the conversation between the three boys seemed to reflect dangerously egalitarian attitudes and a disturbing political outlook. He talked to Vassily about it at length and concluded that much of it was childishness and reflected views the three had picked up from their German tutors at school, and he dismissed it from his mind.

Vassily Ivanovich and his friends returned to school, and the winter seemed endless after Christmas. The bleak, grey, frigid days followed one after the other, and the count often thought of the cluster of frail wagons somewhere on the steppes, where the wind piled up deep drifts and where bones of animals and humans were revealed by the spring thaws. Marya Pavlovna alternated between a cheerfulness which was too demonstrative to be characteristic and a deep depression, at one time talking excitedly to her maids, the count, and everyone else who would listen and then at other times withdrawing into herself and not speaking at all.

Then the days finally began to lengthen. Icicles hanging from eaves dripped during the middle of the

123

day when the weak sun had shone for several hours, and water puddled in the streets from the melting of snow and froze into sheets of ice at night. Then the icicles began crashing down and only a thin coating of ice froze on the puddles in the streets at night, and the midday air was foul with the stench of the refuse of winter thawing. The ice on the river became unsafe to cross, and soon it began rumbling and breaking up. One day the count noticed a bud which had formed on the tip of a tree limb outside the window of his study, and the following day he walked outside and counted several more. Two days later all the trees in the garden were beginning to grow leaf buds, and the next day he went for a ride outside the city and saw that the fields around the city were beginning to turn green. When he returned home, he went to the stables and told the grooms to begin checking the wagons, carts, carriage, and horses.

Marya Pavlovna's pregnancy was well advanced, and she seemed to be in much better condition than during previous pregnancies, except for an ominous lack of motion from the child. The count wanted to take along an apothecary and travel slowly because of her condition, but she wanted nothing to do with an apothecary. She was terrified that her delivery would begin before she could reach Sarhana, and she insisted that they travel at all possible speed. It was well before their usual time of arrival when they reached the village, and the count had warned Marya Pavlovna not to expect the Gypsies to be at the village, reminding her of the time they had come to the village the year before. But she still shouted from the carriage and interrupted Yakovlev's welcoming speech to ask if the Gypsies were there. They weren't, and she wept with disappointment all the way along the avenue to the manor and immediately went to bed when she got inside.

Early the following morning, the count went to the village to begin looking into how the villagers had fared during the winter and how the planting was progressing, and he saw one of Marya Pavlovna's maids in the village. He asked her what she was doing, and the maid told him that Marya Pavlovna had awakened early and sent her to the village to see if the Gypsies had arrived during the night. Marya Pavlovna's anxiety was pitiful, and there were other reasons to see about bringing some of the Gypsies to the village early. The village had been plagued by fire during the winter, two houses being destroyed and the families crowded in with others, and the church had been heavily damaged by two separate fires which had started in the priest's quarters. The villagers were just beginning the planting, one of the periods of heaviest activity of the year, and they didn't have the time to build houses or repair the church. He had a cart loaded with food and other supplies, picked out two house serfs to accompany him, and left that afternoon to travel to Diakonskii.

He intended to stop for the night, but the full moon was bright, lighting the road ahead of him, and he rode on through the night and into the following day. The horses were stumbling with fatigue and the serfs were asleep in the cart behind him as he rode into Diakonskii, and he continued on through the city to the fairground. The maze of tents and booths filled the fairground, and he rode along a narrow aisle between rows of them, the cart trundling along behind him and the yawning serfs sitting up and looking around. The first glimpse of the wagons gave him a curious feeling which was something like a combination of homecoming and achievement of a long-sought objective. There were forges set up at each end of the circle, with crowds of people who had brought things

125

to be repaired, and booths and the stage set up on the side of the circle toward the fairground. He looked around for Saiforella's wagon, but many of them had been repainted and he didn't recognize it among them. Several Gypsies were moving about in the crowd, and they began shouting and pointing toward him. Panna came between two of the wagons and walked toward him with a wide smile. Then he saw her. She was near one of the forges, and she pushed through the people, running toward him. Her previously lithe step had turned into a heavy amble, and the thin, triangular face had filled out as she became heavy with child. But her smile was the same, and she was beautiful. He leaped down from the horse and ran to meet her.

Panna talked with him after he rested, then he held a meeting of the men that night and discussed the work which needed to be done at the village. The following morning, five wagons left the caravan enroute to Sherevskoye. The count rode in the wagon with Saiforella, his horse following along behind the wagon. He was torn between the necessity to get Sarhana to Marya Pavlovna and his concern over inflicting hardship upon Saiforella in her condition, but she laughed at the thought of stopping to rest.

At nightfall he mounted his horse and went to the front of the caravan to lead the way along the road in the moonlight, and the village was quiet and still as he led the wagons down the avenue and onto the tide bank by the river. He roused Sarhana from her doze in the corner of the wagon where she had ridden, and she gathered her pallet and bundle of possessions and followed him up the hill to the manor. The manor was dark, settled for the night, and the footman on watch at the front door blinked sleepily as he opened the door and bowed. The count took a taper from a sconce inside the door and led Sarhana up the steps and along the hallway to Marya Pavlovna's rooms. He went in through her sitting room, knocked on the door of the bedchamber, and opened it.

Marya Pavlovna sat up in bed, blinking the sleep from her eyes, and uttered a wail of relief at the sight of Sarhana. Sarhana darted around the count and toward her, dropping her things on the floor, and she put her arms around Marya Pavlovna and pushed her back into the bed, murmuring to her softly in Romany and patting her. The count lit a couple of tapers on the table inside the door as Sarhana clucked over Marya Pavlovna, and Sarhana motioned him brusquely toward the door as she began feeling Marya Pavlovna's belly.

The weather was still mild, with an intensity to the heat during midday which forewarned of the torrid heat of full summer to come, and the count spent most of his time with Saiforella, his presence unwanted by Marya Pavlovna and Sarhana. They took walks along the riverbank again, with him helping her over small obstructions and making her laugh over his concern each time she slipped or stumbled, and they sat on grassy glades in the reeds and ate the lunches she or her mother prepared. Her girlish attractiveness had changed to a womanly beauty and her wild exuberance had become a serene composure, but her temper was still unpredictable and her mind escaped into flights of fancy when she talked about the legends and the travels of her people. The warm, bright afternoons seemed endlessly long, and he was more contented that he had ever been.

Pavlo still lurked nearby when they walked along the river. When the count was alone in the village or on his way to look at the patches of forest or fields, Pavlo's behavior was as it had always been, his presence unexpectedly announced by a loud shriek as he sprang from a place of hiding and bounded away, but when Saiforella was with the count Pavlo's conduct had inexplicably changed. There would occasionally be a soft rustle in the foliage as he followed them, and when they were sitting and talking he would sit behind a screen of foliage for hours and look at her, sometimes visible as a vague outline or a spot of different color through the foliage, but he was always subdued and quiet.

The rest of the caravan arrived from Diakonskii, nightly entertainment was staged for the villagers, and on Sundays serfs from villages for miles around came to Sherevskoye to attend what was becoming a small fair. Marya Pavlovna's labor began early on a Monday morning, her cries of pain echoing through the manor and awakening the count, and he hastily dressed and went upstairs to make sure Sarhana was with her. The maids were all in the sitting room and all hysterical, and Sarhana's presence was confirmed by a spluttering screech in Romany as he cautiously opened the bedchamber door to peek in. He went back downstairs, finished dressing and had his horse saddled, and rode down through the village to the wagons. Saiforella was also in labor.

Dawn was breaking as he turned his horse away from the wagons, and the headman was stirring people from their houses and forming the traditional procession to go to the church and pray for divine assistance in the safe delivery of an heir. The count rode his horse through the village and up the narrow road between the houses to the church, where he sat and waited. The sun rose above the horizon, its bright rays picking out the repairs the Gypsies had done on the side of the church and making dark shadows behind the tombstones and crosses in the churchyard. The priest came out of the church, bowed to the count,

128

and stood on the steps in front of the church, waiting for the procession. The chant of the villagers echoed between the hills across the river as they came through the village in a long file, carrying household ikons in front. The count reined his horse off the path and to one side as they turned onto the narrow road, and he removed his hat and bowed as the ikons approached and passed him. The priest turned and walked into the church with the procession following him, their chant filling the church with sound, Pavlo bringing up the rear of the procession and glaring wildly at the count.

The count turned his horse and went back to the road, out of the village and up through the fields to a patch of forest. There he tied his horse and sat under a tree, looking down at the village and the river. The day seemed strangely normal in the face of calamitous events. The villagers returned to the houses to eat and then went to the fields, and their songs as they worked sounded as they always did. A girl drove geese along the road, and a half dozen men and women carried bundles of linen from the village and loaded them into a barge. Presently the barge shoved off from the bank and moved toward the middle of the river, then started downstream. The villagers stood on the bank and watched, their thoughts undoubtedly focused on the safety of the cloth over which they had labored. The man in the barge stood in the stern and leaned on the long oar, his thoughts undoubtedly focused on the hazards of the journey. The sun shone down brightly, and the birds sang in the trees as they always did, which was as it should be, Sheremetev thought, but yet oddly inconsistent with the events taking place.

The headman sent a woman with food and drink for him at midday. He ate, the woman returned for the bowls, jug, and cup, and he continued to sit under the tree. Women moved around the wagons by the river, their activity centered around Saiforella's wagon. The sun inched toward the west, and no one came to tell him anything about either of his women. At sunset he mounted his horse and rode back down the hill to the headman's house in the village.

He sat at the table in the headman's house, and the headman sat on his stool in the corner between the wall and the front of the huge stove. The headman's wife put food and a cup of kvass on the table in front of him, then climbed up to her bed on top of the cold stove and lay watching him as the food became cold and dry. The elders filed in, bowing to the household ikons and then to the count and the headman, and sat down in a row along the wall. The villagers gathered outside the house and sat in the street around it. The hours passed in silence except for the soft murmurs, whispers, and shuffling movements among the serfs and the croaking of the frogs along the river.

At midnight there was a stir among the villagers in the street, and the headman rose and went out. He came back in with Panna, Sarhana, and the house steward behind him, the house steward blinking the sleep from his eyes. Panna told the count that Marya Pavlovna had given birth to a daughter and that Saiforella and her infant had died.

It took a long moment for it to sink in, for Sheremetev's mind to assimilate everything, and he sat in stupified silence and stared at Panna. Then the tears came. He drank the vodka the headman poured into the cup, then stumbled along the street toward the manor, the wailing and shrieking from the wagons echoing in his ears as he wept.

The contradictory pressures of the situation had been severe before, but it had been nothing compared to this. The count was joyful that Marya Pavlovna was well and had given birth to the daughter he had

130

always wanted, and yet he felt utter despair that Sai-forella had died.

Saiforella's funeral was at daybreak, by gypsy custom, and the rite was performed by women in a tiny shelter of branches and sticks by the wagons, while the men stood at one side. The count was dazed and numb with sorrow and the vodka he had gulped down, and Panna, the headman, and the house steward stood near him and reached for him when he swayed. His detachment from his surroundings was almost complete, his mind withdrawing from the nightmare into a fog of alcohol, and Panna's murmurs of explanation about the ceremony performed by the women under the shelter were only words to be remembered and pondered later. Too much had happened too quickly for his mind to do more than recoil with horror from the barbarism of the driving of a silver needle through the chest into the heart, the placing of a twig of wolf-bane in the mouth, and of the breaking of the little finger and tying a silver coin to it with a red thread.

Finally the ceremony was ended, and the cloth-wrapped body and the tiny bundle of cloth were borne to the village to be placed in a grave together, because gypsy custom did not allow for coffins. The villagers followed behind, murmuring softly at the strange customs, and when it was over they went to their houses to change into their working clothes. The count stumbled back toward the manor, Panna, the headman, the house steward, and Sarhana following behind him. Panna and the headman turned back at the gate, and Sarhana and the house steward followed him in.

Marya Pavlovna was asleep, and Sarhana held up the infant for him to view. He was afraid to try to hold it in his state of drunkenness and she made on movement to hand it to him, merely holding it up and lifting the covers from its tiny, shriveled face as her

131

beady eyes glared up at him. He nodded and turned away. The infant wailed in a thin, weak voice as he stumbled back out of the room. He went back downstairs to his bedchamber, collapsed on the bed, and sank into a drunken sleep.

During the afternoon he awakened. He bathed, changed clothes, drank some watered vodka, and went back upstairs. Marya Pavlovna was in a state of semiconsciousness from fatigue, pain, and weakness, and she didn't appear to observe his condition. She talked fitfully, dozed off, then stirred and spoke a few words again, each time talking about the urgency of having the naming ceremony performed immediately in the event the infant died. The baby appeared to be healthy and strong enough, slobbering greedily at the breast of a wet nurse from the village and then sleeping soundly in the cradle in the sitting room as Sarhana watched. But life was fragile, as Sheremetev knew to his cost. When he went back downstairs, he sent the house steward to tell the priest to come to the manor and perform the ceremony the next morning.

By the following morning, he was beginning to assimilate what had happened, to place it with the other events of his life and restore some semblance of proportion, and he waved away the vodka his valet poured for him and sat on the stone veranda outside his study as he ate a frugal breakfast. The house steward came to him and told him that Panna and Saiforella's mother had comé to the manor and asked permission to observe the naming ceremony, and he nodded. It seemed strange, but something approaching his close relationship with the villagers had developed between him and the gypsies. He went back inside to dress in the brushed linen trousers, ruffled shirt, silk cravat, and frock coat that his valet had laid out for him.

The ceremony was in Marya Pavlovna's sitting room. The house serfs were in the hall outside, filling the hallway and crowding up along the walls. Inside the room were the headman, village elders, house steward, Panna, Saiforella's mother, the priest, and a couple of Marya Pavlovna's maids. The priest was standing by the silver font on a small table in the middle of the room, and the others were standing around the walls. The count nodded as they bowed, and he walked to the center of the room and stood on the other side of the small table from the priest. The maids went into Marya Pavlovna's bedchamber, and he could hear Marya Pavlovna's voice in a weak, irritable murmur and the thin wailing of the infant. Sarhana came through the doorway into the room, carrying the infant and followed by the wet nurse. The maids helped Marya Pavlovna through the doorway and lay her down on a couch by the door. Sarhana handed the infant to the count, and crossing the room stood by Panna and Saiforella's mother. The priest opened his Bible and began the ceremony.

It was hot and crowded in the room. The infant's wailing was a blur of sound, partially drowning the priest's murmurs. The count pondered who he would ask to be godfather and godmother to the child and in what church in Moscow he would have the ceremony repeated if the baby lived through the summer. And he thought about arrangements for a pension for Saiforella's mother. His infant daughter wriggled in his arms, and he looked down at it as he shifted to support it more firmly. One side of the small blanket slipped off the infant, and the front of the tiny christening gown opened.

There was a dark spot on the infant's thin chest at the edge of the christening gown. Sheremetev opened the christening gown wider with his finger. It was a birthmark in the shape of a *tau* on the child's left breast. The mark of the Hator.

Sheremetev was momentarily stunned. There could be only one possible explanation. Marya Pavlovna's child had been born dead, as he had feared would happen, and the child in his arms was Saiforella's. There had been rapid, furtive footsteps between the manor and the wagons the night it happened. He looked at Panna, Saiforella's mother, and Sarhana, and the truth was written on their faces.

His mind raced, trying to make sense of it. Gypsies prized children highly, yet they had brought this child to the manor. The child was his, but it was more in the nature of a gift. It was against all precedent and his most basic instincts to designate by his family name a child born out of formal wedlock, yet it seemed little compared to what the gypsies had done. He had been concerned that the flesh of his body would be cast adrift as a nomad on the roads, but instead the flesh of a wanderer was being committed to the prison of the cities. More important still, Saiforella was gone beyond reach, but some part of her remained with him still.

There was silence in the room. The priest was looking at him with a puzzled expression. The last words spoken by the priest were still ringing in the count's ears. It was near the end of the ceremony. It was time for the naming. He looked back down at the infant, closing the christening gown and pulling the blanket over it, and held it toward the priest for the holy water.

"This child is called Natalya Ivanova Sheremeteva."

PART II

Natalya Ivanova

CHAPTER VIII

The gnawing irritation surfaced again as Natalya walked down the winding staircase to the entry hall. The long mirrors she had told the housekeeper to have hung between the tall, narrow windows flanking the front door were in place, but the two on the left of the door were higher than the two on the right. The pedestal table on the right of the dais just inside the door was too near the wall, and the drape on one of the windows to the right of the door was sagging. And the four maids further back in the entry hall and concealed by the curving sweep of the staircase sounded as though they were doing more chattering and giggling than work. From their conversation, they had been peering over the garden wall to see who lived next door, because they were talking about a handsome footman who had flirted with them.

There was a crash of china on the parquet floor of the entry hall, and the babble of conversation and laughter abruptly changed to gasps of apprehension. Natalya froze on the staircase, gripping the bannister. Her irritation grew, turning into anger. She clamped a firm control over her temper and continued walking down the staircase, her soft slippers soundless on the thick carpet and the hem of her skirt brushing the edges of the risers.

The housekeeper's firm footsteps came along the hallway from the rear of the house, and she shouted, asking what had been broken. The four maids were silent. Natalya reached the bottom of the stairs as the housekeeper came through the arched doorway at the rear of the entry hall. The four maids were standing by the box of straw from which they had been taking the vases, looking toward the housekeeper. Bits of straw were scattered about on the floor, and about half of the vases had been removed from the box, dusted, and placed on the etagere between the arched doorways on the right of the entry hall. Natalya stood with her hand resting on the richly carved newel post at the foot of the staircase, looking down at a shard of china which had slid across the floor. It was as thin as eggshell, ivory white with a bit of pale blue pattern on it, a piece of what had been a porcelain vase she had bought from an import dealer at the Elisseyev Ryad Bazzar in Moscow, at a price which had made her father wince. The housekeeper's face was red with anger, and she had her finger lifted to begin upbraiding the maids. Then she saw Natalya at the foot of the staircase. She dropped her hand and froze, looking at Natalya. The house steward came through the arched doorway on the right at the rear of the entry hall, glanced quickly around, then stood motionless, staring at Natalya. The maids slowly turned, and their expressions changed from apprehension to fear.

There had been many aggravations during the past weeks. The housekeeper and house steward were competent, ordinarily controlling the household staff effortlessly and having everything done punctually, but the move from Moscow to St. Petersburg had been more of an undertaking than they could handle. The maids, footmen, cooking staff, gardeners, grooms, and others had been both excited and fearful, looking forward to the move even as they were afraid it would adversely affect their personal concerns, and only Natalya could control them. The process of getting things packed and prepared for the move had been tedious, the discomforts and inconveniences of the move and arriving at the empty house had been bothersome, and friends of her father had started arriving at the house to visit with him the day after they arrived, creating panic among the servants as they tried to find furnishings among the contents of carts and wagons to make the drawing room and her father's study presentable. And she had just come from her rooms on the second floor, where she had been hard put to keep from shouting at her personal maids because they couldn't find a box of her books.

A tense, steely silence gripped the entry hall as they looked at her. Anger stirred in her mind, but a safe and moderate anger; the potential of an ecstasy of rage was under firm control. Three of the maids moved stealthily away from the fourth, identifying the one who had dropped the vase. It was Ulyasha, a new girl. She and her mother had been brought to the household in Moscow from Sherevskoye shortly before the move to St. Petersburg, because her father had drowned in the river and there had been no male children in the family to assume responsibility for her and her mother. Ulyasha's face twisted, and she clutched her dusting rag to her lips as she began weeping.

Natalya dropped her hand from the newel post and walked toward the maids. Ulyasha's sobs became louder as she darted a glance from one side to the other. The other maids moved further away from her. Natalya walked up to Ulyasha, who uttered a squeak and flinched as Natalya took the collar of her dress with a firm grip. She was stout and shorter than average, but still taller than Natalya, and Natalya lifted herself on her toes and tugged on Ulyasha's collar to pull her over and glare into her eyes. "Silence! Pay attention to your duties instead of your gossip!"

Ulyasha gulped and nodded rapidly, whereupon Natalya released her and stepped away, her foot crunching a shard of the vase on the floor. The housekeeper bustled forward. "I shall punish her, mistress. I shall make her—"

"I mete out punishment in this household," Natalya interrupted in a firm tone, glancing at her, and she looked back at Ulyasha and pointed at the floor. "Clean that up. And I will deal with you later." She looked at the housekeeper, pointing at the etagere. "That is not evenly positioned between the doorways—it is too far to the right."

"Yes, mistress. I will have it—"

"And those two mirrors there are too high—have them lowered to the same height as the others. Also have someone move that table further away from the wall, and have that drape rehung."

"Yes, mistress."

The maids stooped and began gathering up the pieces of the shattered vase as the housekeeper stepped to the door of a drawing room off the entry hall and motioned to several other maids, and the house steward addressed Natalya. "Mistress, we still have only four gardeners working in the garden at the front of the house . . ."

"The stables come first," Natalya replied, shaking her head. "These four will do what they can until the repairs are finished on the stables, because my horses are more important than the gardens. Have the carriage gates been repaired?"

"Yes, mistress. And the broken paving stones in the courtyard have been replaced. . . ."

His voice faded as he glanced over his shoulder. He had heard the soft sound of the count's cane against the floor in the hallway. The housekeeper was bringing two more maids from the drawing room to move the etagere, and she glanced at the doorway and motioned the maids back. Natalya's father came through the doorway, glancing around, and the house steward and housekeeper nodded respectfully and looked at him attentively. A private soldier in the uniform of the Yamburgsky Regiment of Uhlans followed her father into the entry hall, his kepi tucked tightly under his left arm, his back straight and his steps short and stiff, clearly uncomfortable in his surroundings.

"Natasha, this man brought a message from your brother that he will dine with us and bring a friend from his regiment, Aleksei Andreyevich Orlov."

Her brother had visited the house almost daily during the time they had been there and had taken several meals with them, but the presence of a guest created a more formal situation, particularly in view of the name. Count Andrey Orlov was a powerful man in circles very close to the czar. "Very well, father. Has the soldier had refreshments?"

The man's face flushed with confusion. "I am grateful, but I must return to my regiment," he stuttered.

Natalya smiled and clicked her tongue. "A soldier in the uniform of the Yamburgskys does not leave this house without having refreshments." Her smile widened as the soldier stiffened with pride, and she looked at one of the maids. "Take him to the hall, and give him bread, cheese, and kvass."

The maid murmured an acknowledgement, glancing at the soldier and edging around the housekeeper, and

141

she walked toward the arched doorway on the left. The soldier bowed stiffly to Natalya's father and to her, and he followed the maid. The count turned to go back into his study, then hesitated and looked at the bits of china still on the floor, frowning darkly. "What is this?"

"An accident, and a matter of small concern, father," Natalya replied. "Do you expect other guests this evening?"

He shook his head absently, then looked back at the bits of china and frowned at the maids. "Carelessness," he said in a chiding tone. "I will not tolerate carelessness."

"The household is my responsibility," Natalya reminded him. "If you have comments concerning it, they should be directed to me."

He looked at her, and his mustaches lifted in a grimace as he turned toward the arched doorway. "You are welcome to it," he grumbled, limping slowly through the doorway on his cane.

Natalya turned to the housekeeper. "When you have finished here, make sure the dining room and the main drawing room are clean and in order. Put out the new lace tablecloth and serviettes for dinner tonight." She addressed the house steward. "Have the footmen who serve dinner in fresh livery, and check that their hands and fingernails are clean."

They murmured assent, and Natalya turned back toward the staircase. She glanced into the drawing rooms off the entry hall, then crossed the entry hall and looked into the ballroom. One of the drawing rooms was in order, and the other needed drapes and pictures hung. It also needed an extra piece of furniture or two, perhaps a mirror stand and a shelf or a small table. One of the drawing rooms off the entry

142

hall in the house in Moscow had been smaller, but here both were large, requiring more furniture.

The ballroom was papered with an embossed pink design on a pale green, which clashed with the red in the drapes and in the upholstery on the couches and chairs, and it would annoy Natalya until the room was repapered. Her father would assume an expression of doubtful surprise when she told him that more furniture was needed in the extra drawing room, as well as in several other rooms in the house, and he would protest that the colors in the ballroom looked harmonious to him. But he would eventually give in. She turned away from the ballroom, crossed the entry hall to the staircase, and started up the stairs.

The housekeeper rattled orders, telling a maid to go for a ladder to take down the sagging drape and the two mirrors which were too high, then scolding the maids who were unpacking the vases as she crossed the entry hall and went along one of the hallways. The maids began whispering as the housekeeper's footsteps faded, then they began giggling and chattering again. Natalya hesitated, then sighed with resignation and walked on up the stairs to the landing, wondering hopefully if her maids had found the box of books for which she had been looking.

The move from Moscow to St. Petersburg had come as a result of the czar's granting permission for her father to be received at court, and it had been no less unsettling for Natalya than it had been for the house serfs. She appreciated what it meant to her father, and she also looked forward with pleasant anticipation to being received at court herself, but the house in Moscow, its environs, and the annual treks to Sherevskoye were the focus of her earliest memories, the fragmentary, shadowy images which some feeling or set of

143

circumstances would occasionally bring to life in her mind.

A nurse with a commodious lap, soft, large breasts, and warm arms, deliciously comfortable surrounding her, and the adenoidal serf girl several years older than she who was assigned to watch over her and amuse her. The serfs' hall, bright, loud, and cheerful, and the endless rooms and passages elsewhere, dark, frightening, and gloomy. Snatches of scenery along a high road, her mother's sweaty, fretful face on the other side of the carriage, and the cool greenery of Sherevskoye. Lying on top of a cold stove in a village house and eating a sweetmeat someone had given her while village women with coarse hands and a different odor smiled at her and touched her hair and clothes, and the serf girl remaining outside, neither wanted inside nor wanting to come in. Gypsy wagons with dark, brightly-dressed people towering around her and dark children lurking around corners and peering at her warily, and the hot interior of a wagon where a frightening old woman with piercing eyes and dangling earrings cackled gleefully as she tugged at Natalya's bodice to peer into it at the birthmark.

Leaving the house amounted to the abandonment of a deep emotional investment. It was where her mother had died, an event which Natalya had regarded with unconcern and even a kind of relief that the pallid, remote woman who glared, shouted, slapped, and pinched was gone. Then there had been weeping and sorrow which had been stimulated by the wailing and howling of the women in the serf's hall. Natalya remembered the cathedral and the booming thunder of the music while her shoes pinched agonizingly, and her father's face with tears on his cheeks. And then the graveyard, with lurking grey masses of tombs all about and hordes of people in dark clothes.

Afterwards the house had been quiet and empty-feeling for a time, even the serfs' hall subdued and gloomy.

The maids had found her box of books, and they were putting them on the shelves in the corner of the sitting room with the others. They were exuberantly cheerful in their relief at having found the books and avoiding a situation which might easily have stimulated Natalya's anger. It was the same caution that the housekeeper, house steward, and maids in the entry hall had shown, and for Natalya it was a cause for shame. It seemed that at one level her temper was similar to that of everyone else, resulting in irritation and anger in situations which caused it in others; but at a deeper level there was a demon which could spring to life and possess her if she allowed herself to lose control over it.

It had first shown itself when she was eight, when her father sent her away to boarding school. She had long since known the efficacy of embraces and kisses and then tears in gaining objectives and reversals of undesirable decisions, but for once they had been without effect. He hadn't wanted her to go and had sent her because of some good to which he kept referring and which defied analysis and explanation. Each day had become a torment for her as the time came closer and clothes were bought and letters sent and received, and she had felt suffocated and stifled by his decision, shackled by something she couldn't understand. The last conversation about the hated boarding school had been in his study.

And it had happened. The memory was obscured by a feverish mist born of the fulminating rage which had lived within her, demanding frenzied activity and offering release only when everything about her had been shredded and broken. Her father's face had been aghast as things began flying about the study, and noise

145

had come from all directions, a screeching which had been torn from her by the fury inside her. The faces of the serfs had been grotesquely distorted, their features twisted and their mouths and eyes open wide, and the walls and floors around her had seemed to twist and warp as she raced through the house. Hands had sought to catch her, then shied away from her teeth and fingernails, and a heavy cane in the holder by the front door had seemed to leap into her hands, becoming an extension of them. Glass had shattered from the front door and blood had burst from a footman's forehead under the cane; the cries and shouts of the serfs had added to the uproar in her head, and a rush at them with the cane had carried her into the serfs' hall, where the cane had shattered bowls and dishes and fire had licked up the wall when the pot of oil on the stove was smashed. The demon within her had kept churning, demanding more and more. Other things had shattered around her as the serfs circled, closed in, and leaped back from the cane, shouting hoarsely. Then she had fainted.

The outburst had frightened her more than it had angered her father. There had been no more mention of boarding school, and tutors started coming to the house a few days later. The fury had come again at the summer estate, possessing her when the Gypsies denied her a horse she wished to ride, and they had been strangely pleased, rejoicing in the wild rage which gripped her.

But at about the time when it might have become a means of exerting her will, her father had made it clear that there were penalties attached to misconduct, and responsibilities toward others. He had helped her learn to control her temper by thrashing her soundly with a leather strap, and there had been other punishments for displays of even moderate ill humor. For

146

insolence to a village elder at Sherevskoye, he had made her publicly apologize to the elder, and he had thrashed her with the strap and made her spend two days in her rooms. For striking a maid during a fit of petulance, he had thrashed her with the strap and made her serve the maid a meal at the table in the serfs' hall, with all of the other serfs present and all of them as embarrassed as she.

The wild, unrestrained fury had been controlled, chained and locked away in a recess of her mind where it could not escape, but there had been impulsive actions which seemed to be born of the driving energies which built up within her and lay in wait to feed the lurking fury. At the village one summer, she had escaped the serfs who went with her to watch over her while she rode, and had raced her horse down the riverbank at a furious gallop, making it jump off a low bluff into the river with her, bringing all activity in the fields, village, and among the Gypsies' wagons to an abrupt halt as people streamed to the river and jumped in to rescue her. The Gypsies had reached her first and brought her out, soaked and retching water, and they had laughed gaily and bounced her in their arms as they carried her and led the streaming horse to their wagons. The villagers had been frightened and puzzled. Her father had been outraged, getting out the strap and thrashing her again. But the Gypsies had seemed pleased, and they had also seemed to understand why she had done it, which was more than she did herself.

The maids had put some of the books on the shelves in the wrong order, and she sent them into the bedchamber to work on unpacking more of her clothes and rearranged the books herself.

There were several shelves of them, ranging from Caron, Kotzebue, and volumes of the French *Reper-*

toire, through modern novels in English, French, and German, to volumes of philosophy, political science, and history, as well as a broad selection of classics in Latin and Greek. They comprised an exceptionally large personal library, and they reflected the fact that her tutors had given her an inquisitive thirst for knowledge rather than a veneer of education. It set her apart from others, as did other things in her background. Girls went to boarding schools or day schools, with instruction by tutors normally being limited to boys. French was considered the language of culture, to the extent that children's contacts with serfs were kept to a minimum by watchful mothers so Russian wouldn't become their first language. Natalya's father had more slavophilic attitudes and had been only sporadically concerned with her upbringing, so she had spent much of her childhood life in the serfs' hall. Most girls had French, English, or German nurses and governesses from early childhood, but Natalya had been fourteen before it had occurred to her father to hire one. She had been a German woman who had remained in Moscow when they moved, and during the three years she had been in the household, she had consumed a bottle of cognac every day, spent most of her time in her rooms, and bothered Natalya very little.

As time had passed, there had been a dawning consciousness that the differences between her and others went deeper than her Russian accent in French, that there was a fundamental difference in orientation and values. Contacts with other girls of her age group in Moscow had expanded into the fringes of fashionable social circles as a result of the prestige of the Sheremetev name, and there had been nameday parties and similar occasions at the houses of others when she was a girl. Her father had expected her to go, and sometimes she had found a pleasure of sorts in them. But the other girls had been more interested in comparing dresses, childish gossip, or in playing shuttlecock or quoits, and Natalya had always taken along her sling in her pocket so she could slip away unnoticed and go to their stables to see if they had any rats, the rats around the stables at her house having long since been killed off by the deadly accuracy of her sling.

Once she had enjoyed a party. While the others played croquet in a garden at the side of the house, she had idly climbed into a tree at the rear of the house. The remarks that an older brother resident in the house had recently been married had become a matter of interest when she climbed to the level of an open second floor window and saw a nude man moving about in the dimness of the room. In the gloom on the far side of the room, there had been a bare glimpse of another naked form on a couch. Vague bits of information gleaned from overheard comments between serfs had run through her mind as she waited breathlessly, but nothing had happened. Presently she had become impatient and shouted at them to proceed, causing a panic of scurrying and consternation in the room as the woman on the couch whipped a gown around herself and disappeared, and the man ran to the window in a crouch and shouted for her to get down from the tree. After an exchange of shouts which had rapidly become more heated on both sides, she had started pulling green apples from the limbs of the tree and throwing them at the man until the red-faced governess who was overseeing the party came to the foot of the tree and angrily demanded that she climb down. It had upset the household and caused the party to break up precipitantly, with all the girls crowding around Natalya and questioning her eagerly on what

149

she had seen as they went to their coaches. Her father had gone into convulsions of laughter when she told him about it over dinner.

Natalya finished rearranging the books, then arranged the things on her desk, placing the quills and the graphite and clay pencils in neat rows and the inkwell, sander, and stack of writing paper within easy reach of her chair. She sat down at the desk and absently drummed her fingers on it, thinking about dinner that evening. And about Aleksei Andreyevich Orlov. The prospect of meeting him made her feel both excited and apprehensive. A few friends of her father's had called at the house during the short time they had been there, but she had no friends in St. Petersburg and there would be no social calls or invitations until after they had been received by the czar, for fear of offending him. There had been a time in the not too distant past when it would have meant nothing to her, but new motivations arising within her during the past year or so had broadened her horizons beyond her studies and books, her horses, her target practice with a pistol, and the other things around which her life had once revolved. So the past few days had been lonely and a little boring, despite the work of getting the household organized. A couple of acquaintances in Moscow had known Aleksei Andreyevich Orlov and had mentioned him, gushing over how handsome and personable he was. Natalya thought about what they had said as she got up from the desk, crossed the room, and went into the bedchamber to look through the clothes her maids had unpacked.

Men had been calling on her during the past few months in Moscow, and there had been rides in the park and other occasions approaching courtship, but it had been disorganized and confused. Such matters were usually dealt with by a mother, who placed her

150

daughter in a situation of availability and screened applicants drawn by the bait. In the absence of a mother, the matter was usually taken care of by an older female relative or at least by a governess. Natalya's governess had been disinterested and usually drunk, which had given Natalya independence and freedom of action more valuable than the advice and assistance which would have been rendered by a more effective governess, so she had willingly helped the governess conceal her derelictions from the count. But the lack of a usual channel of communication between Natalya and interested men was less of an obstacle than it might have been for others, because men were stimulated to find a way. Natalya's small stature in childhood had developed into slender, petite beauty at sixteen; men noticed her at parties, at the theaters, and at other places, and they found ways to be received by her father so they could ask for permission to call on her.

The count had been truculent and suspicious about the entire matter, granting permission to only a few, and it hadn't always gone smoothly with them. Once, while riding with a man and two other couples in Sokolniki Park, the men had started tormenting an old Gypsy woman who was sneaking about in the park and selling trinkets, and Natalya had hotly come to the old woman's assistance, much to the amusement of the man with her and the other two couples. Gypsies had been a strong influence and formative element in her life through her association with them at Sherevskoye. It was through their teaching that she could control a spirited horse and ride better than most men, and they had moved in and out of her life at odd times and under what seemed to be strange circumstances. As a child of thirteen, during the flight from Moscow when the French had been advancing on the city, with both

151

her father and her brother with their regiments and accompanied only by the terrified house serfs piled in a wagon with her, four Gypsy wagons had suddenly appeared on the high road, fighting their way through the stream of carts, wagons, and people carrying belongings out of the smoking, burning city, and they had pulled the wagon off the high road and escorted it for what seemed to be an endlessly long time along narrow paths and backroads until they had conducted her to the safety of Sherevskoye. There had been other times when Gypsies had unexpectedly appeared to come to her assistance, almost irrationally grateful for the privilege of camping at Sherevskoye each summer, and Natalya had a deep emotional attachment to them. The old woman in the park hadn't been one of the group which came to Sherevskoye, but she had looked pitiful, helpless, and frightened when the men began badgering her. And there had been a derisive edge to the amusement of those with Natalya over her concern for the old woman, threatening her control over her temper.

There had been other conflicts and problems which had generated sneering gossip and snide comments about her eccentricities. Her concept of manhood was derived from her association with her father, and to a more limited extent with her brother. A man who spent six hours on his toilette was all the rage in fashionable salons, but much too fastidious and effete in her judgement. And she had found that men weren't accustomed to having their pronouncements on the arts, sciences, and the state of world affairs challenged by a woman half their age who moreover had hard facts to support her opinions.

But the men had kept coming, and it had been pleasant, fulfilling a need within her which strangely seemed to be caused by the presence of the means of fulfillment. There had also been a touch of sweet revenge in the satisfaction the situation had brought. Girls who had once exchanged sly glances over her Russian accent in French and the unfashionable but comfortable shoes she had picked to wear to a name-day party were much less attractive than she, turning into fat, petulant clods while she was slender and energetic. And their mothers, who had once sneered down their noses through their lorgnettes at Natalya's conduct, anxiously tried to insert their charges into the clusters of men hovering around Natalya at the parties, poetry readings, music recitals, and other occasions.

Natalya selected a crepe de Chine gown in pale green, and told the maids to prepare her bath. The house was more modern than the one in Moscow had been, and there was a small room off the bedchamber for bathing. It had a large drain in the center of the floor which led into a network of pipes from other rooms in the house and emptied into a ditch at the rear of the back garden, which in turn connected with a canal leading to a branch of the Neva. It was a convenience, and it removed the temptation to dump bathwater out of an upper floor window instead of carrying it down to pour out into the garden, a temptation to which the maids had occasionally succumbed in Moscow. Natalya had traced the powerful stench she had smelled the first time she had entered the house to the drains. Making covers for them had been the gardeners' first task, but the serfs were unconcerned about odors and she was still in the process of making the household staff conscious of the necessity to keep the covers on the drains.

One of the maids took the gown down to the cook house connected to the rear of the house to steam it lightly and shake the wrinkles out of it, and the other maids got a couple of footmen to help them carry water to fill the hip bath. In the bath she usually relaxed in the luxurious comfort of the hot, perfumed water, but she felt tense and anxious about dinner and she wanted to check and make sure everything would be ready. She bathed, put on fresh underclothing and silk stockings, and went back into the bedchamber where she sat on the bench in front of her dressing table for the maids to do her hair. It was thick and heavy, hanging down to her waist, and they always had trouble with it. They took it down and combed it out, then separated it and began coiling it to put it back up again. She became impatient with them and shrugged away from them, taking the ivory combs and pinning it up herself.

The gown was almost new, and it had puffed shoulders, a flounced skirt, and tightly fitted sleeves and bodice, all conforming to the current French fashion, but the neckline was unfashionably high to satisfy her father. He also found ostentatious display of jewelry distasteful, and so she selected a single string of pearls and a pair of matching pearl pendant earrings. The fact that there was going to be a young man as a guest for dinner had spread through the household, and the maids clucked and sighed over how impressed he would be as they put the jewelry on her, tucked wisps of hair under the combs, and plucked the sleeves, shoulders, and bodice of her gown into place. Natalya surveyed herself in the mirror, tugging at the waist and skirt of the gown, then went back downstairs to check on the arrangements for dinner.

Some households she had visited were disorganized and filled with hordes of poorly fed and mistreated serfs whose main occupation seemed to be hiding and evading work, for which she could scarcely blame them, but her father had always insisted on order and discipline in his household. The serfs were well fed, well clothed, and well treated, and they had pocket money to spend as well as presents on their nameday and at Christmas. In return, each had clearly defined duties and responsibilities which they were expected to fulfill. Most women of her acquaintance had little to do with the household, leaving it to the man of the house to issue his orders through the housekeeper and house steward, but Natalya's nervously restless disposition had made her search for things to fill her time. Her father's failing eyesight and diminishing agility had led her into general oversight of the household from the age of thirteen, and she had taken complete control of it by the time she reached fifteen.

For the most part, the house serfs had viewed the transition with satisfaction, because Natalya had grown from a baby to a young woman in their midst, and she had a close rapport with them. The older serfs needed little direction or control, but the younger ones were occasionally inclined to be childishly irresponsible, and she emulated what she had seen her father do in dealing with them. The count had always reacted to laziness or carelessness by scolding them, occasionally taking a male serf by the collar in extreme instances, but never touching a female serf. As a woman, she didn't differentiate between them, and it had never occurred to her to consider that her dealings with the serfs might be anything out of the ordinary until some acquaintances of her father from the English Club in Moscow had dined with them one evening. One of the footmen serving had been negligent, chuckling and whispering disparaging comments about the guests to the other footmen, and when a couple of searing glares had failed to silence him, she had jumped up from the table, taken his collar, and pulled him over to shake her fist in his face and berate him. Her father had continued eating, barely noticing the incident, but the two couples from the English Club had looked at her in shock and amazement.

The mirrors, drape, and pedestal table by the front doors had been put right, the vases had been placed on the etagere, and it was positioned evenly between the drawing room doorways. The parquet floor had been waxed, was a gleaming expanse of richly-colored wood, with a single fringed Persian carpet in a deep red in the center of it. The crystal chandeliers hanging from the lofty ceiling over the entry hall had been lowered and cleaned, and the facets of the crystals sparkled in the light coming through the drapes and through the large fanlight over the front doors. The house didn't have the atmosphere of ancient gentility of the house in Moscow or the one at Sherevskoye, and it had yet to represent home in her mind, but it was spacious, attractive, and comfortable.

She went through the doorway on the right at the rear of the entry hall, walked along the hallway to her father's study, and knocked on the door. There was no reply. She quietly opened the door and looked in. He was asleep in his chair behind his desk, his chin on his chest. She smiled fondly as she entered and quietly closed the door behind her, and crossed the dark, somber room with its heavy, old fashioned furniture and went into the adjoining room, his bedchamber. His valet was asleep on a bench by the hall door, and she crossed the room and nudged him. "Get up and see to your duties, Gavril. Put out fresh clothes for the master, and get him prepared for dinner."

He looked up at her, then slid his feet to the floor and sat up on the bench, yawning and rubbing his eyes. "He told me that he did not wish to be disturbed."

Natalya's lips tightened with irritation. Gavril con-

156

sidered that his position as her father's valet entitled him to special privileges and set him apart from the rest of the household. And she'd had trouble with him several times, including during the move from Moscow. He considered manual labor below him, but Natalya had worked and had put her maids to work, so she had put him to loading wagons. "The master has a guest for dinner this evening," she said in a quiet, steely tone. "He does not wish to remain undisturbed for the rest of his life."

Gavril shrugged and looked away. "The master told me not to disturb him," he said in a stubborn tone. "He said that he wished—"

"Get to your feet!" Natalya shouted at him, leaning over him. "Is it your duty to lie here and sleep while others work? If you have nothing to do, there is plenty to keep you busy in the gardens and the stables!"

He rose hastily to his feet, his expression alarmed. "I have ample duties, mistress, and I work until late at night," he said defensively. "I have done my duties for the moment, and I was only resting until—"

"Have his boots been cleaned?" Natalya snapped.

Gavril cleared his throat and looked away, nodding. "They have been cleaned, mistress," he mumbled.

"Get them, and I shall see if they have been cleaned properly."

He turned and shuffled across the room toward the clothes press. There was a stir in her father's study. She had apparently awakened him when she had raised her voice, and she could hear his chair squeak, a grunt of effort, and the sound of his cane on the floor as he crossed the room toward the bedchamber doorway. Gavril got the boots from under the clothes press and brought them to her.

"I have seen cleaner boots on hod carriers! Would

you send your master to dine with a guest in boots which would be a disgrace for a drover? Clean those boots, then put out a suit for him and brush it!"

Gavril glanced at the doorway as her father stepped into it and leaned on his cane, and he nodded and turned away. "Yes, mistress."

"Is it time to get ready?" her father asked in a mild tone.

Natalya smiled, walking toward him. "There is ample time, father. I was only making arrangements to have you made ready in time."

The count smiled down at her and put his hand on her arm as she started to walk through the doorway. "If there is time, then stay for a moment and let me see you, Natasha."

She smiled up at him, reaching up to pat a few hairs of his mustache into place. "There is time for you, not for me, father. I must see to my duties so that all will be ready and you will not be shamed in the presence of your guest."

His smile widened, and he laughed softly. "He is probably more your guest than mine, or he will be when he sees you. I see you are wearing the pearls I bought for Marya Pavlovna, may God rest her soul."

"Yes," she replied, plucking at them. "They are large for me, but I like them. Do they look as well on me as on her? My hair is much darker, isn't it?"

His smile became thoughtful, and he leaned heavily on his cane and touched the pearls with the tip of his finger. Then he looked into her eyes, patted her arm, and turned away, limping into his bedchamber. "They are very attractive on you, Natasha. I shall prepare for dinner."

There was a note of dismissal in his voice, and she nodded and smiled as she turned away and walked toward the hallway door. It was unusual for him to mention her mother to her, and he had always been vague and evasive when she mentioned her mother in conversation. For a long time, she had assumed that it was a reluctance caused by continuing sorrow over her mother's death, then she had realized that he showed a similar reluctance in discussing her mother with her brother and others. It was puzzling, but it had never aroused her curiosity enough to make her want to risk invading something he obviously considered private in order to explore the subject with him.

She went back along the hallway to the entry hall and started to turn into the hallway along the other wing, then hesitated at the dining room doorway and looked in. The long table was gleaming from fresh wax, and the new tablecloth and serviettes were stacked on one end of it, ready to put in place. Two maids were polishing the silver candelabra which would be spaced along the table and the sideboard, and the silver salvers were stacked on one end of the sideboard. Ulyasha and her mother were polishing the floor, and they glanced up at Natalya and quickly ducked their heads back down. The other maids looked at Natalya, smiled silently in acknowledgement of her presence, and went back to work. The other maids were still avoiding Ulyasha, because her punishment was still pending, and they would continue to do so until Natalya either punished her or publicly forgave her for breaking the vase.

In households where the serfs were treated poorly and there was no loyalty to the house owner, sympathy and support were tendered toward one of their number who was in trouble. In households where the serfs were treated well, they ostracized one of their number who got into trouble. In general, it was a powerful means of discipline, because the conviviality and companionship of the serfs' hall was a fundamental and crucially important element in the life of a serf. Ulyasha's mother had joined her in isolation, as she was expected to do, voluntarily cutting herself off from social intercourse with the others for her daughter's sake. They would eat alone, no one would speak to them except when necessary to perform some duty, and they would live in a vacuum of loneliness while surrounded by others. It was a situation which amounted to cruelty if permitted to continue very long. Natalya turned away from the door, walked along the hallway to the outside door at the end of it, and went out the door and across the covered breezeway to the cook house.

The cook house was a single enormous room with a huge oven at one end, a large, open-top stove and spit at the other, and a long deal workbench against the wall across from the door. Bunches of onions and garlic and bundles of dried herbs hung from the high ceiling on strings, a tall rack filled with loaves of bread filled the corner by the oven, food safes lined the walls on each side of the door; pots, pans, large kettles, and long forks, spoons, and knives hung on the walls, and baskets of vegetables covered the ends of the workbench. There was a penetrating odor of spices, a pungent smell of fresh bread, and an appetizing scent of food cooking. Fires roared in both the oven and stove, steam boiled up from the kettles, and the assistant cooks and helpers were darting about and laboring over mixing bowls and troughs under the scowling direction and snarled orders of the head cook.

He was one of two house serfs who had demonstrated a natural talent for cooking several years before, and her father had paid a fee to have them be trained by a well known French chef at the famous Rostov Restaurant in Moscow. One of the serfs had requested release from the Sheremetev estate, which her father had granted, and had gone into private employment as a chef and had been successful for a time, then he had started drinking to excess and lost several jobs. He had finally ended up in prison for killing a customer who complained about the food at a small café where he was working. The other had remained with the family and had been the head cook from Natalya's early childhood, periodically exploding into tantrums of temperament and consistently producing gastronomic delights. There had been a process of mutual adjustment when Natalya had taken charge of the household. Most of the time she tolerated his volatile disposition without taking offense, and her only serious problem with him had been in getting him to comply with her rule that she was the only one who administered any kind of punishment, because he was given to cuffing his assistants and helpers.

His assistants moved out of her path and gave her harassed smiles as she walked toward the stove, where the head cook was berating two helpers and mixing and stirring a couple of pots. It was easy to tell where all of them worked, because everyone except the head cook was fat, their white blouses soaked with sweat in the hot, humid room. The head cook was thin and angular, his white blouse and dark trousers hanging on him and sweat shining on his craggy features. He was enraged at one of his helpers for breaking his favorite bowl for mixing sauces, a spoon which was crucially important in some process had been misplaced, the only vegetables available at the market were of inferior quality, the ice which had been brought from the entrepreneur who cut it from the Neva during the winter and stored it for summer demands had a strange taste, and the stove was virtually impossible to use, a cheap substitute for a stove compared to the one in Moscow. But everything was on schedule, and dinner would be ready on time.

The heat and humidity in the cook house made prickles of sweat tingle in the roots of Natalya's hair, and she daubed at her temples with her handkerchief and felt her hair with the tips of her fingers as she went back along the breezeway and into the house. She turned into a short corridor off the main hallway which led to the serfs' hall, a long, wide room as large as the cook house. Along the sides of the room there were stools and crude chairs which the serfs had made for themselves for relaxing after their work was done and which they jealously guarded to keep anyone else from using. The continual formation and dissolution of cliques could be traced by the constantly changing arrangement of the chairs as they were moved about by their owners in response to changing alliances.

The center of the room was filled by a massive deal table with benches along both sides; at one end of the room was a huge stove which heated the room in winter and was used for cooking their communal meals, and a large samovar for making tea was on a table adjacent to the stove. The walls were covered with shelves which held cups, glasses, bowls, spoons, and other utensils and personal belongings, the room was cluttered and untidy with the ramshackle stools and chairs along the walls and piles of personal belongings tucked under them, and it smelled strongly of dirty clothes and sweat. It had been clean when they moved into the house, and in less than a week it looked as though the serfs had been resident in the hall for years. From her experiences growing up in the serfs' hall, Natalya knew they regarded it as their territory and resented any attempt to regulate how they kept it, and she always ignored it until it threatened to infest the rest of the house with mice and rats, at which time she had them carry everything outside and thoroughly clean the room.

The house steward and the four footmen designated to serve dinner were in a cluster at the end of the room opposite the stove, making their final preparations. Their faces were still red from the steam bath, a tiny brick building at the end of the back garden with a wood furnace built into one wall, they had on clean shirts and trousers, their boots were freshly blacked, and they were brushing their frock coats and putting them on. They were all a little tense, one in particular. He was only eighteen and new to duties inside the house, the son of a groom and a maid who were married, and Natalya had moved him into the house because he was too slight for the work required of a gardener or groom. Natalya talked to him quietly to reassure him and glanced at the others, flicking bits of lint off their frock coats and adjusting their lapels. They followed her back along the corridor and the hallway to take their positions to wait, the house steward between the two arched doorways at the rear of the entry hall and the footmen just out of sight of the entry hall inside the dining room.

The dining room was now ready, the lace tablecloth on the table, the serviettes, silver salvers, plates, bowls, small dishes, glasses, and silverware in neat stacks and rows on the sideboard, and four candelabra spaced along the table and three along the sideboard, gleaming softly in the diffused light. The floor shimmered wetly from the wax on it, and the chairs were spaced at precise intervals along the long table. The large oil landscape on the wall opposite the sideboard looked a little uneven. She stepped into the room, adjusted it and looked at it critically, and walked back out into the entry hall.

Over a period of time, she had developed what amounted to silent communication with the house steward. As she came back into the entry hall, she looked

163

at him and nodded toward the doorway into the right wing, indicating for him to check on her father, and he nodded silently and walked quietly through the doorway. She crossed the entry hall to the front drawing room. The housekeeper had three maids in it, doing last minute dusting and cleaning. The floor and table tops gleamed, and the wood of the French furniture shone with a satiny luster. The faded rose in the upholstery and in the long drapes over the tall windows harmonized attractively with the wallpaper, an embossed design of dull yellow on off white. It was a comfortable, pleasing room. The cushions on one of the couches were slightly askew, stirring the bothersome feeling that the housekeeper had left something obvious to correct so she would look no further. She pointed toward the couch, and walked into the room to look at the corners and at the chandeliers against the light to see if there was any dust or cobwebs. The housekeeper snapped her fingers at one of the maids and pointed toward the couch, and the maid crossed the room and straightened the cushions. Natalya finished looking around the room. It was perfect. She nodded to the housekeeper, and the housekeeper herded the maids out of the drawing room.

Natalya followed them back out into the entry hall. The house steward was coming back out of the hallway in the right wing, taking his station at the rear of the entry hall again, and he nodded to Natalya, indicating that her father was ready. She took her handkerchief from her cuff and touched her temples and upper lip with it, and the fresh aroma of the rosewater on the handkerchief filled her nostrils with its pleasant scent. The housekeeper and maids disappeared through the arched doorway into the left wing, going to the serfs' hall. The house was suddenly quiet. Natalya considered readiness to receive guests a fundamental measure of order in a household, and she took pride in the fact that scheduled guests never entered her house to find it untidy or in a disorderly bustle of last minute preparations. And she wanted to make a particularly good impression on Aleksei Andreyevich Orlov, in the event that he was as handsome and personable as she had been told.

Natalya felt slightly nervous. She wiped her palms with her handkerchief and pressed it to her nostrils again, smelling the rosewater. A feeling of contained excitement made her heart beat faster. It was time for her brother to arrive, if he came straight to the house from the garrison. But if he and his friend stopped at a *kabak* for a glass of vodka, it might be an hour or even longer before they came. Hopefully it wouldn't be too long, or part of the next day would be consumed in soothing the head cook out of a fit of temperament over his frantic exertions to keep dinner fit to eat.

The drapes on one of the windows flanking the front doors was open a fraction wider than the others, and Natalya crossed the entry hall, lifted the front of her skirt and petticoat and stepped up onto the low dais along the front of the room, pulling at the drapes. She touched her upper lip with her handkerchief again as she turned and glanced around. The pieces of furniture along the walls in the wide, sweeping expanse of the entry hall seemed to her anxious eyes almost disproportionately small, in a way emphasizing the spaciousness of the room, but in another seeming almost spartan. A bust on a tall marble pedestal just at the foot of the staircase would be a pleasing touch, Natalya thought, and would relieve the hint of austerity. The house steward was standing like a statue, arms at his sides and eyes blank, in the mindless reverie which served him better than patience as he waited for a thump of the door knocker to stir him into mobility. Natalya turned and opened one of the tall, heavy doors.

The reddish-gold of the setting sun shone between the tall colonnades supporting the roof of the shallow portico. She stepped outside and closed the door behind her. The air was fresh and cool, smelling of the greenery in the gardens and of woodsmoke, and there were distant, muted sounds from the avenue, the clop of horses' hoofs and rumbling whir of carriage wheels. The gardeners were digging, and their implements made a dull, thumping noise in the soft earth. She crossed the porch, and walked down the steps to the courtyard. The paving slabs which had been replaced in the courtyard were squares of lighter color against the weathered and aged patina of the other blocks of sandstone. The house was surrounded by gardens, and the tall stone wall at the far edge of the garden was barely visible through the tall trees. The wall at the front, along the avenue, was further away and was hidden by foliage, as was the one on the far edge of the garden on the left. A wide paved path led from the left side of the courtyard to the drive which ran along the wall from the carriage gate in front to the stables behind the house, and a path from the center of the courtyard led to the foot gate in the center of the front wall.

Natalya crossed the courtyard to the path leading to the foot gate. Halfway between the courtyard and the front gate, the path branched around a clump of trees with a large fountain and a couple of tall pieces of marble statuary among them, concealing the front of the house from the foot gate. Tall weeds had grown up among the trees, fountain, and statuary while the house had been unoccupied, but it would be attractive when it had been put in order. The gardeners were digging up the thick weeds which had grown up among some of the shrubbery. They greeted her respectfully and continued digging. She started to reply, then she stiffened and her smile changed to a suspicious frown. There were three of them, instead of four. And it was more usual for serfs to acknowledge her presence with a nod than a verbal greeting. Their voices had been louder than necessary, and they were looking at her from the corners of their eyes as they dug busily with their hoes. There was only one explanation. One of their number was hiding somewhere in the weeds, possibly sleeping, and they were apprehensive that her ire would fall on all of them.

All thoughts of the coming evening and of meeting Aleksei Andreyevich abruptly faded from her mind. She moved from side to side on the walk, craning her neck to look into the foliage and gathering her skirts to kneel and peer under the shrubs, then she hurried back along the walk, holding her skirts up with both hands as she searched. She paused where the walk joined the courtyard, looking closer into the foliage on the right. There was a spot of darker color which clashed with the green and brown of the shrubbery and weeds around it. She peered closer. It was the toe of a boot.

She circled around the clump of shrubbery along the edge of the courtyard on her tiptoes. The gardener was lying on his back, snoring softly. She drew in a deep breath and shouted at the top of her voice.

"Lukan!"

A snore changed into a startled snort, and the man's legs and arms thrashed against the ground as he flailed about, leaping hurriedly to his feet. Natalya snarled wordlessly, pushing into the shrubbery and reaching for him. The thickly entwined branches held her back, and she threw herself against them and leaped into the shrubbery, seizing his collar. He squeaked with fright, his eyes bleary and his face puffy with sleep, and she jerked at his collar and struggled to get back out of the shrubbery. A twig snagged the right side of her hair and loosened it and other twigs pulled at her gown, but it barely registered on her consciousness as she threw her weight against him and pulled him out of the shrubbery.

"Lout! Lazy dog! Worthless dirt! Is it your duty to lie here sleeping while others work? Explain yourself!"

"I was very weary, mistress," he mumbled, frightened and confused by being caught. "I have been working very hard, and I—"

"Working hard?" she stormed, pulling harder on his collar and bending him over to thrust her face into his as she shook her fist at him. "Is it work for you to sleep? Perhaps you would be less inclined to sprawl on your back and sleep while others work if you had less skin on your back! Perhaps a taste of the knout would make you a better worker!"

"No, please, mistress, I was only—"

"Silence!" she shouted at the top of her voice, seizing his collar with both hands and pulling his face closer as he tried to edge away from her. "Is this how you repay your master for his care? Would you have your freedom from this estate? We could well do without such a lazy dog as you! Is that what you would have? Merely tell me it is, and you shall be out of the gate before nightfall!"

His eyes refused to meet hers, and he shook his head rapidly, his features trembling. "No, mistress, no . . ."

"Would you go to the village, then?" she demanded. "Would you have an allotment at Sherevskoye? The village headman has less patience with louts than I have, and he would soon put the knout to you! And if you spent the summer snoring, you would spend the winter listening to your belly rumble! But if you would go to Sherevskoye, tell me so and you shall leave for there tonight!"

He glanced at a point behind her as he continued shaking his head. "No, mistress, I would not go . . . no, please . . ."

Natalya released him and stepped back, glaring up at him as she pushed at her hair and straightened her gown. "Then devote yourself to your duties, or you shall regret it, Lukan," she barked, and moved closer to him again, shaking her fist under his nose and raising her voice to a shout. "Do you understand me, lout?"

"Yes, mistress, yes . . ."

"Then be at your duties!"

"Yes, mistress, yes . . ."

He bowed, backing away from her, glancing beyond her once more, and he bowed again as he backed onto the path. He wheeled and ran along the path toward the other gardeners. Natalya glared after him, rearranging her hair and adjusting her gown, and the meaning of Lukan's second bow and his continued glances behind her suddenly dawned on her. At the same time, she heard low, masculine laughter behind her. She wheeled around.

Her brother Vassily and another man were standing in the center of the courtyard, looking at her with wide smiles of amusement, tall and dazzling in their uniforms. The peaks of their kepis were tilted down over their eyes, which sparkled with laughter.

A warm, golden glow suffused Natalya as she looked into Aleksei's eyes. They were a rich, shimmering blue. Those who had described him as handsome had suffered from a deficiency of vocabulary. He had the features of a Greek god, sharply etched to the point of

169

almost being delicate but still very masculine, and his crisp, thick hair was yellow, in sharp contrast to his smooth, tanned face. His mustache was the same color or a shade darker, luxuriantly thick but neatly trimmed and fashioned into a dashing curve on both sides.

Then the glow pulsing within her suddenly changed to an agony of embarrassment. Her hair was coming loose again, and she was disheveled. They had been watching while she stormed angrily at Lukan. Her brother Vassily chuckled again. "If we have need of an extra corporal, Aleksei Andreyevich, all we need do is get a uniform for Natalya Ivanova."

CHAPTER IX

Natalya and her brother were very close and constantly joked with each other, but under the circumstances it stung. She struggled to compose her features as she walked toward them, pushing the comb on the right side of her hair with the tips of her fingers and giving the waist of her gown a final tug. "*Mon Dieu,* Vasasha," she murmured, trying to make her tone light. "You have need of corporals? And you gave me to understand that there was no need for even colonels and generals with *you* there."

Vassily laughed and nodded, turning to Aleksei. "Aleksei Andreyevich, permit me to introduce my sister, Natalya Ivanova. Natasha, this is Aleksei, son of Andrey, the family Orlov."

"*Enchanté, mademoiselle,*" Aleksei smiled, bowing deeply over her hand and brushing it with his lips. "And if we could but have such a corporal among us, we would be so deluged with officers and recruits that we would outnumber the Streltsy."

The blue eyes bored into hers with an expression of extreme interest. His French was perfect, without a trace of Russian accent, and he had the bearing and demeanor, of one who unconsciously takes command of any situation. She steeled herself to keep a pleasant, nonchalant smile on her face as she curtseyed. *"Vous êtes très gentil,* Aleksei Andreyevich. Shall we go in? I have raved at the gardeners sufficiently for the moment, I believe."

"And made me envious. I had thought I would never suffer anyone to take me by the collar, but suddenly I have changed my mind."

It was the usual smooth patter, but somehow his intonation made it sound sincere, as though he really meant it. She wanted to drop a step behind them so she could fix her hair and straighten her gown some more, but Aleksei took her hand and tucked it through his arm as he turned toward the steps, smiling down at her. She kept a faint, polite smile on her face as she gathered up her skirt to lift it away from her toes and walk up the steps. Vassily walked on the other side of Aleksei, making a comment about the house, and Aleksei glanced at it and nodded, murmuring a complimentary remark and dropping his eyes toward hers with a smile which seemed to give her credit for any commendable characteristics the house might have. A flush suffused her throat and cheeks, and it felt as though her loosened hair was getting more disheveled with each step they took. Vassily stepped across the porch to the door and opened it, stepped back to let them go in ahead of him as he held it, grinned comically at Natalya behind Aleksei's back. She bit her lower lip to stifle an impulse to giggle.

As they entered, Aleksei looked around the entry hall with admiration. "This is indeed a magnificent house, Natalya Ivanova."

"It is satisfactory," she replied, signaling the house steward as she spoke. Her palm turned toward him stopped him, a single finger pointing toward the dining room told him to summon a footman, and the finger turning toward the arched doorway on the right at the

172

rear of the entry hall told him to fetch her father. "But we have only just moved in, and I beg you to forgive the grossly untidy state in which you find us."

"Untidy state?" he echoed. "I would our barracks were as 'untidy.' What do you say, Vassily Ivanovich?"

"Indeed," Vassily agreed, then laughed. "But then, we do not have such a stern corporal looking after our barracks."

Aleksei's quiet laugh had a reproachful note, but the reference to her berating the gardener didn't bite as it had before and Natalya laughed, motioning toward the front drawing room. Vassily and Aleksei took off their kepis and tucked them under their arms, and Natalya led the way across the entry hall toward the arched doorway of the drawing room. The officers' boots thudded solidly on the parquet floor with a sturdy, masculine sound. Out of the corner of her eye, she could see one of the footmen crossing the entry hall.

Natalya stopped at the doorway, smiling and motioning the gentlemen in. "*Asseyez-vous*. If you will excuse me for a moment, I will send someone to fetch my father."

Vassily took Aleksei's kepi and put it with his on the table inside the door, and they walked on into the room, unhooking their swords from their belts. Natalya stepped sedately back from the doorway, then turned and rushed toward the footman, frantically tugging at her gown and pushing at her hair.

"Go to my rooms and fetch two of my maids," she whispered. "Then tell the cook to prepare the hors d'oeuvres. Quickly!"

The footman nodded, and hurried off to carry out her commands. Natalya gave her hair a final pat and reentered the drawing room.

Vassily and Aleksei were talking quietly about their

173

regiment, and Vassily smiled up at Natalya absently. Aleksei's eyes followed her from the moment she came into the room, and she could feel him watching her as she moved about. She bit her lower lip to compose herself while her back was turned, and she had an expression of cool insouciance when she faced the young men. She sat down on the end of the sofa, arranging her skirt gracefully about her, and rested her chin lightly on her fingers.

Vassily was saying something to Aleksei, but Aleksei was watching Natalya. He spoke, interrupting Vassily. "Do you find St. Petersburg as pleasant as Moscow, Natalya Ivanova?"

Vassily sat back on the couch, glancing between them and giving Natalya a broad wink. Natalya glanced away from him and shrugged slightly as she gestured vaguely with one hand. "I have scarcely seen enough of St. Petersburg to make a fair comparison, Aleksei Andreyevich, but of all places I have been, I prefer our village of Sherevskoye most."

"Your village?" Aleksei chuckled. "Surely you don't have theaters in your village? And the parties in Moscow must be more dull than I remember if those in a village are as exciting."

His smile was still warm, and the comments were humorous sallies to draw her out, with absolutely no hint of derision or condescension. But he was who he was. He was an Orlov, a name which automatically made him a fixture of fashionable salons. There was a hint of world weariness about him which suggested countless *rendezvous* with women of easy virtue and of nights in the naked arms of beautiful *tzigane* singers. Mothers would scramble to place their daughters where he would notice them, and when the daughters received him they would be reclining lazily on a chaise longue, freshly powdered and perfumed and nonchalantly munching a sweetmeat, not disheveled and with their hair coming down as they collared a gardener and bellowed in his face. Natalya kept her polite smile in place as resentment swelled within her, and she shrugged again and put the tips of her fingers over her lips as though holding back a yawn. "I enjoy the theater and parties, but surely there is more to life. I also enjoy the country. We have gypsies who come to our village each year to camp, and I find them interesting people. And the countryside is more suitable for horseback riding, which I enjoy."

"You are a horsewoman?"

"Natasha is something more than a horsewoman," Vassily said. "She has two saddle horses, neither of which I can ride, but she can control both of them. She would put the best of cavalrymen to shame."

Aleksei's smile indicated he thought his comrade's comments were at least partially exaggerated, but it faded slightly as he looked at Vassily and Vassily nodded firmly to emphasize what he had said. Aleksei lifted his eyebrows, looking back at Natalya. "That is remarkable, Natalya Ivanova."

"The gypsies at the village taught me to ride. They call me Petulengra, which means 'mistress of horses' in their language."

"That is indeed a great compliment, because they are reputed to be very skilled with horses."

"And at other things," Vassily added. "Thievery, for example."

Natalya looked at Vassily, her smile fading and her expression becoming cool. "The Gypsies have never stolen from us or from the villagers at Sherevskoye, Vassily Ivanovich, and thievery takes many forms. I was reprimanding the gardener Lukan for stealing from our father by sleeping when he should have been working, thereby stealing wages. And who among us does

175

not at times steal from His Majesty the Czar by devoting something less than our best efforts toward the Czar's causes? And who does not at times steal from God by devoting less than total commitment to His laws in the Holy Bible?" It was only the beginning of what she wanted to say, but her tongue could easily run away with her and it would be disastrous to scold Vassily in Aleksei's presence. She put the serene smile back on her face.

Vassily smiled ruefully, glancing at Aleksei. "Natasha also has a mind of her own, and she suffers little difficulty in expressing her thoughts."

Aleksei nodded thoughtfully, looking at her. His eyes were penetrating, shining with interest again. "But hardly to be counted as a fault, surely," he murmured. "It is refreshing to meet a person with convictions and loyalties, as well as the ability to express them so aptly."

"You might change your mind if you felt the sharp edge of her tongue," Vassily laughed.

Aleksei's smile widened. "No fear. As I said, I had thought I would never suffer anyone to take me by the collar, either. Natalya Ivanova, perhaps you would favor me with a demonstration of your ability with horses in exchange for my acquainting you further with St. Petersburg. May I ask your father for permission to take you riding?"

It took a moment for the invitation to register, because her mind was occupied by other things, principally the whereabouts of her father, who should have joined them by now.

Then Aleksei's words registered. Aleksei Andreyevich Orlov was making overtures to call on her. He was looking at her with a polite smile which made his eyes crinkle slightly at the corners and showed a gleam of his brilliantly white teeth between his lips, waiting for her reply. She struggled to keep the flush from rising to her cheeks, her mind reeling with confusion. He suddenly appeared even more handsome, and the glow swelled within her again, growing until it enveloped her. Ordinarily there were many meetings on neutral ground and an elaborate ritual of move and countermove before such an overture, and he was rushing into it as though he were afraid she would be captured by someone else. It was extremely flattering, and almost unbelievable, considering who he was. Her first reaction was to say "yes," but it wasn't that simple. Vassily was looking at him with a puzzled expression, indicating that he was also thinking about the most obvious drawback. The two men had been addressing each other as "thou," indicating a close acquaintance, but it appeared that Aleksei didn't have a full awareness of the family situation.

"I am honored, Aleksei Andreyevich," Natalya said, "but I believe it would be appropriate to consider this another time. You see, my father has just been granted permission to attend court after a period of—"

"I am aware of that and of the full circumstances involved, Natalya Ivanova, and it has no bearing on my request. Do I have your consent to ask your father for permission to take you riding?"

Her confusion multiplied, her hands felt damp, she was breathless, and she felt her cheeks beginning to burn despite her efforts to control her emotions. His large, warm eyes seemed to be devouring her. He was clearly stating that he was more interested in calling on her than he was in what the czar might think of his undertaking a social relationship with the Sheremetev family before they were formally admitted to court. Much of St. Petersburg society would wink at it, regarding any relationship between this particular young man and a young woman as outside ordinary

177

considerations, but Czar Aleksander was known to be a stickler for formalities. And so was the Orlov family. Natalya looked away, clearing her throat with a soft sound. "If you wish, Aleksei Andreyevich."

Aleksei's smile became brilliant. "I am very grateful, Natalya Ivanova," he said, quietly emphatic.

"What do we have here?" Vassily laughed. "I did tell you that Natasha was very attractive, Aleksei Andreyevich."

"Your powers of description do you little credit," Aleksei replied, his eyes still on Natalya. "To say that Natalya Ivanova is merely attractive is a veritable insult."

It was banter, with an undertone of seriousness which amounted to a grandiose compliment, and she felt her flush deepening. She felt almost giddy. Things had moved very rapidly for a moment, crowding events which might have taken weeks into seconds. Her attractiveness was a fact of life, and men had been eager enough to crowd about her, compliment her, and ask for permission to call on her, but Aleksei was something apart from other men, both in appearance and bearing and because of his family. What had happened was far more than she had imagined in her wildest flights of fancy.

She heard the tap of her father's cane on the floor outside the door, then remembered to worry about the arrival of the hors d'oeuvres. Her relationship with her father permitted informality in informal situations, but when anyone but the household staff or her brother happened to be present, she automatically and unthinkingly rendered full courtesies. She rose from the couch and curtsied deeply as he came into the room. Vassily and Aleksei rose from the couch, faced her father, and bowed. He limped slowly into the room, reached for Natalya's hand and raised her as he lifted her hand

and kissed it, smiled down at her and patted her cheek with an affectionate caress, then turned to Vassily and Aleksei, returning their bow.

"Vasasha. *Comment allez-vous?*"

"I am well, your honor," Vassily replied, stepping forward to embrace his father. *"Et vous?"*

"I am well."

"You appear well indeed, your honor. *Permettez-moi de vous présenter à* Aleksei, son of Andrey, the family Orlov. Aleksei Andreyevich, allow me to present his honor my father, Ivan Nikolayevich, the Count Sheremetev."

They exchanged felicitations, and the count motioned toward the couch where they had been sitting as he moved toward a chair. "Please make yourselves comfortable. Do we have refreshments, Natalya?"

"Yes, I will fetch them, father."

The count lowered himself into the chair and asked Aleksei about his father's health as Natalya turned and walked toward the door. Aleksei's voice sounded somewhat absent-minded as he replied, and Natalya felt his eyes on her as she walked toward the doorway. She moderated her stride and walked with short, restrained steps, until she was out of their sight. Then she leaned against the wall, drawing in a deep, shuddering breath and clasping her burning cheeks with cold hands.

The house steward and the footmen were standing with the hors d'oeuvres in the doorway of the dining room. They looked at her, blinking, and the house steward moved toward her with a concerned expression as she leaned weakly against the wall. She shook her head and waved him away as she pushed herself away from the wall, and she rushed into the second drawing room. The two maids were waiting just inside the doorway, and Natalya hissed instructions, in-

179

dicating her hair and her gown. One of the maids began jerking the combs out and putting them between her teeth as she unrolled the long, heavy twists of hair, and the other bent over and began adjusting the bodice and waist of Natalya's gown, straightening it and pulling it into a tight, neat fit. Natalya closed her eyes and relaxed, trying to regain her composure as she swayed from side to side from the tugs on her gown.

The maids seemed acutely aware of the situation, and they worked rapidly, their expressions tense and their movements quick and sure. The maid straightening her gown finished, and she turned to a small table where they had put some things they had brought with them. She dampened a fresh handkerchief with toilet water and daubed Natalya's temples and cheeks with it. The other maid wrapped twists of hair around her hand and pinned them up deftly with the combs. Natalya kept her eyes closed, restraining an impulse to snap at them to hurry. The powerful, penetrating odor of smelling salts suddenly exploded in her head, and her eyes flew open as she started to turn her head away. The maid who had straightened her gown was holding the bottle under her nose, and the other maid seized her chin and the back of her neck, keeping her from turning away. She involuntarily inhaled again, and the room seemed to swim around her. The maid released her head and took her arms to steady her as the other maid pushed the cork back into the bottle and began quietly gathering up the things from the table. Natalya wheezed and gasped, catching her breath, and the floor steadied under her again. She nodded and pulled away from the maid, blinking the tears from her eyes and drawing in deep breaths. The maid looked at her hair again and touched one of the ringlets hanging in front of her ears into place, then turned and followed the other maid out of the room.

The house steward was waiting in the entry hall, with the two footmen behind him. One of the footmen was holding a silver tub of iced bottles, the other one was holding a tray of hors-d' oeuvres, and the house steward was holding a small salver on which the plates, utensils, and serviettes were stacked. Natalya drew in a deep breath and straightened her shoulders, and she assumed an expression of pleasant nonchalance as she walked toward the doorway of the front drawing room. The house steward and footmen followed her into the room.

Vassily was relating some humorous incident which had occurred at the garrison, and her father was laughing and commenting about it. She saw Aleksei follow her with his eyes as she walked back into the room, and supervised while the house steward and footmen put the things on the credenza. The large tray held plates and bowls of pressed caviar, fresh caviar, fresh cucumbers, cucumbers in brine and vinegar, herring fillets, smoked sturgeon, sliced suckling pig in horse-radish, patés of meat, cabbage, fish, and eggs mixed with liver, and cold salmon. There was a bowl of lemon wedges and sectioned oranges, slices of white bread with raisins, and white bread without raisins, which her father had gradually grown to prefer during recent years. It had taken some subtle questioning and deduction on her part to determine that his preference for plain bread was a result of his diminished eyesight and a suspicion of dark spots in his food which resulted from a difficulty in keeping mice out of foodstuffs in the household when he was a child. Natalya nodded to the house steward, who nodded to the footmen and they took up their positions by the door.

The conversation between the three men continued as Natalya fixed a plate for her father, picking out the things she knew he liked best, and she could see Aleksei still giving her frequent glances as she turned toward the silver tub and sorted through the bottles in it. Her father preferred *pertsovka,* the fiery peppered vodka, and she took it out of the tub. Her hands were trembling and weak, and the bottle almost slipped from her grasp. The house steward moved silently to her side, loosened the cork, and returned to his place. She filled a heavy crystal goblet with the vodka, put a spoon and small, two-tined fork on the side of the plate, and brought them to the count.

Her father smiled up at her as she put the plate and goblet on the small table by his chair. She turned back toward the credenza, glancing at Aleksei. "What sort of vodka do you prefer, Aleksei Andreyevich?"

"I will have the same as you, Natalya Ivanova."

Natalya shook her head and laughed lightly. "Then you would have kvass, because I am not overly fond of grain spirits. We have *pertsovka, zubrovka,* and white."

"I will have white, please."

She nodded, walking back to the credenza. His tone and expression had attracted her father's notice. He had been lifting his goblet to take a sip of his vodka, and he paused with the goblet halfway to his lips, looking at Aleksei with a suspicious expression. Aleksei returned his regard, and he sipped his vodka and put the goblet down, asking Vassily about a colonel in his regiment who was an acquaintance, and the conversation began again. Natalya prepared another plate with a selection of delicacies and filled a goblet with white vodka. Aleksei smiled up at her as he took the plate and goblet. His fingers touched hers, and she almost jumped. There was a masculine, wholesome scent about him. His skin was smooth and bronzed by the sun, lighter in the hollows of his eyes, cheeks, and temples, and there was a small scar in the edge of his

182

left eyebrow. The barber had made a tiny nick on the point of his left jaw when shaving him. He seemed an even larger man at close proximity, perhaps somewhat taller than her brother. She struggled to keep the polite smile on her face as her hands trembled and her heart pounded. Her father had stopped talking and was looking at them, and he began talking to Vassily again as she returned to the credenza.

Vassily preferred the savory *zubrovka,* and he had a special fondness for suckling pig in horseradish. She filled his plate and took him the plate and goblet. Natalya fixed a plate for herself and poured a goblet of kvass from the bottle in the tub, and returned to the couch where she had sat before.

Aleksei smiled at her warmly as she sat down, and she returned his smile, putting her goblet on the table at the end of the couch and settling herself comfortably. Her father was talking to Vassily, and he hesitated, glanced at Aleksei, then Natalya, and looked back at Vassily and began talking again. Aleksei took a bite from his plate and looked at the count as he chewed slowly. Natalya looked down at her plate and took a nibble of caviar. She preferred the herring fillets over anything she had on her plate, but it was impossible to eat them gracefully. And her appetite had deserted her.

The footmen returned with the bowls, put them on the salver, and took their positions on each side of the doorway again. The house steward moved quietly back and forth, refilling the goblets of vodka and replenishing the delicacies on the plates as the men ate and drank. Natalya kept an expression of polite interest on her face and looked at her father, ignoring the conversation, and she occasionally darted a glance at Aleksei when he wasn't looking at her.

The topic of conversation finally registered. They

were discussing the Greek uprising and subsequent events, her father doing most of the talking, and he was taking his usual insular view of the matter. It was a subject she had discussed with him at length, and they had irreconcilably different interpretations of almost all the facts. She knew that Vassily had little interest in the subject and no particular viewpoint, and Aleksei either had a similar lack of interest or didn't care to dispute with her father. Her expression of polite interest gradually faded, and she moved uncomfortably on the couch.

Her father's eyes were suddenly on her, and he smiled as he forked a slice of cucumber into his mouth and chewed it. "But Natasha has a different view, do you not, Natasha? She sees a grand conspiracy involving half of the civilized world."

Vassily grinned widely as he chewed, accustomed to heated arguments between Natalya and their father. Aleksei looked at her, and his direct gaze made it difficult to concentrate. Natalya smiled lightly and shrugged. "Not that, your honor, but I do see Ypsilanti as more than an adventurer. He was clearly a member of the *Philike Hetaireia*, which has the objective of liberating Greece from Turkish rule. And would you not allow the possibility of a degree of Russian involvement? Ypsilanti was an officer in the Russian Army."

"Russian involvement when His Majesty denounced the revolt?"

"His Majesty the Czar denounced the aims of the revolt, your honor. In his position, he could hardly support an uprising against an established government, could he? But if the revolt had become widespread, he might have sent the Army into the Ottoman Empire to restore order. That would have settled the current and any future disputes between Russian and the Turks, would it not?"

Aleksei was looking at her with a surprised, pleased expression, and he laughed and nodded, looking from her to the count. "Indeed it would have."

The count smiled and shook his head. "It would have been an invasion, and we would have found ourselves at odds with all the European powers, particularly the British."

"Possibly, but possibly not, your honor," Natalya replied firmly. "His Majesty the Czar has made his views on such matters well known. At Aachen he proposed a league of sovereigns to guarantee the political systems of the Quadruple Alliance, did he not? And he offered to send the Army to crush the revolts in Naples and Spain, did he not? It would be consistent with what His Majesty the Czar has said and done before, and it could scarcely come as a surprise to any of the powers that he would wish to settle unrest on our southern frontier."

Her father shrugged, taking a bite of caviar and lifting the edge of his serviette to wipe his mouth as he put his plate down and reached for his goblet. "You have been reading Prince von Metternich too much, Natasha, and you see plots within plots when many things happen of their own accord. However that may be, if we had invaded the Ottoman Empire, we would have been facing the British arrayed by the Turks."

"That is possible, because the British have no desire to see the Czar's warships coming through the Dardanelles. But the British are also realists. They have no desire to war with us, and they respect a firm stand. During the revolt of the British colonies in the Americas, Catherine II promulgated a Declaration of Armed Neutrality when the Briitsh protested our trade with their American colonies, did she not?"

185

"And it was not accepted or recognized by the British, was it?" the count chuckled.

"Small wonder," Natalya laughed. "But trade still continued between Russia and Britain even while we traded with the American colonies. As I said, the British are realists."

The count sipped his vodka, smiling at her, then looked at Aleksei. "You see the result of combining a man's education with a woman's tongue. Each way I turn, she has a reply. Not necessarily a correct reply, but one which is nonetheless based on factual information, of which she has an abundance."

Vassily laughed and Aleksei smiled politely, and Natalya and her father exchanged a glance. His tone was playful and fond, and she was pleased that the exchange hadn't become heated, which frequently happened, and which the count enjoyed. He asked Aleksei about his father's summer estate, and they began discussing it. It was well past sunset and the light in the room was becoming dim. Natalya glanced at the house steward and indicated the chandeliers. The house steward beckoned the footmen to him, spoke to them in a murmur, and they left. They returned a moment later, carrying two heavy candelabra filled with tapers. They quietly lowered the chandeliers, lit the tapers and pulled them back up, and the house steward closed the drapes.

The soft, yellow light of the tapers filled the room, and the facets of the crystals in the chandeliers sparkled. The room was even more attractive in the subdued lighting, the corners fading into dim twilight, the wallpaper, drapes, and furniture becoming more harmonious. Even the atmosphere in the candlelight was different, more warm and intimate. Her father and brother were relaxed from the vodka, and they were laughing and boisterously telling Aleksei about the foibles of some doltish acquaintance in Moscow. Aleksei seemed the same as before, having sipped his vodka sparingly. His eyes were still restless, looking at her father and brother as he listened, nodded, and laughed, and frequently moving toward her. The house steward glanced at her plate and glass, lifting his eyebrows, and she shook her head. The bit she had eaten was burning in her stomach, and she felt strangely hungry but utterly without appetite.

The count drained his goblet and put it down, announcing he was ready for dinner. He picked up his cane and rose, and Vassily and Aleksei stood up as well, straightening their jackets. Natalya put her plate and serviette on the table at the end of the couch and rose, and she smoothed her skirt into place as she moved toward her father. He offered his arm and she put her hand on it, and they walked toward the doorway.

Having her father and brother together and listening to them talk and laugh with cheerful ebullience in the relaxed glow of vodka had always been a pleasure to Natalya, and it was intensified by Aleksei's presence. Vassily and Aleksei walked on the other side of her father as they slowly crossed the entry hall toward the dining room, and Aleksei mentioned something about the Napoleonic War, one of her father's favorite subjects. Natalya listened absently, glancing around and feeling a warm satisfaction. The house looked serenely and quietly luxurious. The parquet floor gleamed in the light of the tapers in the girondoles along the walls and in the chandeliers hanging from the high ceiling, and the room appeared even more spacious in the soft candlelight. In the magic of the evening, the house was beginning to lose some of its feeling of detached and impersonal remoteness, becoming more of a home.

Two footmen stood stiffly against the wall at the opposite end of the dining room, and the flickering light of the tapers played on the snowy expanse of the lace tablecloth and the gleaming surface of the sideboard. By long-established custom, her father seated her on his right even when Vassily was at the table, which was a matter of total unconcern to Vassily but which had occasioned surprised glances from visitors. Aleksei either saw nothing unusual about it or completely concealed his reaction as he and Vassily took their places on the other side of the table, and there was a quiet shuffle of chairs as they sat down and the house steward seated the count and took his cane. The other two footmen came in with the tureen of borsch and platter of rusk bread, and from the way they were moving around, Natalya could see that the new footman was positioned to serve Vassily. She caught the house steward's eye and signalled him to have the new footman serve her instead.

The conversation was still about the Napoleonic War, and Aleksei brought Natalya into it, asking how she had fared with both her father and brother with their regiments. She told him about the flight from Moscow to Cherevskoye, and of the fortuitous meeting with the Gypsies who had conducted her there. The conversation turned to the Gypsies and their annual encampment at Sherevskoye, and the count talked about them and what they had done for the village. Initially, they had provided entertainment and needed services for the villagers, but over the years the encampment had become such an accepted practice that a small fair had started at the village, drawing tradesmen and others from far up and down the river and providing an economic benefit for both the Gypsies and the villagers. As the count talked, Vassily occasionally glanced at Natalya with a sly smile or a wink. He

188

liked to tease her with disparaging remarks about the Gypsies, but years before he had learned to contain such comments in the presence of his father, because the count's reaction was inclined to be even more severe and heated than Natalya's.

The footmen filled the wine glasses. The wine was a tart, full-bodied Crimean to go with the spicy, vinegary borsch, somewhat too strong for Natalya, and she sipped it sparingly as she ate. The conversation turned to the burning of Moscow and to the endlessly-debated subject of whether or not Count Rostopchin had set fire to the city when it became clear that it was lost to the French. The rumor had given Count Rostopchin something of a hero's reputation internationally, the imagination of some being captured by the drama of one who would burn his city to the ground rather than see it taken by the enemy, but the reaction of those whose houses had been burned in Moscow had been understandably different. Count Rostopchin's comments, apparently gauged to maintain his heroism abroad while assuaging the anger in Moscow, had done little to clarify what had happened.

The soup bowls were taken away, and the footmen served the second course, a *kulibyaki* of rice, fish, and vegetables with brioches, and a white Rhenish wine. Aleksei glanced around the long table with its empty chairs and asked Natalya if she had a companion or governess. She told him about the German woman, who had remained behind in Moscow. The count commented that he intended to hire a companion for Natalya, as he had mentioned to her two or three times since they had arrived in St. Petersburg. The point was made was that she had no friends in the city, and it seemed to her an optimum opening for Aleksei to ask her father if he could call and take her riding. Her heart thudded heavily and the wine in her glass trem-

189

bled as she took a sip of it and put it down, waiting to hear the question and her father's reaction, but the conversation continued. She wiped her suddenly hot and damp hands on her serviette, her heart sinking.

The main course was cutlets *á la Russe* with truffles *á la Perigueux,* highly seasoned potatoes, and a mixture of vegetables, with a red Bordeaux. The conversation turned to the Napoleonic War again, becoming less animated as the effects of the vodka and wine became more pronounced. They finished the main course, and the footmen took the dinner plates away and served dessert, pineapple jelly whipped in champagne and topped with fruit macedoine, with a sweet Hungarian dessert wine. The three men began talking about the military operations in the Caucasus under General Yermolov. Aleksei had a friend who was an aide to General Velyaminov, General Yermolov's chief of staff, and the count and Vassily listened sleepily as Aleksei talked about what his friend had written to him about the expeditions.

One of the footmen brought in a small, brass samovar and put it on the end of the sideboard, and the house steward pulled Natalya's chair back as she rose from the table. The house steward took thick glass goblets and heavy silver holders from the back of the sideboard, fitting them together and handing them to Natalya, and she poured concentrated coffee into them from the small pot on top of the samovar, filled them with hot water from the other tap, and stirred spoonfuls of sugar into them. She opened a bottle of framboise and filled four tiny glasses with it, then carried the coffee and liqueur around the table, serving the men. Vassily and her father nodded drowsily in thanks, listening to Aleksei talking about what his friend had written from the Caucasus, and Aleksei looked up at

190

her and smiled as she put his coffee and liqueur in front of him.

He and Vassily had opened the catches and laces on their jackets and were relaxed in their chairs, and her father had opened his coat. She noted that her father's shirt looked wrinkled and made a mental note to speak with his valet about it as she walked back to the sideboard. The house steward opened a drawer in the sideboard and took out a box containing long, dark cigarettes with cardboard mouthpieces, and she lit three of them from a taper on the sideboard and carried them around the table. There was a light, thin scar on the brown, smooth skin at the side of Aleksei's neck which was visible with his collar open, and she had an impulsive urge to touch it. He looked up at her and smiled again as he took the cigarette from her, thanking her quietly, and it seemed that his large, blue eyes were looking so deeply into hers that he knew what she was thinking. A confused flush rose to her face. His fingers touched hers as he took the cigarette, and she almost dropped it.

She had been ten or twelve before she had found out by going to parties that women drank their tea and coffee from cups in polite society, the glasses and metal holders being restricted to men, but she had already formed a habit of drinking hers from a glass by emulating her father, who had a nonchalant disregard for many social niceties and didn't care how she drank her tea and coffee. Similarly, she had been approaching her teens when she found that it was considered risqué for women to smoke cigarettes; she had been smoking an after-dinner cigarette with her father from the age of seven or eight. She had continued her usual practices at home, the after-dinner cigarette somehow cementing a bond of companionship with her father.

With Aleksei there, she had meant to conduct herself in a more conventional manner, at least to begin
with, so he wouldn't get an initial impression of eccen-
tricity, but the house steward had assembled a glass
and holder for her, and she hadn't thought to have
cups available in the room. The footmen had already
taken away the dessert dishes and put small bowls at
each place for cigarette ashes, including one at her
place. She mentally shrugged, fixed her coffee and lit
herself a cigarette, and sat back down with her coffee
and liqueur, the long cigarette held between her thumb
and the tips of her fingers in her left hand, as she
had copied from her father. Aleksei's eyes seemed to
hesitate on the cigarette and glass, but his expression
didn't change.

The footmen put nuts, cheese, and fruit on the table, then resumed their stations against the walls, and
the house steward stood motionlessly beside the sideboard. The conversation was still about the Caucasus.
The hour was late, and presently it would be time for
Vassily and Aleksei to return to their garrison. The
time was very near when Aleksei must ask her father
if he could call on her and take her riding. Her heart
began thumping so heavily that it seemed it must be
audible all over the room. But perhaps he had decided to defer asking until a second visit. The thought
brought a dark cloud of potential disappointment and
a sinking feeling in the pit of her stomach. She pushed
it aside, concentrating on the conversation.

There had been numerous accounts of General Yermolov's achievements in the news sheets, about his
annexation of Shirvan and Karabagh, and the defeats
he had inflicted on the warlike Avars and Chechens.
But his reprisals against attacks on his outposts had
been savage, whole villages put to the torch and their
populations made homeless, and it seemed to her that

a debt of retribution was being accumulated which would eventually be collected if war broke out elsewhere and the strength of the Army in the Caucasus was drawn down to fight in other areas. In discussing it with her father, he had more or less agreed with her general viewpoint, but from Aleksei's comments, the line of thought either hadn't occurred to him or he had a different attitude toward it. It would be an interesting subject to explore with him at length, because he clearly wasn't one of the many men who considered it strange for a woman to venture an observation on something more consequential than fashionable gossip. What Aleksei was saying suddenly registered, and her heart leaped.

". . . be so kind as to grant me permission to take Natalya Ivanova riding, your honor?"

The count's expression of drowsy satisfaction and well-being abruptly evaporated, and his eyes narrowed as he looked at Aleksei with an alert wariness. He glanced at Natalya, looked back at Aleksei, and shook his head. "*Je crois que non.* My family and I will be received by His Majesty the Czar in a few days, and I will speak with you about this again, if you wish."

Natalya's heart sank. Vassily looked at her with a sympathetic expression, and Aleksei glanced at her then looked back at her father. Natalya fought to keep her expression neutral as she looked down at the small bowl in front of her, tapping her cigarette against the edge of it to knock the ashes off the top. Aleksei spoke again.

"I beg you to reconsider, your honor. I am sure the Czar would not be offended by such a simple matter as my showing Natalya Ivanova something of St. Petersburg, and she has no friends here to entertain her. Nor even a governess or companion, as we were discussing."

Her father made an aggravated sound in his throat as though he were going to reply negatively again, then hesitated. The silence dragged out, and Natalya could feel his eyes on her. She summoned her will power and put an expression of total unconcern on her face, and she slowly lifted her eyes to his as she put her cigarette in the corner of her mouth and took a puff. He was looking at her with his lips pursed thoughtfully. She lifted her chin and blew the smoke up at the ceiling. Her father looked back at Aleksei and shrugged his shoulders.

"*D'accord*. But I hardly think your father the Count Orlov will thank me for it."

Aleksei sat back in his chair, smiling widely. "My father will understand completely when he meets Natalya Ivanova, your honor, of that I assure you. And I am grateful for your permission."

Vassily was grinning broadly, looking from Natalya to Aleksei, and he nodded and moved his chair back. "Now that is settled, perhaps we can return to the garrison. I am tired, and I have early parade tomorrow."

The count laughed, pushing his chair back, and the house steward brought his cane and pulled his chair back as he stood. Natalya rose from her chair, struggling to moderate her smile as she put her cigarette out, and Vassily and Aleksei fastened their jackets. They took their leave of the count, Vassily embracing him and Aleksei thanking him for his hospitality, and Natalya moved away from the table and walked toward the doorway. The count sat back down, looking at the house steward and motioning toward his coffee glass, and Vassily and Aleksei followed Natalya through the doorway.

Vassily yawned widely and scratched his head as they crossed the entry hall toward the drawing room, and Aleksei smiled down at Natalya. Natalya glanced up at him, her eyes dancing as she smiled brilliantly, and she looked away and bit her lip to control her smile as her heart pounded furiously. The men went into the drawing room for their swords and kepis, and fastened their swords to their belts as they walked toward the front doors. Vassily opened the door and held it, then followed Natalya and Aleksei out. He closed the door, bent over Natalya and kissed her goodnight, and went down the steps and along the path toward the road to the stables, where they had left their horses.

The lamps at the sides of the doors cast a pool of yellow light, and Natalya walked with Aleksei to the edge of the light at the steps and leaned against one of the colonnades, looking up at him. He tucked his kepi under his arm and released his scabbard, letting the tip of it drag against the step as he took her hand between his. His hands were large and warm, enfolding hers, and his face was in shadow.

"If I was hasty, Natalya Ivanova, it was not because I am a reckless person. It was because it will be difficult for anyone to secure an appointment to call on you after you are introduced to St. Petersburg society."

Natalya shook her head and chuckled lightly. "I daresay you are exaggerating, Aleksei Andreyevich."

His face was unsmiling, and the light of the lamps shone in his blue eyes. He shook his head. "No, I am not exaggerating. You are very beautiful, Natalya Ivanova. More than that, you are . . ." He hesitated, searching for words, then shook his head again. "No, I am not exaggerating, Natalya Ivanova."

His tone was softly and intensely emphatic. Her breath caught in her throat, her heart pounded madly, and she felt a crimson flush rising to her cheeks as she averted her face. He lifted her hand and pressed it to his lips. She wanted to clasp his hand and lift it to her cheek, but she steeled herself and controlled the impulse, letting her hand lie limp and motionless in his as he kissed it.

"May I call for you at two tomorrow?"

She pressed her lips together to stop their trembling and cleared her throat softly, nodding. "If you wish," she murmured, then she suddenly smiled. "But bring a good horse."

He chuckled and nodded, walking down the steps. "I shall. *Au revoir,* Natalya Ivanova."

"*Au revoir,* Aleksei Andreyevich."

A heady excitement churned within her as she crossed the porch to the door, taking sedate, demure steps in case he was looking back at her. She opened the door and went in, closing it behind her. Then she could contain herself no longer. She made a sound of delight, spreading her arms and spinning rapidly across the shining floor until the hem of her skirt and petticoat belled out and lifted from the floor. The room spun around her, the doors and staircase flashing past her vision, and she suddenly saw her father. She froze, clutching her hands to her lips as a giggle bubbled from her throat. He was crossing the rear of the entry hall from the dining room to the hallway to his rooms, and he looked at her and smiled.

"Is he so handsome then, Natasha?"

She laughed gaily, running toward him with her arms outstretched, and threw herself against him, throwing her arms around his neck. "Not nearly as handsome as you, Father."

He lurched backwards as she leaped on him, then regained his balance, laughing and hugging her. "But he is younger, and you might have a care lest you break one of these old bones."

"Old!" she snorted, grinning up at him, and her ex-

196

pression faded to a thoughtful smile. "Thank you for your permission, Father."

He nodded, patting her. "I would rather give permission I should withhold than have a disobedient daughter."

"Disobedient?" she exclaimed. "When have I failed to do as you wish? I am a respectful, obedient daughter to you."

He chuckled tolerantly, bending down and kissing her. "I will agree so I will not force you to lose your respect and debate the subject with me. Good night, Natasha."

She smiled and stood on tiptoe, kissing him. "Good night, Father."

He patted her shoulder, moving away from her and limping toward his rooms, and she walked toward the stairs to go to her rooms. As she started up the stairs, she remembered the incident of the broken vase and Ulyasha. Ulyasha's situation would have to be resolved. She went back down the stairs and crossed the entry hall toward the hallway to the serfs' hall.

The hall was dimly lighted by four lamps with smoky globes in metal holders on the walls, and it was hot and stuffy from the stove, its usual strong odors more penetrating and blended with the smell of food. Many of the serfs were sitting on their stools and chairs, some chatting and others dozing, and a few were still at the long table, eating. Ulyasha and her mother were sitting by themselves in a corner, their expressions forlorn and the bowls from which they had eaten their meal at their feet. The serfs around the table straightened up, looking at Natalya, and the others began stirring. She glanced around at them and nodded, walking toward the table. The end of the bench was empty, and she sat down and rested her elbows on the table.

"Ulyasha?"

Ulyasha looked at her with a terrified expression, opening and closing her mouth without speaking. Her mother reached out and nudged her impatiently, and she tried again, replying in a quavering squeak. "Yes, mistress?"

"Bring tea."

It seemed to take several seconds for the order to register, and Ulyasha continued looking at Natalya with wide eyes. Her mother reached over and nudged her again, and she slowly rose to her feet and walked toward the samovar by the stove, her heavy shoes clumping on the stone floor in the utter quiet of the room. Everyone sat in frozen silence, glancing between Ulyasha and Natalya. Ulyasha took a mug from a shelf, poured tea into it and dropped it. It shattered on the floor, the pieces scattering. Her features twisted, and her shoulders began shaking with sobs. Natalya turned pale and her fingers gripping the edge of the table turned white as she held herself from springing up and racing to Ulyasha. Ulyasha gathered up her apron and wiped her eyes as she turned back to the shelf, and she took down another mug. She poured concentrated tea into it, filled it with hot water from the tap on the side of the samovar, and walked toward the table with the mug in both hands, tea dribbling on the floor as her hands trembled.

She put it on the table and slid it in front of Natalya, her eyes averted from Natalya's and her breath coming in gasps as she held her sobs back. Natalya put her hand on Ulyasha's wrist as she started to move away from the table, and Ulyasha jumped convulsively. She looked down at Natalya, her lips trembling. Natalya tightened her hand on Ulyasha's wrist, pulling her toward the bench.

"Sit."

Ulyasha glanced around with an embarrassed, uncertain expression, still on the verge of tears, and she slowly sat down on the bench by Natalya. She was several inches taller than Natalya and much heavier, and she leaned away and looked down at Natalya from the corners of her eyes as Natalya put her arm around her shoulders, lifting the mug to her lips.

"Drink."

Her expression became one of consternation, and she leaned further away from Natalya. Natalya moved closer, leaning against her and lifting the mug to her lips. Ulyasha took a loud sip and swallowed noisily, and a drop of the tea ran down her lower lip to her chin. Natalya tightened her arm around Ulyasha's shoulders, lowering the mug from Ulyasha's mouth, and she put the mug to her lips and took a drink of the tea.

Ulyasha's eyes became wide with amazement as her mouth fell open. The others in the room uttered a loud gasp of astonishment. It was an ultimately dramatic symbol of forgiveness. Ulyasha snatched at the mug and took another drink to drink after Natalya, then suddenly burst into tears and put the mug down, the tea running down her chin as she snatched up her apron and covered her face with it.

Natalya put her arms around Ulyasha, pulling her head down to her shoulder and patting her. The others looked at each other and at Natalya, murmuring among themselves. Ulyasha's mother crossed the room and stood behind Ulyasha, patting her shoulder. Natalya took her wrist and pulled her down to the bench on the other side of her, putting her other arm around her. She began sobbing. Natalya sat between them, her arms up around their shoulders and her hands patting them, the odor of their hair and bodies familiar from early childhood. On the edge of her vision she saw

199

a suspicious movement in Ulyasha's hair. She looked closer, and she smothered her sigh as she continued patting them. The fine-toothed comb was always painful, but it wouldn't do to give them to Aleksei in event he got close enough to catch them. And hopefully he would.

CHAPTER X

The ride had been dissatisfying. The exhilarating thrill of controlling the massive animal had been missing, and the feel of the horse's powerful muscles gathering and surging hadn't stirred the usual response. Too many things had gone wrong. Aleksei had been required at the garrison and hadn't been able to come and take her riding. The park had been crowded with strolling couples and other riders, which had been bothersome because Orion was highly spirited and needed a fast pace before he would settle to a slow canter or walk. The couples had leaped aside, the women's trailing skirts swirling and the men's tall hats teetering, and the other riders had struggled to control their mounts as Orion thundered by. There had been angry expressions, resentful glares, and a few heated shouts. It had been tempting to take one of the verges along a waterway toward the edge of the city, the route she usually took with Aleksei because they were more isolated and less popular for strollers and other riders, but it was for that specific reason that her father had forbade her to ride along them when she was unescorted.

There had been other irritants. Two young officers in the black pelisses and dolmans of the Aleksandrinsky Regiment of Hussars had followed her for a way, but it would have been construed as bold to let them approach while she was unescorted. So she hadn't been able to let them draw near enough to even get a good look at them. And there had been an argument with one of the guardsmen who patrolled the park over watering her horse in a fountain, but she had no intention of watering one of her horses in a canal. Her hair was coming loose, and her hat kept slipping from one side to the other. One of her boots was pinching across the instep.

And now that she was returning home after a thoroughly disappointing ride, it sounded as though one of Orion's shoes had loosened. She reined him back to a slow walk, gripping his mane with one hand and leaning over to look at his front feet. Her hair and hat slipped forward, and she pushed them back with an impatient shove of her forearm. There was a distinctly hollow metallic clatter with irritation, sitting back upright on the saddle. The shoe sounded very loose, and it was apparent that the grooms hadn't been doing their duties properly or they would have noticed that the nails were beginning to work loose. She glanced around. Her weight was negligible considering that Orion was an exceptionally large horse, but it was contrary to the instincts instilled in her by the Gypsies to ride a horse with a loose shoe on a paved street. But there was no step or wall around of a convenient height for her to dismount.

She was in a quiet, residential avenue, not far from her house, and there were no people around. She reined the horse up, then slid off the horse. The tight boot on her right foot sent a stab of pain through her foot as she landed on her feet, stumbling to regain her balance, and Orion rolled his eyes and shied away, shaking his head and stamping nervously. She straightened her skirt and gathered the reins, talking to him soothingly and searching in her pocket for a lump of sugar. His nostrils quivered as she held it out to him, then he delicately picked up the sugar with his soft lips and crunched it. She leaned over and looked at the shoe, then turned and began leading the horse along the avenue, slapping her riding crop against the side of her skirt irritably. The ride had been disappointing, and instead of quietening the turbulent restlessness within her as riding usually did, it had produced a weary aggravation.

Her hair became looser, wisps falling on her forehead and cheeks, sweat trickled down her face, and her boot pinched. There was the sound of a carriage behind her, the horse's hoofs clopping and the wheels rumbling on the paving stones. It drew nearer, came abreast of her, and began passing. It was a carriage for hire, and the passenger in it was a woman. Natalya looked up at the woman and nodded pleasantly. The woman looked at her with a surprised expression, and turned toward the driver and said something. The driver pulled back on the traces, stopping the carriage.

"Bonjour, mademoiselle. Did your horse throw you?"

Her French was good, with something more than a trace of an English accent. Natalya stopped by the carriage, patting Orion's nose, and smiled up at the woman. *"Bonjour.* No, he has a loose shoe, and he might cast it and injure his hoof if I ride him."

The woman nodded slowly, and suddenly smiled. It was a pleasant, friendly smile, and she had an attractive face. She was about thirty, dressed in a dark grey wool dress which didn't fit her very well and which looked a little shabby. There were frayed spots on the cuffs and hem, the elbows and shoulders were worn and shiny, and it had been sewn in several places. She had the seedy, impecunious look and slightly authoritarian attitude of a governess. "It is very commendable to have such a regard for one's horse, *mademoiselle*. But are you alone?"

Natalya giggled, pushing her hair back from her forehead. "No, I have my horse with me."

The woman chuckled and clicked her tongue chidingly as she shook her head. "You should not be unescorted because you . . . does your mother realize that you are alone?"

The woman was obviously a governess, officiously inquiring into her welfare but meaning well, and Natalya smiled tolerantly. "Perhaps she is looking down on me even as we talk, because she is in Heaven, may God rest her soul."

The woman's expression became apologetic. "I'm very sorry that I—"

"Is this your destination?" the driver interrupted brusquely in Russian.

The woman turned and looked at the driver. Her Russian wasn't as good as her French, because she had to translate the question in her mind and her Russian was strongly accented when she replied. "No, but I am enquiring of this young mistress if she—"

"I have no time to tarry here. Either dismount or let us be on our way."

The irritations of the day suddenly became too much for Natalya, and she lifted her riding crop and pointed it at the driver, frowning at him. "You shall be silent!" she barked in Russian.

He looked down at her with a surly expression. "I shall not. There are others who wish to be transported, and I shall not tarry here to listen to women's gossip."

Natalya snarled with sudden anger, pulling the horse closer and tying the reins to the support bracket on the carriage step. She climbed onto the step up onto the driver's elevated seat, fuming, and the woman moved to one side on the seat and looked up at her with a startled expression as the driver's surly frown changed to alarm. Natalya seized the side of his collar with her left hand as he started to slide to one side, and she shook her riding crop in his face. "By God, I'll not have your insolence, swine! I'll either have a civil tongue from you, or I'll have the skin from your back with a knout!"

The driver looked at her with a frightened expression, pulling away from the riding crop and trying to control his horse as it pranced from side to side. The carriage swayed and lurched as Orion tried to rear and lifted the side of the carriage by the reins. "I meant no offense, mistress," he stuttered. "But a delay costs me money, and I can ill afford to lose a fare in these times when money is so—"

"You can afford the skin from your back less!" Natalya snapped, releasing his collar and standing upright on the seat as she tapped her riding crop against the back of his seat and glared at him. "It will serve you well to learn to control your tongue!"

The driver grinned, a weak grimace, and nodded rapidly. "Yes, mistress," he babbled. "Thank you, mistress. I apologize, mistress. Please continue your conversation."

Her anger faded as quickly as it had risen. The woman was still looking up at her with a stunned expression. Natalya stepped down from the seat, digging in her pocket for a lump of sugar, and she climbed back down out of the carriage, speaking soothingly to Orion and holding out the sugar. He took the sugar, and she stroked his nose and untied the reins, looking back up at the woman. "You are English?" she asked in that language.

The woman was still bemused by what had happened. She looked up at the driver and back at Natalya uncertainly, then blinked in surprise. "Oh, my goodness—you speak English."

"A little. One of my tutors was English."

"Why, you seem to speak it very well . . . you were tutored instead of going to boarding school? That's very unusual . . . you had an English tutor? Perhaps I know him."

"Perhaps, but that was in Moscow. His name was Chumley."

"Chumley? No, I don't believe . . . Moscow? You are visiting here, then? You certainly shouldn't be riding unescorted in a strange city."

"No, my household recently moved here. Do you live nearby?"

"No, I've come to see about employment here." She smiled brightly and motioned toward the carriage seat. "Would you care to share the carriage with me? I would feel much better if I saw you safely home."

Natalya smiled and nodded, and she led Orion to the rear of the carriage and tied the reins to a projection on the rear mudguard on the carriage. The woman moved to one side to make room for Natalya as she walked back around the carriage and climbed in. Natalya looked at the driver. "Sixteen Galernaya Most. And drive slowly—my horse has a loose shoe."

"I am at your command, mistress," the driver replied unctuously, shaking the traces and starting the carriage along the avenue.

"Sixteen Galernaya Most?" the woman repeated as Natalya sat back in the seat. "Then you . . . oh, my goodness. You must be Count Sheremetev's daughter."

The situation was suddenly clear. Her father had again mentioned hiring a companion, and the last time he had sounded definite about it. "Yes, I am Natalya Ivanova. And you are going to see my father?"

The woman's smile returned, and she nodded. "Yes, and I am pleased to make your acquaintance, Natalya Ivanova. My name is Olivia Hamilton, daughter of William."

"I am pleased to make your acquaintance, Olivia Vassilievna."

Olivia smiled and nodded again as they looked at each other with polite inquisitiveness. "You have a lovely name, Natalya Ivanova. And you are about sixteen, I believe?"

"Seventeen, three months gone. Are you are . . . twenty-five?"

"Thirty," Olivia chuckled, patting Natalya's hand. "And you are very kind. I was informed that your father had a daughter, but there was no mention of other family members . . ."

"There is only my brother Vassily, who is a captain in the Yamburgsky Regiment of Uhlans. He stays at the garrison."

"I see."

Natalya studied Olivia's face. "So you are to be my governess," she said in a musing tone.

Olivia laughed lightly, patting Natalya's hand again. "Hardly, my dear. At the moment, I am only on my way to speak with your father. And if he were to engage me for the position, I would consider myself your friend and companion, not your governess. You are a grown woman, much too mature to have a governess. But you've had someone before, haven't you?"

"Yes, Frau Wiegarta. She remained behind when we moved here."

Olivia looked slightly puzzled, her lips moving as she murmured the name, then she smiled and nodded. "Yes, I see. It must have been difficult for you to be separated from her if you had become fond of her."

Natalya shrugged and chuckled wryly. "Frau Wiegarta drunk a bottle of cognac every day, and I rarely saw her."

Olivia frowned and shook her head, clicking her tongue. "That is deplorable, Natalya Ivanova! A young woman requires advice and assistance, and her dereliction was much to your disadvantage."

Natalya nodded and shrugged again, then smiled. "I hope we will be very good friends."

"And I do too, whether your father the count engages me or finds someone he considers more suitable," Olivia replied with a warm smile. She looked at the horse following the carriage. "That is a very beautiful horse. But he seems to be quite difficult to control."

The carriage was turning onto Galernaya Most, and the driver was angling across the wide avenue toward the house. Natalya pointed toward the carriage gate with her riding crop, and turned back to Olivia. "He is at times, but not as difficult as Pegasus, my other horse. Do you ride?"

"I do, but I shan't try to ride Pegasus," Olivia laughed. "You have two horses, then?"

"Yes, and there are others in the stables. Perhaps we will be able to go riding together."

"Perhaps," Olivia replied.

The driver stopped the carriage at the wide carriage gate, and Olivia opened her reticule. Natalya stood, moving toward the step at the side of the carriage, and took out a ruble. She handed it to the driver. Olivia made a sound of protest. "Natalya Ivanova, I engaged the carriage, and I should—"

"It is done, Olivia Vassilievna," Natalya interrupted her with a smile as she stepped down from the carriage. "Come, and I will take you in to meet his honor my father."

The driver looked at the coin with a pleased expression, and beamed as he put it in his pocket, wrapped the traces around the whip socket, and began climbing down. Olivia closed her reticule and stepped down from the carriage. She looked at the horse as he rolled his eyes, snorted, and pawed at the paving stones, and she moved warily away from him. Natalya patted Orion's nose, gave him a piece of sugar, gathered the reins and turned him toward the gate. Olivia took a couple of quick steps to precede Natalya through the gate and stay away from the horse without being too obvious about it. The driver smiled and bowed deeply as he held the gate for them.

Several gardeners were digging and trimming in the shrubbery and flower beds by the drive, and Natalya beckoned to one of them. "Fetch two of the grooms from the stables."

"Yes, mistress," the gardener said, dropping his hoe, and he trotted along the graveled drive in front of them.

"How do you come to be in Russia, Olivia Vassilievna?"

"My husband was a factor at the British trade mission here. He passed away almost five years ago, and I have been working since then."

"I am sorry to hear of your misfortune. Do you have children?"

Olivia shook her head. "No."

They walked on along the drive in silence for a few steps, then Natalya looked at Olivia for a smile. "And you liked Russia well enough that you decided to stay here?"

Olivia opened her mouth, closed it, then smiled vaguely and nodded. "Yes, it is very pleasant here, Natalya Ivanova."

Natalya stopped where a path paved with stones branched off the graveled drive and led through the garden toward the front door, and she murmured to the horse as she gave him another piece of sugar and patted his nose. Olivia looked around the gardens and up at the magnificent house. The horse bobbed his head and bumped Natalya's hat, pushing it forward, and Natalya giggled and shoved it back. Olivia looked down at her, smiling.

"I'm sure you must have many young men calling on you."

Natalya started to reply, hesitated, then smiled slightly and shook her head. "Only one. We have been barred from the Court in the past because of a misunderstanding between his honor my father and his majesty Czar Paul. . . ." Her voice faded, she shifted her riding crop to her left hand and crossed herself, and changed from French to Russian as she murmured in a soft voice. ". . . may God bless his immortal soul and give him eternal rest after his labors in behalf of his loyal subjects. . . ." She took her riding crop back in her right hand, speaking in a conversational tone and in French again. "But his honor my father has now been invited to—"

"Perhaps I shouldn't have asked, Natalya Ivanova. I didn't mean to pry."

"It is something you should know. His honor my father has now won favor in His Majesty the Czar's eyes, and we moved to St. Petersburg because we are to be received at Court next week. But until we are received at court, it is impolitic to deal with us socially. But there is one . . ." Natalya's voice faded into a gusty sigh as she looked up at Olivia with a brilliant smile, her eyes shining and her teeth gleaming.

Olivia smiled widely, and nodded with understanding. "Is he very handsome, then? I'm sure he is. How did you meet him?"

Natalya sighed again, nodding. "He puts the gods to

shame, Olivia Vassilievna—wait until you see him. He is in the same regiment as my brother, and the first night he came to dinner with my brother he asked my father if he could call on me." Her smile became thoughtful, and she looked away, her voice becoming softer. "So tall and handsome in his uniform, and he had no concern that the Czar might find fault with his calling on me before we are received at court. My father almost refused permission, because he has no desire to alienate Count Orlov, and he was concerned that—"

"Count Orlov?" Olivia exclaimed softly. "He is an Orlov?"

"Yes. Aleksei Andreyevich, Count Orlov's son."

Olivia's eyes widened and she looked even more impressed. "His son? Why, that's very . . ." Her voice faded, and she shook her head quickly, smiling warmly at Natalya. "But he is a very fortunate young man for you to find his companionship pleasant. I'm sure there will be others asking to call on you when you are received at court, and I'm also sure you will find the court social life very exciting."

Natalya shrugged nonchalantly. "Social life is a minor matter to me, and I might find others who are congenial, but Aleksei Andreyevich will be first in my thoughts. But I am well pleased that we are to be received at court, because his honor my father will then have the recognition he deserves. And I am pleased that I will be received into the presence of his majesty Czar Aleksander, because I am his loyal and devoted subject."

Olivia smiled and nodded vaguely. "Yes, I'm very sure . . ."

The gardener came back along the drive, followed by two other men, and Natalya's expression became stern.

She pointed to the horse's left front foot with her riding crop, frowning at the grooms. "Look!" she snapped in Russian.

The grooms nodded, approaching cautiously, and one of them reached to take the side of the bridle to hold the horse's head. The horse suddenly squealed angrily, baring his teeth and flattening his ears, and he lunged at the groom reaching for the bridle. Olivia squeaked with alarm, moving rapidly away. Natalya pushed back on the reins, chiding the horse in a playful tone as the gleaming teeth snapped and gnashed together within inches of her face and shoulder and foam spattered down the front of her riding habit. She calmed him, tapping his shoulder warningly with the crop, and the groom darted forward and seized the bridle with both hands, holding it at arm's length so the horse couldn't bite him and standing with his feet well back so the horse couldn't paw him. The other groom bent over the horse's left forefoot, leaning against the horse to make him sift his weight and tugging at the hoof. He lifted the hoof and examined the shoe, moving it with his fingers, then dropped the hoof and jumped back out of the way as the horse pawed at him. He moved forward again, taking a firm grip on the bridle with both hands, looking at Natalya and nodding apologetically.

"We shall replace the shoe, mistress."

"Check the other shoes as well," Natalya said, releasing the horse to them and stepping back, brushing at the foam on the front of her riding habit. The horse immediately began trying to rear with the two grooms holding him, and Natalya moved back to him, putting her hand on his nose and patting him. "Also check the shoes on Pegasus to assure they are sound. And have someone harness a team of horses to the carriage

212

and put on a clean blouse to transport Olivia Vassilievna to get her belongings."

"Yes, mistress."

Natalya stepped away from the horse again, and the grooms turned him toward the stables. The horse squealed again, trying to turn his head from one side to the other to bite at them, but they grimly held onto the bridle and led him along the drive. He began lunging and kicking, as the grooms stumbled and lurched along, holding onto him.

"That is a very dangerous horse, Natalya Ivanova," Olivia said firmly. "I have never seen such a vicious animal in my entire life!"

Natalya laughed, shaking her head. "He does not love the grooms, so he is difficult with them. But he loves me, and I give him sugar." She slapped her riding crop against her palm. "And I also give him this when he doesn't do as he should." She smiled up at Olivia, turning to the path. "Come, I will introduce you to his honor my father."

"Very well. But I believe your ordering the carriage was somewhat premature, Natalya Ivanova."

"I think not, and you must return home in any event."

Natalya pulled the hatpins out of her hat and took it off as they walked along the path, and she fanned her face with it as they crossed the paved courtyard and went up the steps in front of the house. Natalya stepped in front of Olivia to hold the door open. "Welcome to my home."

"Thank you, it is a very beautiful home." She looked around the entry hall as she went through the door, and breathed a soft sigh. "Very beautiful indeed."

"As I said, we have been here only a short time," Natalya said, closing the door, and they stepped down to the entry hall. "There are still things to be done." She pointed toward the foot of the staircase with her riding crop. "It would help to have a piece of statuary just there, don't you think?"

"Yes, that should be very attractive. Do you plan the furnishings of the house?"

"I manage the household entirely, including all of the accounts."

Olivia lifted her eyebrows as they walked across the entry hall. Natalya led the way through the arched doorway on the right and along the hallway on the other side. She stopped at a door near the end of the hallway, rapped on it with her riding crop, and opened it.

"Your honor?"

"Enter, Natasha."

Natalya opened the door wider and held it for Olivia, smiling up at her, closed it behind her, then took Olivia's arm and led her toward the desk. "Your honor, this is Olivia Vassilievna of the family . . . Hamilton. Olivia Vassilievna, this is his honor my father Ivan Nikolayevich, the Count Sheremetev."

Olivia stepped forward to curtsey, and the count bowed over Olivia's hand. They exchanged greetings in French, and the count motioned her to a chair with a smile as he went back around his desk.

"I thought you were riding, Natasha."

"I was, and I met Olivia Vassilievna on the way home. One of Orion's shoes loosened, and I had to lead him, and Olivia Vassilievna came by in a carriage and offered to share it with me. Shall I go have tea and refreshments prepared, your honor?"

"Yes, thank you, Natasha."

Natalya hesitated and turned back to her father. "I will leave you to speak with my good friend Olivia Vassilievna, your honor."

The count smiled and nodded. "Thank you, Natasha."

Natalya gave Olivia a gamine grin as she walked toward the door. They had spoken in Russian and some of the exchange had been almost too fast for Olivia to comprehend, but the reference to her by Natalya as her good friend, which meant somewhat more in Russia than in other countries, had been clear enough. She smiled gratefully at Natalya. The door closed quietly behind her, and Olivia stood, took the packet of references from her reticule, and handed them to the count. He nodded and murmured in French, putting on a pair of wire frame spectacles, and she sat back down in her chair.

The room was cool, dim, and cluttered, the dark, heavy drapes over the windows along one wall open only a crack, and the walls covered with shelves and cabinets of books and rolls and stacks of papers. Olivia studied the count. He was nearing seventy, she guessed, his hair and mustaches a snowy white and his tall form somewhat emaciated and bent with age, and there were lines of authority and of a reserved amiability in the wrinkles on his face. From the conversation between him and Natalya, they were a close family. And from every indication she had seen, they were immensely wealthy.

The possibility of a position after months of unemployment had been a Godsend, and the possibility of being employed in a noble's household had made it difficult for Olivia to restrain her hopes from rising too high so the disappointment would be too crushing if it came. After meeting Natalya, the position seemed even more attractive. She had a sparkling personality, and she was lovely, small and slender, with a mass of gleaming black hair which emphasized her diminutive stature, and a strikingly beautiful face.

But conversely, meeting her had generated just a hint of caution in Olivia about regarding the position as anything approaching a sinecure. A certain pugnaciousness in the line of her mouth and chin had indicated a mercurial temper, which had been amply proven by the way she had clambered up onto the carriage and seized the driver. There was an abundance of masculine influence in her upbringing, and her fluent Russian indicated she had spent a lot of time with household serfs, which could be expected in the absence of a mother or other feminine authority. She seemed to have a strongly Slavophilic attitude, as had been indicated when she spoke of her governess in Moscow. The woman's name was obviously Wiegart, a common German name, and Natalya had added a vowel to feminize the name, as was the custom with Russian family names. And when she had made the introduction to her father, she had hesitated over Olivia's family name, wanting to feminize it but restraining the impulse.

Natalya had assumed that Olivia had remained in Russia because she wanted to. It hadn't even occurred to her that someone might be forced to stay in a place because they didn't have the money to go elsewhere. The ruble she had casually handed the carriage driver had clearly meant nothing to her, and it was difficult to deny the resentment which threatened to come to life when faced with evidence of such plenty. But resentment was nonsensical. Natalya could hardly be blamed for the wealth of her family.

The pages rustled softly as the count shuffled them, and Olivia clutched her reticule in her lap. Since the death of her husband five years before, she had worked in four different Russian households as a governess, three of them merchants and shipping factors associated with the port and one an Army officer at the local garrison. Each of the households had been noisy and crowded, with poor accommodations. It had taken repeated requests for her to get her wages, and a portion from her last position was still unpaid, even after months. Her wages had been far too small to save up enough for the return passage to England, and what she had managed to save had been used up during the past months of unemployment. Economy had become frugality, and her request for assistance from her father had produced edification rather than money, a letter reminding her that one did with what one had and trusted in God, a not unreasonable philosophy from a comfortable farmer in Staffordshire, but hardly helpful to a widow living in a tiny garret over the vicarage of the Anglican Church in St. Petersburg.

There would be many applicants for a position in such a wealthy household, and it was likely that the interview would result in an indefinite answer. It would mean waiting in the garret over the vicarage for an eternity, torn by indecision if a note came from the English Club that a less desirable position had come open for interview, waiting for a message which might never come.

The count refolded the references carefully and put them back into the packet, took off his spectacles, then stood and held out the packet to her. "I was educated at Eton, but that was many years ago and I am afraid I have forgotten my English. Natasha speaks English well."

Olivia put the packet back into her reticule. "Yes, she does speak English well, *monsieur le comte*. She mentioned that one of her tutors in Moscow was English."

"Yes."

"She was taught by tutors rather than at boarding school?"

He smoothed his mustache with a finger and looked away, slowly nodding. "My daughter is . . . different from many her age," he said slowly. "Her upbringing was different. Through ignorance but no lack of love for her, I was deficient in many ways in not providing a background suitable for a young woman." He sighed and smiled whimsically, looking back at her. "But I am far from displeased with her. Many who have large families have less of a family than I do. She has brightened many hours for me, and I find in her more companionship than in my son, although he is a son of which any man would be proud. Her education and intelligence exceed that of many men . . ." His voice and smile faded, and he sighed heavily. The count looked absently at the far wall, still stroking his mustache with his finger, then looked at her again. "Will five hundred rubles a month be satisfactory?"

She gripped herself to maintain her self control. It was a definite offer. There would be no waiting in the garret. And it far exceeded her most optimistic expectations. The most she had been paid before was fifty rubles per month, and five hundred was a small fortune. She smiled serenely and nodded. "That will be quite sufficient, *monsieur le comte.*"

CHAPTER XI

The clear, ringing sound of Natalya's voice raised in an angry shout carried along the wide, long hallway as Olivia came out of her rooms, tugging the coat of her riding habit down neatly and tucking loose strands of hair under her hat. She closed her door and began hurrying along the hallway, the hem of her skirt skimming along the gleaming hardwood floor and her heels clicking. Individual words in the torrent of French became distinguishable as she neared the other end of the hallway.

"Combien jupons? Cinq? Pourquoi? Non! Non!"

It was about the petticoats. Olivia stopped in front of the door to Natalya's sitting room and rapped on it with her riding crop. Silence fell. She drew in a deep breath and composed herself, pushing the door open. Natalya was standing in the center of the sitting room in her undershift and boots, her fists on her hips, her chin thrust out belligerently, and her eyes flashing with anger. Her maids were standing in the bedchamber doorway, looking apprehensive.

"Natalya Ivanova," Olivia said quietly, smiling reproachfully as she closed the door behind her. "This is very unseemly conduct."

"I shall *not* wear five petticoats!" Natalya said slowly

in her heavily accented English, emphasizing each word. "I shall not!"

It was the first time Olivia had seen her in partial undress. The silk pantaloons were knee-length, fitting tightly around her tiny waist and slender hips and thighs, and circled with clusters of crisp, frothy lace. Sheer silk stockings covered her calves, and her boots were sturdy, with heels to add a couple of inches to her diminutive height. Her bodice had short, tight sleeves and laced up the front, the laces drawn tight across her small, rounded bosom. At the top of the bodice, the edge of a dark birthmark on her left breast was visible. The heavy mass of black hair was piled on her head and tied with ribbons, with curled ringlets falling down just in front of her ears. Olivia put her riding crop on the table by the door, and forced a placating smile. "Natalya Ivanova, you can be heard all the way downstairs. Your young gentleman will be here presently, and I know that you wouldn't want him to hear something like—"

"Olivia Vassilievna, if you wished me to wear five petticoats, why did you not tell me?"

Olivia cleared her throat uncertainly. It had been a gross tactical error, that much was plain, but the easiest way of dealing with Natalya was never immediately obvious and at the time she had decided it had seemed best simply to tell Natalya's maids to put them out for her. Or perhaps it had been cowardice, deferring a direct contest of wills. She started to reply and tell Natalya that she had forgotten, then immediately stopped herself. It would be a lie. "I'm very sorry now that I didn't, Natalya Ivanova, and in the future I will discuss things of this nature with you first. I believe four will be sufficient."

Natalya's irritation began fading, and the line of her chin and mouth softened. She folded her arms, and there was a sudden twinkle of humor in her eyes. "I believe *one* will be sufficient."

"No, indeed," Olivia said firmly. "That would be absolutely common, Natalya Ivanova. One must wear at least four petticoats to go riding."

"*Pourquoi*?" Natalya asked in an exasperated tone, changing back to French. "I have worn only one before, and I—"

"*Est-ce possible*! You are no longer a child, Natalya Ivanova, and we must develop a modicum of modesty."

"Two."

Olivia sighed and smiled wearily, walking toward Natalya, and she put her hand on Natalya's shoulder and nudged her toward the bedchamber doorway. "Three, then. And if a wind blows your skirt against you, I shall absolutely *die* of shame."

Natalya looked up at Olivia with a sudden, brilliant smile, her eyes dancing. "Very well, Olivia Vassilievna. I shall sweat, but I will wear three if that is what you command."

The familiar contraction of the patronymic and the smile were peace offerings, and the atmosphere between them was suddenly relaxed and warm again. Olivia shook her head. "I will be satisfied with three and your lovely smile, Natalya Ivanova. Now let your maids finish dressing you so we won't keep your young man waiting too long, my dear."

Natalya nodded and grinned impishly, turning toward the bedchamber doorway. "Yes, I will hurry, because I have a surprise for you that will please you."

"Indeed? What sort of surprise?"

Natalya giggled, shaking her head. "If I told you, it wouldn't be a surprise. You will see."

The maids followed her into the bedchamber, looking over their shoulders at Olivia with arch, knowing smiles. They had said that Natalya wouldn't wear five petticoats when Olivia had told them to put them out. Olivia smothered a sigh as she looked away. After wearing only one petticoat, three had to be accounted as progress.

Natalya's boudoir was an expansive, spacious room, very attractive with the chinoiserie cabinets and screens and the delicate French furniture with colorful upholstery, but it was also generally cluttered and untidy, offending Olivia's sense of order and neatness. Clothes were scattered around and bright, frothy piles of lace and expensive garments and other finery were thrown on the chairs and tables. In the midst of disorder, only the corner of the room occupied by the desk and bookshelves was neat.

Olivia gathered up a handful of combs and a couple of brushes from a chair and put them on a table in a token effort toward making the room neater. There was a pistol case on the table, and she lifted the lid. It contained a matched pair of French dueling pistols, the barrels, locks, and woodwork heavily inlaid with silver and Natalya's name engraved in Cyrillic characters on a silver rosette on the grip of each pistol. A silver plate on the inside of the lid of the box was engraved with an inscription in French. The pistols had been a gift from Natalya's father on her fifteenth nameday. There was a stack of books by the pistol case. It included several volumes of Scott's novels, a couple of volumes by Prince Clemens von Metternich, the Austrian Minister of Foreign Affairs, and Adam Smith's *Wealth of Nations*. Olivia turned away from the table and walked toward the windows.

It was her fourth day in the household, and in many ways the position exceeded her wildest dreams. Her rooms were almost identical to Natalya's, luxuriously decorated, and the count had advanced her a thousand rubles without so much as a hint from her, enabling her to replenish her wardrobe and pay the back rent she owed for the months she had spent in the attic over the vicarage. The household was well organized and disciplined, quiet and orderly, and the meals were punctual, ample, and delicious.

Then there was Natalya. During the time she had worked in Russian households, she had come to accept the fact that Russian children were spoiled beyond reason, and it would have been reasonable to expect Natalya to be more spoiled than most, with dozens of serfs running after her and her only relatives an age-ing, doting father and a brother who adored her. But she wasn't spoiled in the least. She was simply differ-ent from anyone Olivia had ever met before, to a de-gree she wouldn't have thought possible.

Over dinner the first night Olivia had been in the household, Natalya had engaged in a loud, heated ar-gument with her father, and quite beyond the appalling spectacle of a young woman disputing with her father, the subject had been some detail of Peter the Great's foreign policy. Before the shock of that had been as-similated, she had seen Natalya being served coffee in a man's glass and puffing on a huge cigarette as she sucked her teeth and burped, possibly the most incon-gruous sight she had ever seen. After dinner, Olivia had accompanied Natalya to her rooms to chat for a time, intending to make subtle suggestions about how a young lady should conduct herself during discussions with her father, as well as to address the subject of the cigarettes, but Natalya had pushed those aside and had expressed a keen interest in knowing how the cab-inet responsibilities had been transferred during the restoration of the British crown and whether or not Olivia considered Warren Hastings to have been ma-ligned by those who had charged him with malfeasance.

And she had seemed remotely surprised and disappointed when Olivia had known nothing about either subject.

The long, heavy pistols in the case weren't simply an ornament. Natalya's brother had come from his garrison to have dinner with his father and sister on the second evening Olivia had been in the household, and he had brought a pistol with him. He and Natalya had gone to the stables for a pistol match before dinner, and Natalya had beaten him. Earlier that same day, Olivia had gone riding with Natalya in the park, and it had been a disturbing experience, fraught with constant terror that Natalya's fractious gelding was going to bolt, unhorse her, or run over someone in the park, while Olivia raced her mare frantically to keep up with her charge.

Unlike many wealthy Russian women who were indolent, it was only Natalya's need for privacy for four to six hours each day to pore over some book or sheaf of papers and her involvement in the household that made life as her companion bearable, because her days were eighteen hours long. She was a bundle of energy, dashing through the house, gardens, and to the stables and kitchens to oversee things, give instructions, stop to laugh and joke, check foodstuffs being delivered, cast household accounts, order the feed for the horses, and take a brush away from a maid to show her how to scrub a windowsill.

But those around her accepted her as she was. Aleksei Orlov, an extremely handsome and well-placed young man, had come to dinner with Natalya's brother two nights before, and his feelings for Natalya were abundantly obvious, despite the fact that they had been acquainted for such a brief time. He was an exceptionally good catch for any young woman, and he appeared totally enchanted, oblivious to any eccentricities in Natalya's characteristics. Her father also accepted her as she was, as indeed he should, considering that he laughed at her occasional ribald remarks, allowed her to argue with him over which of them would read the evening news sheets first, and had bought pistols for her nameday present and had permitted her to consort with Gypsies as a child. Her brother treated her with deep love as an equal, and the house serfs worshipped her, though she often berated them for neglecting their duties.

It was easy to see why people around her would overlook her failings. In spite of her ready temper which could be dangerous if fully aroused, and perhaps at least partially because of the inseparable characteristics which went with it, she was very engaging. Her Cossack ancestry apparent in the large frame and fair complexion of her father and brother wasn't evidenced in her; she was small, slender, and very beautiful. Her impatient, driving energy and a wild, untamed element in her personality made her scintillating and charismatic. She was exciting, intriguing, and interesting to be around. And in many ways she was still very much a child.

Olivia sighed, moving the drape aside and looking through the window. The trees in the garden and along the stone wall towered high above the second floor window, but she could see parts of the next couple of houses along the avenue through the branches. In the distance the sun gleamed on the huge dome of the Cathedral of St. Issac's and on the other massive buildings along Nevsky Prospekt. She turned her head and looked at the bedchamber doorway. There was still a murmur of voices and rustle of fabric. She sighed again, looking back through the window. It was only a few days before the family was to be received at court, and Natalya had to be coached to get through

225

that momentous event successfully as a credit to her father. Then more basic problems could be attacked. One of the first things to do was to dissuade her from the habit of drenching herself with powerful scent which was much too heavy for her age.

Scents! Olivia turned away from the window and walked rapidly toward the bedchamber doorway, hissing with exasperation at herself for daydreaming, but she relaxed as she walked into the room. Natalya hadn't got around to her perfumes and colognes, and characteristically, she wasn't letting her maids finish dressing her, as a gentlewoman should. She had pulled away from them and was buttoning the coat of her riding habit herself with impatient movements of her small fingers. Olivia crossed the room to the narrow table where the powders, creams, scents, and cosmetics were kept. There were few of them, because Natalya's father regarded them with general disfavor.

"Let us see what scent we should use, Natalya Ivanova. It should be a light one, shouldn't it? Young ladies should always wear a very light scent, particularly during the day."

"*L'eau Coquette*," Natalya said, pointing. "The one in blue glass."

The name seemed hardly promising, and Olivia smiled doubtfully as she looked along the table. "Blue glass? Oh, this one, isn't it? Well, let me see what . . . oh, that seems quite heavy, my dear. Even for a much older woman, that would be extremely heavy for daytime use."

"*Parfume Denise*," Natalya said, shrugging her shoulders and tugging at her coat to settle it on her neatly. "The yellow pot."

"Yellow pot? Yes, this must be . . . that seems quite strong too, Natalya Ivanova. For a young woman, the object is just a delicate touch of fragrance."

226

Natalya sat down in a chair so the maids could put her hat on. "You pick one, Olivia Vassilievna."

Olivia smiled and nodded, opening bottles and jars and sniffing at the nozzles on spray bulbs. They all seemed to be more or less overpowering, but there was a violet-scented paste which was less heavy than most. She took the jar to Natalya and daubed a touch on each earlobe. "There you are, my dear."

Natalya looked up at her from under the brim of the hat as the maids pressed it on and pushed hatpins in, her expression indicating a substantial degree of doubt about the quantity, but she smiled slightly and nodded. Olivia walked back to the table to replace the jar, and Natalya grimaced impatiently, pulled away from the maids and rose from the chair, and went to a mirror to pin on the hat herself. There was a knock on the sitting room door, and one of the maids went to answer it. A man's voice murmured, and the maid closed the door and returned to the bedchamber.

"Aleksei Andreyevich is here, mistress. And he has another man with him."

Natalya nodded. "Get my riding crop, my gloves, and a handkerchief." She turned away from the mirror, pushing the last hatpin in, and looked at Olivia with a wide smile. "*That* is your surprise, Olivia Vassilievna. I told Aleksei Andreyevich to bring a companion for you."

Olivia flushed with pleasure. It had been years since she had been in a situation of social companionship with a man, and responses from years before suddenly returned, curiosity, excitement, and anticipation. "How very thoughtful of you, Natalya Ivanova."

Natalya took her riding crop, gloves, and handkerchief from the maid and looked at Olivia with a grin. "I cannot have you taking Aleksei Andreyevich from me."

"Natalya Ivanova!" Olivia scoffed. "What a thing to say!"

Natalya shrugged and lifted her eyebrows as she walked toward the door. "You are a very attractive woman, Olivia Vassilievna, and any man would find pleasure in your company. Come, let us go see who he is."

Olivia smiled and nodded, looking at her as she followed her through the door. Natalya's riding habit was English style, similar to the one she had been wearing the day they met, a full skirt and matching coat in dark grey linen, with a wide hat of grey felt. The body and sleeves of the coat were tailored to fit her tightly, and the solid grey of the costume was relieved by ruffles of white lace at throat and wrists and by the red ribbons in her hair. She looked small and dainty, her skirt satisfyingly full over the three petticoats and her face almost lost under the bulk of her hair and the large hat on her head.

But as they went through the door to the hallway and walked along the hall, she carried her crop in her right hand and slapped it against her skirt in one of her excessively boisterous and masculine mannerisms. Olivia edged around to Natalya's right side with her riding crop tucked under her left arm to provide an example and to deprive her of enough room to slap her skirt with her crop. Natalya switched the crop to her left hand and began slapping the other side of her skirt.

There was a murmur of masculine voices in one of the drawing rooms as they came down the staircase. Aleksei came out of the drawing room with long strides, looking up at them. Natalya froze, and Aleksei stopped at the foot of the staircase, a wide smile on his face as he looked up at Natalya. He was indeed handsome, the red braid, tassels, and epaulettes contrasting with the dark blue of his jacket, his nankeen trousers skin tight, and his tall boots and sword belt gleaming with polish. Natalya was smiling radiantly at him, her cheeks flushed rosily. Their eyes were shining.

There was a silence. Olivia felt a flush rising to her cheeks. She started to cough politely to break the silence and the almost embarrassing tableau as they gazed and smiled at each other, and in the same instant Aleksei lifted his hand toward Natalya. Natalya was suddenly in motion, skimming down the staircase, her feet barely touching the steps as her skirt brushed along them. For a horrified instant, Olivia thought Natalya was going to throw herself into his arms or he was going to clasp her and embrace her familiarly, then Natalya stopped at the foot of the staircase and put her hand in his. He pressed her hand to his lips as he bowed, looking down at her, and she bobbed in a curtsy.

Olivia coughed, walking rapidly down the stairs. He was kissing her hand much too fervently, and Natalya was standing altogether too near him, her skirt against his boots. She had hinted strongly to Natalya that she should exercise more restraint and conceal her feelings somewhat better, and she resolved to have a straightforward talk with her about it in the very near future. Aleksei straightened up as she approached, his eyes reluctantly leaving Natalya's and moving to her.

"Comment allez-vous, Olivia Vassilievna?"

She extended her hand as she curtsied so he would have to release Natalya's hand and take it. *"Tres bien,* Aleksei Andreyevich. *Et vous?"*

He bowed over her hand and brushed it with his lips. *"Tres bien."* He had a small package wrapped in white crepe and tied with a red ribbon under his left arm, and he turned back to Natalya, handing it to her. "For you, Natalya Ivanova."

She clasped it, her eyes dancing as she looked at it then back up at him. There had been a present every day Olivia had been in the household. When he had come to dinner, he had brought a large box of sweet-meats, and on the other three days there had been baskets of fruit or flowers delivered. Natalya's fingers moved on the wrapping almost in a caress, conveying that the gift was of immense value to her. "May I open it now?"

"Certainly."

She pulled the ribbon off, and gasped with delight. It was a small, calf-bound volume. "Byron! And in English! It is a beautiful present, Aleksei Andreyevich. Olivia Vassilievna and I will be able to read to each other from it." She opened the cover and looked at the title page, her eyes moving over it quickly, and she giggled and flushed as she snapped it closed. "Or perhaps I should read it alone."

Olivia looked at them with a strained smile as they laughed, resolving to read the inscription if she had to sneak into Natalya's room when she was out. "It's a lovely book, Natalya Ivanova."

Natalya sighed with pleasure and nodded, stroking the cover with the tips of her fingers, then she suddenly looked at the drawing room doorway and clicked her tongue. "But we are keeping your friend waiting—how thoughtless of me! Let us meet him."

Aleksei nodded, taking her hand and putting it on his arm as they turned toward the doorway, and he smiled down at Olivia. "You will be pleased to meet him, Olivia Vassilievna. He is a countryman of yours."

Olivia lifted her eyebrows in mild surprise, looking into the drawing room as they approached it. The man was standing in front of a sofa. He was a large man, an inch or two taller than Aleksei and somewhat heavier, and in a green and white military uniform. His expression was one of reserve, and it relaxed only slightly as they entered the room.

"Natalya Ivanova, this is Thomas Greenwood, son of Stephen. Thomas, this is Natalya Ivanova, daughter of the Count Sheremetev."

Natalya smiled up at him, curtsying as he bowed over her hand with a polite, unsmiling expression. "I am pleased to make your acquaintance, Thomas Stephanovich."

"I am charmed, Natalya Ivanova," he murmured in a deep, quiet voice.

"Please permit me to introduce my friend, Olivia Vassilievna of the family Hamilton."

He turned to Olivia and gravely bowed over her hand. "How do you do, Mrs. Hamilton," he said in English.

Olivia murmured a reply as she curtsied. There was no particular disgrace attached to taking a commission in the armed forces of another nation, but it smacked of adventure. And he looked like an adventurer, a dangerous man, large and darkly handsome, with the silvery mark of a saber scar down his right cheek. But she felt a warm gratitude toward Natalya for introducing her as a friend, even though it was a transparent euphemism, because the man was approximately her age, about thirty.

Natalya was still looking up at him with an expression of curiosity, her fingers absently stroking the binding on the book. "Have you been in our country very long, Thomas Stephanovich?"

"For three years, Natalya Ivanova."

"And you have been in the Semenovskys for that length of time?"

"I was an engineer in the Caucasus for a year, and

I was commissioned a captain of horse in the Semenovskys two years ago, Natalya Ivanova. I am flattered that you recognize my uniform."

The replies were in a courteous tone, but terse. And she had addressed him with the familiar "thou" while he had replied in the formal address. Her lips pursed in pique at his solemn manner, then she lifted her eyebrows and smiled slightly. "Who would not recognize a uniform of the Knights Guards?" She turned her head and looked up at Aleksei, her smile brightening, and she touched the metal end of a lace on his jacket into position. "I had it from my brother that he was told by two officers of the Preobrazhensky Regiment that the Count Samoylov had words with his excellency the Grand Duke Nikolas."

Aleksei lifted his eyebrows. "Count Samoylov?"

"Indeed. It was told to my brother that his excellency the grand duke was displeased with Count Samoylov's squadron on parade, and he stopped the count and took him by the collar. And it was further told to my brother that the count said to him, 'Sire, I have my sword in my hand.' "

Aleksei chuckled and looked at Thomas, stroking his mustache with a finger. "There's a hot head for you."

The tall, dark man's expression was inscrutable, and he looked away and nodded noncommittally. Olivia made an uncomfortable sound in her throat; not untypically, it appeared that Natalya had introduced a weighty and unsuitable subject for conversation. Natalya looked back at Thomas, her smile fading slightly. "But surely you heard of this incident before I did, Thomas Stephanovich? Count Samoylov is in the Semenovskys, is he not?"

"I concern myself only with my squadron, Natalya Ivanova."

His tone and manner conveyed a hint that the subject was also inappropriate for Natalya's concern, and Natalya's smile became wider and tense as her eyes narrowed. "Ah, it is always a pleasure to meet one who is dedicated to his duties." She stood on tiptoe, craning her neck to look at his epaulettes. "What battalion are you in, Thomas Stephanovich? Is that the badge of the First?"

"Yes, the First Battalion, Natalya Ivanova."

Natalya's smile became wide and mischievous, and her eyes danced. The first battalion was a prestigious organization, the Czar's Own, but there had been an unfortunate incident in the barracks of the First Battalion four years before, when some enlisted members of the battalion had revolted against their German commander. "I can readily understand why your duties consume your attention, Thomas Stephanovich. The maintenance of discipline and good order requires the dedication of all the officers in the First Battalion, does it not?"

Aleksei looked both amused and slightly reproachful as he smiled down at her. The revolt was the single black mark in the centuries-long history and tradition of the First Battalion of the Semenovskys. It had been forgiven by the Czar, and members of the unit were sensitive about mention of it. He looked at Thomas and smiled apologetically. Thomas looked at him, a hint of a resigned smile twitching his lips, and he shrugged as he looked down at Natalya. "Good order is being maintained," he said quietly, then he looked back at Aleksei. "Natalya Ivanova is uncommonly well informed on the affairs of the Guards, it appears."

Aleksei laughed, shaking his head. "Thomas, that scarcely touches the fact. I know of no subject which Natalya Ivanova has not explored in depth."

"But perhaps I should leave such matters to those

with the wisdom to deal with them?" Natalya asked Thomas quietly.

He hesitated, then shrugged again. "I should think that there are other matters which you would find more interesting."

"Such as what footman got the maid Palashka pregnant or the extent of the duties required of the gardeners of some aged countess?" Natalya replied, her smile fading and her tone flat. "Or perhaps unraveling the indiscretions revealed in the lines of the latest play at the French Theater? Or possibly matters of such moment as my wardrobe? Perhaps I should, Thomas Stephanovich. Or perhaps all minds which are devoted to matters of consequence should, with advantage to all concerned, be devoted to lighter things, to judge from the state in which one can occasionally find matters of importance. I see little good in—"

"Come, Natalya Ivan'va," Aleksei chuckled, taking her hand and patting it. "We came for an afternoon of pleasure, not to debate. Let Thomas see your sweet smile instead of such a scowl."

She looked up at him with the beginnings of an irate expression, then her mood suddenly changed and she nodded. "Then I'll have done with it," she said, looking back at Thomas and smiling slightly. "I referred lightly to the revolt in the Semenovskys, and for that and for being a poor hostess, I apologize. Rather I should have spoken seriously of the idiocy of the German Colonel Gregory Schwarz who ordered floggings for Cavaliers of the Order to St. George among the Semenovskys and caused the revolt. It defies reason how such a man and those who harbor him can consider themselves servants of His Majesty the Czar when they proceed with such folly."

Thomas looked down at her, his lips pursed, and lifted his eyebrows. "And the fact that the colonel is now a general with his excellency the Grand Duke Konstantine in Poland is of no consequence?"

"It is of the utmost consequence, and it supports what I have been saying, if you but listened."

He blinked, frowning thoughtfully, then slowly nodded. "I cannot but agree, Natalya Ivanova. And I should have listened more closely at first." The corners of his lips lifted slightly in a sardonic smile. "But let us hope that you give only your friends the benefit of such views. General Schwarz is said to be an influential man."

Natalya tossed her head back and laughed gaily, reaching out to tap his arm with the book she was holding. "No fear, he cannot hear me. It is said that he has an ear trumpet so he can hear what his aides say to him, and perhaps that is why his army so frequently charges to the rear instead of to the front."

Aleksei exploded into laughter, and Thomas's smile widened slightly and became humorous. The atmosphere which had been tense and strained with friction, was suddenly relaxed again. Olivia sighed with relief. Most of the references in the conversation had been lost on her, but she had found it extremely uncomfortable. Natalya beckoned to the house steward and handed him the book, as he stepped quickly to her. "Have one of my maids put this on my desk." She looked up and glanced between Aleksei and Thomas. "May I repair my deficiencies as a hostess and offer refreshments?"

"A beaker of vodka would be of help in bracing me to assist you onto one of your fiery horses," Aleksei laughed, "but let us wait and have refreshments on the promenade. What do you say, Thomas?"

Thomas shrugged nonchalantly, and they walked toward the table by the door where they had put their swords, Aleksei's kepi, and Thomas's plumed Semenov-

235

sky helmet. Natalya and Olivia pulled on their gloves and moved toward the doorway as the two men hooked their scabbards onto their belts and tucked their headgear under their arms, then they all went through the doorway and crossed the entry hall toward the front door. Natalya and Aleksei walked in front, and Thomas offered Olivia his arm. She smiled and nodded as she put her hand on his arm, then looked back at Natalya and noted with disapproval that Natalya was slapping her skirt with her riding crop again as she chattered to Aleksei.

Aleksei and Thomas had left their horses tethered on the drive, and the grooms had brought a mare from the stables for Olivia and held her by the other two horses. They had also brought the sleek, gleaming black gelding Natalya called Pegasus and tied him several yards away from the other three horses, and the gelding was prancing and bobbing his head impatiently, making the other horses nervous. The grooms were standing nearby, and one of them handed Natalya a handful of sugar lumps to put in her pocket. She tucked her riding crop under her arm, and tugged her gloves tighter as she walked toward the gelding, Aleksei a pace behind her.

Olivia waited by Thomas as he stopped at the end of the walk, looking at the huge gelding and Natalya walking toward it in utter aplomb. His features were in their normal neutral, reserved lines, but the line of his lips indicated bemusement and wonder. The gelding bared his teeth threateningly and flattened his ears as Natalya approached, and she laughingly chided him as she walked up to him fearlessly, taking one of the lumps of sugar from her pocket and offering it to him as she tapped his shoulder with her crop. His ears cocked forward and he took the sugar, as she untied the reins and tossed one of them across his neck. The gelding started to turn his head as she moved back to the saddle, and she held the rein across his neck with a firm grip to keep him from turning his head as she lifted one foot. Aleksei knelt, cupping his hands and putting them under her foot, and there was a brief scramble as he lifted her onto the saddle and stepped quickly back as the gelding wheeled and tried to bite him.

Natalya expertly countered the gelding's attempts to rear as she settled herself in the saddle, then let him trot toward the stables to release some of his energy. Aleksei mounted, and Thomas took Olivia's arm and crossed the drive with her to her horse, looking over his shoulder at Natalya and the gelding. He lifted Olivia onto the saddle and handed her the reins, then untied his horse and mounted it. The grooms swung the gate open, and Natalya turned the gelding at the stables and started back along the drive.

The huge horse sprang ahead, his neck arched, and his tail flowing, sidling one way then the other as he strained against the bit. Natalya's face was flushed and smiling with pleasure and excitement as she controlled the horse's movements with touches of her riding crop, balancing lightly on the saddle and moving with the horse. Olivia glanced at Thomas. He was looking at Natalya and the horse with a clear light of admiration in his eyes. Aleksei lifted his reins and urged his horse forward to trot along beside the gelding through the gate. Thomas wheeled his horse toward the gate, and Olivia touched her crop to the mare's shoulders and lifted the reins. The mare moved forward with a docile gait and began trotting by Thomas's horse.

The clatter of the horses' hoofs on the paving stones echoed between the high stone walls on each side of the street as they rode to the end of Galernaya and turned onto Konyushennaya, and then turned onto Morskaya, a broad avenue lined with luxury shops, hotels, and fashionable restaurants. It was the area for the fashionable strollers, and the pavements were crowded with pedestrians, women in trailing skirts with parasols and men in bright uniforms or the latest styles in mufti. Numerous carriages moved along the street, but there were few riders and people on the pavements glanced at the horses as they passed. Years before, Olivia had seen lords and ladies up from London riding along the streets of Stafford on beautiful, spirited horses, chattering and laughing gaily, and it had seemed that they lived on a different plane which coincided briefly with hers to allow her a glimpse of them as she ran errands for her mother in the city. And what she had felt at the time seemed to be reflected in some of the faces in the street as they rode along Morskaya toward the park. It was very heady and exciting, and Thomas emerged from his reserve, to a considerable extent and talked with her as they rode along.

But the conversation kept coming back to Natalya in one way or another, and she couldn't decide whether it was accidental or by clever manipulation on his part. It was bothersome and vaguely unsettling.

CHAPTER XII

The pale moonlight silvered the long avenue and the meticulously neat squares of shrubbery, gardens, and lawns on each side of it. The lamps lining the avenue faded into lines of yellowish light in the distance converging at the palace, which shimmered and twinkled like stars from the light blazing from its windows. Gleaming white statues or the sparkle of fountains were momentarily visible in the combination of moonlight and cunningly placed lamps as the Sheremetev carriage passed by. A breath of a breeze stirred, carrying the scent of flower gardens and the soft whirring of insects through the open windows of the carriage.

The carriage gradually neared the palace, and the avenue turned into a vast courtyard paved with large blocks of stone so smoothly joined that the wheels of the carriage made a soft, steady rumble, and the palace loomed like a gigantic mountain of marble and granite. The occasion was a relatively minor one, being held in one of the smaller ballrooms, and the carriage angled to the right across the paved area, toward a side entrance. Towering walls filled with dark windows formed two sides of this courtyard and a wide, long expanse of marble steps led up to a lighted portico on the other side. Other carriages wheeled around and stopped at the steps for passengers to alight, and the sound of the horses' hoofs and the carriage wheels on the stove pavement echoed hollowly between the walls. Lighted fountains played along the sides of the courtyard below the two walls, the lamps in them illuminating naiads and cherubs spreading filmy sprays from fingers or outstretched hands and gargoyles belching streams from grotesquely gaping mouths, and the splash of the water into the marble basins blended with the sounds of activity in the courtyard and the music coming from the windows flanking the portico.

· The count dismounted from the carriage first, wearing the uniform of a colonel of the Izmaylovskys that he had worn at the Battle of Borodino, with the Vladimir Ribbon around his neck, then Vassily got out, wearing the uniform of a captain of the Yambursky Regiment of Uhlans that he had worn at Smolensk, where Napoleon had been routed. Vassily turned and took Natalya's hand, and her gown rustled as she stepped out of the carriage. It was of sheer white muslin, with a tight bodice and layers upon layers of skirt over the requisite number of petticoats. The bodice was cut low enough in front and back to have caused Olivia an agony of indecision between the dictates of modesty and of stunning effect. Her hair was piled on her head intertwined with strands of pearls, with curled ringlets falling over her ears, and a necklace of matched pearls encircled her slim throat.

Sentries in the white and crimson livery of the Palace Guard stood between the fluted columns at the front of the portico, and the count spoke quietly to one of them. Other people coming up the steps were entering through the large, double doors standing open in the center, but the guard escorted them to a door at one side and led them inside to a dais elevated above the ballroom floor. There were columns along the front of the dais with thick, heavy draperies between them, and the drapes were gathered and tied, allowing glimpses of the ballroom, ablaze with light from the dozens of chandeliers hanging from the lofty ceiling. There were hundreds of people in the ballroom, chatting and laughing in scattered clusters. Others were walking down the steps between the two center columns along the edge of the dais and greeting friends in the ballroom.

Rows of pillars extended along each side of the ballroom, with low arches of stone latticework between them which made partially-concealed walkways along both sides of the ballroom. The sentry led them along the walkway on the right, and Natalya looked at the people in the ballroom as she passed the openings between the pillars. There were men in the uniforms of various regiments and of the latest fashions from Paris and London, and the women were a symphony of moving fans, bright gowns, and bare shoulders. The murmur of conversation droned under the strains of sedate music coming from the orchestra at the other end of the ballroom.

The count entered a room to the right of the ballroom, and Vassily took Natalya's arm and guided her through the doorway ahead of him.

The sounds of conversation, laughter, and music became distant and muffled as the door closed behind them. It was a large, elegantly furnished drawing room, couches and chairs in bright fabrics and gleaming tables scattered around the walls, and it was richly decorated with tapestries and large oil paintings. A dozen or so people were standing in the center of the room quietly talking, and all but two of them were men. One of them was a churchman, three were in uniform, and the others wore civilian dress. One of the women was about thirty, and the other was a few years older than Natalya. Two of the men walked toward the count and greeted him

241

heartily. Natalya recognized them, because they were among the people who had exercised influence in securing approval of her father's petition to return to court, and both of them had visited several times in Moscow and had been to see her father since the move to St. Petersburg. The count beamed happily, embracing the men, and they moved toward the group in the center of the room. Vassily took Natalya's hand and put it on his arm, and they followed their father.

It was dizzying. The nervousness which had built up over the past days approached a peak, and she steeled herself and exercised rigid self control to maintain her poise and keep her voice steady during the flurry of introductions, sweeping into deep curtsies and murmuring polite responses. Grand Duke Nikolas was in the uniform of his Second Guards Infantry Division, and her estimation of Count Samoylov's courage rose because he had stern, rigid features and towered over everyone in the group except her brother. The churchman was the Metropolitan Seraphim, head of the Church in St. Petersburg, and the men also included Michael Miloradovich, Governor General of St. Petersburg, General Ivan Diebitsch, Chief of General Staff, Shishkov, Minister of Education, and other well known figures. The older woman was the Grand Duchess Aleksandra Fedorovna, wife of Nikolas and a haughty but still somehow motherly-looking woman, and the younger woman was Countess Annya Konstantinovna, daughter of the Grand Duke Konstantine, next in line to the throne and the commander of the armies in Poland.

The introductions over Natalya was left on the edge of the group as her father and brother began talking to a couple of men and conversations they had interrupted resumed. She forced herself to keep her hands loosely at her sides, fighting an impulse to wring them

242

nervously. Annya Konstantinovna moved toward her. A charitable assessment would characterize her as plain and plump; she was tall and had the square face and slightly protuberant blue eyes of the Romanovs. She was dressed in a pale blue satin gown which appeared to be a little small for her and did little to flatter her large build. Her smile of greeting had been polite, but bored. No one had been talking to her when Natalya had entered with her father and brother, and she gave the impression of wishing she were elsewhere.

She looked down at Natalya with an absent smile, plucking and patting at a fold on the shoulder of Natalya's gown. "Do you believe you will like St. Petersburg as much as Moscow, Natalya Ivanova?"

"I hope so, Annya Konstantinovna. It seems to be a pleasant and attractive place."

Annya lifted her eyebrows and shrugged doubtfully, looking away. "I prefer Warsaw." She sighed softly as her eyes moved around the room, and she looked back down at Natalya. "But you will probably enjoy it, because you are very attractive."

"*Vous êtes très gentil,* Annya Konstantinovna. Your gown is—"

"I'm fat," she sighed brusquely, her mouth tightening with impatience. "Anyone can see that I'm fat."

Natalya started to murmur a courteous disagreement, then hesitated. She had less experience than many in social situations, because parties and similar occasions had held little appeal for her until she had become of an age at which men started to interest her. But she did have a degree of intuitive insight under some circumstances, and she could see that Annya didn't like flattery. She was bored in a group where she didn't quite fit in, and she looked as though she suffered from loneliness. Natalya looked up into Annya's pale blue eyes, letting her smile become warm and friendly. "You *are* attractive, Annya Konstantinovna. You are a Romanova and you are large like all the Romanov family, and you are also attractive."

The bored, detached expression left Annya's face, and she looked down at Natalya as though seeing her for the first time, her eyes moving over Natalya's face. Then she smiled slightly and nodded. "Perhaps, but not as attractive as you. Do you have any other brothers or sisters?"

"Only my brother Vassily Ivanovich."

"You don't look like him, do you? Or your father."

"No, I am much smaller and my hair is dark."

"Do you think your mother . . . ? You know."

It was simply a suggestion, if unusually blunt and straightforward, with no hint of malice. Natalya shook her head. "No. I don't remember my mother very well, but I know the serfs would have told my father. They love him very much."

"And do they love you as well?"

"Perhaps even more. I spent much of my time with them as a child, and I still do because I have the responsibility of my father's household."

"Then you speak Russian."

"Yes, I speak it very well," Natalya replied, changing from French to Russian, and she chuckled softly. "Could you not tell by my poor French?"

Annya's smile widened. "You speak French very well," she said in Russian heavily accented with French, then changed back to French. "*Bien.* I believe I like you, Natalya Ivan'va."

In addition to contracting the patronymic, she had changed to the familar "thou," and Natalya smiled up at her and nodded firmly. "I hope we will be friends. Or I hope I will be *one* of your friends, I should say, because I am sure you have many."

Annya's smile faded, and she pursed her lips as she looked down at the floor. "No, not many," she murmured vaguely, then she looked back at Natalya and smiled again as she leaned closer and whispered. "Are you frightened?"

Natalya startled to reply negatively, hesitated, and nodded. "Yes, a little."

"It will be over presently. There is no reason to hide it, because I was frightened when I first came here from my father's household. They treated me poorly, you know. And still do to an extent. His excellency my father has had disagreements with the Grand Duke Nikolas and Czar Aleksander, and it has caused ill feeling for me. But you must swear not to tell anyone about what I have just told you."

The protuberant blue stared down at her demandingly, as though wanting some kind of assurance, and Natalya lifted two fingers, made a surreptitious sign of crossing herself, and touched the tips of her fingers to her left breast.

Annya nodded, looking satisfied, and she leaned closer and whispered softly, "Part of the disagreement was over that Polish whore my father married after he put my mother aside, calling it a divorce." She glanced around and talked in a somewhat louder but still quiet tone. "But I'm not frightened now, because I'm too hungry all the time. They won't let me eat enough, because they say I'm too fat."

A couple of soft gurgles had come from Annya's stomach while they had been talking, which underscored what she said. Natalya lifted her eyebrows, glancing around, and motioned for Annya to lean over so she could whisper in her ear. "The Grand Duchess Aleksandra Fedorovna is heavier than you are," she said softly.

Annya grunted, straightening up. "She also has a husband," she murmured succinctly.

It was a good point. Women of royal families were the pledges which secured treaties and alliances, and it wasn't unknown for some considerations of national objectives to be sacrificed by a ruler with a hot-blooded son who had taken a fancy to a specific eligible, so attractiveness did make a difference. Natalya silently nodded.

Annya nudged Natalya and indicated a door on the other side of the room from the ballroom entrance. It was opening. Two footmen in crimson and white livery stepped in and stood stiffly on each side of the doorway. Annya gathered her skirt to curtsy, and Natalya hastily did the same. She glimpsed Czar Aleksander in the uniform of the Semenovsky Guards as he stepped into the doorway, then he was lost from sight behind the people between her and the door as she dropped her head and curtsied deeply. Annya's gown rustled by her as she swept to the floor in a deep curtsy with a gliding movement surprisingly graceful considering her size and build. The Czar murmured a quiet greeting, and it was echoed from the group as they straightened up again. The group had closed together in front of Natalya, and he was still hidden behind them. Grand Duke Nikolas was visible over the other heads, and he turned to her father and nodded shortly. Her father and the Grand Duke moved forward. There was a breathless silence except for the sound of their footsteps. Then the Grand Duke's deep voice rumbled a formal introduction.

From earliest childhood, Natalya could remember the endless hours her father had spent in his study over letters, drafting, revising, and rewriting them, then sometimes opening the packet just before dispatching it to read something again and perhaps change it once more. The replies had been read and reread, pondered over, and carefully placed with others on a shelf or in a drawer to be taken out and examined again and again. Friends from his regiment and other friends and acquaintances of high station had come to confer with him in his study for hours of quiet conversation, and he had made countless trips to visit others, all for the purpose of being readmitted to court.

Understanding had come slowly and gradually, because it had depended upon an adult grasp of her father's motivations. Natalya's first inkling had come when she placed into perspective all that was involved in the flight to Sherevskoye while smoke from the raging flames consuming Moscow towered into the skies, and why her father and brother had left her alone. After a long time, her father had arrived at Sherevskoye, wounded and confined to bed for weeks, and some time later her brother had come, also wounded. They had told her bits of it, shrugging off most of her questions and turning the conversation to other subjects, but others had told her much more. Visitors had replied to her questions more fully, and there had been tales heard elsewhere by the serfs, which had to be evaluated to extract the kernels of fact from the chaff of fanciful elaboration. But eventually she had learned that her father had held a battalion in place and blocked Napoleon's left flank at Borodino, at the cost of most of the battalion and severe wounds which almost took his life, to allow the Russian armies to disengage and withdraw so they could fight again at a more favorable time. Her brother had been in the arrowhead squadron of the battalion which broke the French line at Smolensk when the stain of the invaders' footsteps on the breast of Mother Russia had been washed away in rivers of French blood, and he had been one of the three surviving members of the squadron.

They had left her in Moscow and joined their battalions to do their duty. Full understanding had come when she perceived that the Vladimir Ribbon awarded her father and the honors and respect accorded her brother were but symbols of the much more fundamental achievement. They had done their duty.

Duty. For her father, a way of life rather than an objective, and the basic consideration around which life was organized. A nebulous web which encompassed all the relationships with those with whom he came into contact, and the first criterion to be applied to any situation. There had been hints that her brother had been frantically concerned about her welfare to the point of coming to her, but he had been ordered to his battalion by his father. And eventually she had arrived at the point of agreeing with her father, if it had in fact happened. Her brother's devotion to her warmed her heart. Her father's devotion to his duty had in large part made the victory at Smolensk possible.

Duty. For her father, it was the organizing principle in the chaos of life, and it was the genesis of morality, ethics, and the other essential characteristics which separated humanity from animals. For him, there was duty to Czar, State, and Church, and duty to those with whom one came into contact. When that was achieved, all else followed.

But the burden had been onerous for him. In his eyes, when one lacked the circumstances or other wherewithal to perform one's duty, the failure was one's own fault. He had alienated himself from the Czar, and being banned from the Czar's presence was his own fault. The commissions and assignments he could have been performing were failed duties, an infinite mountain of failures, because there was no way of knowing what they might have been. So years of effort had gone into soliciting help, advice, and influence so that he might be readmitted to the Czar's presence. And success had finally come.

The bass murmur of the grand duke's voice stopped, and her father's voice cracked with age and emotion as he spoke. Natalya stood with her eyes downcast, staring at the pattern on the gleaming parquet floor without seeing it. Her father stopped speaking. Then she heard Czar Aleksander's voice saying the words for which her father had strived so long.

"Ivan Nikolayevich, Count Sheremetev, our loyal and devoted subject, our brave servant of the Order of Vladimir, we do welcome you most gladly into our presence . . ."

The sob rose so suddenly that it almost escaped her, a choking lump in her throat as she held it back. Annya's large, warm, pudgy hand was suddenly on her elbow, squeezing it firmly, and she looked up at Annya through the tears standing in her eyes. The pale blue eyes were warm, kind, and understanding. Natalya nodded, pressing her lips together and looking back toward her father and the Czar. The Czar kissed and embraced her father. Her father moved to one side, and Vassily stepped forward. The grand duke's deep voice began again. The people moved slightly, and Natalya could see her father clearly. She looked at the tears on his cheeks and on the cheeks of one of his friends standing by him, and an almost unbearable surge of emotion surfaced within her.

She trembled as she struggled to control herself. Annya's large hand tightened and she moved closer to Natalya, standing against her and putting her other arm around her. Natalya looked up at her again. And something happened. The barriers of rank and birth and those which people always erect between themselves and others abruptly crumbled. A casual affinity and mutual liking discovered in a moment of conver-

249

sation abruptly blossomed into something much deeper, something deliciously warm and comforting. Annya smiled down at her, offering support and assistance. Natalya relaxed in the clasp of Annya's strong arm.

To Natalya it seemed that directions of history from the distant past had been brought to focus, that the climax of her father's years of unswerving dedication to one single purpose was only one of the last and most obvious undertakings of generations of ancestors whose efforts were climaxed by her being in this drawing room, with a small group of people in attendance upon the personage who represented all order and supreme authority in Russia. It seemed like a dream, but for the seething turmoil of emotions within her which were much too intense and real for any dream.

And for the supreme irony represented by another hollow rumble from Annya's belly, sublimely ridiculous and hilariously amusing to the extent that the surroundings were once again firmly perceived by the senses and it was a struggle to hold back the giggle which tried to slip through Natalya's clenched teeth. A Romanova, a woman of the family which ruled a gigantic empire encompassing much of the civilized world, and she was denied the satisfaction which was a right of any serf, that of sufficient food for the belly.

Her brother moved away from the Czar. The people in the room turned their heads and looked at her as they parted to make a path between her and the Czar. Her knees were suddenly weak, and she wanted to flee and hide in some dark corner. Annya's hands and arm tightened, urging her forward. Her gown and Annya's rustled softly in the quietness of the room. Annya walked with her until they were by the Grand Duke Nikolas, then she stepped back. The grand duke towered over her, looking down at her sternly, his Romanov features so much like Annya's but at the same time so different because of what she had found between Annya and herself only a moment before. He looked back at the Czar.

"Your Majesty, may I present Natalya Ivanova, daughter of Ivan Nikolayevich, the Count Shereme-tev . . ."

Her limbs seemed to respond of their own will without conscious effort on her part as she swept to the floor in a deep curtsey, bowing her head. The Czar's hand lifted hers in the signal to rise, and she looked at his face for the first time. He looked very weary. Not yet fifty, he looked much older. She had gloried in the details of his success in bringing Russia to the forefront among the nations of Europe during his reign, of changing the face which Russia displayed to the world from that of a great uncouth bear of a nation to the liberator who had crushed Napoleon and the center of a sophisticated, highly developed culture. But his labors had taken their toll. His diplomatic successes as the recognized and respected arbiter among European nations, his reputation for wisdom and judicious advice which had spread from the nations of Asia to the young and burgeoning United States, and his reforms in laws and government structure which had been achieved in spite of conflicting pressures of liberal and conservative elements, all had demanded their price from him.

Aged to the autumn of life while in the summer of his years, consumed by what he had undertaken and achieved, he had done his duty well, lifting Russia to a peak of achievement. His voice was quiet but penetrating, and his words registered vaguely in her mind, as though coming from a long distance away.

". . . Natalya Ivanova, and what would you have of us?"

There had also been an aside comment to her father about her beauty, perhaps sincerely meant or perhaps what he always said under such circumstances when the one before him wasn't so ugly that it would be construed as a subtle insult. He was looking down at her with a detached, polite smile, his blue eyes bored and impersonal. And he looked so very tired. He was obviously anxious to be done with it, to make his appearance at the reception in the ballroom, and then perhaps go to bed and rest.

The question was a courtesy somewhat out of the ordinary but not really unusual, because Olivia had known about it and had forewarned her that it might possibly happen. It was an offer of a bit of jewelry or perhaps even a flower that she could show to people and say that it had been given to her by the Czar, and the offer had been made possibly because he was pleased with her but probably in recognition of her father's long struggle for the moment. And it called for a courteous reply, to give what he would and what he had at hand.

But it wasn't what she wanted to say. The courteous reply froze in her throat, choking her. And the response in French was weak and insipid even as it formed in her mind. The mincing sibilants and honking nasals felt false and insincere even before she uttered them. She replied in Russian, in the hard, hammering consonants and blurred vowels of the peasants of Sherevskoye.

"If Your Majesty will grant me a favor, *batyushka,* I would have prayers said in St. Isaac's on your name-day for the Lord God to give you strength, health, and long life."

The honest and earthy gutterals sounded foreign in the room. His smile faded. There was absolute, ringing silence for two long seconds which felt like an eternity. Then he suddenly laughed, stepping forward and bending over her to put his arms around her. A stir ran through the people in the room, and they murmured in astonishment. If it had been *gauche,* in the tone and words that a serf might ask his master for permission to name a son after him, it had pleased the Czar. The chains, tassels, and starburst medals on his tunic pressed against her face, and the masculine odor of his uniform and body filled her nostrils as he embraced her. He bent lower, and his mustaches brushed her cheeks as he kissed her.

"By God, Sheremetev, we would our own battalion had the loyalty you've instilled in this nippet of yours."

"I did as I could, Your Majesty, but I cannot accept full credit. She has a mind of her own."

"Then she pleases us the more." The fatigue had left his face, and the dull, impersonal detachment in his eyes had been replaced with a twinkle as he released her and stepped back. He looked down at his tunic and took one of the gold buttons in his hand, jerking at it. "We shall grant your favor, Natalya Ivanova, as well as this." The button popped loose and dangled from the gold chain which hung between it and a button on the other side of his tunic, and he pulled at the other button. The threads snapped, and he smiled down at her as he took her wrist, wrapped the chain around it, and tied a loose knot in the links. "There. Tell those who ask that this is a token of esteem from us for your beauty and loyalty, both of which are of rare quality." He bent and kissed her again, and glanced at Annya as he straightened up. "Keep her company, Annya Konstantinovna."

"I shall and gladly, Your Majesty."

He moved around her and was gone, walking rapidly toward the door to the ballroom, with Grand Duke Nikolas walking beside him and the others sorting themselves out to follow. A lot of them glanced at her with expressions of cordial congratulation. Her father and brother smiled proudly. Annya stepped closer, resting her hand on Natalya's shoulder. Natalya beamed up at her and looked down at the buttons dangling at the ends of the chain, studying the imperial insignia. She drew in a deep, shuddering breath and released it in a gusty sigh.

"It's beautiful, isn't it? I shall treasure it forever!"

"By God, His Majesty has done that for no one else. He has as much thought about the appearance of his uniform as his excellency my father, whose concern surpasses belief. And His Majesty did nothing like that for me. He bade Czarina Elisabeth to have a mind to what I was *eating,* is what His Majesty did for me! Here, let us find a thread in this tapestry to hold your chain safely on your wrist, then we will join the entourage. What did you have for supper? I had a piece of fish and a cup of gruel, pitiful fare that it was. But tasty for all of that . . ."

Annya jerked at the edge of a costly tapestry hanging on the wall with her long, sturdy fingers, fraying it and separating a thread, and she broke off a piece of the thread and looped it through two of the links in the chain, tying it firmly to Natalya's wrist. Natalya looked at the chain, fascinated with it, and Annya linked her arm through Natalya's and led her toward the door.

The ripple of activity and attention in the crowd focused around the Czar as he made his way through the people, and Annya and Natalya caught up with the end of the entourage and moved along through the backwater, Annya greeting those she knew and introducing Natalya. She seemed less a woman of around Natalya's age and more a member of the House of Romanov in the presence of others, but she continued to address Natalya familiarly and to walk with her

254

arm linked through hers. It was a scintillating crowd, and there were numerous young officers from various regiments and several civilians in their twenties and thirties. Aleksei had attempted to get an invitation to the function through his father and had been downcast the evening before over his failure to secure one, and he had made a few comments in a wry tone about Natalya's lack of protection. But he had also been resigned, because flirtation was expected to the extent that even young and attractive married women were supposed to respond to compliments paid to their beauty.

Annya knew few of the young officers and civilians, but they boldly crowded around and introduced themselves. As always, it produced a glow of satisfaction in her, but there was a sour note. Few of them were more than courteous to Annya. It was her somewhat dowdy look in the pale blue gown rather than her untouchable station, because any young woman was fair game for flirtation. It was clear that she suffered in comparison with Natalya. She appeared to be resigned, as though she were accustomed to it, and Natalya felt a surge of compassion for her. She had held out her hand when Natalya needed support, and it seemed to hint of deserting her in her moment of need to flirt with the young men who barely noticed her.

There were other reasons. Friendship with Annya was a relationship her father would encourage her to cultivate. Beyond that, and in addition to the multitude of considerations associated with befriending a member of the imperial family, there was something between them that Natalya had never before known, a friendship which had burst to full life with a precious, mutual spontaneity. She wanted to protect it. And she instinctively felt that it would be fragile un-

255

til deeper knowledge and understanding of each other gave it maturity, possibly wilting if touched by a fiery draught of jealousy. Natalya began discouraging the young men, making her smile bored instead of lively and responding absently, subtly turning them away.

Thomas was there, tall and splendid in his uniform of the Semenovskys but as dull as before, with his solemn, withdrawn expression. He was with a Countess Xenia Artamonovna Chernysheva, of whom Natalya had read in the news sheets. She was a very attractive widow in her late thirties, and one of the social lionesses of St. Petersburg. They were a handsome couple, Thomas's dark good looks complementing her blonde, voluptuous beauty, and his remote aloofness balancing her brassy ostentation. And they seemed to match each other at some deeper level which communicated a subtle hint of decadence. Xenia looked jaded and bored, her palate dulled by the taste of too much wine dulled the excitement of lovers spoiled by familiarity.

"You've met before, Thomas Stephanovich? This child?"

It was said with a weary, disinterested smile and a note of sarcasm as her eyes cut acidly up and down Natalya then moved away in search of a more interesting object on which to rest. Natalya automatically clamped a firm control on her temper. The immediate object at hand was to convince her she wasn't dealing with a child and that her advantage lay in sheathing her claws. "We went riding with mutual friends," Natalya replied, cutting Thomas off as he started to mutter a reply. "Do you like horses, Xenia Artamonovna?"

"I can't stand the smell of them," she drawled, letting her eyes flick back to Natalya and move away again.

The question had been carefully phrased and predicated on some negative and disparaging comment, and the bait had been taken. It would hark more of the ribaldry of the serfs' hall than the delicately cutting innuendo of drawing rooms, and it would be more effective because of that. "Well, I was merely referring to riding them, of course," Natalya said in a dry tone. She hesitated to let it sink in, then went on. "My woman tells me that a touch of oil or cream keeps blanc powder more firm by providing a foundation. Do you recommend it?"

Thomas's eyes opened wide for once, and he looked away with his lips twitching slightly. Annya looked blank, then startled, and then giggled heartily. Xenia looked back at Natalya, her eyes narrow and hard. The *jeu de mots* about the horses had bitten deeply. And she used powder heavily to conceal wrinkles and pouches which the unkind march of time had formed on her delicate throat and face, some of which had cracked and dribbled down onto the ample bosom which swelled over the low bodice of her gown. A long second passed as her sharp eyes glared at Natalya in raw hatred, expressing the envy of the exhausted runner for one whose race has barely begun and the jealousy of the timid veteran for the bold recruit. Open warfare hung in the balance for that second, then she blinked, her eyes were hooded, and a polite smile curved her lips.

"You have ample time to experiment before you will need to use powder, Natalya Ivanova. Such lovely hair . . . you might have white bows at the sides to go with your gown, but it is a small matter . . ."

It was a cautious peace offering, and Natalya smiled and nodded in acceptance of it as she made her own. "It is something to consider. The sequins in your hair are lovely. How do you keep them in?"

"With paste, and at the cost of enduring great discomfort when they are removed. What sort of bangle is that?"

"She had it from His Majesty the Czar," Annya said. "His Majesty was so pleased with her that he tore it from his uniform and put it on her arm."

Thomas leaned closer, looking. "I observed that his uniform lacks a chain and set of buttons, which is unusual."

Xenia moved closer and held Natalya's forearm, looking at the chain and buttons. Her fingernails were long and carefully shaped, and her hands were soft and smooth from creams and oils. The tips of her fingers moved on Natalya's forearm, almost as though she were caressing it. Her eyes looked larger because of the dark cosmetics on her eyelids, and her lips were crimson with rouge. A heady, sultry odor of a powerful cologne hung around her, and Natalya could smell the spicy herbs she had put in her mouth to make her breath sweet. Her eyes moved from the chain to Natalya's eyes, and she released Natalya's forearm and put her hand on the girl's shoulder, standing very close to her.

"I am having a small party at my house tomorrow. Just a few friends, and an escort will not be required. Or you may bring one if you wish. Do you have a friend?"

Her father's permission was required to go anywhere, but it would make her appear foolish to say it, and confirm Xenia's original comment that she was a child. The expression in Xenia's eyes was guardedly cordial, and a refusal would be considered a rebuff. An invitation from her was a distinction rendered to few. "Yes, Aleksei Andreyevich."

Xenia's eyes widened slightly. "Orlov?"

"Yes."

Xenia chuckled softly. "I wondered where he . . . well, bring him if he can come, or—"

"The Yamburgskys are on parade tomorrow," Thomas said quietly. "Perhaps Vassily Ivanovich could speak to him at the garrison if he is returning there this evening, and he could arrange to be free."

Natalya shook her head. "I would not have him neglect his duties."

Xenia's smile started to become jeering as she opened her mouth to say something, then she changed her mind and her smile became polite again as she nodded. "You can come alone, then. If you are unengaged tomorrow, that is."

Natalya decided to face her father's displeasure, if necessary, and she nodded, smiling. "I am, and you are very kind to invite me."

Xenia's smile widened, her hand moving along Natalya's shoulder and her fingers touching Natalya's bare shoulder and throat familiarly. "It is very kind of you to accept. At noon tomorrow, then. Do you know where I live?"

It was time for a gesture to seal the peace, at least for the moment, and Natalya nodded again. "Who in St. Petersburg does not?"

Xenia's smile became brilliant, and she bent over to kiss Natalya lightly on the cheek then dropped her hand from Natalya's shoulder and moved away. "Tomorrow, then, Natalya Ivanova." She nodded at Annya. "Annya Konstantinovna . . ."

Annya and Natalya bobbed in perfunctory curtsies, and Thomas bowed to them and turned away with Xenia as she put her arm through his. They moved away, and Annya turned to Natalya, lifting her eyebrows. "She seems to like you, Natalya Ivanova, though I cannot see why . . . God! Where did you hear that about horses? I thought I would laugh aloud!"

"As I said, I spent much of my time with the serfs as a child."

"Perhaps I should have. Let's walk over this way."

The Czar's movement through the crowd had been much more rapid than theirs as he exchanged greetings and asked a question or made a comment here and there, and he and his entourage, which had been supplemented by several hangers-on from the crowd, were on the other side of the room. Annya took Natalya's arm and they moved through the people in the other direction, toward the opposite side of the room. They were stopped a couple of times when people spoke to Annya and she stopped to introduce Natalya and exchange pleasantries, and they worked their way to the edge of the crowd at the side of the room. Annya glanced around, then pulled at Natalya's arm and stepped through the archway opening into the covered walkway at the side of the room. Natalya followed her, looking at her with a puzzled expression.

The walkway was indirectly illuminated by the light from the ballroom coming through the archway openings, and was relatively darker. There was no one else along it, and Annya glanced in both directions as she trotted to a niche in the wall which was occupied by a marble bust. She stood on tiptoe and reached behind the bust, the tip of her tongue in the corner of her mouth as she strained and grunted with effort, then smiled widely as she took a fold of linen from behind the bust and glanced surreptitiously around again, unfolding it. It was a serviette, and it contained two pastries. She licked her lips and swallowed hungrily, gathering one of them in her hand, then she hesitated and offered them to Natalya.

"Will you have one?"

Most of the tension which had kept her from eating during the day had faded and she was hungry, but it was obvious that Annya wanted both of them. "Thank you, no."

Annya nodded, hastily gathering one of the pastries in her hand, and she pushed a large portion of it into her mouth and bit down on it. "Ummm . . ."

Natalya swallowed, looking away. It was a spiced apple pastry, and the smell of it and Annya's hearty enjoyment as she chewed noisily made her even more hungry. "How did they get there?"

"A cook house helper," Annya replied in a muffled voice as she pushed more of the pastry into her mouth. "I have to pay out a fair amount of my pocket allowance just to keep from starving to death . . . these cost me two rubles each . . . they know they'll get the knout if they're caught, and it costs a lot . . ."

"Two rubles *each?* Can't you go out and buy from a shop? You could get them for ten kopecks apiece."

Annya shook her head, chewing rapidly, tried to swallow and almost choked, then cleared her throat, swallowed, and took another bite. "I have duties and someone with me all of the time . . . attendants, my tutors, visitors . . ."

"What sort of visitors do you have?"

"All sorts. Social, do you mean? General Vorontsov has three daughters, and they come on Wednesdays to visit with me, Count Bakhmetev's two daughters come on Saturday, and . . ." Her voice faded as she took another large bite. "There are others."

"Friends, then."

Annya belched, shoved the rest of the apple pastry into her mouth, and shook her head as she chewed. "We play cards and quoits, and we talk about different things, but . . ." She shrugged and shook her head again. "They aren't like you. If they found out that I had something to eat, they would tell someone. But I knew you wouldn't when I first saw you. You're

261

different. They're more like children than you, even though some are older. You're still very young in some ways, but in others you are an adult. You look one in the eyes, you don't smile unless you wish to, you don't say things because you think I would like to hear them . . . except when you said I was attractive, perhaps. Or do you really think I am?"

It took a heavy infusion of love to find attractiveness in the heavy, buxom, and tall young woman in her tight gown and with her protuberant blue eyes. The blocky Romanov face was inspiring on Falconnet's equestrian statue of Peter the Great overlooking the Neva, but less than comely on a woman. But there was an agonizing pathos about her as she stood with crumbs of the pastry on her lips and beads of sweat on her temples, looking down at Natalya, chewing, and waiting for a reply. The blue eyes which in Czar Aleksander oversaw a nation begged for reassurance in Annya. In a way she was so much a Romanova, and in another way she was so pitiful. And pity was a form of love, if nothing else. Natalya stood on tiptoe, pulling at Annya's shoulder, and kissed her cheek. "Annya Konstantinovna, you are an attractive woman. You are also a personable woman, which is much more rare and precious."

Annya grunted, belched, and sucked her teeth, an unsmiling but extremely gratified expression on her face, and she lifted the second pastry on the serviette. "Take a bite and eat with me."

It was an offer to eat food from which she had taken a bite, and Natalya considered the offer sufficient. She smiled and shook her head. "Thank you, but I am not—"

"Eat!"

Natalya nodded, opening her mouth to take a nibble, and Annya pushed the corner of the pastry into her mouth. She bit it off, and Annya grunted with satisfaction as she took a large bite from the pastry.

"I will ask the Czarina if you may call on me, if you wish."

"Of course I do. And if you could visit me, I would have a tasty lunch prepared."

"Her majesty wouldn't let me do that, and for that precise reason. And other things. I have to spend a lot of time learning things which they say I must know in order to perform tasks and commissions. But I will ask. If you are permitted to call on me, please bring me a box of sweetmeats and I will give you the money for them."

Natalya chuckled and shook her head, swallowing the bite of pastry. "That won't be necessary. I owe you much, Anna Konstantinovna."

Annya stopped chewing and looked down at the floor, and she sighed heavily and began chewing again, her eyes looking slightly dewy. She blinked and shook her head. "If you will be my friend, you will never owe me anything, Natalya Ivanova."

"I will that, and gladly. And I'll have another bite of the pastry."

Annya beamed down at her, lifting the pastry on the serviette, and Natalya took a judicious bite, enough to demonstrate she had no qualms about eating after Annya but not enough to deprive Annya of a significant portion of the pastry. She chewed, smiling up at Annya, and Annya smiled down into her eyes, taking another large bite and chewing rapidly. "We must hurry. It is a serious breach of etiquette to absent oneself from the Czar's entourage overly long when one is in waiting upon him, as I am this evening."

"Does court ceremony and etiquette require much of your attention? I suppose it does . . ."

"Most of it," Annya grunted. "When I am not doing it, I am learning about it."

"And are you subject to the authority of the Grand Dutchess Aleksandra Fedorovna as well as Her Majesty the Czarina?"

Annya sighed heavily, cramming the last of the pastry into her mouth. "I am supposed to be subject only to the authority of the Czar. But he deals with me through the Czarina. And when she is not present, then I receive instructions from the dowager Czarina or one of the Grand Duchesses. At times it seems I am subject to the authority of even the footmen in the royal household, because they all watch me. You are fortunate to have the liberty you do, Natalya Ivanova."

"I have constraints upon me, but they seem to be far fewer than yours."

Annya swallowed, touched her mouth with the serviette, and wadded it and tossed it behind the bust. "Pity you, if they are not. Come, let us rejoin the entourage. I hope I haven't been missed, even though the Czar remarked that he could pick me out from one end of Nevsky Prospekt to the other without his spectacles . . ."

The Czar had apparently stood in one place for several minutes to talk with someone, and the end of the room where he was speaking with people was jammed. People were scattered in loose groups around the rest of the ballroom, and they seemed less animated than they had been before, perhaps having failed to achieve some ecstasy of satisfaction they had anticipated from being in the august presence. Natalya and Annya worked their way through the people to the near vicinity of the Czar. Annya smothering belches and introducing Natalya to a few more people, and on the edge of her vision Natalya saw the Grand Dutchess

264

Aleksandra looking at them. Natalya's father and brother were nearby, talking and laughing with several men in uniform, and others moved about, greeting Annya and being introduced to Natalya. Women gasped and men nodded wisely over the chain on her wrist, and there was polite conversation on light subjects. A stodgy, portly man in his fifties started telling Natalya about the history of St. Petersburg, and he looked insulted when she corrected him on some of his dates.

The music from the orchestra had been droning in a pleasant unobtrusive background all the time, and it suddenly swelled and took on a purposeful lilting melody. There was a shuffling movement in the crowd as people sought partners. Most were middle aged married couples, and the young men dashed about in search of unattached women as husbands and wives looked for each other in the crowd. Natalya caught Vassily's eye and looked at him imperatively, darting her eyes toward Annya. He walked over to them with long strides.

"Annya Konstantinovna, would you give me the pleasure of dancing with me?"

"I will, and thank you, Vassily Ivanovich. Let us see who Natalya Ivanova will dance with . . ."

There was a crowd of men closing in around her, several of them speaking loudly to attract her attention, but Thomas was suddenly in front of her and towering over her like a mountain. He silently bowed, took her hand, and put it on his arm. It was far too presumptuous and she had no desire to dance with a partner who had such a funereal air about him, and she stiffened with irritation as she started to draw her hand back. But Annya looked and smiled, commenting cheerfully.

"Where did you come from so suddenly, Thomas

265

Stephanovich? But they make a handsome couple, do they not, Vassily Ivanovich? Let us all stay close together . . ."

Thomas and Vassily were acquainted and they exchanged a cordial nod, and the other men who had swooped down were moving away. The situation was suddenly one in which it would be awkward to make an objection, and Natalya swallowed her resentment and looked up at Thomas with a steely expression. He was looking down at her with an expression not unlike hers, making her wonder why he had bothered.

The orchestra was beginning the *danse polonaise*, and the Czar had taken his position near the center of the floor with the wife of some functionary requiring a mark of special favor, a puffing, bewigged matron of fifty or so who seemed to be comprised principally of a massive bosom and an equally massive bottom, both straining the fabric of her gown. Grand Duke Nikolas was standing near him with Grand Duchess Aleksandra at his side, with the purposeful air of preparing to order an onslaught against enemy ranks. Other couples were moving toward them in a surging shuffle, and those without partners were retiring to the sides of the ballroom. The orchestra leader stepped down from the orchestra dais to assume the function of dance master. He crossed the ballroom floor to the Czar, bowed deeply to him and to the Grand Duke and Grand Duchess, then began forming the traditional court choral procession, bowing the Grand Duke and Grand Duchess into place behind the Czar and waving other couples into position.

Order began to form in the mass of people on the floor, a long line of couples facing each other arranged in a semicircle which covered one end of the ballroom floor. The orchestra leader scurried back and forth, waving his hand and motioning with his baton as he arranged the couples with equal intervals between them, and the orchestra played the opening bars. The orchestra leader had put Natalya and Thomas some fifteen or sixteen couples away from the Czar and Annya and Vassily were on Natalya's left. Natalya hoped that Annya could dance better than her appearance indicated. An indifferent dancer on the side toward the leader made it difficult to follow the steps. Then Annya turned and looked down at her, smiling warmly, and she felt guilty for what she had been thinking.

The orchestra leader bowed to the Czar again from the center of the semicircle of people, and the Czar nodded. The orchestra meshed the announcement smoothly into the opening bars of the dance, and the line of dancers was suddenly in motion. Thomas tightened his hands on Natalya's to signal his first step, and Annya in front of her was surprisingly light and graceful on her feet. Thomas took Natalya's wrist between thumb and forefinger as he lifted her arm, twirling her effortlessly. His eyes were very penetrating as she glanced up at him. He seemed to be looking her up and down, devouring her with his eyes. She looked away, feeling faintly uncomfortable. He was a superb dancing partner, but vaguely disturbing for some reason.

The Czar signalled the approaching end of the dance by moving back along the female partners every five sets of steps and leaving the Grand Duke in front to lead the dance. When he reached Annya, Natalya was pleased to note that he seemed cordial enough, murmuring a polite comment to her as he took her hands. Then he moved on, Thomas moving forward to dance with Annya, and Natalya put her hands in the Czar's and began taking her steps with concentrated precision, conscious of his eyes on her. She noticed the gap in the buttons and chains on his tunic where he had pulled off the set and given it to her. She darted a glance at him. He was looking down at her with a warm smile. She grinned widely, feeling herself flushing.

The orchestra leader watched closely, and the music ended just as the Czar finished the set of steps with the last woman in the line. Applause broke out around the side of the ballroom, and the dancers applauded the orchestra.

Servants had been moving trestle tables into position at the front end of the ballroom and covering them with linen cloths during the final measures of the dance, and they began carrying in salvers of delicacies and tubs of iced champagne. The applause died away, and Annya turned toward Natalya as Thomas stepped over to her and bowed slightly.

"Thank you for the pleasure of dancing with you, Natalya Ivanova."

"Thank you for asking me, Thomas Stephanovich. And the next time, you might speak somewhat louder so I can hear you better."

The corners of his lips lifted in a shadow of a sardonic smile. "I never ask for what I want when there is a possibility of being refused, Natalya Ivanova. Thank you again."

He abruptly turned and walked away. Annya moved closer, taking her arm and sighing heavily. "All that food . . . I can smell it from here!"

"Are you going to eat?"

"How can I? Don't you see the Grand Duchess Aleksandra Fedorovna over there watching me? And a dozen others, doubtless, to make sure I am starved down to my bones. Oh, she's beckoning me. I suppose she wants me closer so she can be sure I don't put any of it into my pocket. If you wish, you could get yourself something and then come and stand with me until the Czar is ready to retire."

The pangs of hunger in Natalya's stomach were so intense she felt weak, but it would be cruel to eat when Annya couldn't. She smiled and shook her head. "I'm not hungry. Come, I'll walk over with you and we can talk."

Annya sighed heavily and shook her head as they began walking toward the Grand Duchess. "It's little wonder that you're so small and slim," she grumbled. "You apparently don't eat."

Natalya smiled again, looking longingly at the trays of food the servants were still carrying in and swallowing hungrily, then she averted her eyes from the food.

There was little conversation between them, because Annya stared hungrily at the tables and licked her lips most of the time. The Czar ate lightly and drank a glass of champagne, and the crowd around him parted and began breaking up as he moved away from the table. The Grand Duke and Grand Duchess moved toward him, as did others in the entourage who had been in the drawing room. Annya sighed and stirred.

"I must go, Natalya Ivanova. I have an audience with the Czarina Elisabeth tomorrow, and I will ask her then if you may visit."

Natalya started to nod, then a thought suddenly occurred to her, causing a sinking feeling in the pit of her stomach. "What if her majesty refuses me permission?"

It appeared that Annya hadn't seriously considered that possibility, and she looked suddenly drawn and grey. Then she shook her head. "There is no reason why Her Majesty should refuse. But rather, there is reason why she should agree, considering the favor you found with the Czar. We shall see. I will send you a message."

269

Natalya nodded, moving closer to her and reaching for her hands. Annya's large, warm hands closed over Natalya's, and she bent over and kissed Natalya's cheek. Natalya pressed her lips to Annya's smooth, rounded cheek, squeezing her hands. The Czar and the others moved toward the side of the room, and the Grand Duchess looked at Annya with an impatient expression. Annya's hands clung to Natalya's for an instant as she moved away, then their hands parted and Annya hurried to catch up with the entourage. A space opened for her behind the Grand Duke and Grand Duchess. The Czar approached one of the openings to the walkway at the side of the ballroom, and the people in the ballroom began bowing and curtsying. Natalya gathered her skirt and curtsied, watching Annya from under her eyebrows as she lowered her head. Annya looked over her shoulder at Natalya as she went through the archway opening.

The place seemed suddenly cold, hostile, and lonely with Annya gone. Natalya turned and walked toward the tables, where her father and brother were standing and talking as they ate and drank. Her appetite had deserted her again, leaving a lightheaded weakness and a sour, empty feeling in her stomach.

The count looked at her with a smile as she approached them. "I see you and the Countess Annya Konstantinovna seem to have formed an attachment," he said in a gratified tone.

Natalya nodded, glancing disinterestedly over the delicacies. "She has an audience with Her Majesty the Czarina Elisabeth tomorrow, and she is going to ask Her Majesty if I may visit her."

"Indeed? I am very pleased, Natasha."

She nodded again, picking up a round of bread and spreading fresh caviar onto it. The smell of the caviar stirred twinges of hunger again, and the first bite

270

brought back her appetite in full force. She took a larger bite.

Vassily stepped to one side, reaching for a bottle of champagne, and filled a glass. "Here, Natasha. You look tired."

She smiled her thanks, taking the glass and sipping it, and she took another bite of the caviar and bread. "And I have an invitation from Xenia Artamonovna, the Countess Chernysheva, to go to a party at her house tomorrow."

"The Countess Chernysheva?" Vassily said, frowning. He glanced around, leaned closer to her, and spoke quietly. "Natasha, that woman's house is a veritable bordello."

Natalya stopped chewing and glared up at him. "Is it now?" she snapped sarcastically. "Are you sure, or might you have it confused with another of your habitats?"

"Who will escort you?" asked Vassily.

"Aleksei Andreyevich is on parade tomorrow, so I—"

"I will speak with him when I return to the garrison," Vassily said. "It could be that he can—"

"No," Natalya interrupted in a firm tone. "I will not have him neglect his duties."

The count grunted affirmatively and nodded. "He should not." He sipped his champagne and sucked his teeth reflectively, frowning, and his frown faded as a thought suddenly occurred to him. "Olivia Vassilievna can accompany you."

Natalya nodded agreement, drained her glass and handed it to Vassily to refill, looking up at him with an arch smile. He frowned, then shrugged in resignation as he took the glass and reached for the bottle.

CHAPTER XIII

Olivia had heard a lot about Xenia through the references to her social affairs in the news sheets and through the considerably less restrained gossip in the city about her, and she had even more reservations than Vassily. She was up and waiting in Natalya's sitting room when Natalya returned home, eager to hear about the reception, and they talked until the early hours of the morning. She was thrilled over the chain the Czar had given Natalya and almost ecstatic about the affinity which Natalya and Annya had found for each other, but darkly doubtful about the wisdom of Natalya's attending a social affair at Xenia's house so early in her introduction into the St. Petersburg social life at large.

But she was also pragmatic. An invitation had been tendered and accepted, and the center of Xenia's clique was a fashionable element in the social life of the city, the edges of which extended into the most elite of social circles. There were both potential advantages and disadvantages in the situation, and Olivia's concern was that Natalya make any valuable social contacts she could at the party while avoiding the pitfall of allowing herself to be drawn into exclusive association with Xenia's circle. And Olivia clearly wasn't displeased that she was going to accompany Natalya to the party.

The following morning started in a rush. Natalya's maids awakened her with a glass of hot tea after a few hours of sleep, sent by Olivia to get her up, and a few minutes later Olivia came in to help her pick out a gown. Natalya was disgruntled by the abrupt awakening, the lack of sufficient sleep, and a nagging headache, but Olivia was irrepressible, pulling Natalya out of the chair into which she had collapsed and taking her into the bedchamber to look through her clothes.

There was barely time to make a cursory round through the house, talking to the housekeeper, house steward, and head cook, and making arrangements for her father's lunch, when it was time to get ready. The gown which had caught Olivia's eye was a fairly old one, a cream chiffon with a high waistline and a demurely high neckline, with pink silk ribbons laced through insertion in the bodice and coming together in a large bow in the back to draw the bodice tight. It seemed much too youthful to Natalya, but ideal to Olivia because of its very youthfulness, and Natalya didn't feel like arguing about it. Olivia went to her rooms to get ready, and Natalya sat down in a chair and let the maids comb out her hair and begin putting it up, tying it with pink ribbons to match those in the gown.

It had rained during early morning and the air was fresh and damp. The carriages moving briskly back and forth along the thoroughfares splashed through the puddles of water standing on the stone pavement. Olivia looked neat and chic in an emerald green dress and bonnet, and she kept up a running barrage of speculation on situations which might arise and suggestions on how to deal with them as the carriage rumbled along the street. Natalya listened and nodded absently, looking at the people, buildings, and other carriages.

Xenia lived in the Novodevichei District, a new and highly fashionable area east of the central part of the city, and the thoroughfare into it led from Nevsky Prospekt and along the embankment of the Neva. The river curved away from the straight, wide thoroughfare for a short distance and was hidden by tall stands of pine and larch, then came back into view, as wide as an arm of the sea. A filmy shroud of mist still hung over it from the rain, moving slowly along in fleecy sheets and billowing folds as a breeze blew along the river, bringing a salty, tangy scent of the open sea. On the opposite shore, the thin, golden spire of the Cathedral of SS Peter and Paul was visible through the mist, overlooking the black, sinister bulk of the SS Peter and Paul fortress. Further along the shore, the arms of the river broke the shoreline into numerous islands which were occupied by the botanical gardens, open air theaters, parks, villas, yachting clubs, and other entertainment areas of the city.

The edge of the street along the wall in front of Xenia's house was lined with barouches, phaetons, cabriolets, and carriages which made the Sheremetev carriage look somewhat lumbering and workaday, but Natalya glanced at them and was contented in her assessment that few of them would be able to traverse the rough road between Moscow and St. Petersburg and arrive in one piece. Other vehicles and men on horseback were arriving at the same time, and the drive between the carriage gate and stables was congested with other vehicles and tethered horses. The driver found an open spot on the edge of the street, and Natalya and Olivia dismounted. Other people were filing through the foot gate as they went in, including a portly count and his wife to whom Natalya had been introduced the evening before by Annya. They greeted Natalya, she introduced Olivia, and they introduced Natalya and Olivia to others around them as they went along the walk toward the house.

The sounds of laughter and conversation and the lively, lilting strains of waltz music came through the open front doors of the large, imposing house at the end of the walk. The sound of music and gaiety stirred a spark of excitement in Natalya as she lifted her skirt and petticoats to go up the steps and cross the portico with the others. Noise and activity surrounded her as she entered. There seemed to be a couple of parties going on at once, a small orchestra playing and people dancing in the ballroom off the right of the entry hall, and something else going on in the drawing rooms off the left of the entry hall. Xenia was at the edge of the dais above the entry hall inside the door, greeting the guests. She looked somewhat brittle and sagging in the daylight, as though she'd had little sleep the night before and perhaps many other nights, and Natalya observed for the first time that her upper arms looked flabby. But the polite smile she gave the other guests as she greeted them warmed appreciably as she moved toward Natalya.

"Natalya Ivanova," she murmured, putting her arms around Natalya and bending to kiss her on both cheeks. "It is such a pleasure to see you again, even though it makes me feel ancient to look at you . . ."

"Ancient? You are angelic, Xenia Artamonovna. May I present my friend? This is Olivia Vassilievna, of the family Hamilton. Olivia Vassilievna, this is Xenia Artamonovna, the Countess Chernysheva."

More guests were coming through the doorway, and they crowded around to catch Xenia's attention as she and Olivia greeted each other cordially, but Xenia ig-

nored them as she turned back to Natalya, putting
her hand on Natalya's shoulder and lifting her forearm to look at the chain around her wrist. "You are
wearing your gift from the Czar, I see. As indeed you
should." She smiled into Natalya's eyes again, then
glanced around, still holding her. "Petr Kirillovich, it
is good to see you again. Have you met Natalya Ivanova? She is the daughter of the Count Sheremetev.
Natalya Ivanova, this is Petr Kirillovich, of the family
Rumyanstev. See the chain Natalya Ivanova has on
her wrist? His Majesty the Czar pulled it from his uniform and gave it to her as a present when he received
her at court last evening. Annya Borisonova, it was
good of you to come. Natalya Ivanova, this is Annya
Borisonova, the Countess Protasov . . ."

People milled around as Xenia introduced Natalya,
and they looked at the chain and at Natalya with interest, exchanging pleasantries with her. Xenia's attention toward Natalya was an indication of special favor
and it was lost on no one. It was a little puzzling to
Natalya, and Olivia looked as though she didn't know
whether to be pleased or wary. The group of guests
who had come in with and behind Natalya and Olivia
were introduced and went in, scattering between the
ballroom and the drawing rooms, and Xenia chatted
with Olivia and Natalya for a few minutes as another
group straggled along the walk. She greeted them and
introduced them to Natalya, and they clustered around
and exchanged pleasantries for a few minutes, then
moved away toward the ballroom and drawing rooms.

Xenia chatted with Natalya and Olivia again for a
moment, then looked out at the walk. "It might be
a time before anyone else comes, Natalya Ivanova, and
you know enough of the guests to be able to flirt and
gossip now, don't you?"

"I do," Natalya replied, smiling in response to the

note of humor in Xenia's voice. "And I am very grateful for your kindness, Xenia Artamonovna."

"I am grateful for your presence. There are refreshments in this drawing room, and Shishkov is in that one giving readings of his poetry. And dancing in there, of course. I will join you when the last of the guests arrive, so enjoy yourselves."

"Thank you, Xenia Artamonovna, we shall."

Xenia smiled and nodded to Olivia, bent down and kissed Natalya's cheek again, then turned away toward the door. Several men crossing the entry hall between the drawing rooms and ballroom immediately rushed toward them, surrounding them and asking them to dance, and they smiled and declined, moving toward the drawing rooms.

Olivia leaned down toward Natalya as the men moved out of earshot. "It appears that Xenia Artamonovna is a somewhat better friend than you told me, Natalya Ivanova."

"It appears that she is a better friend than I knew," Natalya replied dryly. "I had no idea that she would be so kindly disposed to me."

"Particularly after what you said to her. I was shocked by that, Natalya Ivanova. You must learn more subtle repartee."

Natalya smiled, glancing around the entry hall as they walked slowly toward the drawing room doorways. Most of the people at the party were young, with a few older ones moving through the crowd, and there weren't as many uniforms as Natalya was accustomed to seeing at parties in Moscow. But there were a few, and there was suddenly a very familiar one as Thomas came out of one of the drawing rooms. He walked toward them with his long, determined stride, his face in stolidly neutral lines, and he stopped in front of them and bowed.

"Natalya Ivanova, it is a pleasure to see you again. And you, Olivia."

Natalya still felt resentful toward him for the way he had insinuated himself as her dance partner the evening before, and his stern face and dark, probing eyes were still vaguely bothersome. And the way he kept turning up everywhere was becoming disconcerting. She looked up at him in silence, her lips pursed, and nodded her head in a frigid greeting.

Olivia glanced at Natalya as she remained silent, then she looked up at Thomas with a polite smile. "It's good to see you again, Thomas. Are things well with you?"

"Very well. And you?"

"Quite well, thank you." She glanced at Natalya and looked back at him again. "I understand you were at the reception last evening."

"Yes, I was fortunate enough to be invited. And I was even more fortunate in being able to dance with Natalya Ivanova. As I anticipated, she is a most accomplished dancer."

Natalya had told Olivia what had happened, and Olivia nodded uncertainly, glancing at Natalya once more to see her reaction. Natalya sniffed and tossed her head, looking away. Olivia had hinted a few times that Thomas had asked questions about her which could be interpreted as interest, which was ludicrous if true. His compliments were rare, and they always sounded as ponderous and somber as he looked. "Are the Semenovskys still on active duty, or have they by chance been inactivated? Indeed, you seem to have no duties at all beyond attending social functions, Thomas Stephanovich."

He shrugged and the corners of his lips twitched slightly. "I was able to exchange my duty today with

278

another officer who was scheduled for duty tomorrow night."

"Then you will be on duty tomorrow and tomorrow night?"

"I will, yes."

Natalya chuckled lightly. "Xenia Artamonovna's companionship must be an attraction of considerable magnitude for you."

"I wished to attend her party today," he replied gravely, then nodded toward the drawing rooms and glanced between them. "I have been listening to the poet Shishkov, but I must confess a lack of full appreciation of poetry. I'm sure it would have more meaning for you. Or perhaps you would like some refreshments?"

Olivia looked at Natalya, lifting her eyebrows. "Would you care for some refreshments, Natalya Ivanova?"

Natalya had no desire for him to attach himself to them, but Olivia appeared to enjoy his company. It was undoubtedly because they were both English, because there could be no other reason. "If you would, Olivia Vassilievna," she said politely.

Thomas bowed slightly and moved to one side, and they walked toward the drawing room at the end of the entry hall. The furniture had been removed from the drawing room, and trestle tables covered with trays of delicacies and tubs of iced beverages were ranged around three walls, with servants passing in and out of a door on the opposite end of the room and replenishing the food and drink. There were a couple dozen people standing around in groups in the room, laughing and talking as they ate and drank, and Thomas guided Natalya and Olivia through the crush to the relative quietness of a corner.

There was a wide selection of food, and ice champagne, kvass, and several kinds of wine and vodka. Thomas poured champagne for himself and Olivia and kvass for Natalya, and they took serviettes and selected among the trays of food. The conversation and laughter of the others was loud and festive, providing the appropriate background for a feeling of enjoyable excitement, but Natalya felt remotely depressed by Thomas's presence. She thought again about Olivia's delicate hints that Thomas had indicated a degree of interest in the Sheremetevs in general and her in particular. Normally that would be the cause for satisfaction. While Aleksei was first in her thoughts and always would be, interest from others was flattering. Thomas wasn't totally unhandsome in a dark sort of way, and he was a Semenovsky. But his glowering, penetrating looks were unnerving.

Natalya found a tray of brioches stuffed with sliced capon breast in a savory sauce which were delicious, and she concentrated on them and a bowl of cucumbers in vinegar as she listened absently to Thomas and Olivia chatting in English while they ate. Much of their conversation was too rapid for her to comprehend details, but she followed the gist of it easily enough. They talked about recent developments in England, and either Thomas had a much more extensive knowledge of current events or Olivia was deferring to him to be pleasant, because he did most of the talking on the subject. They talked about their homes briefly. In chatting with Natalya, Olivia had mentioned that she had deduced Thomas was from a noble family through his nuances of accent and mannerisms, but he was clearly reluctant to discuss his family in any detail because Olivia did most of the talking on the subject.

The ratio of men to women at the party was high, and Thomas's intimidating size and appearance wasn't enough to keep them trying to pry loose one of the attractive women he had with him. As soon as Olivia's interest in the food began to wane, she was deluged with invitations to dance by a steady stream of men. She would have preferred to not leave Natalya with Thomas, but it apparently didn't occur to Thomas to ask her to dance and her continued refusals began to wear thin. She finally accepted one of them, leaving Natalya still eating and Thomas sipping a glass of champagne.

Most of the conversation had been between Olivia and Thomas, and there was a moment of strained silence. Then Thomas reached for the bottle of kvass to refill Natalya's glass, glancing down at her. "Would you do me the honor of dancing with me presently, Natalya Ivanova?"

She put a slice of cucumber in her mouth and picked up another brioche and took a bite. "At least I heard the request that time," she said. "But you told me last evening that you never ask for what you want if there is a chance of refusal, did you not? Does that mean that you do not really want to dance with me, or does it mean that you consider it impossible for me to refuse?"

He clasped his hands behind his back and looked down at her with a shadow of a smile. "I was speaking in jest, and if I was discourteous or unpleasant to you last evening, I apologize."

She swallowed and took another bite, glancing up at him. "Both your sense of humor and your vehement apologies are overwhelming," she said dryly.

"I might not be as demonstrative as some, but I meant what I said. Or perhaps you would rather listen to the poet Shishkov."

"No. I have a volume of Shishkov on which I wasted two rubles."

"Do you enjoy Pushkin?"

281

"I enjoy Pushkin's poetry."

He lifted his eyebrows. "I would have thought his political views might be opposed to yours, considering that he has been ordered to remain on his country estate by the Czar."

"I said I enjoy his *poetry,* not his political tracts. And it is highly likely that His Majesty the Czar wishes Pushkin to live on his country estate because of Push-kin's interest in Elisabeth Vorontsova, the wife of the governor-general of Odessa, rather than because of his political convictions. The Czar probably wishes to avoid a duel with the possibility of having to find another capable governor-general for Odessa."

Thomas nodded, reaching for the bottle of kvass as she took a drink from her glass, and poured a few more drops. The question about Pushkin had apparently been only a conversational gambit, because he didn't seem to be truly interested in the subject. And it appeared that his store of conversation had been exhausted for the moment, because he stood with his hands clasped and looked down at the floor. Natalya smothered a sigh, taking another bite of the brioche and looking away. He was a very boring man.

"Would you feel more comfortable if I left you?"

The question was discomforting. In a way it was blunt to the point of being aggravating, and in another way it was simply an inquiry into what he could do to make her feel more at ease, one which invited an open rebuff to a greater degree than most men would subject themselves. In a strange way it was also pathetic, revealing very human weaknesses in the man. But that indicated a strength which was gigantic, because he was so strong that he wasn't afraid to reveal weaknesses. She looked up at him, her eyes moving over his dark eyes, thick brows, and lean, tanned features, hesitating on the saber scar on his right cheek. The sounds in the room seemed to fade into the distant background, and they seemed to be isolated and alone as she looked at him. Suddenly he appeared more of a soldier than most men she had seen. His manner was pedestrian in a drawing room, and so was her father's. His stolid features would be in the same fixed lines in the terror and clamor of battle, and he would inspire courage in those around him as he marched forward with his long, determined stride. And it would be forward, always forward. The proud uniform of the Semenovskys was very appropriate on him.

She dropped her eyes, feeling flushed and confused. "If I am such a poor companion, then by all means leave, Thomas Stephanovich," she snapped irritably.

"Indeed, you are not a poor companion by any measure," he said, one of his rare smiles lifting the corners of his mouth. "I take great pleasure in your company, Natalya Ivanova."

She still felt unaccountably disturbed, and she looked down at the brioche on her plate and took another bite. "One would scarcely know it, from the wealth of your conversation," she murmured. She glanced up at him, waiting for him to say something, then looked away with a sigh. "Tell me about your family."

"My father and mother are deceased."

She nodded, waiting again. He looked down at her, silent again. She took a sip of her kvass and put the glass back on the edge of the table. "Were their names Adam and Eve, and were they an original creation by the Lord God, or were they born as other people are and have relatives as other people do?"

He smiled slightly. "We are a family of few children. My grandfather had two sons, and I was the only child of my mother and father. My uncle has two sons who are . . ." He hesitated, then shrugged. "He has two sons. My father was killed when I was a child, and I

283

was reared by my uncle. I remain his client, and he controls my estate."

"One would think you are sufficiently mature to manage it yourself, but I do not wish to pry. Was your father a soldier?"

"No, he was killed in a duel." He hesitated and shrugged again. "He was the younger brother, and something of a wastrel, from what I have been told. My uncle wishes to be satisfied that my estate will be in good hands before he releases it to me, so he has placed certain conditions on it." He smiled wryly and looked away. "One of which is that I must be married before I can inherit."

"I perceive no difficulty there. There are many women who would marry you, I am sure, and you only need to practice some restraint and not be so voluble so they will have an opportunity to accept your suit."

The hint of a smile crossed his face again in response to the humor in her voice, and his eyes were suddenly penetrating as he looked down at her. "To gain control of my estate is not a sufficient reason to marry a woman I do not wish to marry."

The hints Olivia had dropped about his interest in her returned to her mind again, and she felt uncomfortable. He was the antithesis of the fair, smiling Aleksei; dark, secretive, and dangerous. "Is that how matters are managed in England? They are somewhat different here, as you may know. A man of competent age inherits from his father, regardless of what his uncle might wish."

"It is the same in England in most instances, but it is different in some families."

"And what is distinctive about your family?"

"My uncle is . . ." He hesitated, then changed to English. "The Duke of Somerset."

Natalya nodded in understanding, touching her lips with the serviette. "In that event, the same situation could obtain in Russia. In families among the nobility, His Majesty the Czar could be asked to establish conditions for inheritance."

"In England it is the chancery court of equity. My uncle requested that he be appointed conservator of the estate and the conditions of inheritance be established, and his request was approved. That happened when I was a child, and I could solicit a review of the ruling, of course, but . . ." He shrugged whimsically, looking away.

His manner indicated a lack of concern, as though he were contented with his life and what he had. She picked up her glass, taking a drink. "Marriage is an easier way of confounding your uncle's purpose, and there is Xenia Artamonovna."

"Xenia Artamonovna and I are only . . . friends."

His tone didn't change, but there seemed to be ample latitude for a smutty implication. It was a fact of life between young officers and attractive women, particularly widows, and frequently married and unmarried women. But it bothered her for some strange reason, in this particular instance. And she felt irritated that it bothered her. She took another drink from her glass and put it back on the table, shaking her head as he reached for the kvass bottle once again. "No, thank you. Xenia Artamonovna was very gracious to me today."

"She mentioned to me last evening that she would like to be friends with you," he replied, his features neutral but a sudden sparkle of humor in his eyes. "And she mentioned that it might be of value to you to have a sponsor."

Natalya chuckled, reflecting that Olivia, Vassily, and her father would all be apoplectic over the thought of

285

Xenia being her sponsor. "I have learned to do without a sponsor, but I am grateful for her thoughtfulness. And my social life is one of my lesser concerns." She folded her hands in front of her, smiling. "I will entertain an invitation to dance now, Thomas Stephanovich."

He was obviously a man who went through prescribed and dictated motions only on a parade field, impatient of polite social conventions and the whims of others, but his expression didn't change as he gravely bowed. "Would you do me the honor of dancing with me, Natalya Ivanova?" he intoned quietly in his deep voice.

"How could I refuse such an ardent request?" she replied dryly, gathering her skirt in her left hand and putting her right hand on his arm.

Oliva was coming back through the doorway as they crossed the room, on the arm of a man Xenia had introduced as a government functionary. He was in his forties, a little pudgy and ineffectual looking but handsome enough in a wilted sort of way, and he was obviously infatuated with Olivia. Olivia was hiding her reactions behind her usual glacial aplomb and polite smile, but Natalya knew her well enough to see that she was flattered and pleased by the man's attentions, as well as a little flustered and embarrassed. Natalya and Olivia exchanged smiles and nods, and the men bowed shortly as they passed each other. The acknowledgement rendered by the man with Olivia was distinctly absentminded, and he continued chattering to her even as he bowed. It sounded as though his compliments had run the gamut, and he was expounding at length on how well manicured her fingernails were. Natalya reflected that it might be ridiculous, but it was at least more lively than Thomas and his stodgy silence.

All the guests had apparently arrived, because the

286

front doors were closed and Xenia had gone elsewhere. There were about a hundred guests, but it was still considerably less than crowded in the abundantly spacious rooms. The effects of the beverages the servants were constantly replenishing were beginning to show in the people moving about and standing in the entry hall, and the applause coming from the drawing room where Shishkov was reading sounded more enthusiastic and spirited than that usually motivated by the appreciation of poetry alone.

The musicians were French, uninspired but smooth and competent, and Natalya gathered her skirts to lift them clear of the floor, tapping a foot and picking up the rhythm of the music, as Thomas put his right hand on his waist with his elbow turned out at a sharp angle and put his left arm around her, placing his hand against her back. She leaned back against his hand and rested her right arm on his left, poising herself. They stepped off into a smooth glide across the floor in the swaying, circling turns of the dance.

She had anticipated that it might be awkward because of their disparity in size, that he might have to bend over or that the length of their steps would be too different, but none of the problems materialized. Dancing with an unfamiliar partner usually required some adjustment, a few steps of fumbling for rhythm and technique while becoming accustomed to one another, but their coordination was perfect. He had been surprisingly light and agile on his feet the evening before, but the more moderate pace and rigidly dictated steps of the processional hadn't provided a full opportunity to see how smoothly and easily he could move around. It was astonishing, considering his size.

The dance was also different from the processional at a level which went beyond the fact that they were in closer proximity and chose their own steps independently of the other couples. It was a basic and fundamental symbolic difference which had never before occurred to her. Instead of an impersonal partnership with another person while proceeding through the movements and steps established by custom with a large group of people, they were two people isolated and alone to pick and coordinate what steps and movements they wished, restricted only by the rhythm of the music and the necessity of not interfering with the other dancers on the floor as they went their separate ways.

But he was firmly in control of the dance as no other of Natalya's partners had ever been before, which produced ambivalent reactions. The muscles moved in the hard, powerful forearm under her hand as they swept around the floor, and his large hand almost covered her back. His size almost overwhelmed her, and she felt surrounded and encompassed, even her lungs filled with the fresh, masculine odor emanating from him. Her feet scarcely touched the floor in the turns, because he increased the pressure slightly on his hand as she leaned back against it and almost lifted her into the air.

His size was also an asset. The ballroom was large for a private house, but some of the couples had partaken freely of the refreshments and were perhaps bemused by the more intoxicating stimulation of the proximity of the opposite sex, and some of them made wrong turns on the floor or swung in the wrong direction. Thomas seemed to have his attention on everything at once, and in instances when it was impossible to avoid them, he turned Natalya smoothly and presented the offending couple with his side or back, giving them something of the effect of running into a stone wall.

When the dance finished, she felt unaccountably breathless. He seemed to perceive it, and he politely thanked her for the dance and put her hand on his arm to lead her back out of the ballroom instead of suggesting another dance. She was giddy and she felt as though her feet were barely touching the floor as they walked back across the entry hall toward the drawing room. The applause from the other drawing room registered dimly on her consciousness as the tirelessly Shishkov finished yet another recitation.

Olivia and the man who had attached himself to her were in the corner, and the man was declaiming about the beauty of the classic English profile as Natalya and Thomas approached them. Natalya suppressed the impulse to point out to the man that Thomas's profile was possibly more typically English than Olivia's in event he might perceive beauty in it, then had to suppress a giggle. Thomas poured her a glass of kvass, and his eyes lingered on her as she sipped it. Xenia was suddenly there, kissing Natalya's cheek and patting her shoulder, pouting playfully and demanding a dance from Thomas. She leaned forward to say something to the man with Olivia, and Thomas murmured an aside to Olivia in English. Olivia's eyes were suddenly concerned, studying Natalya. Xenia took Thomas's arm and pulled him away toward the ballroom, and Olivia opened her reticule and searched in it as she replied absently to a question from the man hovering around her. She took a small phial from her reticule and took the cork from it as she stepped toward Natalya, and she put it under Natalya's nose.

The powerful aroma of smelling salts filled Natalya's head with the impact of a blow, and she was suddenly in full contact with her surroundings again. She drew in a deep breath and shook her head slightly, then

289

smiled at Olivia. Olivia put the phial back into her reticle, and she daubed with her handkerchief at a spot of kvass Natalya had spilled on her gown.

"Thank you, Olivia Vassilievna."

"You are quite welcome, Natalya Ivanova," she replied, frowning at the spot on Natalya's gown and daubing at it again, then turned back toward the table. "Here, I'll pour you some more kvass, and—"

"Please allow me," the man said, reaching for the bottle. "Are you feeling faint, Natalya Ivanova? I could fetch you a chair . . ."

"No, I'm quite well, Grigory Pavlovich, thank you. I was only breathless for a moment from dancing too soon after eating."

He smiled and nodded, handing her the glass of kvass. "I was just discussing with Olivia Vassilievna that it was an exceedingly unfortunate turn of events which resulted in a woman of her beauty and accomplishments being in the position of a household employee. It seems that it should—"

"Oliva Vassilievna is not an employee in my father's household," Natalya interrupted in a firm tone, frowning. She lowered her glass and looked up at the man stonily. "I introduced Olivia Vassilievna as my friend, and that is what she is."

The man blinked rapidly, taken aback. "Well, I had no intention of making a derogatory—"

"And I do not wish to be unpleasant," Natalya said, her frown fading but her tone still firm. "I only wish to explain a fact. Olivia Vassilievna might have been a household employee at one time, but she is not now." She looked at Olivia with a quick smile, reaching for Olivia's hand and lifting it to press the back of it to her cheek, then she released it and took a sip from her glass. "Olivia Vassilievna is my friend."

Olivia looked surprised by Natalya's vehemence,

then a warm smile of pleasure spread over her face as she reached out and squeezed Natalya's arm affectionately. Natalya smiled up at her and took another sip from her glass.

"Well, I only meant that it was exceedingly unfortunate that her husband passed away . . ."

"Exceedingly," Natalya murmured, nodding and smiling at him perfunctorily to indicate that the disagreement was settled.

He smiled gratefully, and looked back at Olivia. "Did I mention that I am engaged in shipping interests, Olivia Vassilievna? Yes, I am. With various factors, but principally with English. I find them much more honest and fair. And dependable. As well as industrious. More excellent in every way, in fact. The English have always . . ."

The man rattled on, and Natalya exchanged a surreptitious smile with Oliva and looked away. It appeared that Shishkov was either resting and catching his breath or had bored a lot of people, because the drawing room was abruptly more crowded. Natalya took a slice of smoked salmon from a tray and munched it, moving closer to Olivia and the man with her as more people gathered around the table. The laughter and conversation in the room was much louder. Someone's wife was having a baby which would only be a half brother or sister to the rest of the children, someone was in difficulties because of gambling debts, a favorite ballet dancer had been arrested for public drunkenness, the latest play at the German Theater was dangerously pointed in its reference to some highly-placed individuals, and so forth. A few were spouting nonsense on the principles of poetry, unquestionably drawing their inspiration from hearing Shishkov, and others were giving their opinions of current events.

And there was another conversation which immediately caught her ear. It was a one-sided discussion, one man expounding heatedly and a dozen or so others listening silently, on the subjects of promulgation of a constitution and of freeing serfs. They were both subjects which were frequently discussed, and which Natalya had often discussed with her father. Czar Aleksander had commissioned a council to draft constitutional measures early in his reign, over twenty years before, and it had been an exceedingly slow process to develop provisions which would be workable in all the situations and conditions which existed in the vast and varied parts of the nation. A model constitution had been developed and implemented in Poland to see how it would work, and problems had developed in even that relatively small homogeneous area.

Some of her most heated discussions with her father had been on the subject of freeing the serfs. Her father had strong convictions as a result of his years of effort to make the serfs at Sherevskoye learn skills which would make them independent and self sufficient so he could relieve the overpopulation of the country estate by moving them to cities, helping them establish a business, and then freeing them. She had similarly strong convictions, because she believed her knowledge of the serfs and their motivations to be more thorough than his, and she believed her father to be judging the needs and desires of the serfs on the basis of his own motivations. And she believed he was compressing what should be done in two or three generations into one. She was convinced that many of those who had moved to the cities had gone to please her father, leaving the roots of countless generations in the village and sinking into oblivion in the unfamiliar surroundings.

The man doing the talking also seemed to have strong convictions. Xenia had introduced him as Karpovich, a name of no particular distinction, and he was a thin, sallow-looking man in his late twenties. His French was perfect, with an affected Parisian accent, and his appearance went with the accent. He was a fop. His mustaches were heavily waxed and meticulously curled, his hair was heavily pomaded and combed into a high peak on top, with a fringe of short locks plastered across his forehead at exact intervals. The strong odor of his cologne carried to where she was standing, and he occasionally plucked a handkerchief from his cuff and dusted it against his nostrils or waved it to emphasize a point as he talked. His snowy cravat was folded and wrapped with geometrical precision, and he was wearing a cream frock coat and matching cream trousers.

It wasn't difficult to understand why the men around him were more or less silent, limiting themselves to nods of agreement. He was emphatically asserting the necessity for immediately freeing the serfs and immediately promulgating a constitution. And he was making threatening comments about the Czar's welfare if the actions weren't forthcoming.

Natalya put the last of the slice of salmon in her mouth and absently licked her fingers as she listened to the man, her eyes narrowed and her anger building. She felt a touch on her arm, and she looked around. Olivia was holding out a serviette, a gently chiding smile on her face. Natalya took it and absently nodded in thanks, looking back at the man again as she wiped her fingers with the serviette and tossed it onto the table. Olivia glanced at Natalya again and looked from her to Karpovich, listening to what Karpovich was saying, then she frowned in alarm and pushed past the man to reach for Natalya's arm. Her hand closed on empty air. Natalya was pushing between a couple of men and glaring up at Karpovich.

"What do you know of serfs?"

He broke off and looked down at her with a puzzled, startled expression. "Pardon?"

"What do you know of serfs? You have given your views at length on what should be done about them, now what is the basis of your views? What do you know of serfs?"

A supercilious smile spread across his face as he glanced at the men around him, and some of the men chuckled patronizingly, looking at Natalya. Kerpovich looked back down at her. "What are you talking about?" he drawled. "I know what everyone knows about serfs. They are all about us, everywhere one looks. How could someone not know about—"

"There are trees all about us as well," Natalya snapped, elbowing between a couple of men and moving further into the circle around Karpovich. "If you intended to move a tree from one place to the other, would you cut it off at the ground and take it to where you would have it? No, the tree would die. So if one undertakes to change the situation of something, it would be of advantage to know the nature of that which they would change, would it not? Now what do you know of the nature of serfs?"

He glowered down at her with a haughty, angry frown, mixed with a touch of apprehension, and he tossed his head and looked away with a sniff. "I was not addressing you when I was talking, and these gentlemen—"

"You were addressing the state of affairs in Russia, I am Russian, so you were clattering on that which concerns me!" Natalya barked. "Is your valet married?"

The other conversations in their vicinity were dying away, and people were turning to look. Olivia was plucking at Natalya's arm from behind her, and Natalya pulled away. The men in the circle had moved back, and Karpovich looked down at her with an offended, unsure expression. "My valet? André? What has he to do with——"

"André!" Natalya hissed in disgust. "Do you have any *Russians* in your household? The footman who drove you here—is he married? What is his wife's name. Does he have children? What sort of present would he like for his nameday present? When is his nameday? What do you know of him? What do you know of *any* serf?"

He recoiled as she edged closer, firing her questions at him, and he pulled himself up to his full height and whipped his handkerchief out of his cuff, brushing his nostrils with it. "I repeat, I was not addressing you, and this conversation was——"

"Do you even speak Russian so you may talk with your serfs and ask them what they would have?" she spat rapidly in Russian.

He looked at her blankly, blinking, then forced a laugh and looked around again. "What are you saying? Your Russian appears to be excellent, and well it should, considering your abominable accent in French. I have never——"

"You don't even speak Russian," she laughed sarcastically, changing back to French. "How could you know anything of serfs when you cannot even talk to them?"

"I know what everyone knows!" he shouted in an exasperated tone. He waved his handkerchief at a servant bringing in a tray of food. "There is one! Look at him! And he should be free, as I was telling these gentlemen before you rudely——"

"He should be free?" Natalya asked in a suddenly soft tone. "Assuming he is free, what should he now do?"

Her abrupt change took him aback. He blinked and cleared his throat, brushing his nostrils furiously with his handkerchief. "Why . . . he should seek employment . . ."

"And if he could not find it? He would have the freedom to choose a place in which to starve, would he not? And his wife and children, if he has them. But let us say he can find it. Then another freed serf might work for a lesser wage, and he would be seeking employment again. And the serfs on the lands, are they to be freed and thrown from their homes in the villages before or after they have harvested their crop? Are they to carry their food for the winter on their backs? And where are they to live?" She folded her arms, slowly shaking her head. "There are many problems which must be foreseen and resolved before the serfs are freed by edict. And it will take many years, because a course set by centuries is not changed overnight. The eventual freedom of serfs is a most worthwhile objective, and one toward which His Majesty Czar Aleksander has been striving. The immediate freedom of serfs is madness. Czar Aleksander is an exceedingly wise and judicious ruler." She narrowed her eyes, leaning toward him and abruptly raising her voice to a shout. "And you are a fool!"

The room was quiet except for the shuffling of feet as people moved around and craned their necks to get a better look at what was going on. Out of the corner of her eyes, Natalya could see people looking at her with patronizing expressions and exchanging amused glances. Karpovich looked around at the others for support, and laughed weakly as he turned away. "I do not intend to debate with a woman who is scarcely more than a child and who knows nothing of such matters as—"

"And I do not intend to debate with *you,* because I do not debate with fools! But I will correct them when their foolishness impinges on matters which affect me!

You remarked that Czar Aleksander might have a care to his welfare if a constitution is not enacted in the near future. What precisely did you mean by that?"

He pushed his handkerchief back into his cuff and looked down his nose at her, straightening his coat and flicking at his sleeve. "I do not intend to engage in further exchanges with you, because you have no knowledge on these matters and your manner is coarse and—"

"Have you given Czar Aleksander the benefit of your advice?" she shouted angrily. "If you have not, then by God I shall do so for you! Through the agency of his Majesty's prefecture of police! Do you think there are no loyal subjects of Czar Aleksander here so that you may utter threats against him, you seditious dog?"

Karpovich stiffened and turned crimson with rage as he leaned toward her. "What did you call me?" he shrieked in a shrill voice.

"I called you a seditious dog!" Natalya stormed back, pushing closer to him and glaring up at him.

"Come, Natalya Ivanova," Xenia murmured behind her. "Is this not very tiresome?"

Natalya spun around. Xenia's smile belied her words, because her eyes were dancing with pleasure and enjoyment of the atmosphere of conflict. Thomas was standing behind her, an inscrutable expression on his face. Olivia looked mortified. Others were exchanging comments. Natalya drew in a deep breath, controlling her temper.

"Tiresome?" she said quietly, then she slowly shook her head. "No, it isn't tiresome, Xenia Artamonovna." She glanced around at the other people. "Does no one remember Pugachev? Is fifty years so long that the screams of those who were murdered no longer echo in our ears?" A man standing nearby started to turn away, smiling sourly in dismissal, and she stepped toward him, reaching for his arm. "Is this foolishness I am saying, then? If so, disregard it. But consider that some may listen to the words of that idiot there, and you may decide to see to the condition of your pistols. And you may decide to load them and sleep with them under your pillow." She turned toward an older, matronly woman. "Can you defend your children? When Pugachev's mob ran riot, there were children hanging from the balconies in Kazan and Saratov." She looked around again. "Has everyone forgotten? Has the lesson been forgotten?"

Xenia laughed, shaking her head. "Natalya Ivanova, surely you don't believe Bakay Romanovich intends an uprising against His Majesty Czar Aleksander?"

Natalya looked at her, glanced at Karpovich, and looked back at her as she shook her head. "No, Xenia Artamonovna, I do not fear that. I fear the effect of glib words from a foolish tongue on simple minds. Pugachev's mob began with misled people incited by the words of a fool and inflamed with vodka, and it ended in murder, rape, and pillage." She looked back at Karpovich, shaking her head again and chuckling. "This one start an uprising? No, because when it came time for the uprising to start, he would be too busy waxing his mustaches."

There was a murmur of chuckles, and Karpovich stiffened and wheeled toward Xenia, glaring at her. "Xenia Artamonovna, I did not come here to be insulted by some foolish brat with the temerity to wag her tongue on matters of no concern to her! I was having a conversation with these gentlemen, and she interjected herself . . ."

His voice died as Thomas suddenly moved toward him, a muscle twitching in the side of his face. Natalya had started to move toward him again, opening her mouth to shout at him, and she stopped and looked up at Thomas. Thomas stopped by her, his lips in a thin line as he looked at Karpovich. "You will apologize to Natalya Ivanova for referring to her in a disrespectful manner," he said quietly.

Alarm raced through Natalya's mind. Events were starting to move rapidly toward a challenge to a duel. "Here now," she said, pushing in front of Thomas. "This is my affair."

"Leave be, Natalya Ivanova," Xenia laughed gaily, stepping forward and reaching for her arm. "This is no longer your affair."

"I shall not apologize!" Karpovich stormed. "I was having a private conversation, and she interjected herself!"

Thomas looked at him woodenly, and his lips curved in a frigid smile. "In that event, I have no option but to ask you to afford me the opportunity of having satisfaction—"

"No!" Natalya shouted at the top of her voice, jerking away from Xenia and leaping in front of Thomas. "This is my affair, Thomas Stephanovich! And do you think I have no men in my family to protect me?"

"Your brother is not present," he said in a steely tone, looking down at her. "Nor is Aleksei Andreyevich. It is therefore my—"

"And what if they were present? Do you think I would allow a man to shovel dung with his sword on my account? By God, you think little of me indeed! If you would scuffle with rabble, then do so in rags, not in the uniform of the Semenovskys!"

"I cannot let this pass, Natalya Ivanova," he replied firmly.

"And if a dog defecated on the street in front of me,

299

that also could not pass? Would you choose seconds to meet the dog's? By God, you amaze me!" She flung her arm up, pointing at Karpovich. "Am I so shallow that I could be insulted by something from that foolish tongue and feeble mind? If what he has to say aggravates me, I can have an end to it soon enough myself. If I find him bothersome, then I'll . . . I'll . . ." She dropped her arm and looked at Karpovich, searching frantically for words to end the situation, then she darted to him and seized his cravat, and jerked him over and pushed her face into his as she shouted at the top of her voice. "By God, I'll have one of my footmen take the skin from his whoreson's arse with a knout!"

Karpovich lurched backwards away from her, jerking his cravat out of her hands, and it hung out of his coat as he looked down at her in outrage, his eyes bulging. Natalya recovered her balance and glared up at him. There was a long instant of silence. Then Xenia exploded into a shriek of laughter, wrapping her arms around herself and falling against a table. Others burst into laughter as their minds assimilated the ultimate insult. The laughter became an uproar. Karpovich trembled violently, his face turning almost purple then blanching to a sickly white. He lifted his fists over his head and ground his teeth together as he closed his eyes, his face twisting in an agony of speechless fury, then he wheeled toward the door and rushed toward it in a stumbling, running pace with the end of his cravat flapping over his shoulder, shoving people out of his path and screeching wordlessly. The laughter became even louder, a solid wall of sound pushing in on all sides as people leaned weakly against each other and fell against the walls and tables, holding their sides. Thomas stood with his arms folded and looked down

300

at Natalya with a sardonic smile. It took Natalya some-what longer to grasp the humor in what she had said, because she had meant it literally. Xenia pushed her-self away from the table and staggered to Natalya, throwing her arms around her and kissing her as she leaned on her and laughed helplessly.

It took a long time for the laughter to die away. Xenia released Natalya and patted her, then moved away, still shaking her head and laughing. She radiated gratitude and satisfaction, because the incident had made the party a success to an even greater extent than a challenge to a duel. It wasn't at all uncommon for challenges to be made and accepted at parties, and the party at which that happened was a topic of conversa-tion for a few days and then forgotten. But the story of what Natalya had shouted at Karpovich would be told and retold for months. Xenia clapped her hands and shouted for the servants to bring in more wine, then she seized a man's arm and demanded a dance. The other people began moving again as the party re-sumed, talking and laughing among themselves. Olivia wasn't sure whether or not to be displeased, but she put her arm around Natalya's shoulders and patted her as she moved her back toward the table. Thomas took a bottle of kvass from a tub of ice to pour her a glass.

There was one thing left unfinished. In its full im-plications it was a little unpleasant, but it amounted to a debt which couldn't be ignored. The intent to place a sword between her and disrespect had to be acknowl-edged. Thomas filled the glass and turned toward her with it, and she held out her handkerchief.

"I am grateful for your offer of protection, Thomas Stephanovich."

He took the handkerchief as she took the glass, and he silently nodded and tucked it into his jacket with

301

an expression of satisfaction. Olivia glanced between
Natalya and Thomas, with a shadow of a frown on her
face. Natalya took a sip of the kvass and looked away.
The attitude with which Thomas had taken the handkerchief was as disturbing as she had anticipated.

CHAPTER XIV

The sofa was soft under her, with pillows under her head and her knees and the cool cloth over her eyes and forehead was soothing. The scent of lavender water on her temples was strong in her nostrils, and her headache was gone. The fatigue from lack of adequate sleep and the hectic day remained, but it was almost soothing in its own way, making it easy to slide into the dull torpor of a light doze in the twilight between wakefulness and sleep.

The party had ended for her when Olivia had seen a man and woman coming back down the staircase from upstairs in a state of intoxication and deshabille. Olivia had been adamant, emphatic, and unwavering, pulling her toward Xenia for them to make their farewells, and Xenia had been warmly affectionate, kissing her over and over as they walked toward the door. Others had crowded around to speak to Natalya and Thomas had escorted them to their carriage and handed them in, bowing politely. The story had already been spread among the drivers, because they had been clustered together in a knot among the carriages, talking, laughing, and pointing as Thomas walked them along the wall to the carriage, and their driver had hurried in to spread the story through the household as soon as they dismounted at the foot gate.

Olivia had been silent during most of the drive, unsure of what degree of disapproval to radiate. There could be little question that Natalya's entry into the social life of St. Petersburg had been of a character which heralded her arrival to the heavens, but the nature of the reputation which would be forthcoming had been of concern to Olivia. Olivia had come up to her rooms with her and helped the maids to make her comfortable, then she had disappeared. Natalya had assumed she had gone to speak with her father and tell him about the incident, because it was a matter which unquestionably concerned him. Her assumption had been confirmed when she heard her father's roars of laughter echoing through the house. The story had also been popular among the serfs. The voices of a half dozen gardeners working under the open window had been audible as they laughingly discussed which one she might pick to wield the knout.

But it had come perilously close to ending far less satisfactorily. Karpovich was a fop, but he might be able to shoot a pistol and he would have had the choice of weapons. Aleksei would have been resentful that Thomas was in a position of defending her honor. Vassily would have disapproved of her part in it. Olivia would have been horror-stricken. Her father would have been furious that she had precipitated a situation ending in a duel, and he would have been right. There were women who kept score of the gages thrown in their name, as there were men like Karpovich.

And it hadn't ended satisfactorily. Thomas carried her handkerchief, and Aleksei wouldn't like that. If Aleksei had been at the party and had come to her defense, it would have been better. But she might have been so terrified over the thought of Aleksei being wounded in a duel that the outburst which ended the situation might not have occurred to her. Her tongue might have clung to the roof of her mouth at the thought of Aleksei lying with a pistol ball in him as a result of something she had done. So the situation contained an object lesson. There were times when silence was prudent. However unfair it might be, she would have to be on guard in the future.

Natalya lay on the couch, almost asleep and pondering drowsily. It would be good to be able to tell Aleksei about the incident with Karpovich before he heard it elsewhere, but it would be impossible. She wouldn't see him until the next evening, long after he had heard about it. It would be necessary to assure that no ill feeling developed between Aleksei and Thomas over the handkerchief. Thomas was a dangerous man, so dangerous that Karpovich was probably thankful the incident had ended as it had after he had time to reflect on all the possibilities.

Aleksei had mentioned speaking to his family about her several times, and she had hoped to receive a note of invitation to tea from his mother during the day. This lack of contact after she had been received by the Czar could be construed as a cool attitude on the part of his family. Or there could be a simple explanation, and an invitation would be forthcoming after Aleksei spoke to them at whatever function had been scheduled for the evening.

Vassily would be coming to dinner, and it was late afternoon and almost time to consult with the head cook and make the rest of the arrangements for dinner. And she had to talk to her father to make sure he knew precisely what had been said to Karpovich. There was a knock on the sitting room door, and one of the maids came out of the bedchamber and crossed the sitting room with a swish of skirts. She heard whispers at the door between the maid and a footman, then the footman left and ran along the hallway. Curiosity began to stir to life in the languorous, sleepy muddle of Natalya's thoughts. Another maid come out of the bedchamber, and there was a flurry of whispers at the door, then footsteps running back and forth along the hall—the heavy sound of the footman's boots, and the softer, more rapid patter of Olivia's slippers. One of the maids opened the door to look out into the hallway, and Olivia's voice carried into the room in an imperative command.

"Waken your mistress! Waken her! Immediately!"

Natalya lifted her head and took the cloth off her forehead and eyes. The door flew open wider, and Olivia burst into the room, a footman behind her.

"There is an imperial coach coming into the drive!"

It didn't make sense. In fact, it was impossible. She might as well have said that the moon was landing in the front garden. Natalya frowned, shaking her head sleepily. "A state coach?"

"An *imperial* coach! I went to the front window and looked myself! It bears the arms of the double eagles with *crowns*!"

This was something of the utmost importance. And the phlegmatic Olivia was almost frantic, which was a measure of the significance of the situation. Natalya sprang to her feet, collecting her thoughts, and she addressed the footman. "Has his honor my father been advised?"

The footman cleared his throat and began stuttering. "Mistress . . ."

"*Answer me!*"

"The house steward has gone to tell him, mistress . . ."

She nodded, waving in dismissal, and looked at Olivia. Her dress was partially unbuttoned and her hair was untidy, and she had apparently been lying down. "Button her dress and arrange her hair!" she barked at one of the maids, motioning at Olivia. "Make haste!" She turned to the other maids, snapping her fingers. "See to my hair! Fix my dress! Get my smelling salts! Get a damp cloth for my face! Haste! Haste! Haste!"

"You wish me to go down with you, Natalya Ivanova?" Olivia asked, a note of disbelief in her voice.

"Of course! You are my friend, are you not? What transpires here is your concern."

Olivia smiled widely, and Natalya closed her eyes as she tilted her chin up, gathering her self control for whatever the occasion might be. The maids bustled about, pulling at her skirt and smoothing her bodice and wiping her face with a damp cloth. Then she wheezed, choked, and gasped for breath as another maid pushed the smelling salts under her nose. The last shreds of sleep fled from her mind and she was wide awake. She tried to imagine what set of circumstances would bring an imperial coach to her home. A maid arranged her hair, tucking in wisps and adjusting the combs, and another chafed her cheeks with a handkerchief soaked in toilet water.

The seconds passed like hours. She restrained her impatience as long as she could, then opened her eyes and pushed the maids away. "That is sufficient. I will not shame his honor my father by having people think it required hours for his daughter to attend him. Come, Olivia Vassilievna."

Olivia nodded, feeling her hair with the tips of her fingers as she followed Natalya out the door, and they hurried along the hallway toward the stairs. "It is appropriate for me to walk on your right side and one pace behind you, Natalya Ivanova."

Natalya opened her mouth to argue, then threw up

her hands in a gesture of resignation as she continued on along the hallway. As they neared the mezzanine, she could hear the sound of voices in the entry hall—her father's voice, and a familiar feminine voice. She froze, gasping with delight, then lifted her skirt and ran along the hallway, with Olivia trotting along behind her.

Two footmen in palace livery were standing just inside the front doors, each of them holding two large baskets of flowers, fruits, nuts, and the house steward was closing the door behind them. Annya was in the entry hall, curtsying as Natalya's father bowed over her hand.

"Annya Konstantinovna!"

Annya turned and looked up at the top of the stairs. "Natalya Ivanova!"

Her gown was atrocious, a horrible, glaring red, was gathered and flounced in all the wrong places, making her look twice as large. But that somehow added only a touch of extra warmth as Natalya looked down at the joyous smile on Annya's round face. Natalya uttered a thrilled squeak as she lifted her skirt and petticoat up from her toes and raced down the staircase. Annya ran to meet her, holding out her arms.

Natalya's feet swept off the floor as Annya lifted her effortlessly and they kissed, then Annya put her back down, smiling down at her. "Her Majesty the Czarina allowed you to call? This is lovely, and it's far more than I anticipated! But why did you come in an imperial coach? I couldn't think of who it might be . . ."

"Well, it wasn't—"

"Here, meet my friend. This is Olivia Vassilievna, of the family Hamilton. Olivia Vassilievna, this is Annya Konstantinovna, the Countess Romanova."

Olivia was a little breathless and her face somewhat pale as she gathered her skirt and curtsyed, but her

serene, controlled smile was unaltered. "I am delighted to make your acquaintance, Countess Romanova."

"And *I* am delighted, Olivia Vassilievna," Annya replied, smiling at her, and she turned back to Natalya and put her arm around her friend's shoulders, leading her toward the count. "And I am not here because Her Majesty the Czarina gave me leave. I am here and I came here in an imperial coach because I am on His Majesty the Czar's errand."

"His Majesty the Czar . . . ?"

Annya nodded, releasing Natalya. Natalya glanced up at her father. He had been sleeping, because his hair was mussed, his mustaches were untidy, and his smile was drowsy as he looked down at her. She looked back at Annya with an interrogative expression.

"Natalya Ivanova, the Czar called me into his presence an hour ago," Annya said in a tone approaching formality as she looked down at Natalya. "He told me that he had been told a story which reaffirmed your loyalty to him, and he found that gratifying." A slow smile spread across Annya's face, and she chuckled as she continued. "But this story also brightened his day, to the extent that a privy councillor told me that His Majesty was speechless with laughter for the best part of a quarter of an hour. So His Majesty the Czar commanded me hither with a token of his appreciation."

Her father chuckled quietly, Annya giggled, and Natalya glanced between them with a puzzled smile. "So it was that . . . but His Majesty heard so soon? By what means?"

"His Majesty the Czar depends heavily upon the loyalty of his subjects, but he does not depend upon it exclusively," Annya replied dryly. "But to continue." She hesitated, her smile becoming thoughtful. "When His Majesty the Czar commanded me to bring you a present, I asked for his permission to address you as my

309

good friend. His Majesty granted me this permission."

The count's cane tapped the parquet floor as he stiffened. There was absolute silence. Annya stepped back to Natalya. She cupped Natalya's face between her hands and lifted it, kissed her on the lips, then put her arms around Natalya.

"Natalya Ivanova, my good friend."

Annya's strong arms squeezed her tightly in the enthusiasm of her embrace. Natalya drew in a deep breath as Annya relaxed her arms, then a surge of emotion abruptly surfaced, and she almost burst into tears. A sob caught in her throat, and she blinked her eyes rapidly.

"Here now," Annya chuckled, patting her shoulder. "Let us have smiles, not tears."

Natalya nodded and blinked, searching for a handkerchief, and took Annya's as she offered it. She daubed her eyes and looked up at Annya. "You must tell His Majesty the Czar that I am most grateful for his present, and that I am pleased beyond measure that I gave him pleasure. And you must tell His Majesty that I am overwhelmed by his gracious permission for you to. . . ." She choked again, clutching the handkerchief to her mouth.

Annya smiled, putting her arm around Natalya's shoulders. "Indeed I shall, Natalya Ivanova. Here, see what he sent. There are flowers, fruits, the finest nuts . . ." Her voice faded, then became carefully nonchalant. "And a box of bonbons in the bottom of one of them . . . that one, I think."

Natalya collected herself, clearing her throat and wiping her eyes again, and she looked up at Annya. "Will you share them with me?"

Annya smiled casually and shook her head. "No, I must have a care what I eat, Natalya Ivanova, lest I become too heavy . . ."

310

Natalya looked from her to the footmen, thinking rapidly, and nodded. "Very well. Are you free to visit with me?"

"I am indeed, and I have been looking forward to chatting with you."

"Let us go up to my rooms, then. Have I your permission to withdraw, your honor?"

"Of course," her father said, smiling, and he bowed to Annya. "It was a pleasure to see you again, Annya Konstantinovna."

"And for me, your honor," Annya replied, bobbing in a curtsy.

He turned away toward his study, and Natalya took Annya's hand and led her toward the staircase, looking at the footmen and motioning toward a drawing room. "Place those in there, and make yourselves comfortable in the other drawing room." She looked at the house steward. "Have refreshments brought to them."

The footmen bowed and carried the baskets toward the drawing room, Natalya took Olivia's arm and walked between her and Annya, glancing at the footmen to make sure they were out of earshot, then she motioned for Olivia to lean down. "Please go to the head cook and tell him who my guest is, and tell him we must have the best he can put on a dish immediately. And tell him to send it up by the back stairs."

Olivia nodded, turning away, and walked rapidly after the house steward. Natalya put her arm through Annya's, and they started up the stairs. Annya leaned toward her. "What do you think it will be?" she murmured eagerly.

Natalya shook her head doubtfully. "It is well before time for dinner and past time for lunch . . ."

"Perhaps some caviar and white bread, or some fish with pickles?" Annya asked hopefully.

"Oh, certainly," Natalya replied.

"Good, good. It was a cruel punishment to ride in the couch with those baskets on the other seat and knowing those bonbons were in one of them. But the footmen kept looking through the back window . . . and that one dog was rude enough to look in the basket to make sure they were still there when they took them out of the coach, the impudent beggar. I know they would tell if they saw me take a bite of something, but they'll be quick enough to fill their own bellies."

Natalya nodded, reflecting that Annya was beginning to view everyone as a spy. They reached the top of the stairs and stopped for a moment for Annya to puff and catch her breath, then walked along the hallway. "I will have the head cook purchase and put by your favorite treats if you think you will be able to come again."

"Oh, I will—I'm sure of it."

"Really?" Natalya squealed, clutching Annya's arm with delight. "Are you absolutely sure? Have you asked?"

Annya chuckled, patting Natalya's hand. "I haven't asked yet, but I'm sure of it. And you'll be able to call on me as well. His Majesty the Czar is mightily pleased with you, and we'll be together frequently."

"Then tell me what your favorite foods are, and I'll be sure to have them on hand."

They paused in front of the door to Natalya's sitting room as Annya looked down at the floor and thought, and Natalya paused, waiting for a reply. Annya shrugged and giggled. "Anything!" she said.

"That will be easy enough, then," Natalya laughed, opening the door. "Come in, and let us sit down." The maids were in the bedchamber doorway, and she motioned toward a table by the wall. "Move that to the center of the room and put chairs around it."

Annya looked around the room and glanced through the doorway into the bedchamber. "How pretty it is here, Natalya Ivanova!"

"Thank you, but surely nothing to yours."

"Oh, it is," Annya replied quickly, looking at her. "You will see when you visit me." She looked away, sighing. "I brought some pretty things with me when I came, but Czarina Elisabeth had them put in a storeroom and said I could use what was in the apartment. And she took away my nurse I'd had since infantry, as well as my ladies and footmen I brought with me, and assigned different ones . . . to watch what I eat, no doubt."

It seemed an unlikely reason to completely change her staff, and her tone indicated the reason was being provided to avoid a direct criticism of the Czarina or a blunt accusation of arbitrariness. It gave Natalya a brief but shadowy glimpse into the affairs of the imperial family, which was known to be rigorously disciplined. More than one czar or czarina had removed their grandchildren from the control of their children because they were displeased with how they were being reared.

It was yet another thing about Annya which inspired Natalya's pity. The note of sadness in her voice indicated she missed having those servants about her whom she had known for years. She hadn't even been able to keep the treasures she had collected and enjoyed. In some ways, the tall, heavy woman seemed out of place in the imperial family. Yet in other ways she was very much a Romanova. There was a presence about her which evidenced the fact that her bloodlines went back over two centuries of rulers. She was barely more than twenty, but there was something regal about her, an aura of command. Even with her belly growling, it was easy to believe that her strong, pudgy hands might develop a crushing grip on affairs of state.

The maids were spreading a cloth on the table and moving the chairs to it, and Natalya took Annya's arm. "Come, let us sit down. You reside with His Majesty's family, then?"

She nodded as they walked to the table and sat down. "We will be moving to the Winter Palace presently. I had hoped to be able to move into the Anchikov or Marble Palace when His Majesty moves to winter quarters, but it doesn't appear . . ." Her voice faded and she sighed as she shrugged and moved her chair closer to the table.

"The Winter Palace is very grand, I understand. And it will be convenient, if we are to be permitted to visit."

Annya smiled and nodded, starting to reply, then looked at the door as it opened. She sat up in her chair, her smile becoming wide and expectant. Olivia came in, followed by two footmen carrying large salvers filled with covered dishes, serving plates, wine and glasses, cutlery, and condiments. Natalya rose, motioning the footmen to put the salvers on the end of the table, and lifted the cover on the largest dish. A scent of spicy broiled poultry wafted from under the lid.

"Capon à la Kiev," Annya gasped. "Magnificent!"

It was also a little surprising. The cooks had apparently prepared it for their own meal, which explained their generally sleek and rotund appearance, if this was a sample of what they usually ate. Under other circumstances, it would have called for a somewhat closer check on the cook's purchases, but the head cook had shown honesty in sending it and it had come at an opportune time. Olivia set a place for Annya as Natalya put the dishes on the table. The footmen moved around behind Annya into position to serve her, look-

ing apprehensive and shuffling their feet uncomfortably. They weren't among the footmen who usually served at the table, and Olivia had apparently gotten them into special livery for the occasion. Natalya arranged the dishes on the table.

"I shall serve myself," Annya said, moving the plate Olivia had put in front of her to one side and motioning toward the platter. "Put it here."

Olivia looked mildly startled, and Natalya put the platter in front of Annya. The footmen gathered up the salvers and left, radiating relief, and the maids retired into the bedchamber. Natalya sat back down, glancing at Olivia and nodding to the chair on the other side of the table.

Annya picked up her knife and fork and started to attack the capon, then she hesitated and looked at it in blissful anticipation. The skin was broiled to a golden brown, speckled with spices and oozing melted butter and it rested on a bed of rich, savory dressing of rice, bread, and herbs. Annya lifted her fork and knife almost reverently, pushed the fork into the breast, and sliced into it with the knife. The crisp skin made a soft, crackling sound, and butter ran down the breast of the capon. Annya closed her eyes as she chewed. She swallowed, then groaned softly. "Ummmm . . . delicious!"

Natalya poured wine into Annya's glass, a glass for Olivia and one for herself, and sat back down. "I will tell the head cook that you found the food excellent."

Annya was shoveling large spoonfuls of the dressing into her mouth with her spoon. "More than excellent," she mumbled, chewing rapidly. "His Majesty the Czar's chef is from Paris, and yours is his equal."

"He will be pleased to hear that," Natalya said, taking a sip of her wine. "Do you ride?"

Annya began slicing one of the wings from the ca-

315

pon. She hesitated and glanced at Natalya, and shook her head as she looked back at the capon and cut the wing off. "Horses? No, I have no desire to be cruel to an animal."

It was a humorous reference to her weight, and Natalya laughed. Dribbles of butter ran down Annya's chin as she gnawed on the wing, and Natalya shook out a serviette, tied it around Annya's neck to protect her gown, and removed the butter from her chin with a corner of it. Annya nodded in thanks, tossing the stripped wing bone aside and slicing at the other wing. "But we can go for carriage rides, if you wish. And we can . . ." Her voice faded and she stopped chewing, glancing from Natalya to Olivia. "Are you not eating?"

Natalya smiled and shook her head. "We had an ample lunch, and our dinner will be substantial. This is for you."

Annya nodded, cutting the wing off and chewing on it. "I will be forever grateful," she sighed. "This is perfection itself." She stripped the wing between her teeth, tossed the bone onto the plate, and spooned another large bite of dressing into her mouth. "The Baron of Darmstadt-Hesse has expressed interest in me."

Natalya lifted her eyebrows. "Are you pleased?"

Annya shook her head, pointing with the spoon toward the vegetable bowls, and Natalya moved them down the table to her. "Thank you," she mumbled, her mouth full. She put the spoon down and shook her head again as she deftly cut off a drumstick. "No, I saw a picture of him, and he is old and fat. But he might be coming here next year to meet me. If he lives that long. He is quite old."

"Put garlic in the corners of your eyes to make them red, and beef blood in your mouth to make your breath smell foul."

316

Olivia clucked in disapproval. Annya was gnawing energetically on the drumstick, and she giggled and almost choked. Then she stopped laughing and considered the suggestion thoughtfully for a moment, as she took another bite of the dressing. "He might not like me when he sees me anyway."

"Has he not seen a picture of you?"

Annya made a muffled, doubtful sound, then swallowed and shook her head. "The picture was only partially of me. The painter took much of it from my sister Marya Konstantinovna, and she is slender and pretty. He said I moved about too much, but the real reason was probably that he wanted to be paid for his work."

Olivia smiled politely, Natalya tossed her head back and laughed aloud, and Annya chuckled and nodded, pointing at the pickles with her spoon. Olivia moved the bowl of pickles closer and Natalya put the dish of sliced cucumbers by the vegetables, and Annya spooned some pickles into her mouth, picked up the fork, and began stabbing slices of cucumber.

Annya ate the other drumstick, finished off the breast, and picked the carcass clean. Next she finished off most of the dressing and made heavy inroads into the vegetables, pickles, and cucumbers. She pushed aside the platter containing the carcass of the capon and the remnants of the dressing, and began eating the blancmange. Olivia's expression had changed from bemusement to wonder and then to concern as Annya ate, and she looked relieved when Annya finally stopped halfway through the large bowl of blancmange. She put her spoon down and looked at the bowl wistfully. She sucked her teeth and belched gustily, then sighed. "I believe it will give me a stomach burn if I finish it." She sighed again, then looked quickly at Natalya. "Not that I am criticizing the cook," she

317

added hastily. "This meal would have been more than appropriate fare for the Czar's table."

Natalya surveyed the empty platter, bowls, and dishes, reflecting that the Czar and his entire retinue probably wouldn't have been able to do the meal any more justice. "Would you care to sit on the couch and rest, Annya Konstantinovna?" she asked. "Or perhaps you would rather lie down for a time?"

Annya pushed her chair back and rose with a belch and a groan of effort, shaking her head. "No, I must not lie down. It would be better for me if we could walk in the garden, because I must have an appetite for my supper or they will think it strange."

This was something Natalya hadn't considered, and she nodded quickly. "By all means, let us walk in the garden. Would you like to join us, Olivia Vassilievna?"

"Vassily Ivanovich is coming to dinner, is he not? Perhaps I'd better see to the arrangements for dinner first, and join you in the garden later."

Natalya smiled gratefully. "Thank you, Olivia Vassilievna. Come, Annya Konstantinovna. We will go out to the back garden."

Annya yawned, smothered another belch, and linked her arm through Natalya's as they went out the door. They went downstairs and along the hallway past the count's study, and out a back door to the garden. The paths were clean and sharply edged, the flower beds were weeded, the shrubbery was trimmed and shaped, and the trees were pruned.

Natalya moderated her usually brisk pace to Annya's, and they walked along one of the paths, Annya yawning drowsily and smothering belches. The silence between them was comfortable and unstrained. Annya motioned toward a stone bench, and they turned off the walk and sat down.

"I would like to call you Natasha and have you call me Anasha when we are alone," Annya murmured, putting her hand on Natalya's shoulder and running the tips of her fingers through the tendrils of loose hair on the nape of Natalya's neck.

"I am flattered, but is that wise?" Natalya asked.

"You are my good friend, and that is what I would like, Natasha."

"Very well, Anasha."

"And I would have you for a confidante."

"I would like to be your confidante."

Annya nodded, putting her hands in her lap and examining them as she absently picked at her fingernails. She was silent for a moment, then spoke in a low, musing tone. "I was happier in Warsaw, but it was necessary for me to come here after my father married his Polish wench."

Natalya nodded understandingly. It was public knowledge that marital difficulties had developed between Annya's father and her German mother, and he had secured the Czar's permission for a divorce in order to marry the Polish Countess Jeanette Grudzinska. "Did you not get along well with her?"

"No. And there were other reasons. His excellency my father wished me to be familiar with the imperial court and customs. He also wanted me to have a mind toward what was going on around me. Particularly those things which concern people such as the Count Bludsov . . ."

Natalya was familiar with the name from the many times it had been mentioned in the news sheets and in conversation. Bludsov was a withdrawn, retiring man socially, but a powerful one in government. He was a member of the Czar's privy council, with attitudes so conservative that they were regarded by many as

319

reactionary, and it was believed that he and a few others had been a strongly moderating force in many of the Czar's programs of liberal reform.

"He is but one of His Majesty the Czar's advisors who have served him poorly," Annya said in a slow, thoughtful voice. "And they have been attempting to undermine His Majesty's confidence in the Polish constitutional government, which his excellency my father supports, of course. But they are here and his excellency my father is there, and I have been keeping him advised insofar as I can so he will be in a position to defend his undertakings."

Natalya felt a little uncomfortable. When Annya had mentioned confiding in her, she had expected things more on the line of difficulties in adjusting to palace life, her disappointments, and perhaps a little gossip. But not governmental manipulations. On the other hand, it was very interesting. And Natalya suddenly saw Annya in a totally different perspective in relation to the court. Before, she had seemed to be only a relative from the outside who was somewhat mistreated. Now she appeared to be one of those who set events into motion and who was being prevented from acquiring information that might enable her to upset the established balance of power. The sense of having a channel of information which led directly to the center of government was vaguely disturbing to Natalya. But it was also fascinating.

"His excellency your father is fortunate to have such a loyal daughter."

"I have my own objectives, of course," Annya said, her tone indicating qualification rather than disagreement. "Which his excellency my father well knows. In most instances they are in perfect concert with his. As are his with the Czar's."

The perspective changed again. She was a free agent

with purposes and desires of her own, rather than an agent of her father. Natalya nodded. "I am sure they are. I pray the Lord God may give His Majesty health and long life, but it could be that his excellency your father will have the opportunity in his lifetime to change such details in government administration as he wishes, because he is the next in line to the crown."

Annya pursed her lips and slowly shook her head. "I think not."

"You think not? His Majesty the Czar has no son, so it follows that his excellency your father is the heir presumptive. What is there to think about?"

Annya glanced about her furtively, and was silent for a long moment. Then she sighed softly, shaking her head again, and spoke quietly. "Bear in mind that his excellency my father had no son by my mother. And the Polish woman is not of royal lineage. I find much food for thought in these things. And in the fact that his excellency my father is more comfortable at the head of an army than he would be on a throne. So it could be that he may have renounced his claim to the throne in exchange for permission to divorce and remarry."

Natalya was stunned. The pattern of succession to the throne had been as immutable as the firmament in her mind, and what Annya had said made chaos out of order. Her expectations for the central thrust of government in event Czar Aleksander died had been based on her knowledge of Grand Duke Konstantine and his characteristics, but the Grand Duke Nikolas and what she knew of him was suddenly of more significance.

She was about to draw Annya out more on the subject, but at that moment Olivia came along the path and joined them. The conversation turned to life at court, which fascinated Olivia. Annya had limited interest in the social life of the court as such, but she had a keen sense of humor and had accumulated a wealth of anecdotes about the foibles and misadventures of the nobility in the conduct of their affairs with the imperial family. She continued to address Natalya by the affectionate diminutive as they conversed, indicating that her definition of privacy was broader than Natalya's, and Natalya responded with the same form of address, as was demanded by courtesy. It surprised Olivia at first, then she radiated deep satisfaction.

They talked for an hour, then Annya announced that it was time for her to return to the palace, gathering herself with an effort and rising from the bench with a groan. Natalya and Olivia accompanied her to her coach. Once Annya was inside, the coach rumbled along the drive toward the street, Annya leaning out the window to wave and Natalya standing in the drive and waving.

The story of the incident with Karpovich had spread rapidly all over the city, because Vassily came in laughing about it when he arrived for dinner. It was the main topic of conversation at dinner, with Vassily and Natalya's father continuing to discuss it. Olivia listened to the conversation with her habitual quiet, demure smile as she ate, and Natalya heard her brother's comments with growing interest. From his remarks, it was clear that he knew a lot about Karpovich.

The count left the table first, excusing himself and leaving the others over coffee. The room was quiet for a moment after he left. Vassily sat with his elbows on the table, in a glow of pleasant good humor from the vodka, wine, food, and laughter, occasionally smiling to himself as he took a sip from his glass of coffee or a puff on his cigarette. Olivia somehow managed to

322

eat walnuts silently as Natalya sat with her long cigarette trailing blue smoke into the still air.

Natalya glanced over her shoulder at the house steward. "You may go. If we need anything else, I will ring."

Vassily looked up at the servants as they left, yawned widely, and took a sip of coffee. "Dinner was delicious, as always, Natasha. And now I must return to the garrison . . ."

"You could stay the night here."

"And be punished tomorrow," he yawned, shaking his head. "We have an early parade tomorrow."

"Talk with me for a moment then."

He glanced at Olivia, grimacing comically and winking, and looked back at Natalya. "You have a message for Aleksei Andreyevich? You can tell him yourself tomorrow."

Natalya shook her head, taking a puff on her cigarette, and she tapped it against the side of the small bowl in front of her and looked back up at him. "You are acquainted with Bakay Romanovich, then?"

His drowsiness evaporated, and his eyes were alert as he looked at her. He shrugged casually, looking away. "I am acquainted with him. Well enough to know that he is an ass." He smiled, then chuckled. "I wish I could have been there today . . ."

Natalya lifted her glass, and she sipped her coffee. "How did you come to be acquainted with him?"

Vassily's smile faded slightly. "Why do you wish to know?"

Natalya shrugged nonchalantly. "He is not the sort of man you usually number among your acquaintances, so it arouses my curiosity."

"It arouses your curiosity? Why? Do you intend to advise me on who I may include among my acquaintances?"

"Yes, when they are dangerous."

He looked at her with irritation, then suddenly laughed and shook his head. "Natasha, Natasha. Do you envision me as a revolutionary?"

She laughed and shook her head, and took a puff on her cigarette, blowing the smoke up at the ceiling. "Hardly, Vasasha."

"Then what is your concern?"

Her smile slowly faded, and she looked down at the bowl as she tapped her cigarette against the side of it. "You, Vasasha," she replied quietly. "You are my brother and I love you, and I am concerned about you." She stared into his eyes. "It is fashionable to gather and discuss radical politics, this much I know. But that sort of activity also draws the idle and the irresponsible. There is always the possibility that some like Bakay Romanovich will go too far or say too much, and then they will implicate all those with whom they have been associated. His Majesty the Czar overlooks the amusements of the young and hotheaded, but let one hand be raised against him and his forbearance will be replaced by vengeance."

Vassily smiled tolerantly and shook his head. "You have no reason to be worried, Natasha."

Natalya stifled an impulse to shout, "Stop treating me like a child!" She merely nodded and took a puff on her cigarette.

Vassily stubbed out his cigarette, pushed himself to his feet with a weary sigh, and walked around the table to her. She smiled up at him, lifting her cheek, and he bent down and kissed her. "Good night, Natasha."

She patted his hand. "Good night, Vasasha."

He turned away from the table and walked toward the doorway. "Good night, Olivia Vassilievna."

"Good night, Vassily Ivanovich."

His heavy footsteps crossed the entry hall to the front drawing room, then to the front doors. The door opened and closed. Natalya took another puff on her cigarette and exhaled, deep in thought.

"You aren't really concerned that your brother would have anything to do with people such as that man Karpovich, are you, Natalya Ivanova?" Olivia asked.

"Yes."

Olivia's smile faded. "I'm sure Vassily Ivanovich has the presence of mind to realize what that sort of association could—"

"Men go through three stages in life, Olivia Vassilievna. Childish fool, young fool, and old fool."

Olivia clucked in disapproval, shaking her head. "Natalya Ivanova, one must not mock one's elders. In any event, he has satisfied your mind on the point, has he not?"

Natalya looked down at the design on the damask tablecloth, tracing it with a finger, and slowly shook her head. "No," she said quietly.

CHAPTER XV

Under normal circumstances, contact between Natalya and Aleksei's family would be arranged between their mothers, but since Natalya had no mother or older female relative, social convention and custom placed the burden of initiative directly on Aleksei's family. It was one of those delicate subjects which had to be addressed through hints and nuances between Natalya and Aleksei, and it became too raw and awkward to refer to by even this indirect means as the days passed by and no invitation was forthcoming. Natalya received the distinct impression that she was viewed as an unacceptable match, and Natalya's father began to view Aleksei with a touch of hostility during Aleksei's frequent calls. Aleksei's manner expressed an embarrassed distress.

When Natalya finally received a communication from Marie Fedorovna Orlova, Aleksei's mother, it was a curt, cold invitation to have afternoon tea with her two days later. Natalya visited with Annya at Czarskoe Selo the same afternoon she received the invitation, and she discussed it with Annya because it coincided with the time when they had planned to go for a carriage ride and look at Anchikov Palace. Annya suggested that she accompany Natalya to the Orlov residence, overriding Natalya's objections.

The Orlov residence was a short distance from the Sheremetev's and they went in the Sheremetev carriage, arriving promptly at two. A maid showed them into a drawing room, and after fifteen minutes of waiting, Natalya began to lose courage. Annya remained bright and cheerful, chatting and munching pastilles Natalya had provided, and her composure remained unshaken as they waited thirty, then forty five minutes. They had been waiting almost an hour when Marie Fedorovna arrived in a cloud of heavy cologne and a bustle of petticoats, with a supercilious smile on her powdered face and a maid following her with a small tray of refreshments. Her composure was totally destroyed when she found she had committed the politically dangerous social error of keeping the Czar's niece waiting in her drawing room.

Natalya had noticed many indications that Annya had characteristics equal to her station; an education and a keen intelligence which matched Natalya's, a penetrating insight into what went on around her, judgment and maturity far beyond her years, and a formidable will. But this was the first time Natalya had seen Annya shake off her usual cheerful good nature and become the Countess Romanova. The Romanovs in general and the Grand Dukes Konstantine and Nikolas in particular were known for their unwavering, hypnotic glares which could strike terror into all but the most courageous of hearts, and Annya had inherited her full share of that ability. Her protuberant blue eyes fixed on Marie Fedorovna in a penetrating, hostile, Medusa-like stare. The social graces learned in salons and drawing rooms from childhood by the powdered, perfumed, and bewigged matron of fifty or so served only to remind her of the enormity of the gaucherie she had unwittingly committed.

Everything had been prepared to emphasize to Natalya that she was unwelcome. The drawing room was untidy, and the refreshments were an assortment of stale slices of cheese and meat, and a bottle of cheap Crimean wine. Annya used everything as a weapon. When Marie Fedorovna ordered the maid to go for other things, Annya countermanded the order with a motion of her hand and a cutting comment that she had no wish to compound the financial difficulties of the Orlov family. Natalya knew from experience that Annya's appetite for food was catholic, and that under different circumstances she would have fallen on the meager refreshments as eagerly as she would have devoured the most choice viands prepared in the Czar's own kitchens, but she restrained herself taking only a distasteful nibble of cheese and a sip of wine accompanied by a wince. The cold blue eyes moved over the disorder of the drawing room as she remarked on the Czar's penchant for order and cleanliness and how neat and orderly the Sheremetev residence was kept under Natalya's supervision. She emphatically referred to Natalya as her good friend, and she commented on the Czar's favorable impression of Natalya. Then she delivered a broadside. The grand ball given by the Czar every fall upon moving back into the Winter Palace was both the opening of the winter social season and the most scintillating event and Annya casually remarked that the Czarina Elisabeth had directed her to assist the Grand Dutchess Aleksandra Fedorovna in the preparations for the ball, including the invitations. Her tone and attitude left it open to interpretation as to whether she had communicated a thinly veiled threat or a statement of intention to see that the Orlovs would not be invited.

They remained only ten minutes, Annya stating that she had overstayed her permissible time away from the palace when Marie Fedorovna begged them to stay longer. Natalya had the driver stop the carriage at a pastry shop and ran in for a substantial assortment of pastries on their way to Anchikov Palace.

The palace was small but one of the more luxurious of the residences of the imperial family, and it was unoccupied except for a skeleton crew of guards and domestic servants. A guard followed them at a respectful distance as they munched pastries and prowled through the deserted corridors, dark chambers, and spacious, echoing ballrooms and drawing rooms. It was an old building and had acquired a timeless, sleepy atmosphere, a remoteness and detachment from what had gone on within its walls from the lives of those who had pursued their objectives and then had disappeared to be replaced by others.

Annya and Natalya made tentative arrangements to meet again three days later to go to church, and Annya left in her coach for the lengthy drive back to Czarskoe Selo as soon as they returned to Natalya's house. A message from Marie Fedorovna had already been delivered to the house by footman, a long, flattering, and affectionate letter requesting her to come and have tea again the following day. Natalya told Olivia about the visit that day and discussed the invitation with her, and Olivia was enraged, revealing a vindictive facet to her ordinarily kind and forgiving disposition. She wanted to defer a reply until the following day, when she would write a brief excuse herself and have it delivered by footman thirty minutes before the time for the tea, when all the arrangements would have been made.

But there were many considerations involved. Natalya's first reaction was like Olivia's, because a calculated and carefully-arranged humiliation had been set up. But if her romantic hopes were fulfilled, she would be entering into a lengthy relationship with Marie Fedorovna during which an initial display of generosity could be invaluable. After all, the woman *was* Aleksei's mother. Natalya decided to accept the truce, qualifying her acceptance only to the extent of writing her reply in Russian in the certainty that Marie Fedorovna would have to get her house steward to translate it for her.

Olivia accompanied her to the Orlov home, where they were graciously received and entertained. Aleksei's three sisters were there, including the one who was married; the drawing room was fresh, spotless, and decorated with flowers, the refreshments choice and costly delicacies, and Marie Fedorovna was sparkling. The woman had highly developed social talents, smoothing over the initial awkwardness when Olivia and Natalya first arrived, claws in readiness, and she even managed to charm Olivia out of her haughty reserve. It turned out to be a pleasant occasion, and shortly after they returned home a footman delivered a note from Count Orlov to Natalya's father, inviting him and his family to dinner the following night.

Count Orlov was similar in disposition to his son, with indications of crafty depths to his character which had won and secured his political favor, but he was obviously ruled in his home and social life by his wife. Natalya's father got along well with him, reminiscing about past events, and Vassily flirted dutifully with Aleksei's eldest unmarried sister. Olivia spoke at length with Aleksei's younger sister's governess, and Marie Fedorovna was even more entertaining than she had been at tea the day before. Aleksei was exuberantly happy all during dinner, hovering over Natalya attentively under the approving gaze of his mother and father. After dinner, as they sat over nuts, cheese, and coffee and the men were smoking, Aleksei rose from the table with a laughing remark that he wanted Natalya to feel at home, and he exchanged her coffee cup for a glass and brought her a cigarette and a small bowl for the ashes. Count Orlov and Marie Fedorovna looked horrified for an instant, then they beamed fondly and tolerantly at Natalya and the conversation around the table continued.

The preparations for the imperial family to move into winter quarters approached a climax, and Natalya spent much of her time in helping Annya get ready. During the time Natalya had known Annya, she had virtually replaced all the young women who had been previously calling on Annya as a required social activity, and she had occasionally come into contact with other members of the imperial family, the Czarina Elisabeth, Grand Duchess Aleksandra Fedorovna and her children, and Grand Duke Nikolas. At first she had been regarded with something approaching distrust, then with cautious, tentative, and reserved acceptance. But as she acquired insight into the relationships within the imperial family, she realized that the degree of acceptance accorded her had nothing to do with their becoming more accustomed to her presence. It was totally the result of a growing accommodation reached by Annya with the other members of the imperial family.

Natalya gradually came to realize that there were circles of influence and real and apparent lines if authority within the imperial family and the court which were completely without equal in her experience, and that they were interwoven into a complex web of shadowy loyalties and alliances which were predicated on causes and effects completely beyond her grasp. Annya was less than voluble on the subject, and their

331

limited conversations on it indicated that it was impossible to explain to someone of a different background.

But there had been a change, and Annya had come into a position of greater influence. Her involvement in the preparations for the grand ball to open the winter season had been a breakthrough of sorts, and shortly after that Czar Aleksander appointed her a trustee of the Academy of Arts, to the Council of Guardians of St. Petersburg, and to the oversight council of the Society of Natural Philosophy. Evidence of a more dramatic and obvious sort to Natalya occurred when they were taking a carriage ride and were passed by Grand Duke Nikolas and several grand officers on horseback. The Grand Duke hailed the driver and stopped the carriage, and he chatted amiably with them for a few minutes before he went on, a complete reversal of his detached and impersonal attitude toward Annya on the evening when Natalya and her father and brother had been received by the Czar.

The move to the Winter Palace was completed, and the grand ball was held a week later. Annya had seen to it that Natalya and Aleksei were among the twenty couples in the opening processional, and the day of the ball was a blur of frantic activity of preparation, with Olivia hovering over Natalya worriedly and snapping at the maids. Her gown was a confection of lemon yellow tulle, with a low neckline and a skirt pinched in tightly at the waist, then belled out over myriad starched petticoats. The maids piled her hair on top of her head and decorated it with bows which matched the yellow dress. Olivia fussed over her hair, bows, and gown for what seemed an eternity. Then Natalya went downstairs, her arrival announced by the rustling of the starched petticoats. Aleksei came out of the drawing room where he had been waiting. She ran down the last few steps, and he clasped her hand between his and pressed it to his lips fervently, looking into her eyes. A flush spread up her slender throat to her cheeks; she kept her eyes on his and her flush became deeper. He helped her into her ermine-trimmed cape and hood, then escorted her toward the door. Olivia, standing on the mezzanine overlooking the entry hall, looked down at the petite, slender Natalya and the tall, athletic Aleksei in the bright uniform of the Yamburgsky Regiment of Uhlans, and she swallowed a sudden lump in her throat as she turned away toward her rooms.

The square in front of the palace was deserted, but every window was lighted and gleaming in the dusky twilight, stretching out on both sides for what seemed to be an endless distance. The carriage stopped before the left wing, where the main ballroom was located, and Natalya shivered in the chilly air as they dismounted. One of the sentries led them further along the portico, through a door and along a short hallway, and into an anteroom off the main ballroom.

Others were already waiting and more arrived after them, most of them general officers or senior government officials, with their plump, matronly wives. A table at one side of the room was spread with refreshments, and Aleksei tucked his gloves into his belt, put his kepi and sword on a rack at the side of the room, and poured a glass of champagne for Natalya and himself. The stiff, tense, and monosyllabic conversations became somewhat more voluble as the beverages were consumed and replenished by a servant in imperial livery. A few people spoke briefly to Aleksei and Natalya, and a motherly-looking woman fussed over Natalya's hair and adjusted the sleeve of her gown as she looked Natalya up and down with a smile of admiration.

Time passed, and the sounds of the orchestra became audible from the adjoining ballroom, then a murmur of conversation and the shuffling of feet, the droning, swelling sound of a massive crowd growing by the minute. The conversation in the anteroom died away again. Annya came bustling in through the hall doorway, her cheeks flushed and her eyes dancing with excitement, and she greeted Natalya exuberantly and kissed her, cooed and clucked delightedly over her gown, then began making the rounds of the room and consulting a list, telling each couple what position to take along the wall immediately outside the room when they went into the ballroom. She came back to Natalya and chatted for a moment, then kissed her again and left. The rumble of conversation from the ballroom became louder, and those in the anteroom became silent except for an occasional cough or a shuffle of feet.

The conversation in the ballroom quietened. The hallway door opened, and Grand Duke Nikolas and Grand Duchess Aleksandra crossed the room through the door to the ballroom. The other couples began filing after them. Natalya looked up at Aleksei, breathless with excitement. He smiled down at her, taking her hand and putting it on his arm, and they walked toward the door.

The ballroom stretched off into the far distance, the floor gleaming in the brilliant light of hundreds of chandeliers hanging from the high ceiling. The walls were lined with people several deep, totalling thousands. The orchestra, over a hundred of the best musicians in St. Petersburg, was on a dais at the opposite end of the ballroom. The people along the walls were still and quiet, but the occasional movement of feet and coughs from the combined thousands made a constant low background of noise which blended with the soft music of the orchestra. With the Grand Duke and Grand Duchess, the number of people from the anteroom amounted to twenty couples, and they took their places, ten couples on each side of the door.

The music from the orchestra suddenly swelled into a fanfare, and the tiny figures of the Czar and Czarina moved across in front of the orchestra to the center of the ballroom. Natalya sank into a deep curtsy with Aleksei bowing deeply beside her, and a rustling sound swelled and filled the huge room as the crowd curtsied and bowed, then stood erect again. The Czar and Czarina began walking slowly along the center of the ballroom, and men bowed and women curtsied as they passed abreast of them, making a ripple of movement like an undulating wave among the people along the walls which followed them the length of the ballroom. The Czar wore the uniform of the Semenovskys, and the Czarina was wearing a white satin gown which sparkled with brilliants, and a diamond encrusted tiara which glittered in the light of the chandeliers. They stopped a short distance from the twenty couples, who bowed and curtsied again. They turned and faced the opposite end of the ballroom, and the couples formed into a line behind them for the processional.

Natalya was so tense and nervous that she almost missed the first step, and she concentrated grimly on subsequent movements so she wouldn't make a fool of herself in front of thousands of people. Aleksei seemed perfectly calm, his large, gloved hands holding hers warmly and without a tremor, and she glanced up at him. Her nervousness faded somewhat as he smiled down at her, and suddenly the dance became pleasurable, the steps coming to her effortlessly.

The applause from the crowd swelled and ebbed as the line moved slowly back and forth across the room, describing serpentines and geometrical designs as it gradually moved toward the other end of the ballroom, and it rose to a thunderous roar as the line reached the other end of the ballroom, ending the dance. The Czar nodded to the orchestra leader, and the orchestra began playing a waltz. The crowd moved away from the walls, choosing partners, and the floor became filled with people. Natalya felt deflated for an instant as her moment of glory as a member of the processional faded, then Aleksei smiled down at her and the shadow of depression evaporated as they began waltzing.

Servants opened the doors to adjacent rooms along one side of the ballroom, where choice delicacies and imported wines, champagne, and vodka had been put out, and the crowd milled back and forth between the ballroom and the refreshments. Thomas claimed Natalya for a dance, but in the afterglow of Aleksei's presence he was simply another man, rather than being upsetting to her, as he had been before. The dance over, Natalya rushed back to Aleksei, anxious that she might lose him in the crowd, but he was waiting for her where she had left him. She boldly drew him away from the two officers with whom he had been talking, demanding that he dance with her, and he laughed easily as he nodded, taking her arm. The other officers' envy showed through their smiles. Thomas bowed in thanks for the dance, his features in their usual neutral expression, and she hardly noticed him.

The Czar and Czarina retired at midnight, and Grand Duke Nikolas and Grand Duchess Aleksandra shortly after that. At one o'clock many older people began to leave, and by two some of the younger ones left as well. At three, Natalya was in a deliciously numb state from fatigue and champagne, feeling as light as a feather. At four there were fewer than a hundred couples still dancing, and at five, less than a dozen. Daylight flooded through the windows, replacing the light from the candles which were guttering and spluttering, and Natalya and Aleksei left as the sun was rising, munching on delicacies and sipping from a bottle of champagne.

The streets were deserted except for a few workmen and merchants moving about in the chill of the early autumn morning, and the carriage rumbled along the wide, clean streets, the sound of the wheels on the stone pavement and the clopping of the horses' hoofs echoing between the imposing stone facades of the buildings. The empty champagne bottle rolled back and forth on the floor of the carriage.

Natalya, still flushed from excitement and wine, leaned her head against Aleksei's shoulder, savoring the thrill of his nearness. Suddenly he gathered her into his arms, pulling her so close to him that the buttons of his dress uniform dug into her cheek.

"My dearest Natalya—Natasha—my own dear girl, I can contain myself no longer. I want you for my wife. Can you possibly find it in your heart to love me as I love you? Will you marry me?"

Natalya had rehearsed a thousand times what she would say if Aleksei ever spoke those longed-for words, but here in the total privacy of the carriage, pressed so closely against his chest that she could hear the pounding of his heart, her carefully formulated reply went completely out of her mind. All she could do was nod, too full of joy to make a sound. He crushed her lips beneath his, and Natalya came as close to fainting in that moment as she ever had in her life.

Her father proved to be an unexpected obstacle on what her excited imagination had envisioned as a straight path to matrimonial bliss. When Aleksei called on him formally and asked his permission, he replied that he would consider the request after Natalya's eighteenth nameday, the following May. Aleksei's disappointment quickly changed to resigned acceptance and anticipation. Natalya was deeply despondent over her father's unyielding attitude, but Olivia considered the delay no more than proper, pointing out all the arrangements which had to be made. Further reflection during the next few days indicated that Olivia was right. There were a multitude of preliminaries to be dealt with when excitement gave way to considered judgement, and there were problems. Aleksei assumed that they would live in a house which belonged to his father, and it had never occurred to Natalya that she would have to leave her father's household.

Life continued, even though it seemed to Natalya that the sun, moon, and stars should alter their courses in the face of the enormity of her feelings for Aleksei. The Czar and Czarina departed to take a winter vacation in Taganrog on the Sea of Azov, and there was a ball and a smaller gathering to which Natalya was invited before they left. The first heavy snows fell and the Neva froze, and troikas and sleighs decked out with bells replaced carriages and coaches. The streets became too icy to be safe for the spirited Orion and Pegasus, and in any case there was rarely an opportunity to go riding because the winter social season was in full stride, invitations were more abundant than they had ever been in Moscow, and the frequency of visits back and forth with Annya had increased. Natalya's relationship with Aleksei's mother had solidified into a wary, guarded friendship, calling for periodic visits to publicly demonstrate mutual good will.

Grand Duke Nikolas was in command of the local scene and of affairs at large, with communication between him and the Czar maintained by couriers traversing the snowy wastes and deep forests across the vast distance between St. Petersburg and Taganrog. He gave Annya permission to move into the Marble Palace with the Czarina dowager, which gave her significantly more latitude in her activities, and Natalya helped her move. The time of the Winter Carnival came, a week of snatching a few hours of sleep then arising and returning to the sprawling complex of booths, tents, and stands filling St. Isaac's Square and flowing down the embankment to stretch far across the frozen Neva toward the opposite shore. Rows of torches along both sides of the bridge, around the square and the statue of Peter the Great burned through the short winter days, troikas darted in all directions through the milling crowds of people in heavy furs, orchestras played at all hours of the day and night for the dancers on the thick ice on the river, and there were games and amusements which continued through the night. Olivia accompanied Natalya every day and grimly trudged through the snow after her as first one thing then another clamored for her attention. Aleksei was in attendance much of the time and brought Thomas with him to escort Olivia, but Annya could join them only a few times because she was involved in an undertaking to wrest control of the Council of Guardians from some of the other councillors.

News from Taganrog that the Czar had fallen ill was a wind more chilling than the frosty blasts from the North which scoured the broad, icy thoroughfares of St. Petersburg, but Taganrog was far removed and the troublesome news was forgotten in the continuing frenetic swirl of visits, parties, and sparkling evenings at the theaters.

The time for Annya's nameday approached, and Natalya made preparations to get permission from Grand Duke Nikolas to give a party for her. She called on the court chamberlain with a note requesting an audience. The chamberlain left for a moment, then returned and ushered Natalya along a hallway and into the Grand Duke's presence.

The air in the room was thick with cigar and cigarette smoke, and it was crowded with clerks shuffling through stacks of papers and officers talking quietly in twos and threes. A half dozen generals and advisors stood around the table in the center of the room with Grand Duke Nikolas, poring over maps. The grand duke looked immensely large and forbidding in his immaculate uniform of the Second Guards Infantry Division, and Natalya had a sudden intimidating feeling of being at the very hub of the empire. He smiled as he put down a map and turned away from the table, walking toward her with long strides. She curtsied deeply, and he bowed over her hand and lifted her, then held her hand and asked in a congenial tone what she wanted of him. All eyes in the room were fixed on her and her voice suddenly weakened. The Grand Duke had to bend over to hear her soft, trembling words. His puzzled frown changed to a smile, and he chuckled heartily and nodded as he straightened up, patting her hand, then he turned aside and snapped an order.

Men bumped into each other getting to the table where tea, coffee, and vodka had been put out, and one of them filled a glass and brought it to the Grand Duke, who handed it to Natalya. It was the fiery *pertsovka,* and almost choked her, but her voice returned somewhat. The Grand Duke took the glass back from her and drank the remainder of it in a single swallow, then put his huge hand on her shoulder and asked about her father. The room was absolutely silent except for her voice, and she darted a self conscious glance around as she replied. There were a few more cordial exchanges, then the Grand Duke escorted her to the door. She turned and curtsied again, and he raised her, kissed her, and patted her shoulder. The door closed quietly behind her as she stepped back out into the hallway. She drew in a deep breath, then giggled with excitement and relief as she lifted her skirt and petticoats in both hands and began skipping along the hallway. A couple of servants in imperial livery turned a corner and looked at her with startled expressions, and she quickly dropped her skirt and petticoats and began walking demurely, lifting her chin and giving them a haughty glance.

It was Natalya's first big party, and there were decisions to be made and problems to be solved that were completely outside her experience. Olivia was tireless and resourceful, but the magnitude of the party was also somewhat beyond her. Aleksei's mother was a goldmine of advice, all of which was totally useless. But Xenia was priceless, calling unexpectedly one afternoon and bringing the caterer she always used, the leader of one of the orchestras that played at her parties, and a man who had clerks and delivery boys and specialized in preparing and delivering invitations.

The tempo of preparations reached a frantic climax, and somehow everything fell into place. The Grand Duke Nikolas and Grand Duchess Aleksandra arrived in time to lead the first dance, and the nameday presents for Annya grew into a huge mound. The party was a gratifying success by any standard, and the two young officers who squared off to exchange challenges and make the party even more noteworthy were interrupted by Natalya's father, who pushed between them with his cane and snarled that he would fight both of them if they didn't leave immediately.

The house looked like the scene of a pitched battle the next morning. Natalya was out of sorts from lack of adequate sleep and from injudiciously mixing drinks of kvass and champagne during the party. The count was still asleep, and even the indefatigable Olivia looked sleepy over her morning tea. The bustle in the house was bothersome, some of Annya's gifts had been overlooked when they were loaded into her troika after the party, and Natalya felt she needed some fresh air. She sent word to the stables to prepare the troika, and she went back up to her room to get ready and go see Annya.

The frigid air cut between the heavy fur blanket and the high collar of her coat, biting into her face as the troika raced along the streets, the bells jangling, the runners occasionally scraping over patches of rough ice, and puffs of steam coming from the horses' nostrils and the driver's heavy muffler. The temperature had plummeted during the past days, and there was little activity along the streets, a couple of troikas with both driver and passengers buried in fur blankets, coats, and heavy hats, and a few covered sleighs with windows frosted over. The cold cut through the fatigue and lassitude which had plagued Natalya since arising, and she thought about the party the evening before with satisfaction and smiled to herself as she thought about a warm compliment paid her by Aleksei. Then her smile faded and she pursed her lips as she thought about some other parties she had to attend later in the week. And it wasn't too early to begin thinking about Christmas. There would be presents to buy for all the house serfs, her father, Vassily, Annya, Olivia, Aleksei's parents, and Aleksei—something very special for Aleksei.

The driver swung the horses into the side street by the Marble Palace, through the gate leading into the rear courtyard. He reined the horses back to a stop near the rear entrance and climbed down from his seat to assist Natalya out of the troika. She gave him a ruble, then walked toward the entrance, the soles of her heavy felt boots grinding softly in the snow and the hem of her long, fur coat brushing the ground.

She was inside and walking along the lower hallway before the demeanor of the sentries registered. Usually cheerful, they had been unnaturally subdued. There seemed to be a hushed, ominous atmosphere in the palace. She stepped into a cloakroom at the end of the hallway, took off her coat and hat and hung them up, slipped off the felt boots and tossed them into a corner, then took Annya's presents and went along a short hallway to a staircase. A servant coming down the stairs bowed slightly in acknowledgement, and she nodded. The man looked tense and apprehensive. She reached the top of the stairs and turned into the long, wide hallway that led to Annya's rooms.

Two maids were standing in the anteroom, whispering softly, and they turned and looked at her as she came in and closed the door behind her. She put the presents on a small table by the door.

"Is the countess free?"

They looked at each other uncertainly, then looked back at her. One cleared her throat and shrugged silently.

Natalya frowned, then sighed impatiently and walked rapidly across the room to the door to Annya's receiving room. She stepped into the room, closing the door behind her.

Annya was in her dressing gown, looking at a scroll of paper and frowning, deep in thought. Another maid was standing at one end of the room, her hands clutched nervously in front of her and her face pale. A man in uniform was standing near Annya, apparently the man who had delivered the paper.

The scene suddenly had meaning, and the atmosphere in the palace was explained. The scroll Annya was holding was edged in black, and there were black

343

ribbons hanging from the seal on it. The man who had delivered it was wearing the silver breastplate of the Knights Guards parade uniform, with a black cloak and black aiguillettes, and the helmet he held under his left arm was surmounted with a black plume. He looked very fatigued. It had been a long, hard ride from Taganrog. By custom, one of the scrolls would be sent by courier to each member of the imperial family.

At that instant, the bells of the city began tolling in confirmation. Moscow had been a city of bells which had been rung on any pretext, but St. Petersburg was different. They were rung less often and there were fewer of them, making them easily identifiable from their characteristic tones. The deep vibrato of the Cathedral of Kazan began first, setting a bass note for the rest, then the harmonious sound of the matched bells of the Cathedral of SS Peter and Paul carried through the cold air from the other side of the frozen Neva, to be joined by the heavy, pounding, urgent sound of the bells of St. Isaac's Cathedral. The others added their voices to the sorrowful message spreading over St. Petersburg and rising to the heavens.

"Natasha, His Majesty the Czar has gone to his reward."

Annya's voice hung in the air like the dismal sound of the bells coming through the thick walls.

Natalya's tears came in a sudden flood. An agonized wail burst from her throat as she put her face in her hands and began sobbing wildly. Annya looked at her with a stunned expression for an instant, then dropped the scroll and walked quickly to Natalya, putting her arms around her. She began weeping also.

CHAPTER XVI

The social season came to an abrupt end and a sumptuary edict was proclaimed as the nation went into mourning. Several days went by without Natalya seeing Annya, and Annya's earlier comments on the succession to the throne preyed on Natalya's mind. Natalya visited no one, but Vassily and Aleksei continued to come to the house, and from their conversation Natalya learned that the city was awaiting the arrival of Grand Duke Konstantine to assume the throne. Vassily sourly eyed Natalya's and Olivia's black dresses and the crepe hangings on the ikons and in the entry hall, and he grumbled over the cold sausage, dark bread, and watered kvass for dinner each night, observing that Natalya's interpretation of the sumptuary edict was the most severe in all Russia. His visits diminished, but Aleksei continued coming at every opportunity.

Then a proclamation was issued requiring all free male citizens over the age of twelve to attend public ceremonies and swear an oath of allegiance to Czar Konstantine. It was the signal which ended most of the sumptuary restrictions, but the prohibition against public celebrations and social occasions was continued until after Lent, effectively cancelling Christmas, New Year, and early spring festivities. When the day came to take the oath of allegiance, Natalya's father donned his uniform and took the sleigh to a gathering of his regiment for the oath.

Annya came to see Natalya the same day, arriving in a plain sleigh without state insignia and still wearing crepe on her right arm. Her greeting was quiet and subdued, but very sincere and with great relief at seeing Natalya again. Natalya greeted her as a Grand Duchess, and Annya frowned slightly for an instant then smiled wearily and nodded toward the staircase, linking her arm through Natalya's. They walked up the stairs and along the hallway to Natalya's rooms in silence, Annya looking down at the floor with her lips pursed and a moody expression on her face. It was apparent that Annya had something she wanted to discuss, and as they went into the sitting room, Natalya told the maids to leave and have a footman bring refreshments. The maids filed out the door and closed it quietly behind them, and Annya crossed the room and sat down heavily on a couch, heaving a deep sigh.

"I am not a Grand Duchess, Natasha, nor am I to be."

"What is this, then?" Natalya asked in surprise, sitting down by her. "His honor my father left scarcely an hour ago to swear allegiance to His Majesty your father."

Annya sighed again, rubbing her eyes, and shook her head as she dropped her hands into her lap. "It is a plot devised by fools. There was a manifesto in safekeeping in the Senate chambers which designated his excellency Grand Duke Nikolas as heir to the throne, together with a letter from his excellency my father renouncing his claim to the throne. As I suspected there would be. But his excellency Grand Duke Nikolas consulted with Governor General Miloradovich and other advisors on how to proceed, and their advice was that the manifesto is contrary to law. Law establishes succession, and by law my father is heir. So they recommended that my father be proclaimed Czar, that he be requested to come to St. Petersburg and renounce the throne, and His Excellency Grand Duke Nikolas then be proclaimed Czar. I had an audience and recommended a different course of action. That the manifesto be published, and His Excellency Grand Duke Nikolas assume the throne forthwith."

Natalya cleared her throat and shrugged. "But if it is the law . . ."

"Who knows the law?" Annya snorted impatiently. "Senators, professors, and advisors. The Horse Guards and Knights Guards know no law, but they know how to use their swords to settle questions of succession. When a czar is on the throne, they are loyal to the death. When there is no czar on the throne, they are dangerous." She sighed again, lifting her hands and dropping them. "Only yesterday His Excellency Grand Duke Mikhail arrived in Warsaw with letters from my father, one to His Excellency Grand Duke Nikolas and one to me. His letter to Grand Duke Nikolas states he will have nothing to do with the throne, and his letter to me requested me to encourage Grand Duke Nikolas to assume the throne immediately."

It was confusing, and it filled Natalya with a sense of foreboding. "But these are seasoned and experienced men, Anasha. Surely they would not proceed in such a manner as to—"

"They are fools," Annya interrupted her brusquely. "And I had a tête-à-tête with Governor General Miloradovich after he finished dispensing his fool's advice to Grand Duke Nikolas. I told him I'll see his arse in the dungeons of Saints Peter and Paul fortress if mischief comes of this."

Her tone was soft and deadly, reflecting a cold, hard

rage, and the protuberant blue eyes were shining. There was a quiet knock on the door. It opened, and a footman came in with a salver covered with dishes of delicacies, a bottle of wine, a bottle of kvass, and glasses. Annya and Natalya sat in silence as he crossed the room to put them on the table in front of the couch. Natalya waved him aside, and he bowed and withdrew, carrying the salver under his arm.

"Shall I have the cook prepare something more substantial?"

Annya smiled slightly and shook her head, sitting forward and spooning caviar onto a piece of bread. "This is more than sufficient, Natasha. And I apologize for being such a poor companion."

"You are troubled, Anasha, not a poor companion," Natalya replied, pouring the wine for Annya. She opened the bottle of kvass, and filled a glass. "But will all this not be resolved if your father will come and renounce the throne?"

"It is a moot question, because he will not," Annya replied, chewing a bite of the caviar and bread and taking a sip of wine. "My father has said he will have nothing to do with it and that he has no intention of coming to St. Petersburg."

Natalya sat back on the couch and looked at Annya. "And he will not change his mind?"

"He will not," Annya said emphatically, shaking her head. "My father never changes his mind. And I talked until I was breathless trying to convince Grand Duke Nikolas and that fool governor general of that. My father does not swerve once he sets his course. There are thousands of enemy dead who would testify to that, if they could. When he has determined to do battle, nothing will stand in his way. His cannon will fire until there is no more shot or powder, then his rifles will do the same. If there are enemies left, then his soldiers will advance to do battle with swords, bayonets, and the butts of their rifles, with him at their head. If all of his soldiers are killed and the enemy still stands, he will fight by himself. And if his sword is broken, he will leap on the enemy still standing and bite them with his teeth. The flight of a cannonball is like the zigzagging of a swallow in comparison with how his excellency my father proceeds to do his will. As I well know, because I am much like him myself."

"Then we are undone," Natalya said quietly. "Today we have a czar who will not be czar, so we have no czar."

Annya lifted her eyebrows and shrugged, pushing the rest of the bread and caviar into her mouth. "We shall see. Grand Duke Nikolas meets again with the privy council tomorrow morning, and I will try once again to persuade him to publish my father's renunciation and assume the throne."

Natalya looked at her in surprise. "You sit with the privy council?"

Annya shrugged again, chewing and swallowing, and took a drink of wine. "I have not been formally appointed to the privy council, but I have been sitting. Grand Duke Nikolas likes a variety of opinion, and he listens to me." She chuckled wryly. "He does not do as I say, but he listens." She finished the wine and put the glass down, and smiled at Natalya as she patted her knee. "I must go. Come and see me tomorrow afternoon and I will try to be a more pleasant companion."

"I will come gladly, and you are always a pleasant companion, Anasha."

"No, but I always leave you feeling more pleasant than when I greet you," Annya chuckled, leaning toward Natalya and kissing her, then she took her hand and stood. "Come, I must go."

Natalya went back downstairs with her and helped

her on with her felt boots and furs, then stood shivering in the doorway and waved as Annya walked along the path toward her sleigh with her driver and footmen. She stepped back inside and closed the door, and wrapped her arms around herself, looking down at the floor and frowning worriedly as she thought about what Annya had told her. An hour later her father returned from taking the oath of allegiance, and he had stopped to buy copies of etchings of Czar Konstantine, which were being sold in shops. Natalya took them without comment and began going through the house and putting them in the frames to replace the pictures of Czar Aleksander.

When Natalya visited Annya the following afternoon, she heard news which seemed more promising but yet other news which was even more disturbing than what Annya had told her before. Grand Duke Nikolas had been swayed by Annya's arguments and had agreed on a schedule to publish Grand Duke Konstantine's renunciation and his assumption of the throne. The renunciation would be published three days later, on Friday, together with a proclamation requiring an oath of allegiance, and the ceremonies for swearing the oath of allegiance would be on the following Monday, December fourteenth.

But dispatches had come from General Diebitsch at Second Army Headquarters in Tulchin that investigation of suspicious activities immediately subsequent to Czar Alexander's death had led to the discovery of a secret revolutionary organization which had been plotting the overthrow of the Czar. The initial findings had indicated that the organization had been in existence for some time, included dozens of people, and was in contact with a similar organization located in St. Petersburg.

The dispatches confirmed what a Lieutenant Jakob

Rostovtsev of the Palace Guard had reported the day before to Grand Duke Nikolas. He had related that he had been present at a meeting where plans had been discussed for a revolt, that the conspirators included both civilians and officers, and that the leader of the conspiracy planned to establish himself as an interim dictator until a constitutional government could be elected. The lieutenant named all the civilians involved, declined to name the officers because of his code of honor, and further announced his intention of informing the conspirators that he had performed his duty as a loyal subject by betraying them.

Natalya was stunned by Annya's offhand, almost nonchalant attitude as she talked about the conspiracy. "How can you be so casual about such plots? Such men intend the destruction of the nation, and they—"

"Natasha, Natasha," Annya remonstrated, patting her shoulder. "The existence of this group has been known for some time. It was known to His Majesty Czar Aleksander, God rest his soul."

Natalya crossed herself as Annya murmured the benediction, then frowned again. "Then they should have already been arrested!" she said heatedly.

"What would you do, Natasha?" Annya sighed. "Arrest every man who returns from Germany or France where his parents have sent him to me educated and where he has been filled with foolishness in those hotbeds of radical teaching? That is what the universities are there, you know. Or have such restrictions placed on foreign travel that they could not go?" She shook her head firmly. "No, that is no cure. Tyranny and despotism beget their own end. The only cure is that which has been practiced. Let them have their meetings and rave to each other about their plots, and eventually they will mature. Today's judicious councillors are yesterday's revolutionaries."

"But now they are dangerous."

Annya hesitated, then nodded. "They could be. We are at a critical juncture of events."

"Yet they are not now being arrested?"

"Many of them are known, and they are being watched. We trust that any actions they are planning will be cancelled when Rostovtsev advises them that he has reported their undertakings to Grand Duke Nikolas." She smiled wryly and shook her head. "And Grand Duke Nikolas has been assured by Governor Miloradovich that no danger exists." Her smile faded, and she shrugged slightly. "His Excellency Grand Duke Nikolas fears arrests might inflame the situation, and he may be right. He knows the temper of the garrisons much better than I."

Natalya lifted her hands and dropped them in a gesture of despair as she shook her head worriedly. "Then we wait for Monday to see whether we have a government or a revolution."

"Uprising," Annya corrected her quietly. "If there is any untoward incident, it could only be minor. But even that would be too much. It would be an inauspicious beginning for a reign, and the punishment would be severe."

Natalya nodded silently, thinking of the conversation she'd had with Vassily in which she had indicated that some of his associations might be dangerous. If there was any show of resistance to Grand Duke Nikolas taking the throne, there would be an exhaustive investigation and everyone involved to any degree would be arrested, tried, and punished if convicted. It didn't seem possible that Vassily could be implicated, but she couldn't be sure. For several days after the conversation with him, she had debated discussing it with her father to see if he thought he should concern himself with it. But she had been reluctant to cause fric-

352

tion and incur Vassily's resentment. And she realized that she had succumbed to weakness instead of deciding on the basis of facts.

It also seemed ominous that Vassily didn't come to the house for dinner that night or the next, even though Aleksei came both nights. She called Vassily's absence to her father's attention to see if he attached any significance to it, but he shrugged it off. On Thursday she asked Aleksei to tell Vassily to come to dinner the following night, and she had the head cook prepare some of Vassily's favorite foods. He came, but he was silent and withdrawn, listening most of the time as Aleksei and Natalya's father discussed the Grand Duke Konstantine's renunciation and the Grand Duke Nikolas's proclamation which had been issued that day.

Aleksei came to dinner Saturday night, but he remained in barracks Sunday night to prepare for the parade formation to take the oath of allegiance early the next morning. It was a quiet meal, with Natalya, her father, and Olivia alone at the table. The count retired early so he could rise for the ceremony the following morning. Olivia tried to make conversation for a time with Natalya, then she also retired. Natalya remained up late, pacing restlessly back and forth in her sitting room, and when she finally went to bed she stared sleeplessly up at the ceiling in the darkness. Presently she gave up trying to sleep, got out of bed and put on a dressing gown, and went downstairs to see that her father had hot tea before he left for the ceremony.

At six o'clock, almost seventy thousand privates and noncommissioned officers were in parade formation in the grey, frigid dawn at the garrisons in the city. Their company commanders were with them, and the flag grade officers were in formation in the main ballroom of the Winter Palace, listening to Grand Duke Nikolas

353

explaining the facts leading up to his accession of the throne. He finished talking and reading the documents, and asked for comments or questions. There were none. The officers took the oath of allegiance to him, hailed him as Czar, then filed back out to their horses to return to their regiments and administer the oath to their subordinate officers.

By seven, the regimental commanders had administered the oath to most of their subordinates, and the process was beginning to trickle down to the battalion and company level. In the barracks of the First Battalion of the Semenovsky Guards, three enlisted men began shouting, "Hail to Czar Konstantine," when the battalion commander started to administer the oath. Captain Thomas Greenwood broke formation from the front of his platoon, spurred his horse through the ranks of men, and cut the three men down with his sword. He wheeled his horse back around and rode out of the ranks, which closed and reassembled behind him, then took his position again, holding his sword at present arms to take the oath as blood ran down the blade. The battalion commander administered the oath, then the formation was dismissed. One of the three men was dead, and his body was carted away. The other two were taken away to be treated and confined.

In some garrisons across the city the oath was administered without incident, and in others there were scattered rebellions. In the barracks of the Second Battalion of the Chernigovsky Regiment, three company commanders ordered their men not to salute and take the oath. One of the company commanders was shot in the back of the head by a soldier in the front rank, and another was wrestled from his horse and mauled by his men until he was unconscious. The battalion commander shot the third, and the oath was administered. In the garrison of the Moscow Guards, two companies followed the orders of their commanders and stood in silent repudiation of the oath. The battalion commander sent for the regimental commander, and when he arrived the two companies were marching out of barracks. The regimental and battalion commanders placed themselves in the path of the two mutinous companies and ordered them to halt. The company commanders ordered their men to fire, but there were only a few scattered, ineffective shots, slightly wounding the regimental commander and killing the battalion commander's horse. The two companies marched on out of barracks, firing their muskets at random and shouting, "Hail to Czar Konstantine!"

Czar Nikolas was still in the Winter Palace, where the flag grade officers and other officials were gathering to attend the traditional *Te Deum* to celebrate his accession to the throne. The regimental commander of the Moscow Guards hurried to the palace and informed Czar Nikolas of what had happened, and Governor General Miloradovich, who was standing nearby, castigated the regimental commander for permitting a misunderstanding to develop among his men and allowing them to get out of control. The Czar ordered the governor general to proceed immediately to the two companies to correct their misunderstanding and return them to their garrison, and he ordered other nearby officers to place the Second Guards Infantry Division, First Battalion of the Semenovsky Guards, and a company of the Horse Artillery Guards on alert in their barracks. The governor general and the officers left, and the Czar ordered the Metropolitan Seraphim to proceed with the celebration of the *Te Deum*.

The two companies, eight hundred men, marched along Gorokhovaya Street and formed up in the Senate Square. Shouts of "Hail to Czar Konstantine!" rang out among them, and they occasionally discharged their muskets over the heads of passers-by. The square was rapidly vacated. The governor general arrived on his horse, accompanied by two aides, and approached. He was shot and killed. The aides picked up his body and went back to report to the Czar.

The *Te Deum* over, the Czar received the governor general's aides, then dismissed them and joined the officers and officials at the buffet which had been served after the service. At twelve noon he ordered three officers present to proceed at once and bring the Second Guards Infantry Division, First Battalion of the Semenovsky Guards, and the alerted company of the Horse Artillery Guards out of garrison and to the Senate Square, and he ordered the other officers and officials to remain where they were as he left.

The Czar rode alone along Nevsky Prospekt and Gorokhovaya Street to the Senate Square. The men in the two companies became silent as he came into sight. His horse approached them at a slow walk. Several muskets were raised, then slowly lowered. He stopped in front of them, glaring at the company commanders. They looked away. His eyes moved slowly over the men. The men in the ranks moved restlessly.

The frozen silence which lay over the Senate Square was broken by the distant sound of boots pounding in a steady cadence. The sound gradually came closer, then the first companies of the Second Guards Infantry Division came into sight along Gorokhovaya Street. Presently the entire division, eight thousand strong, were spread out along the street. The first companies turned into the Square and began marching around it, and the division formed up on the three sides facing the Neva. The First Battalion of the Semenovsky Guards clattered along the street at a trot, turned into the Square, and formed into ranks on the far end of the Square facing the Neva, in front of the ranks of the

Second Guards Infantry Division. The cannon of the first company of the Horse Artillery Guards turned into the Square, the wheels of the carriages rumbling briskly, and they formed up in front of the Semenovskys. The Square became quiet again, the stillness punctuated by the occasional movement of a restive horse and by coughs in the ranks of the Second Guards.

The Czar Nikolas turned in his saddle and his voice carried across the Square in the frozen stillness as he ordered the commander of the cannon to load with short powder charges and grapeshot and to depress to point-blank range. There was a flurry of activity around the cannon, then a series of ringing shouts as corporals reported their cannon ready. Silence fell over the Square again. The Czar ordered the two companies to return to barracks and take the oath of allegiance. There were stirs and shuffles in the two companies, then they became still again. The Czar Nikolas wheeled his horse toward the cannon, shouting the command to prepare to fire. The two company commanders repeated his orders. Several shots rang out from the two companies as they fired at the Czar, one of the horsemen among the Semenovsky Guards slumped from his horse, another one fell to the ground as his horse collapsed under him, screaming shrilly and thrashing about, and two in the ranks of the Second Guards fell. A half dozen men in the ranks of the two companies broke ranks and fled toward the river embankment, followed by another dozen in scattered twos and threes. The companies began disintegrating. The Czar reined up by a cannon, pushing the gunner out of the way and reaching down from his horse for the lanyard, and he shouted the command to fire as he jerked the lanyard. The sixteen cannon thundered, belching smoke and a hail of grapeshot into the scattering ranks of the two companies. The Czar shouted at the Semenovskys to charge, and their horses sprang forward as their swords cleared the scabbards. They thundered across the Square and raced through the remanents of the two companies, leaning down to slash and stab; then chased those fleeing along the embankment. The Second Guards came forward with bayonets, and their ranks closed together across the Square.

The arrests began before dark and continued into the next day as the details of the plot unfolded. The conspirators had counted on widespread support from the soldiers by telling them that Nikolas was seizing the throne from Konstantine in his absence, intending to seize power as soon as the existing authority was overthrown. But some company commanders involved had lost heart because of Lieutenant Jakob Rostovtsev's report, and others had found that their men either didn't believe them, felt a sublime unconcern whether Nikolas or Konstantine was czar, or were reluctant to revolt against authority. The contingent of the Naval Guards which was to have attacked the Winter Palace and other palaces in the city to kill all members of the imperial family had refused to act at the last moment. Sergei Trubetskoi, the organizer who was to assume position of dictator, had quietly withdrawn from the plot when he saw that it was failing, and he had taken refuge in the Austrian embassy, where his brother-in-law was ambassador. He was located and arrested Tuesday evening.

Arrests continued on into Wednesday as more names were gathered from those who had been arrested on Wednesday afternoon. Vassily Ivanovich Sheremetev was arrested at the garrison of the Yamburgsky Regiment of Uhlans.

PART III

Love's Gentle Agony

CHAPTER XVII

The wall hung over the edge of the river like a black cliff, the rows of huge stones darkened with age and marked by the tides which had come and gone. The boatman struggled with the oars, fighting the current as the boat approached the wall. The bow of the boat bumped solidly against the stones, and the boatman dropped the oars and scrambled to slip a rope through a rusty metal ring anchored between two stones. The stern of the boat swung around on the current, the boatman let out slack on the rope, and it settled against the bottom of the steps built into the wall, thumping against them with a hollow, wooden sound as the boat rocked on the waves.

Natalya picked up one of the baskets and cautiously stepped over the gunwale to the steps. The tide was going out, and the first half dozen steps were wet and slimy from the receding water. She put the basket down and turned to take the others, and Olivia silently shook her head as she took both of them and moved toward the gunwale. Natalya picked up her basket again and began climbing the steps.

At the top, the massive, ponderous walls of SS Peter and Paul fortress loomed over the narrow street along the edge of the quay, dark, grim, and threatening. They crossed the street to a sentry box by a large, rusty gate, and Natalya took the pass from her reticule and gave it to the sentry. He looked through the thick bars of the gate and called for the corporal of the guard. The corporal came to the gate, looked at the pass, and unlocked the gate. The heavy hinges groaned as he opened it barely wide enough to let them through, and Natalya handed the sentry a ruble as they went through the gate. It was an investment. The guards rotated between sentry duty and guard duty in the dungeons, and the coins she dispensed might buy a kindness for Vassily when he needed it.

They crossed a small, bare courtyard and through a doorway into the guardroom. It was small and dirty, smelling strongly of cheap tobacco and sweat. Guards lounged about on benches, and the lieutenant sat behind a battered deal table which served for a desk. His uniform was shabby, his French was worse than Natalya's, and he was always determinedly gallant, as though to demonstrate that a plebian Streltsy could flirt as well as an officer of the elite Guards. Money would be an insult to him, even though he could unquestionably use it, but she always brought caviar, vodka, or sweetmeats for him, which could assume the guise of a friendly rather than functional gift. He glanced through the baskets perfunctorily, going through his small repertoire of gallantries, thanked her for the vodka, and pointed to one of the guards watching expectantly. It was a choice assignment, because it was always worth a ruble.

The weak, yellow light from the smoky lantern made a pool of murky light around them as they went down the curving stairs which descended into the dungeons. The edges of the stone steps had been worn over the years by countless footsteps, the fearful and reluctant shuffling of prisoners and the indifferent tread of jailors, and the walls were spotted with mildew and streaked with moisture. The stench of the dungeons rose up the stairs, a dank, fetid, choking effluvium which seemed to permeate the clothes and leave a residue on the skin, lingering for hours after leaving.

They turned into a narrow corridor at the bottom of the stairs, and the guard lifted the lantern over his head to light their way through the refuse and filth which had been pushed out of the cells on each side. Flickering, wavering shadows played along the floor and walls, rats squeaked and raced ahead of the light, and occasionally dim, bearded visages peered out from between the bars in the anxious hope that someone had come to see them. The guard stopped in front of a cell, rattling the keys and searching through them. He unlocked the door, took the baskets and put them inside the cell, re-locked the door, then put the lantern on the floor in front of the cell and moved a few steps away.

"Are you well, Vasasha?" Natalya asked, pressing her face to the bars.

"Yes. Are you?"

"Yes."

"Are you well, Olivia Vassilievna?"

"Yes, thank you."

Silence fell. During the first visits, the realization that they had nothing to say to each other had come as a shock. His honesty had disallowed protestations of innocence, her love had been a barrier to recriminations, and what had happened had been of an enormity which completely owershadowed all their shared experiences, diminishing their relationship to that of a brother accused of crime and a sister suffering the anathema of his guilt. The bars cast dark shadows on his face as the light from the lantern on the floor shone into the cell. It was tiny, a wooden bunk built against one wall and a shelf on the other, and a single small, barred window high above the floor. His hair was unkempt and he had grown a matted beard; his clothing was soiled and disheveled, and the hands gripping the bars were grimy, with long, dirty, and broken fingernails.

"Thank you for coming and bringing these things."

"It is nothing, and I am more than glad to do anything to make your lot easier. Have you thought of anything in particular you would like to have?"

"No."

Silence fell again. There was no mention of their father. And her father never referred to her visits to the fortress or asked about Vassily. He had initially forbidden her to go, but her burden of love and duty had been a much more demanding imperative than her father's command. She had obtained a pass from Annya and crossed the frozen Neva in a sleigh to the fortress, bringing food, blankets, and other necessities to supplement that provided prisoners. When she returned, she had found the strap and gone to his study and given it to him so he could thrash her for disobedience if he wished, and he had burst into tears and taken her into his arms. But he had never asked about Vassily, he had coldly ignored a single chance comment she had made about him, and he pretended that her visits to the fortress did not exist.

Vassily began weeping. It was the way the visits always ended. Natalya stepped back and glanced at the guard. He moved forward and picked up the lantern, and they walked back along the corridor. Pale, ghostly faces peered from between the bars to catch a glimpse of the visitors who broke the ennui of countless hours of misery in the long night of their lives. When they reached the top of the stairs, Natalya touched the guard's sleeve and handed him a ruble.

Despite Natalya's continuing depression, the fresh, clean, early spring air sweeping along the river gave something of a lift to her spirits after the unwholesome stench of the dungeons. The oars rattled in the locks, the afternoon sunlight gleamed on the surface of the water, and the gulls screamed as they circled and swooped after one of their number which had found a tidbit to eat. Olivia's face was set in its usual somewhat prim and withdrawn lines as she sat by Natalya in the stern of the boat. The past months had brought them much closer, and had revealed a depth of character in Olivia that Natalya had never suspected. She had long since saved enough money to return to England, and when the full extent of the cataclysm had started sorting itself out in January, Natalya had suggested to her that she might find the circumstances at the Church of England vicarage or English Club more congenial while awaiting the breakup of the ice in the port and the resumption of shipping. Olivia had wept, deeply disturbed that Natalya had even considered that she would think of leaving. It had been a deeply revealing moment. The Englishwoman's aloof, poised manner concealed a heart more warm and loving than most. Once secured, Olivia's loyalty was like tempered steel, remaining steadfast through all disaster.

Which was much more than could be said of those who had been far more demonstrative. Aleksei Orlov had been posted to the armies in Poland the week after Vassily's arrest, and hadn't even come to the house to say goodbye. There had been no communication or word from him since. Annya had dismissed him summarily with a scathing remark about cowardly puppies, and Olivia had been silent about him, which was her form of condemnation. But Natalya considered their reactions simplistic, not taking into account all the ramifications of the situation. Aleksei's father was an influential and willful man, and he might well have obtained the posting and ordered Aleksei to leave without communicating with her. Aleksei would have obeyed in order to let circumstances sort themselves out. It would be foolish of him to alienate himself from his father and be disinherited; there had been too much between them for it to end so quickly, and it was inevitable that he would contact her sooner or later.

Natalya's friendship with Annya remained firm, though not without risk on Annya's part, because the Czar's rage had been dangerous. But not irrational. Privates and noncommissioned officers involved had been transferred to other organizations, and only the commissioned officers had been arrested and imprisoned. Countries harboring those few who had escaped had found their diplomatic and commercial interests with Russia in jeopardy, and the most conclusive expression of the Czar's concern was that the traditional coronation in Moscow had been deferred until all investigations, trials, and sentences had been completed.

Others had been understandably reluctant to chance the Czar's displeasure, and not surprisingly Natalya had received no visits or invitations after the ban on public gatherings had been lifted. What had happened had spread its ripple of effects far and wide, and Annya had sarcastically remarked that whereas previously mildly seditious and heretical comments had been considered chic, it was now both fashionable and politic to express a pious horror of anything hinting of disrespect to the State or Church. The continuing friendship with Annya had been priceless, brightening many dark hours, and Natalya had done her utmost to protect it. She had carefully avoided situations which might lead to her being seen in public with Annya and undermine her influence with the Czar. The visits back and forth between them had diminished in frequency, but that was more a result of Annya's busy schedule than anything else. Natalya still went to the Marble Palace occasionally, but more often Annya came to her home.

Her only other contact was with Thomas Greenwood, and it was something of an enigma. Her suspicion that he might have a romantic interest in her had faded with time and the lack of any overt signal which could be construed as evidence. On the contrary, everything indicated that he was content with his life as a soldier and considered that dalliance with women such as Xenia an amusement which was less than distracting. So there was no obvious explanation for his frequent visits. He appeared to be visiting her father, and her father found him interesting, so she was grateful for that and for the fact that his visits to some extent dispelled the deadly boredom of remaining in the house most of the time. But only to an extent, because he was still hardly a sparkling companion. Now and then he brought a present for her when he came, always a practical gift such as a package of Italian writing paper or a box of eucalyptus pastilles for the sniffles she had developed during the winter, and they were always delivered with less grace than the sweetmeats or flowers brought for her by the friends of her father who still came to see him.

The possibility that it was Olivia who attracted him to the house hadn't escaped her. What he had said about the necessity of being married in order to come into his inheritance came into focus with the fact that Olivia was English and of approximately his age. But when she had suggested the possibility to Olivia, Olivia had responded in a huffy, almost indignant tone that their different social stations ruled out anything closer than friendship. But, thought Natalya, her response could have been motivated by defensiveness or a wish to keep her hopes from rising.

Or it could have been based on knowledge. Olivia seemed obtuse much of the time and Thomas all of the time, sharing a common national charactertistic of concealing their reactions and feelings, but there were hints that they understood each other well enough.

A couple of ships were anchored in the river, with lighters plying back and forth between them and the piers along the cargo docks, and there were other boats and barges of various sizes and types moving about. The boatman weaved through them toward the embankment at the side of St. Isaac's Square, where stone steps came down to the edge of the water. The trees along the edge of the embankment were in full leaf, and the daytime temperature had risen rapidly during the past two weeks. Over dinner two nights before, Natalya had asked her father if he wanted to go to Sherevskoye before the heat and disease of the summer began, hoping that the rest and fresh country air would take his mind off Aleksei's imprisonment and rid him of the congestive illness which had remained with him since the winter. He had replied morosely that the result of the trials might bring him a message from the Czar which would send him to Sherevskoye for the rest of his life.

Natalya paid the boatman, and they climbed the steps to the top of the embankment. The carriage was waiting a short distance away, and the driver climbed down from his seat to open the door and hand them in. As the carriage rumbled along the wide, straight, immaculately clean thoroughfares, St. Petersburg had never seemed more impersonally hostile, and she had never been more homesick for the gaudy and cluttered but simple and traditional Moscow, where the markets were brawling, seething panoramas of humanity, and where a stroll along an unfamiliar mews off one of the tortuously winding, congested, and grubby streets could lead to the discovery of a beautiful jewel of a tiny church with gilded turrets and ancient ikons or a carved stone bridge which dated from the time of the Ivans across a small canal.

A horse was tethered in the drive of the Shermetev house. The neatly cropped mane and tail and the plain, sturdy saddle identified it as a garrison horse, and the blanket under the saddle was edged with the green, crimson, and white of the Semenovskys. It was Thomas's horse.

Natalya had expected to find Thomas with her father, but he came out of the front drawing room as a maid and the house steward were taking their cloaks and bonnets. He looked as solemn as always, but she smiled brightly as she walked toward him, feeling a little guilty about some less than subtle gibes she had made about his funereal mannerisms the last time he had come.

"*Bonjour,* Thomas Stephanovich."

"*Bonjour,* Natalya Ivanova," he replied, bowing over her hand. He released her hand, turning and bowing to Olivia. "Good afternoon, Olivia."

"Good afternoon, Thomas. Are you waiting to see Count Sheremetev?"

"I have already spoken with him." He looked back at Natalya. "And he would like you to come and see him upon your return, Natalya Ivanova."

It seemed a little unusual. And there was a suggestion in his manner that a course of events about which she knew nothing was in process. But it was impossible, as usual, to read his expression. His ponderous, plodding demeanor could frequently lead to a misapprehension of significance in the most commonplace remark or situation. She nodded, turning away. "Very well. Will you stay for dinner?"

His hesitation was so long that she paused and looked back at him. He bowed slightly. "If you wish."

369

She fluttered her lashes in mock, exaggerated flirtation. "Of course I do, Thomas Stephanovich. Your lively conversation would charm the birds from the trees. Would you entertain Thomas Stephanovich while I see what my father wants of me, Olivia Vassilievna? And do try not to go to sleep."

Reproachfulness and mirth struggled on Olivia's face as she nodded. "Very well, Natalya Ivanova."

Natalya giggled, turning toward the hallway to her father's rooms, and she heard them murmuring as they went into the drawing room. She walked along the hallway to his study, and knocked on the door. There was no reply, and she opened it and looked in, hearing a hoarse cough from his bedchamber. She entered, closed the door behind her, and frowned worriedly as she crossed the study toward the bedchamber doorway. He had been spending more and more time in bed, his appetite had been getting progressively poorer, and his strength seemed to come and go. It appeared that he had received Thomas in his bedchamber, which evidenced that he felt very ill indeed, because he shunned a show of weakness.

"Father?"

"Come in, Natasha."

The effort of replying made him cough again. He was propped up in bed reading a book, and he took off his spectacles and put the book aside as she came into the room. She automatically glanced around to see if it was neat. His valet was lying on a bench by the hall door, and he put his feet on the floor and sat up. Natalya looked back at her father. "Abed again, Father? You were up this morning, were you not?"

"I felt tired, Natasha. Bring a chair over and talk to me." He looked at the valet. "You may go to the hall."

The valet silently rose and left, closing the door quietly behind him. Sending the valet away indicated a discussion of the most personal nature. The first thought which flashed through her mind was that it might have something to do with her brother's trial. But it was much too soon for any kind of conclusive result. Then she reflected that Thomas had been talking to him and he had told Thomas to send her in when she arrived. There were implications she didn't like, and she frowned slightly as she carried a chair from the corner, put it by the bed, and sat down.

"How well do you know the Englishman, Thomas Stephanovich?" the count asked.

Her frown became darker, and she looked at him for a moment in silence. "Why do you ask?"

He coughed again, a deep, rasping noise, and cleared his throat. "Because I wish to know," he said impatiently.

She looked away and shrugged. "Not well at all. Who does? He stands about with his surly looks and makes one word suffice for forty, so I doubt if anyone knows him well."

"Is that the extent of your feelings for him?"

A cold hand seemed to clutch her vitals. They had been discussing her. Then anger stirred. Her frown became a scowl, and she thrust her chin out. "Has he spoken to you about me?"

He licked his lips dryly and nodded. "Yes."

"That sly dog!" she spat. "He well knows what he would hear if he had spoken to me instead!"

"He will, but I asked him to let me speak with you first. And in his country, it is acceptable for a man to make his intentions known to a woman's father first."

"Such barbaric proceedings suit him well," Natalya growled. "And you have your answer, as he will shortly. The only one for whom I have feelings is Aleksei Andreyevich."

He uttered a disgusted sound and gestured irritably.

371

"Have you no pride? How can you have 'feelings' for a man who—"

"You do not understand the circumstances, Father," she interrupted him firmly.

He frowned darkly, snowly nodding. "Then perhaps you would be so good as to explain them to me."

The conversation was closing in on her. And the situation. From his expression and manner, her father had made a decision. Fright swelled within her, smothering her anger, and she tried to think of things to say. "It could be that I do not know the extent of them myself. There are many reasons why he could have left without speaking to me. His father could have ordered him to have no contact with . . . us . . . until the situation is settled, and it would be unfair to criticize a son for obedience to his father. Or it could have been that—"

"It could have been anything," her father interrupted brusquely. "No one knows the full circumstances of another, but in this instance I know the facts involved. He left for Poland without explaining himself to you or to me. He has been there for months without communication with either of us. That is all I need to know, and it should be sufficient for you as well."

She sighed and shook her head. "I do not wish to debate with you, Father, and it is clear that you do not understand."

"I do not intend to debate with *you*, and I believe my understanding exceeds yours. And I want no more discussion of the Orlov pup. I want to talk to you about—"

"You have no call to refer to him in such a manner!"

"I have call to try his blade for how he has dealt with you, were he here!" her father retorted heatedly, then began coughing. The spasms shook him, and he gripped his chest and winced with pain. Natalya moved toward him, an expression of deep concern on her face, and he waved her back to her chair, gasping for breath and reaching for a bottle on the table by the bed. He pulled the cork out of it and took a drink, and pushed the cork back and put it on the table, controlling his cough with an effort. "I am concerned about your welfare," he said in a choked voice.

"My welfare?" she said indignantly. "By God! You have been discussing me with a man for whom I have no feeling, and this is in the name of my welfare? Have you also by chance been bartering with the owners of brothels for me?"

He frowned darkly, glaring at her. "You shall not speak to me in such a manner as that, Natalya Ivanova!"

"Then how should I, your honor? Am I to be grateful to you for talking to some hulking brute of a foreigner about me behind my back?"

His frown faded into a grim, weary expression and he looked away, shaking his head. "This is not the way I would have it, but I have little choice. I am an old, sick man. There is every reason to believe Vassily Ivanovich will be found guilty, and if he is found guilty and I die, then all the property I own will go to the State. You will be destitute, because a child cannot inherit. But a married woman can." He coughed weakly and controlled it again, looking back at her. "And he is a good man, as well as a good soldier. I have spoken with others about him, and everyone speaks well of him. He comes from a good family, and he is a man of substance. Beyond all that, there is the consideration that there is no one else. And you must be married."

She stared at him, appalled. His voice had a firm, definite tone. He had decided. It seemed as though an abyss had opened up beneath her. She slowly shook her head, gazing at him with a horrified expression. "You cannot do this to me," she gasped.

"I have always tried to give you your way, Natasha," he said sadly, shaking his head. "But this time I cannot."

Tears of despair filled her eyes, and she put her face in her hands as she began sobbing. "Do not command me to marry him, Father," she whispered in an agonized tone. "Do not do this to me!"

"Do not make me command you, Natasha," he murmured, his voice suddenly breaking. "This is what you must do, and I ask you to do it in love for me. Do not make me command you."

She lifted her head and looked at him through her tears. There were tears in his eyes and on his cheeks. He looked very old, tired, and ill. And sorrowful, although his torture could hardly be as great as hers. The decision had been made, and it had the force of a command. Her only option was to accept it or make him force her into it. She swallowed and nodded. "Very well, Father," she whispered.

He lifted his arms toward her, his hands trembling and tears running down his cheeks. "Kiss me, Natasha."

She pushed herself up from the chair and moved leadenly to the side of the bed, and she bent over him and kissed him as he embraced her. Then she straightened up and turned away from the bed, stumbling toward the door as she wiped her eyes with the back of her hands. She felt numb, totally unreal, as though this were some horrible nightmare from which she would presently awaken. She opened the door and stepped out into the hallway, pulling the door closed behind her, and walked blindly along the hall. When Vassily had been arrested and Aleksei had left, it had seemed that she had plumbed the depths of depression and sorrow. But this despair was greater. There was nothing left. She crossed the entry hall toward the drawing room, where Thomas's and Olivia's voices were still murmuring. The house steward came out of the ballroom and started to walk toward her, then turned away, looking at her with a concerned expression. She swallowed and wiped the tears from her eyes again, and stopped in the doorway and looked at Thomas. Olivia sprang to her feet, frowning with concern. Thomas stood and looked at her with an unfathomable expression.

Natalya felt only a dull, seething hatred for this man. "You have had your will with my father, and I must do as he commands," she said in a quiet, trembling voice. "But you will never have your will with me. The only thing which will ever await you in my bedchamber is a pistol ball."

"Perhaps in time the situation will be less distressing for you, Natalya Ivanova," he said quietly.

"Less distressing," she hissed sarcastically, and she lifted her fist and shook it at him. "You whoremonger's whelp! You will rue this day!"

She wheeled away from the door and ran across the entry hall to the staircase. She needed to flee, to hide in the security of her rooms. Her toe caught in her petticoats as she started up the stairs, and she almost fell, jerked her skirt and petticoats out of the way, and began stumbling up the stairs. She heard Olivia's running footsteps behind her. Her legs suddenly became rubbery and weak. Tears blinded her again, trembling on the verge of breaking through. Olivia caught up with her, and her arms were warm and friendly, offering comfort. The tears exploded. She sagged against Olivia, weeping wildly, and Olivia helped her up the stairs, murmuring in a soothing voice.

CHAPTER XVIII

The wedding was a tawdry, shabby charade in Natalya's eyes, pathetic in Olivia's attempts to provide something of the appropriate symbols and attributes of the occasion, rawly awkward in its hurried and inelegant execution and embarrassing in the pitifully small gathering assembled to witness the event. It was a cruel humiliation in the absence of love, that most basic and fundamental necessity to the joining of a man and woman, in the presence of which they could be truly wedded by only smiling and reaching out to each other, and without which all the trappings and ceremony the human mind could devise must utterly fail in its undertaking to join two souls.

Besides the priest, there were three of her father's oldest friends, Annya, Olivia, and the count, leaning on his cane and trying to keep from coughing, his frock coat dingy because his valet had overlooked brushing it or hadn't wanted to exert the effort. And of course Thomas, who hadn't had sufficient respect for his uniform to dress in mufti and save the proud unform of the Semenovsky's from involvement in such shameful hypocrisy.

The wedding took place in the front drawing room,

the priest muttering the words, her voice whispering and Thomas's deep voice intoning the responses. It was an abbreviated form of the service which was soon over. The wedding breakfast was held in the dining room, and the obligatory toasts were excruciatingly difficult to struggle through. But the hastily gulped glasses of champagne provided a buffer to bolster Natalya's feeling of detachment from reality so she wouldn't burst into tears and shame her father.

The priest made his excuses and left. The three old men talked and laughed with her father for a time and also left. Her father had spasms of coughing and went to his rooms a couple of times for his cough elixir, and the third time he didn't return. Thomas's lack of sensitivity made him apparently oblivious to the awkwardness of the situation, and he appeared perfectly at ease as he sat at the table and sipped a glass of champagne, listening to the conversation maintained by Olivia and Annya and replying briefly when addressed. Olivia showed small indications of strain, but her almost superhuman control provided a facade of poise.

Annya's aplomb never deserted her, and from her behavior and attitude it could have been any small gathering of friends as she sat by Natalya with her hand on her shoulder, sipping champagne, nibbling delicacies, and chatting with Olivia. Both she and Olivia had been deeply sympathetic in their discussions of the situation with Natalya, but both of them had also accepted it with surprising readiness. Natalya felt alone and deserted in the calamity which her father's decision had brought upon her.

Natalya lifted her glass and drained it again, and a footman stepped forward and refilled it. Annya's breath was warm against the side of Natalya's face as she talked to Olivia. Thomas sat with one arm over the back of his

377

chair and the other resting on the table in front of him near his champagne glass, listening to Annya. He looked very smug and self-satisfied, and her hatred flared.

"I would not want to keep you from your duties at your garrison."

Her flat, quiet voice cut through the conversation between Annya and Olivia, and a sudden silence fell. Thomas pushed his chair back from the table and rose, bowed slightly, and turned toward the door. Olivia made an uncomfortable and mildly reproachful sound in her throat. Annya looked from Thomas to Natalya with bemusement as he walked through the doorway.

"By God, you have him answering to rein quickly enough," Annya chuckled quietly as his footsteps crossed the entry hall. "But you might have a care that your hand is not too heavy at first."

"He has what he wants," Natalya replied in an even tone. "A paper which says he is married to a woman of good family so he may come into his inheritance."

"I'll be surprised if he's satisfied with that," Annya laughed, a ribald grin spreading across her face. "If he is, I've misread his looks at you."

"If you can read his looks, Euripides in the original is child's play for you, gloomy brute that he is. Here, have some of this caviar. Perhaps it will take the taste of this sorry affair from your mouth. A funeral would have undoubtedly been more pleasant, and I've never had clearer evidence of your friendship than your presence here today."

Annya smiled fondly, putting her arm around Natalya and smiling down at her. "I am always glad to see you, Natasha. And, as I told you, I am troubled that you are miserable. But give it time, little one. Captain Greenwood is a good soldier and a good man, and there are many women who would wish to do as well. Love and respect will follow if you let it. Love is pleas-

378

ant, but it makes thin gruel when other things are absent. A good man of good station is first, and other things will come later."

"You are marvellously comforting about my pinching shoe when you are barefoot, Anasha," Natalya replied sourly, then she forced a smile and patted Annya's cheek. "But I will not debate with you, because you are my friend and I love you. Here, have some more caviar."

Annya smiled and shook her head, patting her stomach and sighing. "I have eaten my fill, Natasha, but I will have another glass of champagne."

Natalya glanced at a footman as Annya picked up her glass and drained it, and the footman stepped forward to refill it. She looked back at Annya. During the past weeks, there had been a gradual but steady diminishment in Annya's previously ample bulk, and she was beginning to look as trim as she could, considering her large, heavy-boned frame. During their visits back and forth, there had been a marked reduction in Annya's appetite. Her gown was in characteristically poor taste, a lavender silk which was expensive but which didn't suit her at all, and it looked as though it had been altered to take it in.

Natalya was struck by a sudden, chilling thought. Annya had mentioned possible matches for her several times. If she had been losing weight to be more presentable to a suitor, with an immediate prospect of marriage, it would almost certainly mean that she would be leaving the country. "You've lost weight, haven't you, Anasha? Have you prospects of marriage yourself?"

Annya shook her head. "No. The Baron of Darmstadt-Hesse died during the winter, and Czar Nikolas has withdrawn other possibilities. He has shown an inclination to keep me about." She looked down at her-

379

self with an expression of satisfaction, nodding. "And I have lost weight. It's been His Majesty's doing, but not by starving me—he has been giving me so much work to do that I hardly have time to eat." She sipped her champagne and put the glass back down, looking at it with a musing, reflective expression. "But somehow I also want less to eat now. My work seems to be more of a pleasure, and one which suffices me. And one which I might with advantage be now engaged, by the way." She looked down at Natalya, smiling apologetically. "May I leave, Natasha? As much as I enjoy your company, I risk the Czar's displeasure if I fail to finish a task which he gave me to complete today."

"Of course, Anasha. I am very grateful for the beautiful presents, and even more so for your presence to make the day lighter for me."

Annya chuckled and patted Natalya's shoulder as they pushed their chairs back and rose. "The day is as light or heavy as you make it for yourself, Natasha, but I hope my company is as pleasant for you as yours is for me." She turned toward Olivia and smiled at her. "Goodbye, Olivia Vassilievna."

"Goodbye, Annya Konstantinovna," Olivia replied. "It was very pleasant talking with you again."

"And for me," Annya said, taking Natalya's hand as they walked toward the door.

They walked out of the dining room and across the entry hall, Annya holding Natalya's hand as she talked to her softly. It was more of the same. A good attitude and positive approach would bring happiness. Thomas was an excellent match, and he would be a good husband. Her situation was secure, and in due time the social activities of the city would be open to her again if things went well, and her life would be complete. She had much for which to be thankful. Natalya didn't want to argue with Annya, so she listened patiently with a

380

neutral smile as she helped her into her cloak and let her out the door.

The footmen were carrying the wedding presents upstairs as Natalya walked back across the entry hall from the door. The three old men had brought the usual things, silver and porcelain. Olivia had given her a set of vases in blue Delft. Annya had brought a beautiful ikon of St. Aleksander Nevsky which dated from the past century and a large dinner service of Meissen which filled several boxes. Her father had given her a bill against the State treasury for two thousand gold rubles. It was a handsome present, a massive amount of money, but it was somewhat diminished by the fact that she had found out he had given Thomas twenty thousand gold rubles as dowry, probably a more substantial sum than would be given to Annya's husband when she married.

Natalya walked slowly up the stairs, feeling weary, gloomy, and out of sorts from the champagne so early in the day. Her maids were sighing rapturously over the presents, and Natalya dispiritedly crossed the sitting room to the bedchamber as they rattled on. She went into the bedchamber, fell onto the bed and buried her face in her pillow, weeping.

Thomas came back for dinner. Her father had frequently been having dinner in his rooms if he was feeling too ill or weak to dress for dinner, but he was obviously feeling better and joined them. His mood was jovial, with something of an air of relief in his manner, and he addressed Thomas as one of the family. Olivia was her usual serene self. Natalya had awakened in the middle of the afternoon with a headache from the champagne, and the champagne she had gulped to cure the headache made her feel disorganized and more than slightly addled. The headache was also trying to return, and she soothed it with two glasses of vodka during the hors d'oeuvres. The vodka helped the headache, but she rocked on her feet as they got up to go into the dining room, bringing a quick glance from Thomas as Olivia took her arm to steady her.

He sat where Vassily usually sat, with Olivia down the table from him. Her father's mood had become even more expansive with the vodka he had drunk, and he laughed and talked with Thomas. Thomas conversed in his usual terse, quiet manner, but somehow it seemed that both of them enjoyed the conversation. Natalya wasn't hungry, but she drank several glasses of wine as she picked and nibbled at her food. Coffee was served, and her father excused himself from the table with clumsy nonchalance to have his coffee and cigarette in his study. Natalya tried to glare threateningly and belligerently at Thomas, but her eyelids were so leaden that they kept closing, and the room seemed to be revolving slowly around her. Presently he rose, said good night in a quiet voice, and left. Olivia came around the table, and she helped Natalya out of her chair and assisted her up the stairs to her rooms.

The count had never been acutely sensitive to or curious about what went on in the household or among those around him, and a sudden worsening of his congestive illness sent him back to bed and kept him away from the dinner table for a time. As a result, it was several days before he found out that Thomas was still staying at the garrison. It troubled him, and when he began having dinner with them again he tried to explore the subject with what were meant to be delicate and subtle hints, bringing no response from Thomas and cold, hostile glares from Natalya. After a time, he gave up.

A routine resumed, not markedly different from the

382

routine which had existed before, with some minor adjustments due to Thomas's daily presence in the house. On some evenings he had duty in his garrison, and he would come to the house during the afternoon for three or four hours, sometimes seeing Natalya while he was there but making no obvious effort to do so. His actions around the house seemed designed to insinuate himself into the household and establish a clear claim as the son-in-law, because he occasionally gave the serfs small things to do, called the gardeners' attention to roses which needed trimming, and had the grooms clean out the feed bins and do repairs in the stables. During a day off, he worked with a couple of serfs in repairing a fountain in the front garden. He wasn't backward about doing manual labor, but on the other hand it didn't seem to be a demonstration of willingness to do such work. It appeared that he had simply observed that the fountain needed repair and had decided to do it.

While he was working on it, Natalya passed an upstairs window and stopped for a moment to look. He was wearing a linen shirt with the sleeves rolled up, his uniform trousers and a wide belt, and work boots. As she watched, two serfs struggled to put a slab of marble back into place, and Thomas took it from them and lifted it back into place with no apparent exertion. But the bulging of the muscles in his powerful shoulders split the shoulder seam on his shirt. The serfs laughed and exclaimed admiringly, and he smiled slightly and nodded as he pointed to the smaller slabs of marble for them to lift them into place. As she turned away from the window and walked along the hallway, she reflected that he wasn't an unhandsome man, large and strong, and she could see how he would be attractive to a woman such as Xenia.

When it became clear that he had no intention of forcing himself on her, she became more adjusted to his presence. He began taking her riding occasionally and they went to some of the smaller and more private theaters, and it was very enjoyable. While he was as dull as he had always been, she was at least assured of a lack of advances from him, and he was impressive enough in his uniform to do her credit. Olivia communicated concern about the continuing platonic nature of her marriage, and Annya inquired bluntly and made ribald suggestions and comments on the subject when they visited each other. Natalya dismissed Annya's remarks, and she disregarded Olivia's troubled air. She had given the matter full consideration, and she found ample reason to be satisfied with the situation.

She was totally secure, regardless of what happened, and there was also a way out. An unconsummated marriage was less than complete by law, and it could be annulled. Once Vassily's trial was finished and sufficient time had passed, her situation would be almost as it had been prior to his involvement in the uprising. Except that she was married. But her connections with the imperial family were firm, and she could petition the Czar and the Metropolitan Seraphim through Annya to get an annulment. And then she would marry Aleksei.

But other less complicated and far less important plans had gone awry in the past, particularly when they involved other people. Thomas might conceivably interpose an objection, but he had his twenty thousand gold rubles and his inheritance, which should satisfy him. It was tempting to sound out Annya on the idea but it would be premature, considering the current state of things. Natalya was also tempted to discuss it with Olivia, but her horrified indignation was predictable. Her father had clearly stated that her welfare was his only concern, so it should make little difference to him to

384

whom she was married, provided she was indeed a wife. It was likely that he would object to providing another dowry, considering his grumbling and muttering about household accounts—fifty rubles for a gown, thirty for a vase—but he undoubtedly could be persuaded.

By far the greatest imponderable in the situation was Aleksei. His continued silence was inexplicable. His fervent expressions of undying love were still fresh in her mind, returning with agonizing clarity each time her eye fell upon some reminder of him in her room. She had selected a choice blossom from each bouquet of flowers he had sent and placed them in a book to press and dry. Virtually each time she opened a book she would find one. There were boxes which had contained bonbons and pastilles and which she kept small trinkets in. Books he had bought for her were in a prominent place on the top shelf of one of the bookcases, and a swatch of ribbons he had brought for her was in her pillowslip, carefully removed by the maids and replaced each time the pillowslip was changed. In her mind's eye, she could picture his handsome, smiling face on each occasion when he had uttered some poignant phrase which had set her heart to racing madly. She could touch her mouth and recall the pressure of his lips on hers, a gentle caress increasing to a passionate intensity which made her flush and her breath catch in her throat even in memory.

But he was silent. It was impossible in the face of what had existed between them, but it was a fact. But if he was compelled by a command from his father to remain out of contact with her until Vassily's trial and attendant difficulties were settled, he could be depending upon what existed between them to provide her with faith, trust, and understanding. A love of such boundless strength could surely bridge the gap of a lapse in communication. In which event, her marriage—

of which he had undoubtedly heard—would seem the ultimate perfidy.

The idea of writing occurred to Natalya. If Aleksei were under an edict by his father not to communicate with her, it would present him with an opportunity to rationalize his way around the command in order to be courteous. Also, if her marriage had created doubt in his mind as to her willingness to communicate, a note would resolve that in his mind. And it would only be a note, short and simple, a few words about the weather, a comment on a couple of books she had recently read, and so forth. A polite chatty note from one friend to another. Once the silence was broken, there would be opportunity to gradually lengthen the letters and go more deeply into what she wanted to say. She would explain the circumstances of her marriage, and she would very carefully phrase hints as to the precise nature of her marriage. And eventually, of course, she would sound him out on his reaction to an annulment of her marriage and marriage to him in order to realize the happiness they had planned to have together.

The first note was twenty pages long. And, in re-reading it, it seemed to Natalya to delve too rapidly and too deeply into matters she had meant to address in subsequent letters, when communication had been firmly established. After marking out many passages and condensing and rephrasing others, the second try brought it down to ten, which still seemed too long. It took a lot of paper, but Thomas had fortunately provided her with a couple of packages not long before, and she finally got the note down to six pages by keeping a fine trim on the quill and spacing the lines closely. She let it wait for a day and read it over again to make sure she was satisfied with it, then sealed it in a packet, addressed it, and sent it by footman to the military courier station to be taken to the garrison in Warsaw.

CHAPTER XIX

Almost immediately after sending the letter, doubts about the wisdom of writing began to occur to Natalya. If her father found out that she had written to Aleksei, he would be apoplectic with rage. And there was an incident with a soldier at SS Peter and Paul which gave her reason to give at least passing consideration to Thomas's possible reactions.

There had been occasional remarks or comments by the guards at the fortress which bordered on insolence when their officer wasn't present, and Natalya had always contained her temper and held her tongue in event any retaliation by her would be passed on to Vassily. Such incidents always enraged Olivia, who was extremely apprehensive when around men who might be uncouth or forward, and another occurred which was so irritating that Natalya was provoked to the extent of snarling at the soldier. He was unimpressed by the rebuke, laughing rudely, but he didn't make any more insolent comments.

On Natalya's next visit to the fortress, the guards were obviously frightened of her and went to great lengths to be polite. It was a marked change in attitude, and at the same time Olivia seemed to be very complacent about it. It took Natalya some prying to find out from Olivia what had happened, and when she did it revealed a hitherto unknown facet of Thomas's personality.

Olivia had told Thomas about the incident, and the following day, Thomas had gone to the fortress, hunted the soldier down, and thrashed him soundly with a riding crop. Natalya had always been accustomed to handling her own affairs, but it gave a not displeasing sense of being looked after and protected. But it wasn't the usual way of handling such a situation. Most men, Aleksei for example, would have gone to the soldier's officer and demanded he be punished. It showed a tendency in Thomas to go straight to the source of a problem and take the most direct sort of action. And it also showed a streak of viciousness. For the first time, it occurred to her that Thomas might have something to say about her letter to Aleksei if he found out about it. He *was* her husband. But the post would be delivered while he was at the garrison, and there seemed to be small likelihood that he would find out.

During a late afternoon some two weeks after she had dispatched the note, she was reading a book in her sitting room. There was a quiet knock on the door, and it opened to reveal Thomas was standing in the doorway. It was earlier than he usually arrived from the garrison, and he had apparently come straight upstairs to her room, because he was still wearing his plumed helmet and the straps for his scabbard were still hooked to his wide belt. He removed his helmet as he stepped into the room, and tucked it under his arm, closing the door behind him. Both his actions and manner seemed highly presumptuous, and Natalya stiffened and frowned darkly.

"You will wait until you are invited to come in my rooms. And it promises to be a wait of some length."

"I will come here when I have matters to transact with you," he replied tersely. He looked at the maids as

388

they came curiously to the bedchamber doorway. "Wait outside."

The maids rushed hurriedly toward the door without waiting for her nod to confirm the order. Natalya dropped her book on the sofa and stood. Something about his demeanor stirred a feeling of disquiet. Before, he had always been scrupulously courteous in his quiet, withdrawn way. He didn't seem precisely discourteous, but there was a hard edge to the way he looked at her which she hadn't seen before. It took her aback for an instant, then she took the offensive.

"You shall not come to my chambers and order my maids about! And if you have something to communicate to me, you shall tell the house steward, he will advise me through my maids, and I will wait upon you when the opportunity presents itself!"

He looked at her in silence. The door closed quietly behind the maids. He turned, opened the door, and looked into the hallway. There was a flurry of footsteps as the maids scuttled away from the door, where they had been waiting to listen. He closed the door firmly and unbuttoned his tunic pocket as he walked toward her, and he took a letter from his pocket and held it out to her.

"Read this."

The letter was addressed to him at his garrison, and it was in an unfamiliar hand, one accustomed to writing in formal German script by the way the letters were formed. She turned the packet over, and a cold wave of apprehension raced through her. It was from a general in Warsaw, a Baron Gniessen. Thomas was standing a short distance away, his eyes on her, and she felt overwhelmed by his size and presence. She moved away from him, shrugging nonchalantly. "I have no particular objection to reading it. You may ask me to, and I will do so. When I have time."

389

"Read the letter, Natalya Ivanova."

The tone was no more forceful and his voice was still quiet, but it was more compelling. And her apprehension was growing and would continue to do so until she knew what was in the letter. She sighed impatiently, jerking the letter out of the packet and unfolding the pages. It was in French but written in the alphabet of German script, and she frowned slightly as she began deciphering it. The baron was evidently Thomas's friend, because the salutation was familiar. He was also wordy, because the letter was several pages long. There was a reference to a party they had attended together the last time he had been in St. Petersburg, and then a paragraph about disciplinary problems in his regiment. Her apprehension faded and she relaxed, reading a couple more lines, then she shrugged again and looked up at him.

"What has this to do with me?"

"Read the letter, Natalya Ivanova."

She glared at him, then sighed again and shuffled the pages, reading on. Halfway down the second page, she stiffened with shock and her mouth fell open. It was only a couple of lines, tossed in quite casually, then the letter went on about something concerning the lack of sufficient supplies of uniforms and other items of equipment. But the two lines were like a bombshell to Natalya.

A Lieutenant Orlov, a platoon commander in one of his companies, had received a letter from Captain Greenwood's wife, and Lieutenant Orlov had asked the baron to advise his friend Captain Greenwood of the fact, because Lieutenant Orlov did not consider it appropriate to communicate directly with Captain Greenwood's wife.

It was so stunning that her mind reeled for an instant, trying to assimilate it. And suddenly everything had a different perspective. Aleksei's abrupt departure and long silence had indeed been a rejection of their love and of her, as her father had indicated. His devotion amounted to a modicum of feeling fleshed out with glib talk, and had utterly collapsed in the face of the first breath of scandal. He was a cad who had exposed her to ridicule and shame, so shallow had been his feelings and so precipitant his flight. As the ultimate rebuff, he had replied to her ill-considered note through a third party to her husband, to the effect that he did not wish to communicate with her. She had been made a fool of.

She stared up at Thomas with a stricken expression as the awful realization dawned on her. There was resentment in his eyes, and she realized that what she had done had exposed him to insult, even shame. But the shuddering collapse of all she had felt for Aleksei was so cataclysmic that she gave only a passing thought to Thomas's concerns. That which she had dwelt upon for months and which had been so much a part of her was suddenly gone, leaving a hollow, gaping emptiness. Tears flooded her eyes.

His features softened as he looked down at her, and he sighed as he stepped to her and put his big hand on her shoulder. "Natalya Ivanova, you are a very young woman and I have no wish to—"

"Get out!" she screamed, knocking his hand away and leaping away from him. She pointed to the door, sobbing wildly. "Out! Get out!"

She was still holding the letter, and she began tearing the pages into pieces as she wept brokenly. Through her tears, she saw Thomas turn and walk toward the door. He opened it and beckoned to her maids as he went through the doorway, and she continued shredding the pages of the letter into tiny pieces and weeping. The maids filed back into the room and closed the

391

door, looking at her and at the snowfall of paper with wide eyes. She threw the last of the letter down and ran to her bookcases. She began taking the once-precious flowers out of the books and throwing them among the bits of paper in the middle of the room.

There was a light knock on the door, and Olivia stepped in. The maids glanced worriedly up at her and continued gathering up the pieces of paper and dried flowers from the floor. Natalya sniffled and sobbed like a miserable child, snatching the books Aleksei had given her from their special shelf, tearing the inscribed pages and shredding them, and hurling the books across the room. When she finished with the books, her eyes lit on a tin box on her desk. It was a pastille box from Aleksei in which she kept her knife for sharpening quills and other small things. She opened the box, dumped the things out of it and flung it to the floor, then crushed it underfoot. Olivia went back out and closed the door quietly behind her.

Natalya searched out all her beloved mementos—the flowers put away to dry, the books passionately inscribed to her, theater programs, champagne bottle corks—and threw them away. As the maids were collecting up the last of them, she remembered the ribbons in her pillowslip. She raced into her bedchamber and threw them out the window, then stumbled to her bed and fell on it, sobbing bitterly.

Natalya's emotional investment in her love for Aleksei had been massive because she had held nothing back, and the sudden collapse of his golden, shining image erected in her mind was devastating. Her faith and trust had remained solid and untarnished until the instant they had turned to dust. Her father had warned her that her faith and hope were misplaced, but she had disregarded his words in the light of his lack of understanding of the immortal love on which they had been based. In retrospect, it appeared that his understanding had been less deficient than she had supposed.

Natalya was prostrate with shame and humiliation. In her mind's eye, she could picture the face which had seemed godlike, but which she now realized lacked character, and the smile which had glowed down at her upon greeting actually needed little alteration to become sarcastic and sneering. It was probably the same smile he had worn when telling his comrades of the one he had wooed and won in St. Petersburg and who had endeavored to remain in contact with him even after her marriage. No doubt he had joked about her with some Polish woman of uncouth manners, no education, and low morals.

Along with the seething turmoil of her emotions, there was also a cold touch of fear. Her father would be in a rage if Thomas told him. She pulled herself together and slid off the bed, drying her eyes with her sleeve. Her maids had returned from burning the things, and she motioned them in to get her ready for dinner.

Her father had dinner with them and his good mood was abundant evidence that he didn't know. But Olivia's demeanor telegraphed that she did. During the past weeks, Olivia had been subtly disparaging about Aleksei, and Natalya searched Olivia's face for indications of satisfaction that her opinion of Aleksei had been confirmed. She found none, but it occurred to her that Olivia's expression was often as hard to read as Thomas's.

By the following day the event had assumed a more reasonable proportion in her mind, subordinate to what had happened to Vassily and becoming even more minor in relation to that disaster as she thought about it. But the pain remained. And while it wasn't precisely Thomas's fault, he was involved. It was *his* friend who had addressed the matter so callously in his letter. His

393

approach to the matter had been reminiscent of his dealings with the insolent soldier at the fortress, figuratively drubbing her with the letter instead of a riding crop. If his only objective had been to inform her of the matter, he could have given the letter to the house steward to give to one of her maids, saving her the embarrassment of his presence in her distress.

And then there was the matter of the books. Thomas had apparently stopped the maids before they burned them to look at them, or had asked Olivia the titles, and the next evening the house steward handed one of her maids a heavy, paper-wrapped package containing a new copy of each one of them, the Byron, Racine, Voltaire, and the two volumes of Rousseau. It was a pleasure to have them back, but to Natalya's wounded spirit it seemed that replacing them was an oblique and cunning tactic of Thomas's to assure she would remember the incident of the note each time she looked at her bookshelves.

Two days later she found a means of reprisal while reading through a news sheet. At first she was enraged, determined to meet him at the front door and berate him about it, then she thought again. It would be more effective to coldly present the matter and demand an explanation. She thought about it for a moment longer, then smiled grimly and nodded to herself as she tore the piece out of the news sheet, folded it, and put it in her pocket.

It seemed for a time that it was going to be one of the evenings he remained at the garrison, and she would have to wait to confront him until the next day. He came in, however, while they were having hors d'oeuvres in the drawing room, apologized quietly for his tardiness, and sat down. Natalya glowed with satisfaction as she rose from where she was sitting, and he looked closely at her expression. She hadn't told Olivia about it, but Olivia had apparently concluded that she had something on her mind because Olivia's eyes followed her as she went to the credenza. Her father began talking to Thomas, referring to a subject they had discussed a couple of days before. Natalya filled a plate, poured a glass of the white vodka he preferred, tucked a serviette under her arm, and went around the couch to him. He held his serviette on his lap instead of around his neck, as Olivia did, and he shook it open on his lap and took the plate and glass, thanking her gravely. She silently nodded, her satisfied smile still in place, and went back and sat demurely down on the sofa. Her father asked Thomas a question, but his eyes were still on her with a bemused expression, then he looked back at her father and asked him to repeat the question.

The meal seemed to take a long time, but she found she had a good appetite and she ate heartily as she listened to Thomas and her father, with occasional remarks from Olivia on some subjects. The conversation touched on the Caucasus and her father confused the provisions of the Treaty of Bucharest with that of Gulistan, and Natalya automatically corrected him in a loud voice through a mouthful of food. It almost developed into one of their frequent heated arguments, with both of them changing to Russian, leaning toward each other, and thumping the table for emphasis; then she became aware that she was delaying her father's departure from the table and her confrontation with Thomas. She subsided and began eating again, surprising and disappointing her father and bringing long, thoughtful looks from both Thomas and Olivia.

When the meal was finally over and coffee served, her father excused himself and withdrew. Natalya took her cigarette from the footman and puffed on it, feeling gratified and contented as she savored the glow of anticipation of what the next few minutes would bring. Both Thomas and Olivia were silent for a moment, glancing across the table at her, then Olivia said in English that she had received some journals from England which he might find interesting. He replied in English, and they began discussing the news.

Natalya put her cigarette into the bowl in front of her, untied her serviette and dropped it onto the table, and pushed her chair back and rose. Olivia and Thomas immediately became silent, looking at her. She walked slowly around the end of the table, taking the piece of newspaper from her pocket, and she unfolded it and put it on the table in front of him. "Read that, Thomas Stephanovich," she said triumphantly.

He glanced at the piece of paper, and looked back up at her. "What is this, Natalya Ivanova? A piece of a—"

"Read that, Thomas Stephanovich," she said in a louder voice.

He pursed his lips and looked at her with an inscrutable expression, then looked at the piece of paper, turning it to the light of the candles. Natalya moved closer to him, the front of her skirt pressing against the legs of his chair, and she leaned on her right hand on the table and put her left hand on her hip, looking at him with an indignant expression.

"Well?" he murmured, looking back at her and shrugging slightly.

"Well?" she exploded in a shout, leaning closer and taking his collar with her left hand as she glared into his eyes. "Is that all you have to say? After skulking off to a party at Xenia Artamonovna's house? Or do you deny what is printed there?"

He straightened up slightly in his chair, his eyes fixed on hers, and he lifted one hand, removed her hand from his collar and put it on the edge of the table by her other hand, and replied in a quiet voice, "I deny nothing, Natalya Ivanova. I attended a reception for my battalion commander at Xenia Artamonovna's house."

"With your wife remaining at home like some whore you found on the streets?" she shouted at the top of her voice, seizing his collar again. "Do you take me for a child or a fool that I cannot perceive the relationship you have with that woman? Is it your intention to make me the laughing stock of St. Petersburg? By God, you might have a care lest I do the same for you!"

He lifted his hand to move her hand again. She tightened her grasp, but he effortlessly picked up her hand and put it by her other hand again. "In the future, I will not attend social functions to which you are not invited, if you construe it as a slight, Natalya Ivanova," he said in the same quiet voice.

It was difficult to maintain a proper attitude of belligerent aggressiveness in the face of the level, unswerving look from his eyes. And the combination of his glacial calm and large size made him seem overpowering, towering over her and surrounding her even while sitting. She turned away, then wheeled back toward him and slammed her fist down on the edge of the table. "*Slight,* you say?" she stormed. "*Slight?* A deadly insult, I'd say!"

"No other wives were invited, Natalya Ivanova. If they had been, I would not have gone."

"And that is your excuse?" she shouted, thumping her fist on the table again. "I should have expected as much! By God, you're loath to leave the riotous life to which you're accustomed, are you not? You worked your way into my father's confidence and persuaded him to force me to marry you, and you still pursue the wild ways of a garrison soldier!" She leaned toward him, drumming her fist on the table. "I'll not have it! Do you understand me?"

"I will move into the household forthwith, if that is what you wish, Natalya Ivanova."

It wasn't exactly the conclusion she had intended, but it seemed logical enough. And it would be a positive way of keeping up with his activities. "Tonight!" she shouted triumphantly. "You shall do that *tonight*!" She turned toward the house steward, pointing to him. "Go tell the housekeeper to prepare the chambers across the hall from Olivia Vassilievna's for immediate occupancy."

The house steward bowed slightly and walked quietly toward the doorway. Thomas pushed his chair back and rose. "I will take a wagon from the stables, and I shall return presently, Natalya Ivanova."

"Very well," she sniffed, nodding her head in. satisfaction. "I have no desire to be unreasonable, but I believe due consideration for my feelings is no more than my right." She lifted her hand and pointed at him as he walked toward the doorway, raising her voice again. "And bring the lout who is supposed to be your valet with you. There is a room for him in those chambers, and I will have a word with him. The insignia on your epaulettes is uneven, and your laces are a disgrace. Unless someone makes him have a care to his duties, your commander will have you by your collar."

He turned at the doorway and looked back at her. "In all of my life, only one person has ever had me by my collar, Natalya Ivanova," he said in a soft tone, then he turned and disappeared through the doorway.

Natalya looked at the doorway blankly, thinking. The comment hadn't sounded like a rejoinder, and his precise meaning was obscure. She shrugged and walked back to her chair, sat down with a sigh of satisfaction and took a sip of her coffee. "He will think twice before he trifles with me again," she muttered.

Olivia looked at her in silence for a long moment, a smile playing around the corners of her mouth, then nodded. "Yes. But I would like to suggest a less . . . *aggressive* approach in dealing with him, Natalya Ivanova. There is a possibility that you may strain his patience."

"Patience?" Natalya snorted. *"I* was the one who was patient. *I* waited until my father left the table before I discussed the matter with him, did I not? And that took all of my patience. But I had no desire to risk a misunderstanding between him and my father, who is very protective of my feelings, protective to the extent that he told me he would try Aleksei Andreyevich's blade for the way he dealt with me, were the devious whoremonger's pup here so he could." She took her cigarette out of the bowl, stood up and lit it at one of the candles in the candelabrum in front of her, and sat back down, exhaling the smoke and tapping the cigarette against the edge of the bowl. "He said only one person has ever had him by his collar," she murmured in a musing tone. "I wonder who it was."

Olivia lifted her eyebrows and looked at her, then lowered her eyes to her coffee cup as she picked it up and took a sip. She made no reply.

CHAPTER XX

Having Thomas's valet in the house produced an unforeseen benefit. Natalya had found out a few more things about her husband as a result of comments he had made to her father during conversations over dinner, but in many instances she had found out just enough to stimulate her curiosity. She was reluctant to reveal her curiosity to him or to deepen the personal aspect of their relationship by asking him about himself, even though she was sure he would tell her whatever she wished to know, but she found that his valet was very well informed about Thomas. Her first contact with the valet was when she berated him about his indifferent performance of his duties, after which he avoided her when possible and communicated in monosyllables when she cornered him. He spent all his free time in the serfs' hall. Everything he had to say about Thomas became household gossip among the serfs, and Natalya heard all of it by simply listening to her maids gossiping among themselves. And one of the first things she heard about was the impending duel.

It was set for four days away when she heard about it, a day when both Thomas and the other man would be off duty, and the reason was a remark the other man had made about Thomas's marriage.

She considered the possibility that her letter to Aleksei had been the actual cause of the duel, the other man having heard about it and making some comment which angered Thomas, but it didn't seem likely. Her curiosity was thoroughly aroused when she heard about it, and she manipulated the conversation at dinner to try to draw Thomas out. It only served to start her father off onto duels he had fought and other duels which were prominent in his memory, but it brought no desired response from Thomas.

Natalya's worry grew as the day for the duel approached. She disapproved of duels in general, and she discovered she had a specific distaste for Thomas's involvement in a duel. Distant though their relationship was, she had no desire to become a widow. Thomas had become very comfortable to have in the household. His wasn't the most engaging personality she had ever known, but her father enjoyed conversing with him, she was finding him more congenial than before, and he had dispelled much of the continuing gloom in the household since Vassily's arrest. Natalya was even getting to the point that she could detect tiny nuances of expression which gave some indication of his moods and what he was thinking.

The day before the duel arrived, and Natalya had still found out no more about it. The day was fraught with a dull, heavy sense of foreboding, and Natalya also had a growing feeling of pique toward Thomas. She felt that he should have told her about it without being asked, considering the fact that she was his wife. Olivia knew nothing about it, and Natalya hadn't told her because she knew it would only worry her. But it was difficult to maintain continued silence, because she wanted desperately to discuss it with someone.

The day seemed endless, the hours dragging even more slowly because of her uneasy restlessness, then late afternoon finally arrived. Natalya dressed for dinner and went downstairs to check on the final arrangements. The house steward told her that Thomas had come in a few minutes earlier and was in his rooms preparing for dinner, and that her father had sent word that he would have his meal in his rooms. She sent a footman to take her father's dinner in to him, then joined Olivia in the drawing room. Thomas came down a few minutes later and they went into the dining room. It was impossible to keep from admiring Thomas's courage and self control. Nothing about his quiet conversation and demeanor suggested that he was going to fight a duel the next morning.

Dinner over, the footmen cleared away the plates and started to bring the coffee and cigarettes. Thomas looked up at the footman serving him, shaking his head as the footman started to put the coffee in front of him, and spoke at Natalya. "I will excuse myself, if I may, because I wish to retire early. I have an early appointment tomorrow morning."

"So I understand," Natalya said quietly. "It is an affair of honor, is it not?"

There was an instant of silence, broken by Olivia's gasp of horror and astonishment. She turned and looked at him wide-eyed. "An affair of honor? Not a . . . duel?"

Thomas glanced at her and nodded, then looked back at Natalya with a sparkle of wry humor in his eyes. "It appears that very little escapes you, Natalya Ivanova."

Natalya took her cigarette from the footman and lit it from the candle he held for her. "Why did you not tell me? I am your wife."

He shrugged nonchalantly. "Is it a matter which interests you?"

"What a thing to say, Thomas!" Olivia barked at

him angrily in English. "Of course it's a matter of interest to her!"

It was the first time Natalya had seen anything but cordiality between them. Olivia glared at him. Thomas looked at her with his lips in a straight line and a glow of anger in his eyes. Olivia looked down at her coffee cup and cleared her throat, and the corners of Thomas's lips lifted in a hint of an apologetic smile. "Perhaps that was unfortunate phrasing on my part, Natalya Ivanova. I did not wish to trouble you."

"What is the reason for the duel?" she asked. "Or is it a private matter?"

"I have nothing I wish to keep secret from you, Natalya Ivanova. The man I am to duel commented that I married you for your dowry and your father's property. I asked him to retract the statement, he refused, and I challenged him."

Natalya took a sip of her coffee, avoiding his eyes. "And why did you marry me, Thomas Stephanovich?"

"Because I love you, Natalya Ivanova. I have loved you since the first time I saw you."

The phrasing lacked the flowery grace with which such sentiments were normally expressed, but somehow the impact on Natalya was greater because of their unadorned simplicity. He meant it. Others had told her of their love in fanciful figures of speech, but in retrospect they seemed more artful than truthful. Aleksei had composed a multitude of pretty speeches about his love for her, and each of them had been a lie. For the first time, Natalya was absolutely positive that the words meant what they said. Thomas had not spoken to please her or make her smile. He had made a bald, straightforward statement of fact. He loved her.

And only a moment before, he had expressed doubt that she would be interested in the fact that he was engaged to duel. He loved her, and he believed she did not care whether he lived or died. There was suddenly an agonizing pathos to his courage in going through the routine of this evening before the morning on which he would meet with another man with death hovering close in the mists of the morning. He was very much alone, loving a woman and unsure that she even felt for him as any human being should feel for another. He had interpreted her silence on the matter as lack of interest. And perhaps she hadn't been as interested as she should have been. Perhaps she hadn't cared as much as she should have. But suddenly she did.

Utter terror sprang to life within her. She looked down at the table in front of her, controlling herself as best she could, and she swallowed to make sure her voice would be steady as she lifted her eyes and looked at him again. "Is he a large man?"

"Count Delyanov is somewhat smaller than I am, with a shorter reach. He chose pistols."

That was worse, much worse! With swords, death or serious injury usually resulted only rarely. Once blood was drawn, the arbiter would usually adjudge the duel was over. And once a sword arm was injured, the duel was finished without exception. But a pistol ball knew no degrees of pain and injury. When the pellet of death spat from a pistol barrel, it flew to its mark. The most awkward hand could send a pistol ball into a heart when guided by chance. And the most sure hand could tremble in the face of death in the cold of the morning.

"Where is it to be?" she whispered.

"Off Mariinsky at Smolny Canal."

A green sward where she had ridden numerous times, and a place, she had heard, favored for duels because it was convenient to Mariinsky Hospital. And to St. Basil's. She took a nervous puff on her cigarette.

"Thomas, you cannot proceed with this," Olivia said

firmly. "You have responsibilities, and I cannot believe that you—"

"That is wasted talk, Olivia Vassilievna," Natalya interrupted her in a quiet tone. "The fool's part was played when the gage was cast. Now it cannot be changed. And Thomas cannot withdraw and show his face again where men go." Olivia subsided with a resigned, disgusted sigh, and Natalya looked back at Thomas. "What sort of pistol will you take?"

"A cavalry issue Tower."

Natalya shook her head firmly, pushing her chair back and stubbing out her cigarette as she rose. "You shall use my pistols. Come, and I will get them for you."

He looked as though he were going to demur, then nodded and followed her around the end of the table toward the doorway. The house seemed very quiet around them in the semi-darkness. Tapers burned in the wall sconces in the entry hall and up the staircase, and the solid tread of Thomas's footsteps behind her stirred echoes across the entry hall and along the hallway to her rooms. The maids had retired to the hall, leaving a single candle burning in a holder on a table by the door, and she picked it up and shielded it with her hand as she crossed the sitting room to a chiffonier in the corner. She put the candlestick on top of the chiffonier, opened a drawer, took out her pistol case and opened it.

He made a startled sound when he saw the pistols, and he took one out of the case, balanced it in his hand, then held it out at arm's length and sighted down the barrel into the darkness in the corner of the room. "I thought you were sending me to duel with a lady's pistol, Natalya Ivanova, but these are some of the finest weapons I have seen. Are you able to hold them at arm's length?"

It occurred to her that she had known Aleksei for

only a very short time before she had shown him her pistols and other treasures, and she had known him only a couple of weeks when they had gone together to the stables to shoot pistol match. And she suddenly felt guilty. "Only when I use both hands, and then not for very long. I shoot as the sight crosses the target. And I would not send you to a duel with a lady's pistol. Or shame you in other ways. To that end, I will not beg you to forego your fool's errand."

He looked down at her with a slight smile, taking the case from her and fitting the pistol back into it. "There is no one whose concern means more to me, but this is not my first duel, Natalya Ivanova."

"It is the first since I have known you. Stay a moment. See the mark on this one? I marked it because it shoots a thumb's breadth to the left of center at twenty paces. *My* thumb I should say, which is on the order of your lesser finger. The other one shoots fair to center. There is fresh powder in the flask and balls in the pouch."

He nodded, closing the case and snapping the latch on the front of it. She picked up the candlestick, carried it back across the room and put it on the table by the door, and he opened the door and followed her out into the hallway, closing the door behind him. They walked back along the dark hallway to the mezzanine, and she paused at the top of the staircase. He stopped, the pistol case under his arm. She felt as though there was something else she should say and wished he would say something to ease the dark foreboding which hung in her mind like a somber, threatening cloud.

"I shall wish you good fortune in the morning."

"I shall rise early," he replied, an apologetic note in his voice.

"So shall I." She looked searchingly at him for an instant. "Good night, Thomas Stephanovich."

"Good night, Natalya Ivanova."

She went back downstairs to the dining room. Olivia was sitting over her cold coffee, staring morosely down at the table. The house steward and footmen were still in attendance, and Natalya dismissed them, got another glass of coffee and a cigarette. They sat in worried silence for some time, and presently Olivia said good night and left.

Natalya went back to her rooms, lit the candles in a candelabrum and put it on the table by a couch, and tried to read. Her eyes moved over the words, but they didn't register in her mind. She concentrated harder, and the thoughts expressed on the page seemed pointless, like a load of nameday decorations she had seen a porter struggling to carry along a crowded street during the flight from Moscow when sht was a child. She put the book aside and sat staring at the wall. Two of the maids came in to get her ready for bed, and she sent them away.

Time passed, the seconds dragging and the minutes flying, and she pushed herself up from the couch and walked around the room. She felt too restless to go to bed, and she took a candlestick and went back downstairs. The entry hall was lost in darkness, the only light two single tapers in sconces near the door, and the two footmen on watch inside the door leaped to their feet as she came down the staircase. She silently motioned them to sit back down, and walked to the rear of the entry hall and into the hallway on the right, the pool of light from her candle moving along the gleaming floor around her.

Light was shining from under the door of her father's bedchamber, and she could hear the muffled sound of an occasional cough as she approached the door. She tapped on it quietly, then opened it and looked in. He was lying in bed and holding a book to the light of a

407

candle on the table by his bed as he peered at it through his spectacles.

"How do you feel, Father?"

He looked at her over the top of his spectacles as she came in, and he smothered a cough and nodded. "I will live though the night, if for no other reason than the Lord God would have little use for me, as ill as I am. It is time you were abed, is it not?"

She shrugged, walking to the side of the bed and straightening the covers. "I am restless . . ." Her voice faded, and she looked into his eyes then looked away. "Thomas Stephanovich has an affair of honor at dawn."

He coughed again, then drew in a deep, ragged breath and pursed his lips, looking at her closely. "Indeed? Well, I have no fear that he will acquit himself well, Natasha."

"I have no fear of that either. I am concerned about how well his opponent may acquit himself."

He reached out to pat her hand. "Worry will not help. No more than what I say will keep you from worrying. There is a sleeping draught there, if you would like to take some."

She shook her head, shielding the candle with her hand as she turned back to the door. "You could do with some yourself."

"I will have an abundance of sleep soon enough."

"Soon enough is long enough, and you will probably attend the funeral masses for everyone in this house. Good night, Father."

"Good night, Natasha."

She went back out into the hallway, closed the door behind her, and walked to the end of the hall. She put the candlestick on a table by the door and went outside.

The sky was clear, a large, bright moon lighting the garden with its pale glow and stars twinkling in the

408

velvety sky. The air was uncomfortably chilly, and thin tendrils of mist hung close to the ground among the trees and shrubs. Natalya wrapped her arms around herself as she went down the steps and along a path through the garden. She heard a sound from the cook house, and sparks and smoke came from the chimney at one end as the helper on duty through the night put wood into the oven furnace. Natalya looked up at the rear of the house. There was a dim glow of a candle in a window in Olivia's rooms. A sudden shiver raced through Natalya, and she walked back toward the house.

She went back up to her rooms and tried to read again, then dropped the book and folded her arms, staring at the wall. She had no consciousness of the passage of time, but the candle was suddenly burned low and the flame was guttering, and the back of her neck ached. She sat up straight, yawning and rubbing her neck, then stiffened and turned toward the door as she heard footsteps in the hallway. She opened the door and looked into the hallway. Thomas's valet was walking from the other end of the hallway toward the stairs, the lantern swinging in his hand casting grotesque patterns of light and shadow on the walls. He was on his way to saddle Thomas's horse. Natalya hurried after him.

A half dozen of the serfs were already in the hall, making tea. Natalya got a pot of tea, went into the dining room and took a tray and a glass out of the sideboard, filled another glass with vodka and put it on the tray with the tea. Thomas's valet was coming back through the front door as she came out of the dining room with the tray. He took the tray and she took his lantern, and he followed her up the stairs.

Natalya opened the door to Thomas's room and held it for the valet, pointing to a table, and she closed the door behind him. The atmosphere in the room was distinctly male, with a characteristically masculine odor of mingled leather and tobacco. She put the lantern down and crossed the room to the table to pour the tea as Thomas came into the room.

He was wearing only his trousers and boots, and he was drying his face and neck. Without his shirt in the dim light by the doorway, he looked like a giant. His shoulders, chest, and arms were powerful, the bulging muscles rippling. He slipped the shirt on and came toward her with a pleased smile. She suddenly realized how handsome he was, the saber scar on his right cheek accenting the smooth regularity of his features. A warm, throbbing glow suddenly sprang to life within her. She felt her cheeks turning crimson and she avoided his eyes as she poured tea into the glass. The spout of the pot rattled against the glass as her hand shook.

"Good morning, Natalya Ivanova."

"Good morning, Thomas Stephanovich." She took the glass of vodka off the tray and put it on the table. "It is a cold morning."

He nodded, lifting the glass and taking a polite sip, then put it back on the tray. The valet brought his tunic and held it while he slipped into it, and Thomas fastened the frogs and laces as the valet fetched his belt. He put the belt on, then drank some of the tea. Natalya moved closer to him, straightening the metal ends of a couple of laces and touching the fringe on one of his epaulettes into place. He smiled down at her as he put the glass down and took his helmet from the valet.

"Will you have something to eat?"

He shook his head, his white, even teeth shining in the soft light of the candle as he smiled. "Breakfast and a pistol ball make poor company. I will wait until later."

She tried to smile, then stopped trying and merely nodded. The valet brought the pistol case, and Natalya took it from him and held it against her. Thomas took another drink of tea and tucked his helmet under his arm, and they walked toward the door.

The footman unbolted the front door as Natalya and Thomas came down the stairs. They crossed the entry hall, and one of the footmen opened the door. Thomas took Natalya's arm and guided her through the door ahead of him. The footmen's eyes fastened on the pistol case Natalya was carrying as they went out the door.

The moon had set, it was darker, and the low-hanging mist was thicker. The horse tethered on the drive moved restlessly, and the stirring of its hoofs on the gravel was loud in the dark quietness. Thomas slipped his helmet on and adjusted the wide chinstrap. Natalya moved closer to him and leaned against him. He put his arm around her.

"Good fortune, Thomas Stephanovich."

"Thank you, Natalya Ivanova."

It was the first time he had kissed her since the marriage ceremony, when she had glared at him defiantly and silently dared him to take undue familiarity as she lifted unwilling lips, but this time the gentle pressure of his mouth against hers was markedly different. He took the pistol case and walked down the steps. Natalya hugged herself and stood on the edge of the porch. His footsteps faded along the path. A moment later the horse's hoofs clattered along the drive, then she heard the carriage gate rattle and clank as it opened and closed. The sound of the horse's hoofs gradually faded, and she turned back toward the door.

The footmen shot the bolts as she walked across the entry foyer toward the staircase. She stopped and looked down at the floor, thinking, then turned back suddenly and spoke to one of the footmen. "Go find three of the grooms, and have them saddle my horse Pegasus."

The footman nodded. "Yes, mistress."

Natalya turned toward the staircase again, then hesitated, pondering the advisability of what she intended to do. The presence of women in the vicinity of a duel was regarded with extreme disfavor. She shrugged the thought off and ran up the stairs. Her mind was made up, and speed was now essential.

She took out a wide, grey felt hat and hastily pinned it on, threw on a heavy grey cloak, gathered up her gloves and riding crop, and went back downstairs. The grooms were in the process of bringing Pegasus along the drive, and he snorted irritably as he stamped, pulled against the reins, and tried to rear. He was even more nervous and high-strung because of the darkness, and the lanterns which the grooms had placed at the side of the drive seemed to irritate him. He snapped at Natalya, and she stepped back to avoid his teeth and moved toward him again, scolding him quietly. She held out a lump of sugar in her hand, he looked at her warily, then took the lump of sugar and crunched it as she patted his neck and talked to him to calm him.

One of the grooms handed Natalya up to the saddle, then leaped back as the horse wheeled and tried to bite him. Natalya let him trot along the drive for a few yards in the darkness. The gate rattled open, and she guided him between the two lanterns and out onto the street.

In the thick, impenetrable darkness just before dawn, Natalya could see virtually nothing. The horse was agitated, fighting the bit ferociously, and she kept him in the middle of the street by listening to the echoes of his hoofbeats off the walls at the sides of the street. In the first grey light of dawn, she could see the bright pieces of metal on the bridle as he tossed his head. A moment later dark, shapeless masses of the trees in the gardens behind the walls became visible against the sky. The sky began growing lighter rapidly, and the mist rose about her on the street. The chill intensified as daybreak approached, and she pulled her collar up and tugged her cloak tighter as she urged her horse forward through the deserted streets.

A blush of reddish-gold touched the sky in the east as she turned onto Nevsky Prospekt, and she let Pegasus out to a canter. A detachment of the watch was on a corner, but they made no movement to hail her. As she cantered by them, the officer smiled and saluted. His face was vaguely familiar to Natalya, and she smiled and waved her riding crop. The rich, fresh colors of sunrise spread further across the sky, deepening toward a thick, bloody crimson. She let Pegasus out into a run. His shoes clattered on the stone pavement in a rapid tattoo. She leaned forward over his withers, clutching the brim of her hat so it wouldn't blow off and holding the reins taut.

The cold air burned against her cheeks and brought tears to her eyes as the horse raced along the street. She gathered the reins and slowly pulled the horse back to a canter, then to a trot, and finally to a walk as she turned onto the street which paralleled Smolny Canal. The horse panted for a moment, then quickly caught his breath, and she reined him over to the grass verge by the street and let him trot again. The massive domes of St. Basil's came into sight over the roofs of the other buildings as she approached Mariinsky, a wide thoroughfare which met the street paralleling the canal at a right angle. The verge between the street and the canal became wider, and she saw figures in the distance. She reined the horse back onto the street to keep out of sight, rode along to a point parallel to a copse of trees along the edge of the sward, and turned the horse toward the trees.

She was too far away to see their features distinctly or hear their voices, but they were clearly visible through the thin screen of foliage. The seconds were two groups of three men each, all of them Semenovskys, and the arbiter was a portly man in civilian dress. The horses were tethered at one side, and there was a carriage near the horses. Thomas and the other men had removed their helmets and tunics, and were standing together talking to the arbiter. The arbiter stepped back a pace, motioning to the seconds, and the seconds moved toward him for the inspection of the weapons. One of the men was carrying Natalya's polished wood pistol case, and a man in the other group was carrying a larger, dark leather pistol case. The arbiter looked closely at one, then at the other, and he nodded and motioned with his hands. The seconds removed a pistol from each case and began charging them as the arbiter watched.

The last of the stars faded and disappeared in the west, and the sky became a canopy of crimson, as the sun seemed to poise just below the horizon until all was ready. A thin mist hung over the canal, floating a few feet above the dark, featureless surface of the water. Two wild ducks soared in a circle and banked toward the canal, then glided onto the water. The arbiter looked to the east. The sun broke above the horizon in a silent symphony of brilliant color to herald the new day.

Thomas and the other man took the pistols and moved a short distance away, standing back to back, and the two groups of seconds moved apart. The arbiter's voice was barely audible as he counted, and Thomas and the other man took steps in cadence with the man's voice. The cold was intense, and Natalya shivered uncontrollably. Her teeth began chattering. After ten steps, they stopped with their backs to each other. The arbiter's voice rose louder in a command. They turned to face each other. The arbiter's voice rose even louder, and she could hear the command to cock weapons. They cocked the pistols and lowered them to their sides. Her shivering made it difficult to see, and the scene was also obscured by the tears gathering in her eyes. Pegasus was moving about and shaking his head, and she had to keep turning him to keep them in view. The arbiter shouted the order to aim, and Pegasus fidgeted as their arms came up. The arbiter's voice echoed across the sward in a penetrating command to fire. The crack of pistol shots broke the dawn silence. The wild ducks squawked with alarm and took flight. Natalya couldn't see. She wiped at her eyes frantically with the back of her hand. When her vision cleared, she saw that Thomas was standing, and the other man was lying on the ground. She slumped in the saddle, bursting into tears.

Pegasus began stamping impatiently and prancing about, and she controlled her weeping as she gathered the reins closer and talked to him to calm him. On the green the other man's seconds were helping him toward the carriage. There was a large stain of blood on the right side of his shirt, and his right arm was dangling. Thomas walked toward him with long, rapid steps. He stopped in front of him, talking to him. The atmosphere seemed strangely friendly. The wounded man lifted his left hand and slapped Thomas familiarly on the shoulder, and his seconds supported him into the carriage. Thomas joined his seconds, and they all huddled together, examining the pistols.

Still hidden by the trees, Natalya looked at Thomas more closely and frowned as he turned and his right shoulder came into her line of sight. There was a dark patch of blood on his sleeve from the point of his shoulder halfway down his bicep. She lifted the reins and touched the horse with the crop, and rode out of the trees and across the sward toward the men.

The arbiter looked at her with a dark frown of surprise and disapproval. The three seconds grinned widely and looked at Pegasus with admiration. Thomas looked at her with the same satisfied smile he'd worn when she brought in his tea. Natalya's answering smile was brilliant, her cheeks flushing and her eyes shining. The arbiter grunted a farewell and turned toward the horses. Thomas glanced at him and thanked him, and he nodded silently as he continued stalking toward the horses. Pegasus kept prancing and wheeling about, and Natalya kept turning him back and smiling silently at Thomas.

One of Thomas's seconds walked toward her. "I will hand you down, if you wish—" He broke off and leaped back with a startled exclamation as Pegasus stretched his neck and snapped at him. "By God! The beast almost had my arm!"

The other two seconds exploded into laughter at his expression, and Thomas chuckled quietly as he walked toward her. She tightened the rein on the other side and kept Pegasus from turning his head as Thomas reached up with his good arm to lift her down. For a moment she leaned her head against his chest, too overcome with relief to speak. Then she remembered the blood.

"Are you wounded badly?"

"Only a scratch."

"I'll bandage it, nonetheless."

"Very well."

She led Pegasus toward the other horses, tied him well away from them, and walked back toward Thomas. He was bending over his tunic on the grass and opening the pocket, and he took out a small, folded square of cloth. As he handed it to her, she recognized it. It was the handkerchief she had given him at Xenia's party. He had been carrying it ever since. A lump formed in her throat and her eyes stung. She shook her head and handed it back to him, turned her back to the other men and bent over, lifted the front of her skirt and tore the hem out of one of her petticoats, ripping a length of cloth from it.

"By God, I'd be shot any day for such a pretty bandage," one of the seconds commented enviously.

They all laughed, and Thomas smiled down at her as he leaned over so she could reach his shoulder easily. She stood on tiptoe, looking at the wound and tearing the hole in his shirt wider. It was a minor wound. She slid the strip of cloth in through the hole in his shirt and wrapped it around his arm, pulling it tight.

"Was Count Delyanov wounded seriously?"

"No. The ball passed through his shoulder without striking a bone."

"You didn't aim to kill."

"Neither of us did."

She tied the strip of cloth into place and tucked the ends under, then stepped back and looked up at him. "Will you come home now?"

"I must report to my commander, then I will come home."

She nodded, turning toward her horse. He handed her up, then stood back and smiled up at her as she settled herself on the saddle and turned the horse toward the street. Pegasus began prancing impatiently away, he lifted his hand and waved, and she waved. The three seconds waved, shouting a farewell, and she waved her riding crop in salute. Pegasus strained at the bit and shook his head, and she let him stretch out into a pounding run across the sward. The sun was coming up over the line of buildings on the other side of the street. The sky was a clear, deep blue. It was a beautiful day.

Olivia was waiting for her, torn between anxiety to know how Thomas had fared and distress over her riding out into the pre-dawn darkness alone. Her father's valet was also waiting in the entry hall, sent by her father to bring word about Thomas as soon as he found out. Olivia's relief was so great that it overcame her indignance over what Natalya had done, and she embraced her warmly. Natalya hurried along the hallway to her father's room to tell him the good news, but his valet had already told him and he had composed himself to go back to sleep. Natalya talked to him for a few minutes, then went to join Olivia at breakfast.

Fatigue from her sleepless night descended upon Natalya all at once. Her eyelids became heavy and she nodded over her plate. She went up to her rooms and bathed, put on a dressing gown, and lay down in her sitting room. The events of the past hours raced through her mind in a mad swirl. Time had become distorted and weeks seemed to have passed since dinner the evening before. The soft sounds the maids made as they moved quietly about and whispered to each other registered dimly on her consciousness. She suddenly thought of Thomas's wound; he would need a fresh bandage on it. She opened her eyes and told a maid to fetch a phial of antiseptic and a roll of linen bandage, then closed her eyes and settled her head on her pillow again.

It seemed only a moment later that a maid was bending over her and shaking her shoulder. Thomas had returned. Natalya got up, stretching and yawning wearily, washed her face in cold water to take the sleep from her eyes, pushed her hair into place, and took the antiseptic and bandage and walked down the hallway to his room.

She rapped on the door, and entered. There was no one in his sitting room, but she heard a slight noise from the bedchamber. She crossed the sitting room to the bedchamber. Thomas had taken off his tunic and was standing by the bed unbuttoning his shirt. His smile made her feel confused, and she lowered her eyes as she walked toward him.

"Was your commander angry with you?"

"No," he replied, then he chuckled. "He was more interested in your pistols."

She put the phial of antiseptic and bandage on the table by the bed, motioning toward his shirt. "Take it off, please."

He smiled and nodded, obeying her instructions and dropping his shirt onto the bed. Natalya untied the knot in the makeshift bandage and untied it, dropped it onto the table by the bed, and opened the phial of antiseptic. She experienced a sudden extreme awareness that they were alone. Her confusion increased, making her fingers tremble as she pulled at the cork in the phial. He didn't appear to notice. She daubed the tincture on the wound, replaced the cork, picked up the bandage roll and unwound part of it. She pulled at it, trying to tear it in two, and he took it between his hands and tore it effortlessly. She put the remainder of the roll on the table, wrapped the bandage around his arm, and tied it.

"There, that should do."

"Thank you."

She smiled, avoiding his eyes as her confusion mounted even more and she felt a hot flush stealing up her throat to her cheeks. His proximity created a wild, surging rush of violently disturbing emotions, making her heart race. He was suddenly closer, one of

419

his large arms was resting lightly around her, and he was bending down to kiss her.

He seemed to be surrounding her with a feeling of protection, the gentle pressure of his arm a proffered comfort. His lips touched hers. The warm, masculine scent of his body filled her nostrils, and she felt his bare skin under her hands. Her heart raced madly, and the glowing, golden warmth surging to life within her made her weak. She opened her lips under his, pressing against him.

His arms gathered her closer, and she felt an instant of panic, an impulse to delay this ultimate commitment, but it was swept aside by the rush of her feelings which carried her along, making her completely helpless. His touch brought to life a bittersweet need which seemed to spring from the very core of her being.

The quick stab of pain and fleeting sense of invasion disappeared into the feeling of oneness, a triumphant and exhilarating fulfillment in which his hard, lean body was part of hers and his strength was her joy, and there was partaking and mutual joining rather than giving and taking. Then she was possessed by a deeply satisfying afterglow, pressing and snuggling against him as he held her. His fingers moved over the birthmark on her left breast.

"Does it make me ugly?" she whispered.

"No, you are beautiful, Natasha. You are the most beautiful woman in the world."

"The old women among the Gypsies who camp at our village used to look at it when I was a child. It appears to have some special significance to them. But they are a superstitious people. Or perhaps they are wise, and we are unwise."

"How did they know about it?"

She was silent for a moment, thinking, then shook

her head slightly. "My father might have mentioned it to them. He likes them very much."

They were silent for a moment, then she stirred. "You are a cunning dog," she murmured drowsily.

"How so?"

"You contrived to get yourself wounded so you could lure me into your bed, didn't you?"

He laughed softly, pulling her closer to him and kissing her, and there was no more need for conversation.

CHAPTER XXI

Vassily became ill with a wasting fever which gradually became worse, sapping his strength and reducing him to a gaunt, skeletal shadow of his formerly brawny and robust physique. Natalya brought an apothecary to the fortress with her, and he examined Vassily and left tisanes for him to take every day. The medicine seemed to help somewhat, but the illness came and went and each time she arrived at the fortress it was with a dread that he might be too weak to see her. She began visiting twice each week, taking the apothecary with her on every other trip, and she brought fresh fruit as the apothecary recommended and gave the guards extra money to assure Vassily had fresh water every day.

Then her father became worse. His cough was almost constant, and the congestion in his chest became so bad that he had difficulty breathing. The apothecary was in and out of the house at all hours, boiling infusions of eucalyptus and fanning the steam into his face, smearing pastes and salves on his chest, and giving him tisanes. Natalya was torn between wanting to stay with her father and wanting to visit Vassily, but Vassily's need was greater, ill and lonely in the cell in the dungeons. She returned from visiting him one afternoon, and the wailing and shrieking of the serfs resounded through the house and carried out to the front garden as she walked along the path. Thomas met her at the door, his expression confirming her worst fears.

At first it was impossible to accept. Of all the fundamental and basic assumptions around which her very existence were based, one of the most stable was the presence of her father. At every turnng point, he had been there. When decisions had been puzzling and problems had arisen, she had turned to him. He had been ill before, and her concern over his illness had been because of his discomfort, not from apprehension that he would die. She found it impossible to accept. The pain of her sorrow tore at her like some inimical force which was consuming her. At some deep level there still existed a belief that she would enter a room and he would smile at her and greet her, that she would hear his voice calling for her from some other part of the house. She could not believe that he was gone beyond her reach.

Vassily had to be told, and Thomas and Olivia went with her to the fortress when she went to tell him. But his fever was at its peak, he was unable to arise from his bunk, and it was questionable if the outside world was penetrating the delirium and registering in his mind. She told him of their father's death, kneeling at the side of the bunk with his thin, limp hand between hers as she talked. His hand was burning hot between hers, and her tears flowed freely again as she told him over and over that their father had died. And while her words did not seem to penetrate the fever which confused his mind, they penetrated hers. The sorrow she had suffered before was a mild and transient disturbance in comparison with the sheer agony which seized her as the effect of what she told Vassily brought full realization of the finality of her loss, and her own contact with the world around her became tenuous. Impressions were vague and indistinct—the fresh air sweeping across the water during the boat ride back, Thomas's and Olivia's voices murmuring, the feel of Thomas's tunic and laces against her cheek as he carried her to the carriage, and Olivia's arms around her helping her up the stairs to her rooms.

The funeral was at St. Augustine's, and a surprisingly large number of people attended, considering Vassily's involvement in the uprising and his imprisonment. But the imperial coach Annya had come in was prominent in the square outside the church, and she had arranged for a bishop to conduct the service. After the funeral, the coffin was taken on a gun carriage and placed in a niche in a mausoleum reserved for State officials in the square behind Kazan Cathedral.

The next few days passed for Natalya in a numb daze of wandering through the rooms and hallways of the silent house, dark and quiet with its mourning crepes, and of going into his chambers and looking at his spectacles, books, and papers, at the things he had touched and used. Sorrow returned at the sight of a pair of worn boots in a corner or from opening a book to a page and resurrecting a memory of passages they had discussed together, and heavy, continuing melancholy sapped her strength and made her weary but kept her from resting or sleeping.

Then some essential rhythm between her body and the cycles of the universe surfaced, and almost against her will Natalya searched for order and meaning in what remained to her. Thomas and Olivia were content to help her as they could and let her participate in or withdraw from what went on around her to the extent she wished, but there were ways in which she had to stand alone, unassisted and independent, and there were rules of responsibility by which she had lived too long to abandon.

Olivia had been ordering the household to the best of her ability, but Olivia was an outsider and couldn't communicate with the serfs. Natalya put her will into the household and made her presence felt, and the weeping in the serfs' hall diminished and the pulse of the household became firm and even again. And there was Vassily. Natalya and Olivia went to the fortress again, and Natalya was relieved to find that his health seemed to be much improved. He knew now that their father was dead, and she didn't have to go through the pain of telling him about it yet again.

Natalya's nameday approached, and she was firm in expressing her conviction that any celebration would be inconsistent with the state of mourning in the household. But Annya came to the house for dinner that evening, and there were presents. All the serfs had made and bought small things, Olivia had bought her a locket, Annya brought her a set of hair combs crusted with gems, and Thomas had bought her an opal ring. It was a pleasant evening, bringing back something of the lighthearted happiness she had known in years past.

Events began to move rapidly, as though some kind of momentum had been accumulated and was beginning to be released, and a multitude of things began happening with bewildering speed. Rumors circulated that the judges' deliberations over the evidence accumulated against those accused of involvement in the Decembrist uprising were drawing to a close, and Annya confirmed the rumors. They were further confirmed when Czar Nikolas ordered his staff and advisors to begin preparations for the ceremonial and traditional coronation in Moscow, a ceremony he had delayed until after the trials were completed. As one of the preparations, the Horse Guards and the Knights Guards were ordered to Moscow.

Thomas wanted to take Natalya with him, and she wanted very much to go. Her attachment to him had become deep and meaningful to her, sustaining her through the loss of her father and the essential loss of her brother, but also comprised of a world of precious meaning quite apart from that. At the same time, she felt that the atmosphere in the quaint and provincial Moscow would offer refuge from the misfortunes which had overtaken her in cold and impersonal St. Petersburg. But it was out of the question. She couldn't leave and abandon Vassily to the misery of solitude and loneliness in the dungeon.

There was a bittersweet character to Thomas's departure, the heavy sadness of separation combined with a glowing pride as the Horse Guards and Knights Guards departed the city in all their glory, massed battalions and wave after wave of thundering horses and marching feet, with banners, guidons, and helmet plumes waving and fluttering in the breeze, and Thomas at the head of his platoon and turning his head to look at her with a most unmilitary smile as she waved. Then the house was even more empty and quiet.

Shortly after Thomas left, contingents of the Czar's inner circle began leaving to make preparations in Moscow for the coronation, and Annya left. There were frequent and hurried visits back and forth between Annya and Natalya during the last few days before her departure, then Natalya saw her off early one morning and St. Petersburg seemed even more dismal. During the next few days more and more people left for Moscow, and the wide thoroughfares took on a semi-deserted aspect.

Then the sentences were handed down, a day was spent while the Czar studied them and set mitigations, and they were published in a news sheet. The judges had decreed death by quartering for the organizers of the plot and those who had planned to murder the imperial family, which totalled five of the conspirators. Another twenty-four who had been instrumental in the plans and had suborned other persons were sentenced to death by decapitation. The eighty five who had contributed to the uprising were sentenced to exile in Siberia for varying periods, depending upon their involvement. The Czar reduced the deaths by quartering to death by decapitation, the deaths by decapitation to exile for life in Siberia, and made a proportional reduction in the periods of exile for all the rest. When Natalya got a copy of the news sheet, she searched feverishly down the list for Vassily's name, then found it. His sentence was exile to Siberia for one year.

There were other provisions. All those convicted were stripped of rank and titles. Vassily had automatically become the Count Sheremetev upon his father's death, so for the first time in centuries there was no Count Sheremetev. All those convicted were banished from court for life and denied imperial commissions or service in the Army. But after the months of waiting, it was a relief to find out the extent of punishment to be inflicted. And it wasn't nearly as bad as it might have been.

The family property was safe, willed to Thomas as conservator until Natalya attained the age of twenty, at which time Vassily's share could be deeded back to him, because it would be immune from confiscation once his exile was completed. A year in Siberia, then another year or two in Moscow or at Sherevskoye to allow the immediacy of the situation to die away, and he could petition the Czar for reinstatement of his title and restoration of his court privileges and commission in the Yamburgskys. Considering her influence with

427

the court through Annya, and the previous good will she had won with Czar Nikolas, the chances of approval of such a petition were good.

A great weight seemed to have been lifted from Natalya's shoulders. After such a series of misfortunes and calamities, there seemed to be a firm path forming in the quaking bog over which she had been passing, and the future promised some semblance of normality. Those whom she loved would be in agreeable circumstances, and her crushing isolation from others would be lifted. Olivia had a similar optimism when she talked with her about it, and Vassily seemed cheerful and confident.

But there was one serious problem. Vassily's feverish illness continued. Once the year of exile in Siberia was completed, his prospects would be favorable. But in his state of health, the possibilities of living through a winter of the cold and hardships of Siberia appeared poor. It was possible that his health would improve once he was out of the foul dungeons under SS Peter and Paul fortress and in the fresh air and sunshine enroute to Siberia. But it was also possible that his health would deteriorate further as a result of the hardships of the trip. He would need care along the way, as well as the exercise of influence and judicious distribution of money at the other end of the trip to assure that he had the best of accommodations and food to last through the severe Siberian winter.

Natalya pondered each aspect of the situation thoroughly, and each time she came to the same conclusion. It was inescapable. She was well aware that there would be resistance, but the situation had minimized it. Thomas was in Moscow, where he would be for another month. Annya would have voiced strong objections and possibly brought her authority into play if she had been present, but she was also in Moscow.

That left only Olivia to deal with, which would be a sufficient task. Natalya carefully picked a time and place, the privacy of the back garden while walking after dinner, and the reaction was what she had anticipated.

"Siberia?" Olivia exploded, aghast. "Natalya Ivanova, after all the madcap things you have done, I thought I was beyond being surprised! But this time you have outdone yourself! Of all the . . ." She tossed her hands up and dropped them as she shook her head in despair, her voice fading into an exasperated sigh.

Natalya took the offensive, looking at Olivia with an insulted frown. "All the madcap things I have done, Olivia Vassilievna? What things are these? I have always considered myself a person of adequate judgement."

Olivia shook her head irritably. "Don't try to change the subject, Natalya Ivanova. I want you to have no doubt in your mind that I absolutely refuse to even contemplate the possibility of your going to—"

"I am not changing the subject, I am referring to what you said. You spoke as though I am an immature, spoiled child, which I am not."

Olivia looked at her with an aggravated expression, then smiled wearily and shook her head, patting Natalya's arm. "I didn't intend to offend you, Natalya Ivanova, but the first day I met you, you took a carriage driver by the collar while you shook your riding crop in his face and threatened him. Now don't you think that could be considered somewhat out of the ordinary? And if that were the only time, it would be another situation altogether, but—"

"It could be considered out of the ordinary only by someone who failed to consider his insolence."

"Then how about the letter to Aleksei Andreyevich? If that wasn't ill-considered, then I don't know what—"

"It was not a letter, it was a note. And I see nothing wrong with the exchange of notes between friends. The only difficulty with that particular note arose from the fact that the Orlov pup is a churlish whoreson bastard, a fact which had not been presented to me. And if your judgement and discrimination are of an order so superior to mine, you might have warned me about his undesirable characteristics."

"I tried to, but you acted as though you were going to bite my head off every time I suggested he was anything less than an emissary from Olympus."

"I recall no such discussion," Natalya replied coldly. "And now you are the one who is changing the subject. We were discussing Vassily Ivanovich and Siberia."

"Very well," Olivia said, nodding firmly. "That is a subject which may be disposed of with few words. You are *not* going to Siberia."

Her tone had the force of a command, and Natalya looked at her with a nettled frown. "Olivia Vassilievna, you are my friend, not my mother!"

Olivia sighed heavily, taking Natalya's hand between hers and patting it. "I am your friend, Natalya Ivanova, and that is why I said what I did. There are a multitude of reasons, any one of which is sufficient to keep you from going. To begin with, Thomas would never allow it."

"Thomas Stephanovich is not here." She lifted her hand and shook her head as Olivia started to say something. "No, hear me out. I have given this some thought, Olivia Vassilievna, and I also thought about that. Does he ask my permission before he casts or picks up a gage? No, nor would I expect him to. Nonetheless, he might at this moment be facing another man with a sword or a pistol. And there is another point. Do you think Thomas Stephanovich would sentence my brother

430

to death? Hardly, but that is what it would amount to in denying him care on the journey and someone to see to his needs at his destination."

"But you could give some money to the guards who will be conducting them there, or to their commander, and have him—"

"Money to be spent for vodka at the first shop they pass," Natalya interrupted impatiently, shaking her head.

"Well, there must be some other way. You simply don't know what is involved in going to Siberia, Natalya Ivanova. The very idea of a young woman by herself among all those soldiers . . ."

"It appears that I know more than you, Olivia Vassilievna. To begin with, I would not be by myself. I know of eight other families which are accompanying the prisoners to Siberia, wives and children of some of the prisoners, and there are undoubtedly more that I do not know about."

"And how would you get back? Or do you propose to spend the winter in Siberia?"

"There are several convoys back and forth each year, and I would return with a convoy bringing back people released from exile and their families. And I wouldn't go alone, of course. I would take a footman with me, and perhaps a maid."

"I cannot believe what I am hearing," Olivia sighed, shaking her head. "Ride to Siberia and back in a wagon with a footman and a maid? Natalya Ivanova, I have a very deep affection for you, but that doesn't blind me to some things about you. You have an entire staff of maids to do your hair, bathe you, and dress you, and an entire household at your beck and call. You have a cooking staff to prepare dinner, and to clean up after dinner you look at the housekeeper and point your finger at what needs to be done. And you tell me that

431

you intend to ride to Siberia and back in a wagon with a footman and a maid?" She shook her head and laughed wryly again. "My dear, you wouldn't get ten miles from St. Petersburg."

Natalya let her finish, looking at her with a slight smile, and slowly shook her head. "You do not understand me as well as you think, Olivia Vassilievna. In fact, you hardly understand me at all. You have only seen me here, and you know only what you have seen. And perhaps you are judging me by others you have known, expatriate French rather than Russian. Olivia Vassilievna, I am Russian. I eat from gold or silver plate when I can, and I will eat from my hand when I must. I will have delicacies prepared by a master chef when I can, but black bread and gruel will suffice if that is all I have. To understand me, you must understand what it means to be Russian. This great land of mine stretches from the seas which never thaw to deserts where the sun bakes the life from the body. It has mountains so high there is no air to breathe at the top of them, bogs without bottoms, and steppes so vast the mind cannot encompass them, much less the eye. To be Russian is to be like Russia. To be Russian is to be a part of all of these. And I am Russian, so I am many things."

Olivia looked at her in thoughtful silence, her eyes moving over Natalya's face, then she looked away and nodded. "Perhaps I was being hasty in my judgement, Natalya Ivanova," she said quietly. "Perhaps I did underestimate you." She smiled wryly. "As a minimum, I must say that you are different from others I have known, and that I have continually been surprised by you. In a way, it seems that I have found out something new about you each day I have spent here." She looked back at Natalya, her smile fading. "But Siberia is out

432

of the question. It is absolutely out of the question."

Natalya took Olivia's hand and laced her fingers through Olivia's. "Tomorrow we go again to visit Vassily Ivanovich. While we are there, look at that pale face and at that frail body. Remember he is my brother. Remember that I love him. And then we will talk again."

They did, discussing it quietly in the boat as the boatman rowed them back across the river, then in the carriage and over dinner after Natalya had sent the house steward and footmen away so the household serfs wouldn't find out what she was planning to do. As point after point was satisfied, Oliva began wavering. Natalya's primary purpose in telling Olivia had been so she could leave Olivia in charge of the household, but on that point Olivia was adamant, refusing even to discuss it.

"I?" she snapped. "You intend that *I* should be the one to tell Thomas Greenwood that his wife has left in a wagon for Siberia?" She uttered a short, barking laugh and shook her head. "Not I. No indeed, Natalya Ivanova. This much I know—that man has sides to him that you haven't seen and probably will never see, but I am in a less enviable position and I am not going to put myself in the way of his wrath. And in addition, I wouldn't contemplate letting you go unescorted. If I permitted you to go, you would have to leave money with the house steward to maintain the household until Thomas returns, and I would accompany you."

Natalya smiled and nodded. "Then it is settled. You may go with me."

"I didn't say that," Olivia said hastily. "What I said was, *if* I permitted you to go. And that isn't the same as saying that I intend to permit it. But Vassily Ivanovich is ill, and there are points favoring what you say.

433

I still regard this as a madcap undertaking, and we will have to think about it and see if there is another solution . . ."

She continued talking, and Natalya listened to her absently as she pondered. The bill for two thousand rubles which her father had given her was in her room, and that was several times the amount of money she would need. The logistics of the situation eliminated the possibility of a middle ground in the size of retinue. Taking several servants would dictate several wagons for belongings, which would require more drivers and others to take care of the animals, and more wagons for their belongings. The only other possibilities were a full retinue of twenty-five or thirty wagons and carts used for the trip to the summer estate, which would empty the house of servants, or a single wagon. A single wagon was the logical and economical course, and it would be ridiculous to set out with a retinue as large as the rest of the convoy.

She would have to look through the wagons behind the stable and pick out the best one, and she would select the best of the draft horses. With Olivia going along, a maid and her belongings would make the wagon too crowded for such a long trip, so they would take only a single footman. Olivia's voice continued as she talked herself into it, and Natalya began to consider what clothes and other necessities she would need for the journey.

CHAPTER XXII

The sound of the wagons was a constant din in Natalya's ears, a combination of the wheels jolting over rocks and through ruts, the boards and crossmembers of the bed rattling and squeaking, the heavy canvas covering the bows billowing and the harness clanking and jangling, a steady level of noise which made conversation difficult.

Over the sound of the wagons, she could hear a baby's shrieks and wails from the wagon directly behind theirs, one driven by a large, silent woman of forty or so who had four children, including the baby of six months. The woman's husband had been sentenced to Siberia for ten years, and somehow Natalya knew the woman would endure those ten years in the same taciturn, capable way she went about her tasks when they camped each night, feeding and caring for her children, and taking food to her husband. She would survive.

But others would not. After a few days on the road, it had come as a shock to Natalya to realize that she could with certainty pick out those who would return from Siberia and those who would die there. Of the fourteen families, at least a half dozen of the women were frail and incapable, at a total loss for what to do in the face of hardship. Some of them couldn't even speak Russian adequately enough to barter with the villagers for food.

When she could, she helped them. But she observed that the woman in the wagon behind theirs conserved her energy for her own tasks, asking for nothing and offering nothing. And there were others like her, instinctively reverting to the most primitive selfishness in the name of survival.

She had forced herself to face the question from which her mind had kept recoiling, that of whether or not Vassily would be among those who returned. He had still been ill when they left St. Petersburg, the Army wagons had been overcrowded, and the first few days had been very hard on him. Then the wagon train had started leaving a trail of small crosses in the village churchyards as the weaker of the prisoners succumbed to their illnesses and the poor food provided them by the Army cooks, and there had been more room in the wagons. With his share of the food she and Olivia cooked each night and took to him, he had improved somewhat until they came to a dry stretch where the road had been covered with a thick coating of fine dust. It had been hard for her to endure, and it had almost meant the end for Vassily during the three days they had traveled through the boiling clouds churned up by the wheels and the horses' hoofs. Then they had passed beyond it, and he had recovered somewhat. But he was still very weak, and they were still west of the Urals, with a long distance left to travel.

The noise in front took on a slightly different sound, and Natalya pushed herself up from her pallet at the side of the wagon, braced herself with one hand on the side against its lurching and swaying, and moved to the front of the wagon, leaning on Danilo's shoulder and looking out. There was a small village ahead, and adjacent to it was one of the caravansaries maintained by the Army for their wagon trains and couriers passing back and forth along the road. The detachment of soldiers at the front and the first couple of Army wagons were turning into the courtyard in front of the long, low building, all of the soldiers out of step and their muskets on their shoulders at different angles, as usual. They were Streltsy, poorly disciplined and only marginally controlled by their officer.

"Are we stopping?" Olivia called over the noise of the wagon as she sat up on her pallet, pushing the hair back from her forehead. "It is early."

Natalya nodded, moving back to her pallet and sitting down on it. "There is a caravansary ahead."

Olivia looked relieved, brushing at the sleeves of her dress and arranging her hair as best she could. Natalya straightened her dress and brushed at it half-heartedly, then gave up. The meticulous care and attention her appearance had once received from the full time attention of four maids had quickly become a thing of the past after leaving St. Petersburg. Her adjustment to the trip had been more extensive that she had anticipated, because she now seized part of the chores from Olivia and had willingly neglected her appearance. She and Olivia helped each other do their hair, so it was done only once a day and much less expertly than it had been done before, and changing into a freshly ironed dress whenever one became soiled or wrinkled was an impossibility, because clothes were simply washed out and hung up to dry. But the situation wasn't without its favorable aspects. All of her life, it had been drummed into her that presenting a favorable appearance was a major part of her function in life, and she had been relieved of that. Comfort had become the main criterion, limited only by the dictates of modesty, which represented a freedom of sorts.

The caravansary, village, and squares of tilled fields

around the village were a tiny speck in the vast emptiness of a stretch of grassy plain which extended to the
horizon, with the road fading off into the distance, carving the world into two halves. Towering masses of
clouds filled the sky to the north, giving an oppressive,
apprehensive atmosphere of an impending storm, but
to the south the sky was clear and tranquil. The soldiers
who manned the caravansary milled around among the
Streltsy, chatting and laughing, and the prisoners were
herded out of the wagons and into sheds at one end
of the long building, their chains rattling and clanking.
The officer of the Streltsy talked to the soldier in charge
of the caravansary, and began shouting at his soldiers.
A forge in one of the sheds was glowing, and the soldiers began removing one of the wheels from an Army
wagon to repair it and unhitching the horses to lead
them into the stables in the long building to feed them.

Danilo parked Natalya's wagon at one side of the
wide expanse of paved area between the road and the
caravansary building, and they got out of the wagon.
It was a hubbub of activity, people leading horses
around, gathering to chat, going about their chores, and
walking toward the village, and children raced back
and forth and laughed gleefully at their release from
the confinement of the wagons. Danilo unharnessed
the horse and led it into an adjacent field to crop the
grass, then came back to the wagon and took buckets
to the well for water. Natalya and Olivia took one of
the bundles of wood from under the wagon and built
a fire at the side of the wagon, then sorted through the
pots and pans and supplies of food. The early stop for
the night gave time to do washing which had been put
off, and they took all the dirty clothes out of the wagon,
washed them in the buckets, and hung them on the side
of the wagon to dry.

The thunderclouds moved further to the north, a

brilliant rainbow forming below them and the rays of the sun gilding them with scintillating colors as it declined toward the west. Natalya walked down the road to the village and bartered with the villagers for bread and vegetables. She haggled with them, enjoying the friendly give and take and their bemusement over the fact that she spoke in the accents and earthy metaphors of those who worked the land. It was necessary to avoid a display of wealth. The rigidly established system of law and order of the cities had been left behind, and the caravan had a precarious system of its own which was much less dependent upon traditional authority and which could easily slip into primitivism. Those with a high survival quotient had sharp eyes for anything which would give them an advantage, and they would steal food, clothing, or anything else if given an opportunity. The soldiers were scarcely more than rabble, barely controlled by their fear of the officers. A couple of them had got drunk a few days before and raped one of the women, resulting in a lashing with the knout. But the officer had also delivered a stern lecture to all of the women on conduct and behavior which might incite the soldiers.

Insolent, lascivious stares from the soldiers had been infuriating to Natalya at first, but she had developed the capacity to ignore them. And they hadn't gone beyond stares, because she made a point of having Danilo with her when she was in the immediate vicinity of the soldiers and sending him with Olivia when she would be among them. Danilo had been the perfect choice for the trek, a mute but a massively powerful man of forty-five or so, and utterly devoted to her. His affection for her went back to when she was a small child, when she had become angry at others for ridiculing the strange sounds he made in trying to attract the attention of others, and through the years it had deepened. She had always seen that he had something extra on his nameday and that his shirts and boots were somewhat better than average, and the whistles and rattles he made for her namedays as a child had gradually changed to ribbons and handkerchiefs bought with carefully hoarded kopecks as she grew older. He had a fierce protectiveness toward her, and the burly Danilo with a glower on his face and a stave in his hand was accorded respect by the soldiers.

Natalya bought two large loaves of black bread, a half dozen large potatoes, a couple of turnips, and an onion, and she walked back along the road to the caravansary. Fires were burning by all the wagons and the soldiers had a large fire blazing, and the pungent odor of woodsmoke and the appetizing smell of food cooking blended with the fresh, sunny scent of the breeze moving across the open plain. Olivia's face was taut and shiny from being scrubbed and from the heat of the fire as she knelt by it and stirred the kettle suspended on an iron tripod. Natalya put one of the loaves of bread and vegetables in the wagon, washed her hands and face in a bucket of water, and sat down by the fire between Danilo and Olivia.

Dinner was a stew of vegetables and fish thickened with oats, with black bread and kvass. They served Vassily's first, and Danilo got his stave from the front of the wagon and went with Natalya as she took it to him. The Army cooks had already distributed what they had cooked among the prisoners, a weak gruel and lumps of soggy bread. Some of the wives and children were among the prisoners, having brought what they had cooked, and they were sitting with their husbands and talking and laughing as they ate, while the other prisoners looked hungrily at the food and women or sat and stared into space. Natalya weaved through them to Vassily, stirred him from his weary doze, and sat down on the straw floor by him. One of the most marked characteristics she had identified among those with high survival quotient was a hungry intensity and alertness, a constant watchfulness, hoarding their energy while their eyes roved restlessly, shouting at the Army cooks for a piece of potatoes or an extra spoonful of gruel, and snatching up a piece of hard crust discarded by another. But Vassily seemed apathetic about everything. His smile was absent and his attitude was indifferent, and she had to cajole him into eating his food while others stared at it ravenously.

He ate most of it, and she gave the remainder of it to the man chained next to him as she checked Vassily's manacles to make sure the rags she had put under them were keeping them from galling him, and gave him a drink of the infusion for his fever. They were chained in pairs, and she had been doing what she could to cultivate the good will of the man next to him in event it would prove of benefit to Vassily, after having brusquely cut off a sarcastic remark about the Czar's justice from him with a scathing reminder of the state to which his attitudes had brought him. Vassily lay back down and dozed off again, Natalya chatted with the man chained to him for a few minutes while he finished the food, then she gathered up the bowl, cup, and spoon and went back through the prisoners to the front of the shed.

The soldiers in the detachment assigned to the caravansary were pleased by the break in the lonely ennui of the isolated post and excited by the presence of the women, and they were sharing vodka with the Streltsy as they sat around their fires in front of the long building. They were louder than they had been before, and a lot of them looked at Natalya with salacious grins as she came out of the shed. Danilo walked behind her, so close that his toes brushed the hem of

441

her skirt, and he tapped the heavy stave against his leg as he glared around at the soldiers.

The setting sun made the clouds in the north glow with a rich, golden light which faded into shades of red as it slipped below the horizon, and they sat around the fire and ate. The traveling produced fatigue which seemed far out of proportion to the amount of physical activity involved, and Natalya's shoulders slumped as she sat with her legs folded under her and her bowl and piece of bread on her lap. Her spirit was heavy. She was worried about Vassily, the recent death of her father giving her an acute awareness of how fragile life could be, and she missed Thomas far more than she had anticipated. Up until the time they had left, she had known intellectually that they would be separated for two to three months, but still felt that they would shortly be rejoined. Then the knowledge had penetrated to the depth of the feeling after they left St. Petersburg, and it had been almost crushing. He would be angry, which was a matter of total unconcern because she knew she could cajole him out of it, but he would also be worried. That bothered her. And she missed him, much to her surprise.

Leaving the serfs had also been more of a wrench than she had anticipated. The memory of their expressions when she called them together to tell them was an aching torment. Their very existence had been shaken by the death of her father no less than hers had been, and they had viewed Thomas, their new master, with suspicion. But as long as she had been there, a known and established order had been present. She had always been among them, and during the past years they had looked to her more than to her father. They had understood why she had to go, they had understood that the household would still be a functioning entity under the control of the housekeeper and house steward, but they had still been dismayed and fearful.

And yet there were also positive aspects. Vassily would be in a position to come through his exile satisfactorily, if only he could shake off the lassitude which plagued him and his health would improve. What she had thought was a close friendship with Olivia had been little more than a passing acquaintance, compared with the attachment which had developed since leaving St. Petersburg. Her respect for Olivia's strength of character had increased manyfold, because her endurance seemed unlimited and she was always determined in the face of any adversity. With such an example before her, Natalya had forced herself to be cheerful and companionable regardless of the circumstances, and she knew Olivia's respect for her had increased as well.

Beyond that, the trek had represented a break from routine, refreshing in itself. Surprisingly, she had found that traveling across vast distances and living in a carefree, day-to-day fashion struck some responsive chord deep within her, enabling her to quickly adapt to the situation.

Darkness fell, and the fire made a pool of warm flickering light at the side of the wagon as they sat around it. Olivia scraped the rest of the stew into Danilo's bowl and gave him another piece of bread to go with it, then rinsed out the kettle and put it to one side. The breeze fanned the coals of the fire, making them glow from dull red to bright orange as it freshened and waned, and the ruddy light highlighted the planes on Olivia's face as she looked silently into the fire, and Danilo's honest, craggy features.

Natalya glanced around almost furtively as she got up and reached into the wagon for two cigarettes. These were among their few luxuries, and were kept out of sight of others. Any number of people in the caravan knew who she was, and among those who knew the name Sheremetev, there were presumably those who would link the name with wealth. But there were other names among the prisoners which had once been associated with wealth and whose wealth had been forfeited to the crown upon their conviction, and Olivia and Natalya had been careful to give the impression of financial difficulties. The bags of rubles hidden in the wagon amounted to more than a vast majority of people could earn in years, and any hint of their existence could place their lives in jeopardy.

Some who had talked to her in the wagon train had thought she was unmarried, because she continued to use her maiden name in referring to herself. Olivia expressed mild disapproval about it, but Natalya had found it fundamentally impossible to devise a feminine form of the name Greenwood, a blur of sound in her ears which began with a gargle and ended with a thud. And she refused to be known by what she thought of as a man's name. But that was only one of her problems with English names. She would have long since begun addressing Olivia by an affectionate diminutive except for the fact that Olivia's name in that form closely resembled a slang vulgarism. And she had continued addressing Thomas by full name and patronymic because an affectionate diminutive of his first name sounded like a sneeze to her.

Danilo smoked half of his cigarette, pinched the burning end off it, put the remainder in his pocket, and brought the horse back to tether it to the rear of the wagon. He took his blanket and stave out of the wagon, then he crawled under it to go to sleep. Natalya and Olivia chatted quietly as Natalya smoked her cigarette. The fire died down and the breeze became cool, and Natalya tossed the end of the cigarette into the coals of the fire. They climbed into the wagon and lay on their pallets, pulling their blankets around them. Natalya rooted under the bundle of clothes she used for a pillow, checking her pistols, then composed herself for sleep.

The day began early. Danilo crawled from under the wagon well before daylight, built up the fire and put water on to heat, and rapped on the bed of the wagon to waken Natalya and Olivia. They climbed out and made tea while Danilo harnessed the horse, then he took a cup of tea and a piece of bread to Vassily. The three of them breakfasted on tea and bread, and the first of the Army wagons were rumbling out of the courtyard by the time they were finished and preparing to leave. The caravan formed along the road by the village in the grey light before dawn, and the village was out of sight behind them by the time the sun rose.

Natalya and Olivia changed into clean clothes and helped each other with their hair as the wagon jolted along, then they read and dozed on their pallets until the midday stop. Danilo went with Natalya to take Vassily a piece of dried fish, a slab of bread, and a cup of kvass for lunch, but he would only drink the kvass. The wagons started along the road again, a line of motion which was almost lost on the broad plain, with the massively dark and threatening thunderclouds moving across from the north again. Natalya and Olivia discussed Vassily above the noise of the wagon during the afternoon, wondering what they might be able to do for him. During late afternoon the caravan came to a stop at the side of the road near a village, and Natalya bartered for a chicken. They made a savory stew of the chicken, vegetables, and onions, and Vassily ate part of what Natalya took to him. The next day he seemed in better spirits, but the following evening his appetite was poor again.

The thunderheads continued building up in the north every afternoon, appearing as though they were going to sweep across the road and the caravan, then in the evenings they would drift back to the north and in the mornings the sky would be clear. The road started down a long, slow incline, and in the distance a blue shadow appeared on the horizon—the Urals. Then they went across another stretch where the soil was exceptionally dry. The surface of the road was covered with a light, powdery dust. The first wagons churned it up, and by the time it reached their wagon it was a thick cloud which reduced visibility to a few feet. It came in through all the openings in the wagon to sting the nostrils, clog the throat, and penetrate all of their belongings and into the tightest container. They kept damp cloths tied over their faces to filter the air, and during each of the frequent stops called by the officer to let the horses blow, Danilo took a freshly dampened cloth to Vassily. The dry stretch lasted for two days, during which they suffered the misery of the dust while the thunderheads hung almost over them and drenched the plains just to the north of them with rain. When they were finally out of it, Vassily's fever had returned and his breathing was a hoarse, choking rasp.

Then the rains descended, with lightning bolts dancing along the ground and reverberating claps of thunder making the horses shy, and the downpour turned the road into a sea of thick, clinging mud. During the first afternoon of the heavy rain, they dismounted in the pouring rain to tie ropes to the shafts of the wagon and help the horse pull it. The fury of the storm burst around them in a wild maelstrom of lightning, thunder, wind, and rain as they fought their way through the mud, and twice they had to edge the wagon to the side of the road to get around other wagons which were hopelessly mired, with women standing by them and weeping in despair. The rain stopped when evening approached, and they were staggering from exhaustion, soaked through, and plastered with thick mud up to their waists. They rested for a few mintues, then grimly went about their tasks. And Natalya found that what she had done for the man chained to Vassily had paid a rich dividend. The prisoners had been unloaded to help the horses pull their wagons, and the man chained to Vassily had pulled the rope for both of them and carried Vassily along. Natalya went back to the wagon and got more food for both of them.

It rained again the next day, and the end came for Vassily the day after that. They didn't know until the midday stop, when Natalya and Danilo went to take his meal to him, and the guards told her that he had died in the middle of the morning. The officer let them put his body in their wagon to travel on to the place where they stopped for the evening, a small village at the base of the foothills of the Urals.

The caravan traveled on the following morning, without Natalya's wagon. Two others had died during the past three days and had been carried along until a convenient churchyard was found, and Natalya, grief-stricken, paid the priest for a funeral service and burial for all three. They spent two more days at the village, resting the horse and washing and drying their clothes as they discussed waiting for a westbound caravan, and on the third day they decided to start back.

CHAPTER XXIII

Natalya woke abruptly as the wagon stopped and she heard the man's voice in a thick, gutteral, Southern Volga dialect.

"Do you not need an escort for your wagon, pretty woman?"

Olivia was sitting on the front seat with Danilo, and she had been reading to him. There was a quaver of fright in her voice as she dropped the book behind her, replying in French. "I cannot understand you. Get away from my wagon."

There was coarse laughter from several men, and a shout. "She is French! Get her down so we can see her better!"

Natalya sat up, digging under the bundle of clothes at the end of the pallet for her pistols as she looked out the front of the wagon between Danilo and Olivia. A man in the uniform of the Streltsy was holding the horse's head, and two more came into sight as they climbed up onto the front of the wagon, leering at Olivia. All three of them looked drunk. Olivia shrank back from them as they reached for her, then screamed piercingly as one of them seized her arm. Danilo looked back at Natalya for instructions, his expression wild and distraught. She shrieked a single word.

"Kill!"

Danilo whipped the stave off the floor of the wagon under his feet and clammed it down onto a man's head, crushing it, and the other man fell back off the wagon as he dodged the stave, still holding Olivia and dragging her with him. She screamed again, and Danilo gathered himself to spring after her, holding the stave over his head. A musket barrel came into sight, pointing toward Danilo at point-blank range, and it fired as he knocked it aside with his stave. Another rifle fired, and Danilo staggered and fell off the wagon. Olivia screamed again. Natalya cocked the pistols, pushed herself to her feet and started toward the front of the wagon. Another man leaped onto the wagon, looking through the opening in the front with an excited grin, then his mouth dropped open as he saw the pistols pointing toward him. Natalya squeezed the trigger. There was a metallic snap. It had misfired. The man's expression changed from terror to triumph, and he moved toward her. Consternation spread across his face again as she lifted the other pistol. She squeezed the trigger. It went off with a deafening roar in the interior of the wagon, filling it with thick, black smoke. The impact of the ball threw the man backwards across the seat and he fell to the ground, blood gushing from a large hole in his neck.

There was a bellow of pain from outside the wagon, another rifle shot, and the thin, animal-like hissing sound Danilo made when angry or agitated. There was more harsh laughter, a sound of tearing fabric, and Olivia screamed again from further away from the wagon, a piteous wail of despair. Natalya knelt over the pistol case, jerking it open and working frantically. Years before, Vassily had frequently campeted with her to see who could reload faster, and her trembling fingers flew through the motions she had learned then

449

as the swirling smoke in the wagon burned her eyes and stung in her nostrils and throat. She took two caps out of the box in the pistol case, pressed them down onto the nipples under the hammers, leaped to her feet and rushed toward the front of the wagon, cocking the pistols.

Another man's head came into view as he climbed onto the front of the wagon, and she lifted the pistol which had misfired and pulled the trigger. It thundered, and a large red hole appeared on the man's forehead as the ball knocked him off the wagon. She dropped the discharged pistol and held the other one in both hands as she leaned over the seat and looked out.

Seven or eight drunken soldiers had pursued Olivia into the field by the road, and they were tearing her clothes from her and pushing her to the ground. Danilo was a few yards away from the wagon, his right arm dangling uselessly and blood streaming from his limp hand, and there was a deep cut on the side of his head, but he was still fighting furiously with his stave. Two soldiers were at his feet, their heads broken, and he was parrying the bayonets of two more with his stave. As she watched, he feinted and punched one of the soldiers in the stomach with the stave, then brought the stave down on the soldier's head as his bayonet lowered. The other soldier drove his bayonet into the side of Danilo's chest. Danilo raised the stave with an effort, trying to fight on even as his knees sagged. The soldier stabbed him again. Natalya lifted the pistol, aiming down the barrel. Danilo slumped to the ground. The soldier jerked his bayonet out and drove it in once again. Natalya pulled the trigger. The soldier fell on top of Danilo.

The soldiers who had chased Olivia had dropped their muskets by the wagon, and Natalya dropped the pistol and leaped out of the wagon toward them. She landed on top of the soldier she had shot through the neck, who was still kicking and writhing, and fell flat. There was a shout of alarm from one of the soldiers around Olivia. Natalya jumped to her feet and seized one of the muskets, and looked at the cap under the hammer. It had been fired. She dropped it and picked up another one. It was charged. Two soldiers started running toward her. She dragged the hammer back with her right hand and awkwardly shouldered the long, heavy musket, the barrel weaving from side to side. One of the soldiers running toward her turned to the other one with a laughing shout. The musket boomed. His laugh changed to a cry of pain as the ball hit him in the stomach, and he went down. The other soldier stopped. Natalya dropped the musket and picked up another one, cocking it. The soldier began moving back toward the others, looking at Natalya apprehensively. The musket boomed, and he shrieked with pain as he fell.

All of them except one in an officer's uniform began scattering and running. He pulled a pistol from his belt and aimed it at Natalya as she picked up another musket. Olivia pushed herself up from the ground, her clothes torn away from her to her waist and her skirt hanging around her in shreds, and she threw herself at the officer. The pistol cracked, and Olivia fell back, shot through the chest. Natalya aimed the musket at the officer, pulled the trigger, and missed. He began running across the field, shouting and waving at the soldiers. Natalya picked up another musket, cocked it and took careful aim, and squeezed the trigger. The officer went down.

There were five soldiers left, and they made a wide circuit around the wagon and through the field to the road, then began running along the road in the direction from which the wagon had come. Natalya looked at Danilo. He was dead. She ran out into the field to Olivia and bent over her. Olivia was dead. She pulled Olivia's clothes together over her as best she could to conceal her nakedness, then stood erect and looked around. It looked like the scene of a massacre. Her expression was blank and she felt numb, her mind refusing to assimilate what had happened. It was too enormous, too much to grasp. She looked at the road again. The five soldiers had disappeared over a low hill a short distance away. A couple of the soldiers on the ground were moving feebly. She bent over Olivia's body and began dragging her to the wagon.

Pulling Olivia across the field almost exhausted what little strength Natalya had left, but somehow she managed to lift her into the back of the wagon. When she went for Danilo, she could hardly move even his limbs. She unhitched the horse and put a rope around Danilo to pull him to the rear of the wagon, ran the rope through the wagon and pulled him up into it, and hitched the horse back to the wagon. A soldier who had been shot though the stomach sat up and watched her, breathing with a loud, hoarse sound as he held his stomach. When she climbed onto the seat of the wagon and started the horse along the road again, he fell back over on the ground.

During the late morning she passed by a village. It was a sparsely populated area, with villages scattered at wide distances apart, and the villagers working the fields and those in the village looked at the wagon curiously. A couple of them called out and waved. She looked straight ahead, driving on. A couple of hours later the wagon topped a rise, and the dim track of a woodcutter's road branched off to the right and went into a thick stand of trees. She turned the horse onto the narrow, rutted road. The wagon rattled and bounced heavily, and the horse struggled along. The road went into the trees, and branches brushed against both sides of the canvas as the wagon swayed from side to side. The road narrowed as it went along the side of a ravine, then there was a deadfall across it and the horse stopped. Natalya stirred, looking at the ravine. She sat for a long time and looked at it, then she dropped the traces and climbed back into the wagon, found the shovel among the other things and threw it out, and began pulling Olivia and Danilo out of the wagon.

The soil in the ravine was damp and soft and her hands had roughened from the work during the trek, but blisters formed on her hands and broke as she dug feverishly. She deepened the hole until it satisfied her, slid them into it side by side and covered them, then climbed back and forth on the wall of the ravine, rolling rocks down and piling them onto the mound of soil.

She climbed through the wagon and went through the things in it methodically, putting them in piles then going back and forth and looking at them again for long moments as though it were a mental effort to identify them. She collected all the money together, put it with some rope, clothes, a blanket, and food, reloaded her pistols again, found the flint, steel, and tinder box, and made up bundles. Then she took the harness off the horse, put the bundles across its back, climbed up behind them, and rode on into the forest.

The forest deepened, then thinned out at the top of a hill above a shallow valley which stretched away on both sides. The forest began again at the top of the next hill, and the horse ambled slowly down into the meadow, drank at a creek which ran through it, and climbed up the next hill and went into the forest. The forest continued for a long distance, with occasional small openings and glades. The horse began walking slower and slower, stumbling with fatigue. He almost fell at the edge of one of the glades, and she reined up and looked blankly around for several moments. Then she slid down and pulled the bundles off, put the horse on a long rope, sat down by the bundles and leaned back against a tree, staring vacantly into space.

The light reddened as the sun sank into the west. The horse finished eating and rested, his head hanging and his eyes closed, and his rear quarters canted to one side as he turned a rear hoof onto its edge. Darkness fell. Natalya continued to stare in front of her. A breeze moved through the trees, and they whispered softly overhead. Her hands crept up her arms in a habitual and instinctive movement to protect herself against the chill. The moon rose over the horizon, and stars twinkled overhead. Natalya began shivering with cold. The breeze freshened, and the limbs overhead swayed. Natalya began trembling convulsively, and her teeth began chattering. Her eyes suddenly focused, and she looked around. She reached toward the bundle for the blanket, then hesitated, looking around again and studying the horse and bundles in the pale light of the moon as though she had never seen them before. Then she burst into tears.

She lay against the bundles, weeping bitterly, her sobs lost in the rustling and creaking of the branches overhead. Self-recrimination over Olivia's fate burned within her. She had precipitated the situation by deciding to accompany Vassily to Siberia, Olivia had come with her out of loyalty, and she had paid for that loyalty with her life. Her last living act, even while wracked with terror from the men tearing at her clothes to rape her, had been to throw herself between a pistol and the object of her loyalty. She had died far from the geren fields of her native England about which she had spoken so often, and she lay in a cold and unhallowed grave in a briar-filled ravine because of her love and loyalty.

And Danilo. He hadn't even had the option to go or not to go. Her finger had pointed him out among the assembled serfs. He had smiled with pride and joy, but that meant nothing. Her father's dictum that the responsibility for a serf's welfare lay with the master was a fundamental tenet in her life, and she could not escape it. The fault was hers. She had failed in her responsibility. The times he had come to her with a nameday present or a small gift of thoughtfulness in his large, knobby hands with a gentle smile on his homely, trusting face raced through her mind. In return, she had brought him to his death.

It was too much for even Natalya's indomitable spirit. The blows had been too cruel and too frequent, and she felt herself collapsing inside. Her father, Vassily, Olivia, and Danilo. Death's scythe had cut down too many from her side. There seemed to be no limit to her pain, but there had to be a limit to what one person should have to bear. And that limit had been overreached by far in Natalya's case. It was too much.

Her body began shaking violently, and she fumbled with the bundles, dragging out the blanket and pulling it around herself. Then she curled up again, still weeping. The horse lifted his head and cocked his ears, looking at her, then closed his eyes and hung his head again. Natalya's sobs became dry, shuddering gasps, and her mind began going over what had happened on the road, searching for some reason and trying to make some order out of the chaotic events. The soldiers couldn't have been deserters from some garrison, because an officer had been with them. Most of them had been drunk. A lot of the Streltsy were notably ill-disciplined. There had been a small garrison in the large village they had passed shortly after dawn, and the soldiers could have been relieved from duty at a caravansary or on a training march. They might have approached the wagon thinking it was a villager's wagon. What had started as drunken amusement had turned into tragedy.

But she had killed several soldiers. That was an inescapable fact, and while life seemed to have become too much to bear, ending it in a district prison seemed worse. And that would happen if they caught her. Annya and Moscow were a long distance away, and a lot could happen to her before Annya and Thomas found out where she was. The instinct which had led her to leave the scene and abandon the wagon while in her numb, addled state had removed her from immediate danger, but she was still in an extremely perilous situation.

She sat up, pulling the blanket around her, and began feeling around on the ground for twigs and breaking them up. Her hands shook uncontrollably from the cold, and she could hardly hold the flint and steel. She pulled the blanket around into a tent to shelter the tiny pile of twigs, and knocked the flint and steel together over the tinder box. The flint fell from her numb, trembling fingers, and felt around on the ground for it, found it, and tried again. Sparks fell into the punk, then died. She knocked them together frantically, and several more sparks fell into the punk. They began glowing. She bent over and blew on them until they glowed hotly, then picked up a small twig and touched it to the fire. It burst into flame, and she sheltered it with her hand and pushed it under the pile of twigs. Flame leaped up among the twigs, and she closed the tinder box, pushed the blanket to one side, and began searching for larger pieces of wood.

The fire began burning brightly as she piled wood

onto it, and it cast dark, leaping shadows among the trees and made a circle of light on the edge of the glade. The horse edged closer to the fire, the flames glowing in his eyes. She had no appetite and didn't feel like eating, but she felt weak from the lack of food. She searched in the bundles for a loaf of bread, pulled a piece off it, and began eating it slowly as she looked into the fire and thought about her situation.

Arrest was a virtual certainty if she remained in the area. She had to get to Annya, who would be able to advise her what to do and who could exercise influence in her favor. But getting to Annya would be a problem. They would be looking for her, and even though communications were slow and tedious, a woman traveling alone bareback on a horse was an unusual sight. Also, her papers wouldn't stand up to the most cursory check even by an official who wasn't looking for her, because they included Olivia and Danilo. There was also the distance involved; Moscow was far away, to the south and west. For the most part, she could travel backroads and cross country to evade officials, as long as the horse didn't go lame, but crossing the Volga would be a problem. There were a limited number of crossings, with officials at each one. Food would also be a problem, because she would excite curiosity in any village she entered. She searched in the bundle and took out a piece of dried fish, and she took a bit of it and another bite of the bread. It would be difficult, but she would do it. The night seemed very dark and vast and she felt like a tiny speck in it sitting by the fire. But she had to get to Annya, and she would do it.

At dawn things seemed much less promising. The ease with which things had slid into place in her mind the evening before was lacking in the cold light of morning, and the problems and difficulties seemed much greater. The gripping sorrow and self-blame over what had happened to Olivia and Danilo returned. The forest seemed hostile and threatening around her.

There was a small brook at the bottom of the open glade. Natalya took the horse to it and let him drink, washed her face and hands in the icy water, then let the horse crop the fresh grass along the side of the water. The bundles on the ground looked very pitiful and paltry when she led the horse back up the hill. And she felt very lonely. She sighed, folding the blanket and tying it in one of the bundles, then she lifted the bundles onto the horse's back and pulled herself up behind them.

What had seemed a meticulously detailed knowledge of geography of the area for the purposes of discussion and the understanding of history was markedly deficient for the purpose of getting from one place to another. She knew the general direction to go, but nothing of the details of the topography or the roads to Moscow. The forest opened into scattered stands of trees among meadows and crop fields, with small villages dotting the countryside. It was distinctly open country, where she would be visible for a long distance. But it had to be crossed. She restrained the impulse to make the horse trot, aware that her situation would be virtually hopeless if the horse went lame, and conscious that those who saw her would interpret hurry as furtiveness. People working in distant fields stopped and stood erect to shade their eyes against the sun and look at her, and a few of those who were near waved at her. She returned the waves, hoping it would give the impression of nonchalance.

At midday she stopped in a meadow out of sight of houses and villages to let the horse drink, eat some grass, and rest for a few minutes, and she ate a piece of bread and some cheese. There was a half loaf of bread left, a piece of dried fish, a small cabbage, and some turnips. But she had no utensil to cook vegetables. She tossed the cabbage and turnips to the horse and let him eat them, then put the bundles back on him and pulled herself up behind them. On the other side of the hill, there were fields with a village in the distance; the workers either weren't working the fields that day or had gone to the village for their noon meal. She stopped the horse at a stone fence and climbed over, and took a stick and dug among hills of potatoes. There had been innumerable occasions when she had seen the villagers at Sherevskoye digging potatoes, and as a child she had helped them while they laughed among themselves and joked with her. But they seemed much deeper and harder to dig than she remembered. She managed to root up half a dozen of them, and climbed back over the fence and went on.

During the afternoon she came to another belt of forest. She rode through it, then reined up and looked around on the other side. Rolling hills with fields, pastures, and small villages extended far into the distance, and darkness would overtake her in the open countryside if she went on. She turned back into the trees.

All but one of the potatoes were disappointingly small, but that turned out to be an advantage in baking them in the coals of the fire, because the small ones baked through within a short time while the large one was still hard. They were tasteless but filling, and distinctly more appetizing than the fish which was slightly rancid and the bread which was dry and hard. Natalya finished eating and pulled her blanket around her, looking dispiritedly into the fire and thinking of the innumerable glasses of tea she had barely sipped and the bottles of kvass she had turned away in easier times. Then she thought of Olivia and Danilo again, and her eyes filled with tears. It had been a long, hard day, but she had come such a short distance. She felt very alone in a cold, hostile, and inimical world. She pillowed her head on one of the bundles and sobbed quietly.

The large potato baked through in the hot coals during the night, and there was a heel of a loaf of bread to go with it. It was tasteless, but she was ravenously hungry. She finished eating, watered the horse and washed her face and hands in a brook, fixed her hair and brushed her dress as well as she could, then put the bundles on the horse and pulled herself up behind them.

During midmorning she reached the top of a hill overlooking a moderately large village. Pastures and fields associated with the village and tiny, outlying clusters of houses here and there stretched for a long distance, and there were many workers in the fields digging vegetables and reaping grain. They were taking the crop, which meant that all able workers were in the fields. Most important of all, there was no manor house or official-looking building in the village. It was as safe a place as she would find, and it was the safest time for her to enter the village. Natalya rode down the hill along a path by a stone fence. Workers in the fields turned to look at her, and she forced a smile and waved to them. She reached the road and turned the horse toward the village, tension and fear gripping her. Several dogs raced out and ran around the horse's heels, barking and snapping madly, and the horse kicked irritably. Children and a few older women were moving around the village, and they stopped to look at her curiously. The smell of fresh bread and food cooking wafted along the street, making her weak with hunger.

An old woman was standing in the doorway of a house, and Natalya reined up and greeted her, using the French-accented Russian of landlords, and the old woman replied, stepping out of the doorway and looking at her curiously. Natalya smiled down at the old woman and chattered, slurring her words with the French accent so the old woman would have difficulty understanding her precisely, and she told the old woman she had wrecked her phaeton and was riding her horse home. A less ignorant person would have looked at the state of her hair and clothes and would have wondered about the bundles on the horse, but the old woman appeared to accept the story at face value, clucking sympathetically and asking where she lived. Other women were moving toward them and gathering around, and Natalya replied vaguely, rattling off a name and waving toward the east, then she asked the old woman if she would sell her some food. The old woman was taken aback by the question, and she told Natalya that she probably didn't have anything she would like, but she could dismount and have some of the stew she was cooking. Natalya refused graciously, telling the old woman her mother would be worried about her, and she asked if she had anything she could take with her. The old woman was doubtful, but she went into her house and came back out with a loaf of bread, a small bladder of curd, and a sausage, offering them hesitantly. Most of the money was in one of the bundles, but Natalya had a few rubles tucked in her belt and she took out a ruble and gave it to the old woman. The old woman was astounded by the amount, and she thanked Natalya profusely. Natalya shrugged off her thanks as she turned the horse back into the street. The old woman and several others tried to walk along and chat with her, their curiosity still not satisfied, and Natalya repeated that her mother would be worried about her as she thumped the horse's side with a heel and made him trot for a distance.

It was an exercise of will and restraint to keep from

attacking the food until the village was out of sight behind her. She tore open the crust on the bread and ate bits of it as the horse plodded along the road between the fields and outlying clusters of houses, and when the last of them was behind her she broke open the bladder of curd and began ravenously eating it and the bread.

The road went up a long, slow incline, and it was late afternoon by the time she reached the top. There was a belt of forest off to the right along the top of the ridge, and she looked at it thoughtfully as the horse started down the road on the other side of the incline. She turned her head and looked along the road ahead, then reined up. A dozen wagons were in a circle in a field adjacent to the road. Gypsies. She had often argued hotly with Vassily and others when disparaging comments had been made about Gypsies, but there were elements of truth in what they had said. Those who had camped at Sherevskoye had been friends. Gypsies who weren't friends had to be treated with caution, particularly by a lone woman. She turned the horse back, looking over her shoulder at the wagons. Fires were burning inside the circle and a few people were moving about them, but no one appeared to have observed her. She went back over the crest in the road, then turned the horse off the road toward the belt of forest.

The sausage was delicious, hot and strongly flavored with garlic. She remembered the times she had passed over slices of such sausages on trays of delicacies in favor of pieces of dry and flaky salmon, chunks of ham dotted with cloves, or tiny cakes of pressed caviar, and the memory seemed very remote and dim. The tactic she had used to buy the food had been good, but she would have to think of some reason for buying in

462

greater quantity. There was bread left for breakfast, then she would be out of food again and would have to buy more. The more often she entered villages, the greater her danger would be.

The horse was restless. He kept lifting his head and cocking his ears, looking around with his nostrils flared. Natalya looked at him, frowning. Wolves could be a danger during winter, but rarely during summer. She turned her head from side to side, listening, then moved closer to the bundles and began fumbling in one of them for her pistols.

There was a distinct sound of a twig breaking behind her and she felt hostile eyes on her. A stab of fear raced through her, and she looked over her shoulder into the darkness as she frantically dug for the pistols. A thicker shadow in the darkness turned into a man rushing toward her. Her hand found the grip of a pistol, and she jerked at it. He was suddenly upon her, a huge, burly figure with a dark beard and long dark hair, with a gleam of a gold earring. A gypsy. And another one behind him.

Natalya screamed in panic, and his teeth shone in a triumphant grin as he knocked the pistol from her hand and seized her, lifting her off the ground and pinning her arms to her sides. The other man uttered an exultant whoop, coming around from the other side. She drummed her feet frantically against the man's legs, throwing herself from side to side and twisting, and she got one of her arms loose. Her fingernails gouged into his face, and he bellowed with pain as he snatched at her hand and jerked his head back. She got her other hand loose and clawed at him in a frenzy of terror. The other man seized her hands and pulled them around behind her, twisting her arms painfully, and she leaned back and bit at him. Her teeth closed on the side of his hand, and she put all of her strength into her jaws. He shrieked shrilly, and she felt a sudden stunning blow on the side of her head.

The ground seemed to come up and hit her solidly, knocking the breath from her. Fury mingled with the fear gripping her, and she sprang to her feet, tearing with her fingernails and searching for something to bite with her teeth. There was another blow to her head, and Natalya fell to the ground once more.

CHAPTER XXIV

She returned to consciousness slowly, in stages. At first she felt only a numb, bewildered perplexity over the strange surroundings and people. Her head ached, and the strange language was gibberish in her ears. Then memory returned. She started to sit up, and everything around her swam giddily and she fell back to the ground. The conversation suddenly stopped as they looked at her. She braced herself with her hand as she sat up and shook her head to clear it.

There were twenty or more gypsies, men and women of different ages, and a few children peering out from behind adults or from under the wagons. The fire in the center of the circle leaped up, throwing shadows along the sides of the wagons. All the people looked dark and dangerous. A half dozen men were looking through her things, and several women were watching them. One of the men was counting the money, an expression of astonished delight on his face. Another was holding her pistols. The horse was standing at one side. Two of the men were dimly familiar. One of them had a bandage on his hand, and the other's face looked as though he had run through a briar patch.

An older man with an authoritative air about him

looked at her and spoke in heavily accented Russian. "What is your name?"

She steeled herself to keep her voice from trembling and lifted her chin. "I am Natalya Ivanova Sheremeteva."

They looked at each other and murmured softly in their language. The wood on the fire crackled, and sparks flew up. The men continued searching through the bundles, and counting the money. The older man looked at her with a stolid, impassive expression. "What are you doing alone?"

She cleared her throat, pulled her legs up under her, straightened her dress, and put her hands on her lap as she looked into his eyes. Gypsies had little contact with authorities, none if they could manage it, and there was a bare possibility that she could talk herself out of this situation if they hadn't heard of the incident with the soldiers. "I find myself in unfortunate circumstances. I was on my way to Moscow, to meet my friend Annya Konstantinovna Romanova, His Majesty the Czar's niece. If you will assist me, you will be paid well." She nodded toward the money. "You may keep that—it is nothing. And it is but a small portion of what you will be paid if you assist me."

"We will keep it," the man replied in a grimly emphatic tone. "If you are the friend of the Czar's niece, why are you sleeping in the woods like a wild animal?"

Natalya licked her lips and swallowed dryly; there was disbelief in his voice. And in the faces looking at her. "You shall not omit the honorific when referring to His Majesty the Czar in my presence," she said firmly, a quaver creeping into her voice despite her best effort. She cleared her throat and lifted her chin again. "I find myself in my present situation because my traveling companions and I were set upon by brigands." She turned her eyes toward the two who had captured her. "As I was myself again not an hour ago."

One of the men snorted and snarled something in his language. A woman chortled, pointing to his face. He snarled back in a defensive tone. A ripple of laughter ran through the group. The older man looked at the two men, then looked back at her. "If this happened as you said, why did you not go to the authorities?"

"The governor general of this district has an enmity toward my family."

It wasn't a very strong reason, and it didn't convince him. He looked at her doubtfully, scratching his beard. One of the men murmured a question, and he shrugged and replied quietly. Two or three other men murmured in agreement. He looked at Natalya thoughtfully, his lips pursed, then shrugged in dismissal and turned toward the man who was counting the money, looking at the money.

"You have not replied to my request. If you will assist me, you will be well paid."

He shrugged and shook his head, glancing at her and looking back at the money. "We will talk later," he replied in an indifferent tone.

It seemed to be the best she was going to get. And it was far from reassuring. Several of the men were looking at her with lustful expressions. Anything could happen to her, and it seemed that rape was only part of it. It had taken an extreme effort of will to maintain control while talking to him, and it was rapidly running out. Natalya wanted to burst into tears and beg them, promise anything if only they wouldn't hurt her and would see her safely to Annya and Thomas. The pain in her head swelled, so intense that it made her dizzy. Escape was impossible, because they were all around her. The darkness outside the ring of wagons looked inviting, but they would catch her before

467

she could get between two of the wagons. And the facade of poise she had painfully erected would be destroyed if she tried.

They moved around the fire, looking at the money, pistols, and other things, and a couple of men looked at the horse. The children peered at her curiously, and some of the women looked at her and commented to each other. A couple of the women went to a larger fire in the center of the circle and stirred a large kettle hanging over it on an iron tripod. A large, stocky woman of forty or so with a cruel, spiteful face approached, looked at her with a sneering comment to a couple of others, then leaned over and pulled at the reticule on Natalya's belt. It was where she kept her chain from Czar Aleksander. She pushed the woman's hand away, opened the reticule and took out all of the coins and handed them to the woman. The woman made a laughing comment to the others as she straightened up and looked at the coins in her hand. Natalya put her hands on her lap and gripped them together to keep them from shaking, and she placed her forearm on the reticule. The woman put the coins in her pocket and leaned over again, pushing at Natalya's arm and plucking at the reticule. Natalya silently shook her head, pushing the woman's hand away. The woman snarled angrily and slapped Natalya's face.

The woman's hand was heavy, and the pain in her head flared. But the pain was minor in comparison with the insult. Something snapped inside her. She had been pushed too far.

She leaped to her feet, snarling like a wild animal.

The woman sprang back with a cry of alarm and pain as Natalya's fingernails gouged deep furrows down her face. Her arm came around in instinctive protection, and her hand slammed into the side of Natalya's head and knocked her to the ground by the fire. People leaped out of the way, some of them laughing and shouting encouragement to the woman. Natalya gathered herself to get back to her feet. The woman rushed toward her, screaming with rage. Natalya gathered a double handful of the hot coals from the fire as she rose to her feet, unconscious of the searing pain in her hands, and threw them into the woman's face. The woman's scream changed to one of agony as she stumbled backwards, clutching her eyes and smoke billowing from her clothes and hair. There was motion all around, the laughter abruptly dying away and shouts ringing out, and Natalya seized the end of a large piece of wood sticking into the fire, jerked it out, and swung it around her. The people rushing at her jumped back, and Natalya raced toward the woman pawing at her eyes, and slammed the burning end of the piece of wood down on top of the woman's head.

Sparks and pieces of burning wood flew, and smoke boiled up from the woman's hair as she uttered a shrill, piercing shriek and fell to the ground, flailing at her hair and clothes. Men closed in on all sides of Natalya, and she whirled the firebrand around her again. They fell back, and she jumped at a man and hit at him, scraping across his shoulder and chest and spreading smoldering sparks down his clothes as his beard turned into a cloud of odorous smoke. A man snatched at her from behind, and she wheeled and hit at him. He dodged the firebrand and gripped the shoulder of her dress, trying to grapple her. She jerked away from him, hitting at him again, and her dress tore loose from her shoulder. He held onto it, dodging the firebrand again and reaching for her with his other hand, and the dress ripped down to her waist as she leaped backwards to break his grip on her. Other men closed in, and she beat at them.

An old woman's excited scream carried through the

hubbub, and the people began spreading back away from her. They shouted back and forth, and the old woman kept shrieking. Suddenly they were in a wide circle around her looking at her, and the old woman was still shouting. Natalya raised the firebrand over her head to strike and rushed at one side of the circle, her torn dress and petticoat flapping around her. The people dodged back out of her way. Her charge had taken her to the side of the large fire in the center of the circle, and she stopped and looked around.

The pain in her head was agonizing, and her hands felt as though they were on fire. The circle of wagons seemed to be swaying around her. She panted hoarsely as her lungs labored for air. Her limbs were trembling violently, and nausea churned in her stomach. They had stopped, and they were all looking at her. Their behavior seemed odd, but they were leaving her alone. They were attentive rather than threatening. The old woman was talking excitedly, pointing at Natalya, and the older man who had spoken with Natalya before was asking the old woman questions.

She had won. But it wasn't enough. She moved closer to the fire, lifting the piece of wood, and hit at the iron tripod holding the kettle. The piece of wood seemed very heavy. She hit at the tripod again. And again. It finally fell over, and steam and sparks boiled up as the kettle emptied into the fire with a loud hissing sound. Natalya almost fell, and she caught herself with the piece of wood and leaned on it, panting. The people were still standing and looking at her, a few of them commenting quietly and a couple of them chuckling. The older man and old woman were still talking. The woman with the burned hair was kneeling on the ground by a wagon, holding her head and whimpering, and another woman was bending over her. Natalya moved closer to the fire again, and she leaned

470

on the piece of wood and bent down, pulling a piece of smoldering wood from the edge of the fire. She straightened back up, summoning her strength, and she threw the piece of wood at a wagon. It slammed into the wagon and fell to the ground, flames licking up from the grass at the side of the wagon. The older man shouted something, and a man ran and poured a bucket of water on the grass. Natalya pulled another piece of wood from the fire and threw it at him. He dodged, it hit a wagon and fell to the ground, and he poured water on it.

Natalya leaned on the piece of wood again, looking around. Her strength was fading rapidly. The pain in her head and hands was almost unbearable, increasing as her contact with her surroundings returned. Her knees were shaking uncontrollably, and her teeth were chattering. The old woman was moving toward her with a placating smile, holding her hands out and saying something. The older man shouted at the old woman, and she began speaking in heavily accented Russian. "Come here, daughter. We will not harm you, daughter. Come and let me—"

She broke off and ran back as Natalya lifted the piece of wood and rushed at her with it. A few steps was all Natalya could manage, however, and she leaned on the piece of wood again, swaying on her feet and staring dizzily around at them. The large fire was almost out, a few flames licking up around the liquid which had spilled out of the kettle, and the smaller fires made the people standing and looking at her seem only shadows. Their behavior made no sense to Natalya.

The older man looked at a woman and snapped an order. The woman ran into a wagon, then emerged with a bottle and a cup. She walked hesitantly toward Natalya, put the cup and bottle on the ground, then

471

backed away from it. Natalya looked at the bottle, licking her lips dryly. It was kvass. And it was obviously meant for her. Her knees were shaking so hard that she could hardly stand, and the nausea was more pronounced. She panted weakly, looking at the bottle, then stumbled toward it, dragging the smoking firebrand along the ground. Suddenly she became aware of her state of deshabille. Her dress and petticoat were torn almost off her down to her waist, and her breasts were exposed. She pulled her dress up in front and held it against her as she lowered herself shakily to her knees, and she splashed some kvass into the cup and drank it greedily, spilling it down her chin and throat as the cup rattled against her teeth.

The older man who had spoken with her before moved toward her. "I would speak with you again."

Her voice caught in her throat, and she cleared her throat and tried again. "Speak from there."

He sat down on the ground, looking around, snapping orders and motioning. A couple of women circled around to the large fire, and Natalya watched them warily over her shoulder. They began dragging the tripod and kettle out of the fire. Others moved around, but no one approached her. The old woman who had been doing the excited chattering looked at Natalya with a wide smile. A man of about her age stood by her, murmuring to her.

"My name is Paspati. I am leader of this band. What is your name?"

"I told you my name."

Paspati looked up at the old woman and the old man by her and had a short exchange with them, then looked back at Natalya. "What is your mother's name?"

"Her name was Marya Pavlovna Sheremeteva, may God rest her soul."

Paspati looked back at the old man and woman, and

they started talking again. The old man explained something in an emphatic tone, saying the masculine form of Natalya's family name several times as he talked. Paspati said something in a musing tone, looking at the old woman, then turned and waved at a child, snapping an order. The child trotted to where Natalya's belongings were, picked up the blanket, and brought it to him. He handed it to the old woman.

"This woman will bring you your blanket."

Natalya silently nodded. The old woman walked toward her with slow steps and a wide smile, her demeanor appeasing. She shook the blanket open and knelt near Natalya, scooting toward her on her knees. The old woman put the blanket around her shoulders, looking at Natalya's torn dress and clucking sympathetically. She plucked at the torn fabric, then she suddenly pulled it away and stared at Natalya's birthmark intently. Natalya pulled away from her, jerking the blanket around her and scowling at the old woman, and the old woman backed away from Natalya, smiling and nodding again. She pushed herself to her feet and trotted toward Paspati, chattering rapidly.

He silenced her with a wave and motioned for her to sit down by him, and looked at Natalya again. "Do you know any of our people?"

She pulled the blanket closer around her. Her head was swimming giddily as the pain in it throbbed, and his voice seemed to come from a long distance away. She picked up the cup, her hand trembling and spilling the kvass down the side of it, and took a drink. "I know the band of Panna, which comes to camp every summer at Sherevskoye, the village of my family."

It caused a strong reaction. Several people uttered exclamations, nodding to the old man and woman, and they looked at Paspati with triumphant expressions. He slowly nodded, talking in a musing tone to the

473

group at large and motioning toward Natalya, then a note of humor came into his voice as he motioned around the circle and pointed to a couple of men with singed beards and the woman with the singed hair. There were chuckles and nods of agreement. He snapped orders, pointing at a couple of people, and they began moving around. A woman picked up Natalya's bundles, carried them toward her, and put them down near her. A man added her pistols to the pile. Another man brought her money and put it on a cloth by the bundles. The woman with the singed hair dropped the coins Natalya had given her on the rest of the money, and returned to her place and sat down, holding her head.

"These people tell me they have heard of you," Paspati said, indicating the old man and woman. "They tell me that your mother was Saiforella of the family Hator, a family of kings among our people. They say that the woman Saiforella was the second wife of a man called Sheremetev, and that she gave him a daughter. I have heard this story also at the winter camp, and I heard that the daughter was reared among the *gadjo* as a *gadjin*. You have the birthmark of the Hator, so you must be that daughter." He smiled and chuckled wryly. "And you conduct yourself like a Hator. Rael Hator, your grandfather, had a temper which would make Ivan the Terrible seem as mild as a priest in comparison."

There was a murmur around the circle. Natalya glanced around, then looked back at him blankly. His words were totally senseless, but his attitude and that of the other people was friendly.

"You are of the tribe Halebi, as are we, so you are kin to us. You are also of royal blood, and you will be treated accordingly. I apologize for the treatment you received when we did not know who you were, but . . ." He hesitated, smiling wryly again. "But it appears that you avenged yourself." He motioned to the old man and woman. "This is Corwen, and this is Mara. They have no children, so you may live in their wagon until we can contact Panna and make arrangements to transport you to his band."

They were going to help her. She nodded numbly. Everyone was suddenly in motion around her. The old woman came to her and helped her up, and led her toward one of the wagons. Men collected up her belongings and carried them after her.

The smell of the wagon was familiar from early childhood, a warm and comfortable odor. The old woman led her to a pallet, and the men put her belongings down at the foot of the pallet and left. The old man hovered around, and the old woman hissed at him impatiently until he left. She clucked worriedly over the blisters on Natalya's hands and took out a pot of soothing ointment and smeared some of it on them, then she brought a cool cloth and wiped Natalya's face and neck. Peace, calm, and quiet replaced wracking terror and turmoil. More than that, Natalya's loneliness was gone. The old woman took advantage of every opportunity to peek at the birthmark again, and presently it became too much trouble to keep pulling the torn dress back together. She closed her eyes and went to sleep.

CHAPTER XXV

The lurching of the wagon as it jolted through the ditch and turned onto the road awakened her. She snapped up to a sitting position, looking around wildly. Mara was kneeling by the pallet and smiling at her, and she reached out and patted Natalya's shoulder. Natalya looked at her without recognition and shrank away from her touch, then memory returned and she smiled faintly. The wagon rumbled noisily along the road, a deafening uproar of rattles, clatters, and squeaks. Mara said something which was lost in the noise, moving away from the pallet, and she got to her feet and crossed the wagon, her feet wide apart to balance herself against the motion of the wagon. Natalya leaned on her elbow and pushed at her hair, then winced and looked at her palms. There were several large blisters on them, and they were painfully tender. But it was only one pain among several. There were sore places on her head where the men had hit her, she still had a pounding headache, she felt weak, and there was a queasy feeling in her stomach.

Mara came back to the pallet with a cup, a pot of tea nested in a basket lined with cork to keep it hot, and a bowl of a thick paste of rice and oats. It was delicious, and Natalya identified a lot of her weakness

476

and nausea as hunger as she ate ravenously and drank cups of tea. Mara nodded and chuckled with pleasure over Natalya's appetite, then she took the bowl, cup, and pot away and brought a basin of water and a cloth for Natalya to wash her face and hands. Natalya washed, then sat up and rummaged in the bundles at the foot of the pallet for a dress. Mara clucked and shook her head negatively as Natalya took a dress out of the bundle, and she went to a chest in the corner and began lifting out skirts and blouses and examining them critically, putting them aside, and looking for others. She found a low necked lavender blouse and a skirt in green and black stripes, holding them up and looking at Natalya with a hopefully interrogative expression. Natalya smiled and nodded, and Mara took scissors, needles, and thread from another chest and sat down by the pallet again and began altering them to fit Natalya.

She chattered incessantly as she snipped, sewed, and held the blouse against Natalya, reiterating and enlarging upon what Paspati had said the night before. Her accent was very strong, and the constant din inside the wagon as it bumped along the road made it difficult to hear her clearly, but she spoke on the subject authoritatively, telling Natalya that she personally knew her grandmother.

What Paspati had said the night before had made little impression upon Natalya in her state of virtual collapse, but it had remained in her memory. And as Mara talked on and Natalya thought about it, she had a feeling of confusion and readjustment. At first she was certain that they had her confused with someone else. Then she realized they knew too much about her. They hadn't made a mistake. Things finally began to fall into place.

They knew her father's name, where and when she

had been born, and other things. Mara rattled off names of people in Panna's band which Natalya remembered. Then there was the birthmark, and the intense interest the old woman in Panna's band had displayed about it when she was a child, and the exceptional interest in general the gypsies had shown in her.

Her father had always been reticent about discussing her mother with her, and in retrospect she could see that it must have been from a reluctance to lie to her about her birth. Most of all, there was her physical appearance. The woman she had believed to be her mother had been a Muscovite, from a family of large, fair people, and her father and brother had shown clear Cossack ancestry, whereas she was small of stature and dark haired.

There was an aura of romantic mystery about the entire affair. The idea that her mother had been a beautiful gypsy woman wasn't at all displeasing. She began asking Mara about Saiforella, and Mara sighed gustily and rolled her eyes as she began describing Saiforella's breathtaking beauty and fiery temper.

Mara cut and sewed on the blouse and skirt all morning, and at midday the wagons stopped for a time. Natalya started to put on the blouse and skirt to follow Mara, but Mara wanted her to stay inside. Mara went out, and Natalya heard other people moving around the line of wagons and calling to each other. Mara came back in with a bowl of cabbage and potato soup and a loaf of bread, apologizing for the poor food, and Natalya shrugged off the apologies and ate hungrily. There had been a time when she would indeed have regarded it as poor, but it tasted delicious. When she finished eating, Mara carried in buckets of water and had Natalya undress and stand over a grating in the corner, and she poured the water over Natalya as she scrubbed herself with a cloth.

478

The wagons started out again, and Natalya put on the blouse and skirt. She felt almost naked without petticoat and pantaloons, but there was a light and carefree sense of comfort, freedom, and lack of constriction she hadn't known since childhood. Mara made a few final alterations, then took a bowl of oats from a chest, laid down a large cloth for Natalya to sit on, and began working the oats into her hair and combing them back out. She was tireless, working carefully around the sore places on Natalya's head and gathering the oats back up to start over again. After two hours of it, Natalya's back began to ache and she suggested her hair had been combed enough, and Mara smiled coaxingly, telling her it would take only a short while longer, then she combed the oats through Natalya's hair for another hour. She took a pot of olive oil from a chest and put a small amount in the oats the last couple of times she combed them through Natalya's hair, and she sighed and clucked with admiration as Natalya's hair began to shine glossily.

It was evident that Natalya's appearance was a matter of pride to her, so Natalya endured it. Mara parted her hair in the center, letting it fall over her shoulders to her waist like a thick, heavy scarf, gleaming with the olive oil. The wagons swayed and jolted off the road into a field and stopped, and people began moving around them and unhitching the horses. Mara rooted around in a small chest and found a pair of large hoop earrings and put them in Natalya's ears, then took out an assortment of bangles and sighed with disappointment over the fact that only four of them were small enough to stay on Natalya's wrist. Natalya took out the chain Czar Aleksander had given her to put on her other wrist, and Mara nodded in approval and took out some rouge and a stick of charcoal to tint Natalya's lips and darken her eyelids.

479

Corwen came to the door of the wagon and called a couple of times, and Mara replied with an irritable monosyllable each time. She finished shading Natalya's eyelids, then dug in the clothes chest again for sandals. The smallest pair was slightly too large, and Mara wrapped the straps around Natalya's ankles an extra turn to keep them firmly on her feet. Then she took Natalya's hand and motioned toward the door.

The women were building fires, and the men were moving about and doing their chores. All movement stopped when Natalya appeared, and they all looked at her. A flush began to steal up her throat to her cheeks. But it wasn't unlike being on display in a drawing room, a familiar situation, so she assumed an expression of unconcern, looking around. Paspati said something in a laughing tone, nodding emphatically, and she picked out the name Hator in the sentence. The others laughed and nodded, turning back to what they had been doing. Mara put her hand on Natalya's shoulder and motioned toward the fire in the center of the circle of wagons, and they walked over to it and sat down.

There was a communal meal of stew, bread, and kvass, and Paspati sat by Natalya and talked to her. She told him candidly about the incident with the soldiers and why she had to get in touch with Annya, and he listened closely, nodded thoughtfully, and brought a couple of other men into the conversation to discuss what they would do. The caravan would cross the Volga at Kazan, closely approaching the circuit of Panna's caravan in Novgorod District, and she would be transferred to the other caravan at that point. Paspati didn't know the details of the route Panna's caravan took on its circuit beyond the fact that it approached his at one point and ended where his did at the winter camp, but he thought that Sherevskoye was the nearest that Panna's caravan approached Moscow. Natalya started to tell him about the time when some of the wagons in Panna's caravan had come to Moscow and she had happened on them during the flight from Moscow from the advancing French, then she thought again. The wagons had obviously come to Moscow for the specific purpose of seeing her to safety.

The interest some of the younger men showed in her changed when she told Paspati she was married and told him about Thomas. Paspati chuckled humorously, wondering what her husband must be thinking about her long absence, then he guffawed and looked around at the younger men, telling them in Russian that their despair needn't be total because she might be divorced when she got back to Moscow. Natalya joined in the general laughter, then she sobered, bringing an explosion of hilarity from the group around the fire.

Several men brought out instruments and there was dancing and music for a while, then the people began to drift away to their wagons. Natalya and Mara returned to the wagon and chatted for a time, then Mara hung up a cloth partition around Natalya's pallet to give her privacy and she went to bed. She lay and looked up at the ceiling in the darkness, thinking. Her plans had to be revised. There was no question that her safety lay in staying with the caravans, but their itinerary didn't coincide with her needs. By the time she would get in the vicinity of Moscow, Annya and Thomas would have long since gone back to St. Petersburg. Her best course of action would be to write to Annya, explain what had happened, and ask her advice.

The wagons were back on the road again at sunrise, stopped at noon for a rest, then continued on until sunset. It developed into a routine, then they reached Dvorovye, where there was a fair. They remained there for three weeks, during which Natalya was confined to the wagon for the long, stifling hot days and could leave only after dark to walk around the wagon for exercise. She gave Corwen money to buy caviar, kvass, pork, white bread, and other things, as well as cloth, bangles, earrings, and other presents for Mara, but it was poor compensation for the boredom. The wagons got underway again at the end of three weeks, traveled for five days, then stopped at another fair. It was for only two weeks, but it seemed endless because the next leg of the circuit would take them across the Volga. Finally the stay at the fair was over, and they passed through an area of rolling hills and descended to the flood plain of the Volga.

It was unusual for two gypsy bands to meet before the winter camp, and everyone began making preparations after the rider was sent out to intercept Panna's band and deliver the message. The paint on the wagons was touched up, harness was cleaned, repaired, and polished, new clothes were sewn, and musical instruments were polished and tuned. The rider returned, and the rendezvous was set. Preparations became more feverish as the rendezvous approached, and on the last night the wagons were washed, the horses groomed, and other final preparations made. The wagons were back on the road at daybreak, and Natalya sat patiently in the flickering, yellow light of a lantern swinging from the ceiling of the wagon as Mara combed oats through her hair.

Panna's caravan was encamped in a meadow off the road, and people began rushing from the wagons as Paspati's caravan came into sight over the hill. The wagons picked up speed down the hill, the drivers shouting at the horses and snapping the reins for them to break into a trot, men shouted at each other, and dogs raced back and forth, barking madly. The sounds were clearly audible over the uproar in the wagon as it jarred along the road, and Mara almost wept with frustration as she braced herself against the lurching of the wagon and put the finishing touches on Natalya's lips and eyelids. Paspati's caravan turned off the road, then stopped. Men and women rushed together, embracing and greeting each other, and children raced back and forth, screaming gleefully. Mara was frantically nervous, looking Natalya over and touching her hair into place, smoothing an eyebrow, and tugging the neckline of her blouse down so the top edge of her birthmark would show. Then she drew in a deep breath and took Natalya's hand, leading her toward the door.

The noise diminished as they walked between the wagons into the circle. Men and women turned toward them and shuffled from side to side to get a better view. Children stopped running. Dogs stopped barking. Silence fell. Natalya looked around, the sunshine gleaming on her hair, on the large earrings and on her bangles, and intensifying the bright colors of her blouse and skirt. The faces all around were warmly familiar from her childhood; Panna, wizened and white-haired, but like seasoned oak; the younger Fignon, with hands like a smith which somehow became magically nimble on the balalaika; Bediya, the mother of the finest dancers; Hamza, shriveled and leaning on his cane, looking as though the winter had been hard on him. Kostich. Sincani. And Bala. Bala, snowy-haired, her small face a maze of wrinkles. Natalya's grandmother. Bala uttered a choked sound, wailing something in Romany, and she hobbled toward Natalya, her arms extended. Natalya rushed to her. Bala fell to her knees, kissing Natalya's hands and shaking with sobs. Natalya put her arms around Bala and lifted her, embracing her and kissing her. It broke the spell. Everyone began crowding around Natalya and greeting her. And it wasn't until later that Natalya found out that Bala had thought her daughter had returned to her.

There were two days of celebration, music, and dancing, then preparations were made to leave. Bala had her own wagon which she shared with a childless widow who looked after her, and Natalya hid a hundred rubles in Mara's wagon where she would find them later before she moved her things into Bala's wagon. On the third morning, there were hurried farewells in the darkness before dawn, and the caravans parted to go their separate ways until they met again at the winter camp.

Bala's mind wandered, the effects of age and hardship warping time in her mind so that the events of years gone by were intermingled with those in the recent past and her memory operated in planes and rhythms meaningful only to her. At times she would address Natalya by the affectionate Romany name the band had given her in childhood, Petulengra, Mistress of Horses, and at times she would address her as Saiforella. Sometimes she would remember to speak in her halting, faulty Russian, and at others she would speak in Romany and interpret Natalya's lack of understanding as obstinance. It took several days to develop the understanding relationship dictated by the close confines of the wagon, with the widow who cared for Bala assuming the role of interpreter at those times when Bala thought she was addressing her daughter.

Natalya wrote two letters, one to Annya at the court in St. Petersburg and one to Thomas at his regiment, explaining everything that had happened, her circumstances, and the itinerary of the caravan. Panna dispatched the letters for her when they reached the fair at Diakonskii. He accepted Natalya's faith in Annya, but he shared it to a degree which was tempered with a large measure of caution, and he made arrangements within the band for Natalya's escape at the first indication of trouble, designating two men who were to immediately flee with her on horseback.

The fair at Diakonskii seemed intolerably long, each day a misery of sitting in the oven-like wagon and waiting for dark and a chance to walk about under the watchful eye of the widow who looked after Bala, but the end of each day brought a heightening of the exhilarating anticipation of being that much closer to the time when she would again be at Sherevskoye, the scene of childhood memories, and eventually rejoined with Thomas. Then the last day finally came to an end, and the wagons filed out of the city and along the road in the darkness to travel through the night.

After sunrise, each stone along the road marking the distance from Moscow stirred pangs of nostalgia. A creek in a valley was where they had once stopped while traveling to the estate because she had felt ill, and her father had dipped his handkerchief in the cool water and wiped her face. A peculiar rock formation on a hill a short distance away from the road brought back the memory of the time when her father had lifted her up behind his saddle so she could look at it.

Then the wagons turned off the road and along the drive lined with tall limewood trees, the wheels rumbling over the fascines embedded in the road. Natalya left the tiny window and sat on her pallet at the side of the wagon, gripping herself as her heart pounded furiously. If there had been time for the letters to reach St. Petersburg, there would be some word for her at the village. Her long journey was nearing its end. The thought that Panna had sent out a rider to check the village for trouble flashed through her mind like a dark cloud, then disappeared; Annya was her friend. The wagons started down the other side of the hill, and she could hear the villagers shouting gleefully in greeting and the drivers replying. The wagons picked up speed, then slowed again and the noise from the wagons in front diminished as they turned off the road onto the grassy strip by the river.

The villagers knew from the rider that Natalya was with the caravan, and they had collected around the wagon. Many didn't recognize her at first, blinking at her with vacant expressions and thinking she was a gypsy woman. But others recognized her, and their cries of greeting rang out, spreading through the crowd.

Then she saw him, and she realized that she hadn't even let the hope form within her for fear of the shattering disappointment if he wasn't there. Thomas was walking with long strides across the grass, and he towered over the villagers as he pushed his way through them toward her. He was smiling widely, the sun shining on his white teeth and in his eyes. She gasped with ecstasy, leaping down from the steps of the wagon and rushing toward him.

His strong arms swept her off the ground and held her to him, his lips covering hers, and he crushed her to him. She kissed him eagerly, her hands moving over his shoulders, neck, and face, touching and feeling to give the reassurance her swelling heart demanded. He lifted his head and looked down at her, his eyes moving over her face as he held her to him. She started to speak, then all she had to say and tell him seemed to swell up at once, choking her. Tears came in a sudden flood. He lifted her in his arms and cradled her against him, kissing her forehead lightly and murmuring softly to her as he turned and walked away with her.

There were no recriminations, only love, understanding, and sympathy. His efforts to locate her were referred to with wry humor and characteristic self deprecation, but his eyes reflected the sleepless nights and agonies of despair he had suffered. And he flatly contradicted her self-recriminations about Olivia and Danilo, sitting with her on his lap and her head resting against his chest on a bench in the quiet, cool garden behind the manor. It had been misfortune, the result of the violence which could strike in any life, leaving scars of pain and sorrow. His presence, his protection, and his love enfolded her.

Then he gave her the letter from Annya. There were expressions of affection and relief that she was safe jumbled together with admonitions for what she had done, then pages on what she must do. The district governor had sent the Czar a report that a group of roving bandits accompanied by two women had attacked a patrol of soldiers and killed eight of them. The wagon had been found, her name was known, and there was an order out for her arrest. She must flee the country until such time as the soldiers could be forced to tell the truth or a pardon could be secured from Czar Nikolas. To attempt to clear herself through the courts at the present time would be extremely unwise, because there was mountainous evidence against her.

There were practical matters. Annya would take title to the house in St. Petersburg and the village, and credit in the amount of twenty-five thousand gold rubles would be placed in a bank in England in Natalya's name. The serfs would be treated well and the property would be maintained in good order, and it would be returned to her for the same amount plus accrued interest when she returned to Russia. There were more expressions of affection, of sorrow at being parted, and an emphatic reiteration that she must flee the country.

Natalya crumpled the pages in her hands, leaning back against her husband and burrowing her face in his shirt as she began weeping again. "I cannot leave Russia, Thomas Stephanovich! I cannot!"

He sighed heavily, one of his hands patting her

gently. "You must, Natasha. To resolve this by trial would mean your going to prison, because they have the evidence of several men against you. As Annya Konstantinovna says, you must."

"But for how long? And you cannot leave your regiment . . ."

"I spoke with Annya Konstantinovna, and she wouldn't say for how long. She will have to work through others to get some of those soldiers transferred to St. Petersburg, and then she will have them questioned. But there are those in St. Petersburg who try to undermine her influence with His Majesty the Czar and she can't put herself in the position of appearing biased on a matter of justice, so it will take some time. Alternatively, she will solicit a pardon from the Czar, but much time would have to pass before that could be considered. It might take years. As for my regiment, I no longer have a regiment. With Annya Konstantinovna's assistance, I gained release from my commission."

She looked up at him with a horrified expression, then began sobbing harder. "What have I done to you, Thomas Stephanovich?" she wailed. "Because of me, you have resigned your commission . . ."

"There are other reasons," he replied, smiling down at her as he lifted her chin and wiped the tears from her cheeks. "My solicitors have advised me a number of times that my affairs in England require my presence. So it is perhaps time that I should forego the pleasures of a man's younger years and attend to the duties of maturity."

She nodded, looking down and controlling her tears with an effort as she straightened and folded the pages of the letter. "When must we leave?" she asked softly.

"The order for your arrest is being pursued less than vigorously, as is fairly obvious, so there is no immediate danger. However, we could have an early winter. I shall make the arrangements as soon as possible."

She looked down at the letter, nodding slowly, and burst into tears again. He gathered her in his arms and lifted her, and walked along the path toward the house with her.

The house had an empty, deserted feeling, with only Natalya, Thomas, and a few villagers the headman had sent to do what they could. Thomas had brought some of her things from St. Petersburg, and she bathed and dressed in a gown to have dinner with him, a village girl awkwardly trying to help her. Her ambivalent emotions—joy at being with Thomas again, sorrow at having to leave her beloved homeland, made her moods vaccilate rapidly between exhilaration and depression, but she tried to present a cheerful attitude for Thomas. The facade became unnecessary when she lay in his arms, her moods compressed into a calm, serene exhaustion from love.

He left early the following morning to return to St. Petersburg. She visited with the villagers and the gypsies, watched the entertainment, and sat with her grandmother and listened to her memories. The days began to melt into each other as she waited for him; then the gypsies left and there were agonizing farewells and a feeling of loneliness after their wagons had moved along the road and disappeared from sight. Natalya felt a hollow, empty feeling of loss from fear that she might never see them again. She walked along the river the next day, and the grass was already springing up where it had been crushed down by their wagons.

The leaves began to acquire autumn tints. The mornings became crisp, and the afternoons golden, with woodsmoke hanging in the air over the river and the sunsets brilliant cascades of color. Wild ducks came to rest in the reeds along the river before continuing on their journey, and she startled them into frightened flight as she walked along the river, looking at the ancient stone walls among the willows, wondering as she had when a child whose hands had put them there.

A few leaves began falling, and the villagers began the final plowing of the season. She walked along the roads and paths where generations of Sheremetevs had walked, savoring the smells, sights, and sounds so she would be able to remember them. Then Thomas returned with a covered carriage, and it was time to go.

CHAPTER XXVI

The dark was impenetrable, as though some powerful force had absorbed all light from the earth and all creation was enshrouded in darkness. The fog was damp against Natalya's face, the salty smell of the ocean tingled in her nostrils, and the only sound was a light slapping of waves at the foot of the stone wall, sounding remote and far away with the thick fog blanketing the noise. She shivered, tugging the collar of her thick cloak higher and moving closer to Thomas. He put his arm around her shoulders, pulling her against him. The rhythm of the waves changed, and there was a wooden thud. Thomas's arm tightened fractionally. A moment passed, then they saw a hazy spot of yellow light, moving up and down. It brightened and became larger, moving off to one side of them. Thomas spoke quietly in English. The light hesitated, then moved toward them, raising higher. It turned into a hooded lantern, lighting the side of a man's face as he held it at shoulder height. He was wearing a sailor's coat and round, black hat, with a tarred pigtail sticking out at the back of his head. He peered closely, lifting the lantern higher to look at Thomas's face then glancing at Natalya. He said something in English, in an accent she couldn't understand, and Thomas replied. The man turned, holding the lantern for them, and Thomas led her after him, his arm tight around her shoulders to keep her from slipping on the damp stones under their feet.

The stone steps were barely visible in the dim light of the lantern, and Thomas walked down them ahead of her, half turned and holding her with both hands as she followed. There was a rowboat at the bottom of the steps, bobbing up and down on the waves, with another sailor crouching in the bow and holding the rope. Thomas turned and picked her up, then stepped into the boat and around the other sailor. He carried her along the boat, feeling with his feet and taking careful steps in the darkness, then put her down on a seat and sat down by her, tucking her cloak around her legs and pulling the collar up around the sides of her face. There was a metallic rattle as the hood on the lantern snapped down, and total darkness descended again. The sailors murmured to each other in soft voices, and the boat swept away from the steps on the current.

The oars were muffled with rags and made only a soft, grinding noise, hardly louder than the rhythmic breathing of the sailor pulling them. The fog caressed Natalya's face delicately from the slight wind of the boat's motion and the breath of breeze on the water. The breeze freshened after a few minutes, and she pulled her collar across her face. The sailor in the bow of the boat hissed something, and the other sailor shipped the oars. A yellow glow of lights became visible through the fog and darkness, resolving into three lanterns on a larger rowboat. Voices carried across the water, men's voices laughing and joking. She pulled her collar away from her ear, listening. It was the port inspector and his assistants. The boat passed several yards away and disappeared again. The sailor in the bow spoke, and the sailor at the oars began pulling in long strokes again.

A long line of lights several feet above the water became visible, rapidly brightening as the rowboat approached them, and turned into lanterns hanging on the rail of a ship. The sailor in the bow of the rowboat called out, and other figures became visible in the light of the lanterns on the ship. Ropes dropped down, and the sailors in the rowboat fastened them to the bow and stern of the boat. Orders rang out on deck. The ropes tightened, then the rowboat began lifting out of the water and bobbing upward a few inches at a time as men's voices on the ship chanted in unison, hauling in the ropes.

Thomas lifted her out onto the deck, then leaped lightly down beside her. The fog swirled around the yellow light of the lanterns, and there were many sailors moving about, some of them looking at her curiously. She held her collar over her face. A tall, authoritative-looking man approached, speaking to Thomas in the strangely accented English which was unintelligible to her. Thomas replied that they would remain on deck for a time. Thomas put his arm around her and led her along the deck.

He led her along the rail, in front of the bridge, and stood by the opposite rail with her. Lanterns were glowing on the bridge, and there seemed to be motion everywhere in the darkness. Bare feet ran back and forth on the deck, and the ropes fastened to the rails vibrated as men climbed them. Orders rang out, and voices replied.

The fog. acquired a rosy, opalescent quality, as though glowing with a light of its own. She looked up, and she could see the masts jutting out of the fog, with tiny figures of men moving back and forth along the spars. Then she could see for a distance along the deck in the swirling fog, men running back and forth on obscure tasks in a confusion which seemed to have a pattern of its own. An order rang out on the bridge, amplified by a speaking trumpet. It was repeated on the deck in a loud shout, and a group of men raced across the deck with heavy sticks of polished wood. They plugged them into the holes around a large, barrel-like structure on the deck, then another order rang out and they leaned against the sticks. The round structure began turning, groaning heavily, and the men began stamping their feet and chanting in unison as they walked around it, turning it more rapidly. A breeze moved across the deck, whipping the fog, and it began thinning. The anchor rope became visible, vibrating as the men turned the round structure on the deck. Their chant filled the air, echoing back from the shoes. The ship crept forward on the anchor rope, the deck trembling slightly.

An interrogative shout on the bridge carried over the sound of the men chanting, and a thin, distant voice from the spars replied. The men turning the round object suddenly lurched forward and it began turning loosely. The ship began edging backward with a sagging motion in the current. An imperative order rang out on the bridge, and one of the massive rolls of canvas on the spars spilled loose and unrolled with a rumble which made the deck vibrate. A series of shouts sounded back and forth, and the sail tightened. It suddenly filled with wind and bowed outward with a booming report. Another sail spilled downward. Then another. The ship began to move in the water with the breeze.

The sun began rising over the horizon, and the breeze dissipated the fog, whipping it into filmy shreds scattered along the surface of the water. The ship was picking up speed and moving with a steady, bobbing motion, still a hubbub of activity as orders rang out and men raced back and forth.

Natalya looked back at the buildings, at the huge bulk of SS Peter and Paul fortress and at the majestic beauty of SS Peter and Paul Cathedral. The statue of Peter the Great overlooking the Neva was already only a speck in the distance. And the sun was glinting on the massive dome of St. Isaac's. Natalya looked up at her husband.

"Thomas Stephanovich, now I go with you to your country. I love you, Thomas Stephanovich, and I will be a good wife to you. But know this. I am Russian. When I leave this great land of mine, much of me remains. Wherever I may go or whatever I may do, I am Russian. And much of me will remain in Russia."

He looked down at her with a gentle smile, and he nodded as he tightened his arm around her shoulder and turned to lead her through the passageway to their cabin.